Susanna Gregory was a police ~~officer in~~ Leeds before taking up an academic career. ~~She~~ conducted postgraduate studies at the ~~University~~ of Durham before earning a PhD at the ~~University~~ of Cambridge. She has spent seventeen field seasons in the polar regions, and has taught comparative anatomy and biological anthropology.

Aside from her two popular series of historical mysteries featuring Matthew Bartholomew and Thomas Chaloner, she has also written books on castles of Britain and cathedrals of the world. She now lives in Wales with her husband, who is also a writer, and the two have published another series of medieval mysteries under the pseudonym Simon Beaufort.

Also by Susanna Gregory

The Matthew Bartholomew Series

A Plague on Both Your Houses
An Unholy Alliance
A Bone of Contention
A Deadly Brew
A Wicked Deed
A Masterly Murder
An Order for Death
A Summer of Discontent
A Killer in Winter
The Hand of Justice
The Mark of a Murderer
The Tarnished Chalice
To Kill or Cure
The Devil's Disciples
A Vein of Deceit
The Killer of Pilgrims

The Thomas Chaloner Series

A Conspiracy of Violence
Blood on the Strand
The Butcher of Smithfield
The Westminster Poisoner

A MURDER ON
LONDON BRIDGE

Susanna
Gregory

sphere

SPHERE

First published in Great Britain in 2009 by Sphere
This paperback edition first published by Sphere in 2011

Copyright © 2009 Susanna Gregory

The moral right of the author has been asserted.

*All characters and events in this publication, other
than those clearly in the public domain, are fictitious
and any resemblance to real persons,
living or dead, is purely coincidental.*

A CIP catalogue record for this book
is available from the British Library.

ISBN 978-0-7515-4182-3

Typeset in Baskerville MT by Palimpsest Book Production,
Falkirk, Stirlingshire

Printed and bound in Great Britain by
Clays Ltd, St Ives plc

Papers used by Sphere are natural, renewable and recyclable
products sourced from well-managed forests and certified
in accordance with the rules of the Forest Stewardship Council.

Mixed Sources
Product group from well-managed
forests and other controlled sources
www.fsc.org Cert no. SGS-COC-004081
© 1996 Forest Stewardship Council
FSC

Sphere
An imprint of
Little, Brown Book Group
100 Victoria Embankment
London EC4Y 0DY

An Hachette UK Company
www.hachette.co.uk

www.littlebrown.co.uk

For Captain Dick Taylor

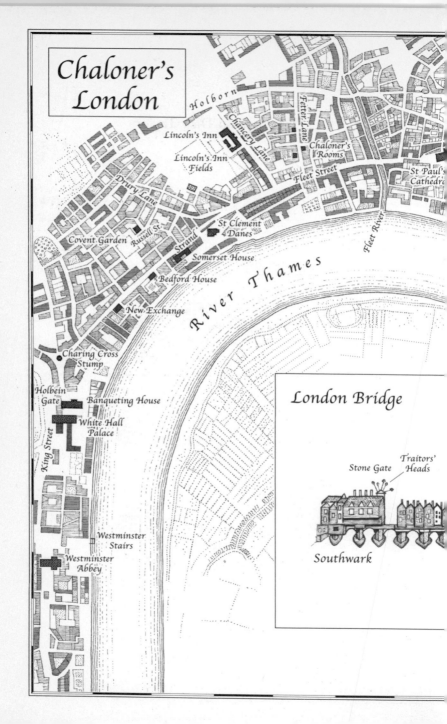

Chaloner's London

Holborn

Lincoln's Inn

Chancery Lane

Fetter Lane

Chaloner's Rooms

Lincoln's Inn Fields

Fleet Street

St Paul's Cathedral

Drury Lane

St Clement Danes

Russell St.

Covent Garden

Strand

Somerset House

River Thames

Fleet River

Bedford House

New Exchange

Charing Cross Stump

Holbein Gate

Banqueting House

King Street

White Hall Palace

Westminster Stairs

Westminster Abbey

London Bridge

Stone Gate

Traitors' Heads

Southwark

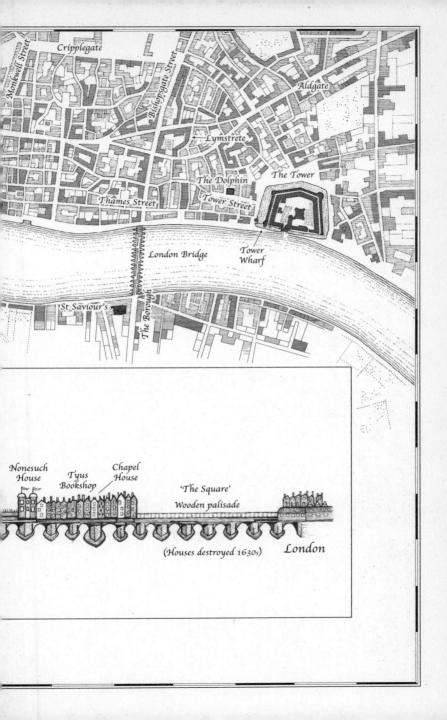

Cripplegate

Mortkwell Street

Bishoppsgate Street

Aldgate

→ Lymstrete

The Dolphin

The Tower

Thames Street

Tower Street

Tower Wharf

London Bridge

St Saviour's

The Borough

Nonesuch House

Tyus Bookshop

Chapel House

'The Square'

Wooden palisade

(Houses destroyed 1630s)

London

Prologue

The Reverend Richard Culmer loved the sound of smashing glass. And when that glass was the stained type, bursting with idolatrous images of popish saints, then the sound was even more satisfying. He stood on top of a ladder with a pike in his hand, and gleefully jabbed out as many panes as he could reach. His bright blue cloak swung around him as he worked, the trademark garment that had earned him the nickname 'Blue Dick'.

Below him, steadying the swaying steps, were two of his most trusted henchmen, although both looked as though they wished they were somewhere else. Blue Dick grimaced. What was wrong with them? Could they not see that Canterbury Cathedral had far too much in the way of nasty Catholic regalia? Did they not understand that it was their moral duty to destroy it all?

He gave a last, vicious poke at a window depicting pilgrims at the shrine of St Thomas Becket, then scrambled down from his precarious perch. There was so much to do – everywhere he looked were statues that needed

1

their heads knocked off and paintings to be slashed. And then there was the body of the saint himself – the long-dead archbishop who had defied his king and been murdered for it. The cathedral's clergy had assured him that Becket's bones had been destroyed more than a hundred years before, but Blue Dick did not believe them. Before he left, he planned to open the tomb and pulverise what he found inside, to make sure Becket's relics really were gone for ever.

When he reached the ground, he stood for a moment to admire his handiwork, pleased to note that the once-ornate windows were now reduced to a series of gaping holes. Through them he could see outside, to where a large crowd had gathered. He rolled his eyes: they wanted him to leave Canterbury and spare its treasures. But that was too bad, because he was not going anywhere until his work was finished. And they would accept the righteousness of his actions in time.

Breaking windows was hot work, so he started to remove his cloak. Unfortunately, the blue garment made him easy to identify, so when a stone sailed through one of the broken windows, he knew it was meant for him. It missed, but only just, and the crack it made when it hit the wall left him in no doubt that it had been intended to kill.

Blue Dick smiled: God had protected him. The knowledge gave him the strength to continue, and as he attacked a stone bishop with a mallet, grinning his satisfaction as the ancient face dissolved into shards and dust, he began to sing. Well, why not? It was, after all, one of the happiest and most fulfilling days of his life.

Bonfire Night. The time when effigies of Guy Fawkes were burned all over the country, to remind good Anglicans of the danger posed by religious dissenters. Recently, some folk had even taken to creating images of the Pope to go on their pyres, filling them with live cats to howl as the fires consumed them. For a reputedly civilised country, England could be a barbaric place, thought the Green Man, as he waited in the cellar for the occupants of the house to go to bed.

He took no pleasure in what he was about to do – it was just necessary. People needed to be shaken from their smug complacency, and made to sit up and listen. And his message was clear enough: before Charles II had been given his throne back in 1660, he had promised that all his subjects would have the right to worship God as they saw fit. The whole country had breathed a sigh of relief – Charles's reign was going to be one of tolerance and reconciliation.

But the King had gone back on his word, and laws were being passed that were making life intolerable for non-Anglicans. These repressive decrees were known collectively as the Clarendon Code, and the Green Man was outraged by them. He had decided it was time to make his objections known, and if a few innocent souls had to die in the process, then so be it.

He glanced at the barrels of gunpowder he had smuggled inside the house, and experienced a warm glow of pride. It had taken six weeks to accumulate enough of the stuff, and every tortuous journey had carried with it the risk of capture and death. Fortunately, the house had plenty of pantries and storerooms on the floor above, so the servants never bothered to visit the cellars.

Outside, he heard the night-watchman call midnight: it was time. He stood, stiff after his long wait, heart hammering in anticipation. He smiled grimly to himself. In moments, the house and its sleeping occupants would be nothing but smouldering rubble.

He had prepared his fuses earlier – three long trails of powder that would take several minutes to burn their way across the floor, giving him time to escape. His hand shook as he lit the first one. Immediately, it began to hiss and smoke. Quickly, he ignited the others, then turned to bolt up the cellar steps. He ran across the garden, and darted into the street beyond. His stomach churned with the enormity of what he had done as he ducked into a doorway and waited, holding his breath and clenching his fists tightly enough to make his knuckles hurt. Any minute now.

But the seconds ticked past, and nothing happened. He gazed at the house in bewilderment. What was wrong? Had his fuses failed? Was the powder damp? He supposed he should go back and look, but he had no wish to share the fate of his intended victims. He stayed where he was.

More time slipped away, and eventually he was forced to concede that nothing was going to happen. Bitterly disappointed, he started to walk home. He was vaguely aware of shadows in the street ahead, but he paid them no heed. All he could think about was the fact that he had failed.

'Give us your purse or you are a dead man.'

The voice so close to his ear shocked the Green Man from his reverie. He tried to back away, but someone shoved a dagger against his throat. He struggled frantically, but there was a sudden blazing pain in his neck, and he could not breathe. As he gagged and choked, deft hands moved across him, removing purse and jewellery.

The attack was over in a moment, and the robbers did not linger once they had what they wanted. As his life ebbed away, the Green Man was overwhelmed with the futility of it all. He had been so close to achieving his goal! If only the gunpowder had ignited, if only his disappointment had not caused him to lower his guard, if only . . .

London Bridge, late January 1664

The Earl of Clarendon hated the London Bridge. He disliked the way its narrow-fronted, teetering houses loomed over the road, meeting overhead to turn it into a shadowy, sinister tunnel. And he disliked the fact that it was always so busy – thick with carts, people and animals. Usually, he hired a boat if business took him south of the river, but a spate of abnormally high tides recently meant they were not always available – and then he had no choice but to brave the Bridge.

He sat in his fine coach and glowered out of the window, furious that no oarsman had been free to ferry him across the churning brown waters that morning. Then he remembered the last time it had happened. It had been a few days before, and as he had been driven along the Bridge's potholed, stinking roads, he had been somewhat startled to see several of his enemies loitering around one of the Bridge's rickety houses. Moreover, he had also been told that dubious characters had taken to lurking there of late – men such as the infamous iconoclast 'Blue Dick' Culmer.

And if that were not enough to raise eyebrows, there were the Bridge's two wardens. The Earl did not trust them, mostly because they were rumoured to be incorruptible. Who was incorruptible in Restoration London, where only the devious and dishonest could expect to prosper? As far as the Earl was concerned, anyone extolled as men of honour automatically earned *his* suspicion!

He narrowed his eyes as he passed Chapel House, a shabby affair that had been built on the site of a church dedicated to St Thomas Becket. It was swathed in scaffolding and canvas, because someone had decided it needed refurbishing, which effectively shielded it from passers-by. But the material was poorly secured, and through a gap the Earl glimpsed a gaggle of his enemies' servants. They were huddled together, speaking in low voices.

He experienced a surge of unease. What were they doing? Hatching another plot against him? After twenty years of civil war and military dictatorship, England was an unstable, restless country, full of shifting loyalties. Uprisings occurred on a weekly basis, and no government minister who valued his life and his position ignored that fact. It was not impossible that his foes were planning some sort of coup that would see him discredited – or worse.

The carriage rattled on, passing Nonesuch House, a fabulous jumble of onion domes and great glass windows, currently rented by a fellow named Sir John Winter. The Earl pursed his lips. Not only was Winter a Catholic, but he was reputed to be an authority on gunpowder, too. And if *that* combination was not sinister, then the Earl did not know what was. He would have ordered Winter put under surveillance, but the only man he trusted to do it – Thomas Chaloner – was in Wimbledon on other duties. Still, Chaloner would be back soon, and then he could look into whatever dark business was fermenting on the Bridge.

Finally, the coach reached the Stone Gate, where the Earl's eyes were drawn upwards, to the severed heads that had been impaled on spikes above the arch – traitors, all executed since the monarchy had been restored three and a half years before. Some were men the King would have spared, but the Earl had urged him against clemency, lest it was seen as a sign of weakness. He felt no remorse, though, as he stared at the blackened, unrecognisable features. It was hardly his fault they had backed the wrong side.

As his carriage passed under the arch, there was a sudden violent thud that made him jump and set his heart racing. Immediately, people started to shout, then laugh. It did not take the Earl long to realise what had happened. One of the heads had come off its pike, and had landed on the roof of his coach. The vile things dropped not infrequently, especially during windy weather, but the Earl was seized by the immediate and unshakable sense that it was an omen of evil to come.

He could not prevent a shudder as the head was brandished outside his window by a grinning apprentice. He told himself he was being fanciful – that the falling skull was a chance event, and meant nothing at all. But his stomach continued to roil, and gradually he accepted what he knew to be true, deep in his heart – it *was* an omen, and it boded ill for him, for the people who knew him, and for London.

Chapter 1

London, February 1664

Everything about 'Blue Dick' Culmer said he was about to do something illegal. He slunk along Thames Street in a way that could only be described as furtive, stopping every so often to duck into a doorway or lurk behind a stationary cart. Then he would peer back the way he had come, to see whether he was being followed.

Thomas Chaloner, spy for the Earl of Clarendon, was better able than most to melt invisibly into a crowd, but even he was struggling to stay out of sight. Unfortunately, the man who had been assigned to work with him that day was worse than hopeless, and Chaloner thought Blue Dick would have to be blind not to know Humphrey Leigh was on his tail.

'I am getting tired of this,' grumbled Leigh, as Chaloner hauled him out of sight behind a dray. He staggered slightly; Chaloner's exasperation – with Leigh's ineptitude as well as their quarry's antics – had made him heavy handed. 'We do not even know what he is supposed to have done.'

Leigh was the Earl's Sergeant at Arms, a small, trim, truculent martinet, who had seen fit to wear an eye-catching scarlet coat that day. It was a spectacularly inappropriate choice of garment for surveillance work, and Chaloner could only suppose he was new to the business. Chaloner's own clothes were an unmemorable shade of grey, and his brown hair was tucked under a nondescript wig – he had learned years before that intelligencers tended to live longer if no one noticed them, and he attributed reaching the grand old age of thirty-four to having perfected the art of ordinariness.

'Well?' demanded Leigh irritably, while they waited for their target to begin moving again. 'Why did our Earl order us to follow him? It is a filthy morning, not fit for a dog to be out.'

Leigh was right about the weather. It was one of those dark, dreary, dank days Chaloner had come to associate with London. The sky was an unbroken dome of grey, and drizzle fell in a misty pall. It was cold, too, and the shallower puddles were turning to ice around the edges.

'I imagine because he was one of William Dowsing's cronies.' Chaloner saw Leigh's blank look, and elaborated. 'Dowsing was the man appointed by Oliver Cromwell to destroy images of—'

'Oh, *that* Dowsing,' interrupted Leigh. 'The iconoclast, who ruined our best churches by knocking the heads off statues, slashing paintings, and setting fire to altar rails and pulpits.'

Chaloner nodded. 'Blue Dick was responsible for despoiling Canterbury Cathedral.'

'Was he, by God?' Leigh's eyes flashed with righteous indignation. 'Then why are we skulking behind him?

We should be chopping off his villainous hands. Damned fanatic!'

Chaloner also deplored what Dowsing and his zealous comrades had done, but there was no time to discuss the matter, because their target was on the move again. Chaloner began to follow, indicating with a wave of his hand that Leigh was to cross the street. Leigh either did not see the gesture, or chose to ignore it, because he fell into step at Chaloner's side instead.

'I know the iconoclasts have not plied their nasty trade in years, but they still deserve to hang,' he declared. 'So why does the Earl not order Blue Dick's arrest? Is it because he is a vicar?'

'The Earl did not say,' replied Chaloner shortly, wishing Leigh would shut up and concentrate on the task in hand. The road was busy, and they would lose their quarry if they did not pay attention.

'*I* would arrest him, if I were the Earl,' Leigh went on, worrying at the subject like a dog with a bone. 'Fanatics should not be allowed to wander around London as they please. It is not right.'

Chaloner was spared from having to comment, because Blue Dick had turned into Fish Street Hill, a wide thoroughfare with Leadenhall Market at one end and London Bridge at the other. The noise there was deafening – traders yelling, iron-shod wheels rattling on cobbles, and above it all, the river roaring under the Bridge like a never-ending roll of thunder. The racket was amplified by the tall houses that lined either side of the road. The assault on their ears was rivalled only by the one on their noses – unwashed bodies, horses, sewage, stagnant water, and the fish that was for sale in the line of makeshift booths that ran from one end of the road to the other.

11

'He is going over the Bridge.' Leigh was forced to bawl in Chaloner's ear to make himself heard. 'He must have business in Southwark, which does not surprise me. It is the place of choice for dark dealings.'

He and Chaloner joined the stream of folk aiming for the city's only crossing of the mighty Thames. There was an unspoken, but universally agreed, law that kept everyone to the left. It did not always work. Sometimes a stranger or an obstreperous local ignored the rule, which invariably resulted in chaos. That dismal winter morning, however, traffic was moving fairly smoothly, and although the Bridge and its approach were tightly packed with pedestrians, livestock and vehicles of all descriptions, there was still forward momentum.

'I dislike the Bridge,' Leigh declared, stopping dead in his tracks to regard it in distaste. He ignored the jostles and resentful mutters of the people who were obliged to funnel around him. 'So, I shall hire a boat and meet you on the other side. Blue Dick is less likely to spot us if we separate.'

It was a little late to be worrying about that, thought Chaloner acidly, but he nodded agreement, relieved to be rid of the irascible little soldier. He walked on alone. The ground rose sharply, and then he was on the Bridge itself. The roar of water was louder here, and he fancied he could feel the stones reverberating under his feet, shaking with the sheer raw power of it.

Londoners were proud of their Bridge. It spanned a river that was both wide and deep, and boasted nineteen arches, each a different shape and size, which stood on boat-shaped feet called starlings. Above the starlings were houses, some five storeys tall. As the city imposed no restriction on size or style, the result was a chaotic jumble of rooftops and chimneys. Many leaned towards each other, and structures called 'haut-pas' had been built between them, serving not only to shore them up, but providing additional rooms, too.

The northern end of the Bridge was devoid of buildings though, because a fire some thirty years before had destroyed them, and they had not yet been rebuilt. Traders had set up in the open space – Londoners called it 'the Square' – their stalls perilously close to the great cartwheels that lumbered past. Chaloner blinked when he reached the first of the houses, and their looming shadows turned the road from broad daylight into a murky gloom.

About halfway across, Blue Dick ducked into a building – a sign nailed to the wall outside declared it to be Chapel House. It was surrounded by scaffolding, which was a problem, because the bulky wooden struts did not leave enough room for two large vehicles to pass each other – one would need to yield, and no self-respecting London driver liked to demean himself with gratuitous courtesy. Chaloner glanced casually at it as he passed. The door was ajar, and he saw Blue Dick lurking in the shadows beyond. Feigning disinterest, he walked on.

After a few moments, he turned and retraced his steps. He passed Chapel House again, but the door was now closed. When he reached the Square, he stopped and pretended to inspect a display of dolphin tongues, keeping the building at the periphery of his vision. It was not long before his quarry emerged and began to head back towards the Square. Chaloner tensed. Had he been spotted, despite all his care, and Blue Dick was coming to confront him?

The iconoclast was pale and nervous, eyes darting

everywhere. But they did not linger on Chaloner. Relieved, Chaloner let him pass, and was about to set off in pursuit again when the hairs on the back of his neck began to rise. Something was wrong! He stayed put for a moment, and then saw it: Blue Dick was being followed by a man swathed in a dark cloak.

As if he sensed he had company, Blue Dick stopped and peered behind him. It was then that the cloaked man made his move. A knife flashed. Horrified, Chaloner broke cover and raced towards them. But it was too late. Blue Dick was toppling forwards with an agonised expression on his face. He was dead before he hit the ground.

There was nothing Chaloner could do for the hapless Blue Dick, so he turned to follow the killer instead. The man was moving at a rapid clip towards Southwark. Carters and carriage-drivers yelled angrily as he cut in front of them, startling their horses and making them swerve. The killer ignored them all, careful to keep his face hidden beneath his broad-brimmed hat.

Chaloner moved more discreetly, fast enough to keep up with his new quarry, but not so quick as to draw attention to himself. The killer broke into a run, but to leave the Bridge, he had to pass through the Stone Gate, and the Stone Gate was a bottleneck – not just because it constricted the road, but because pedestrians and drivers alike enjoyed slowing down to admire its display of traitors' heads. Chaloner did not. Most of the skulls belonged to regicides – men who had signed the old king's death warrant – and some had been friends of his family.

The killer was brought to a virtual standstill as the crowd filed through the narrow opening, but his agitated jostling did nothing to hasten his progress. Indeed, people stopped walking to shove him back, retarding the flow even further. But he managed to squeeze through eventually, racing ahead the moment he was free of the press. Chaloner was not far behind.

Leigh was on the far side of the gate, brazenly scanning the faces of those who passed. Chaloner supposed it was just as well Blue Dick was beyond caring, because Leigh would have given the game away in an instant. The scrutiny made the killer uneasy, too, because he edged away, to avoid passing the little soldier too closely.

'Where is Blue Dick?' Leigh demanded, when he saw Chaloner alone. 'Did you lose him?'

'Dead.' Chaloner indicated the killer with a nod of his head. 'Stabbed by him.'

Leigh's jaw dropped in shock. 'What? But why would—'

'That is what we need to find out.' Chaloner began to run, aware of Leigh turning to follow. He skidded to a standstill when the killer darted into a nearby church, and was almost bowled from his feet when Leigh barrelled into the back of him. He regained his balance without taking his eyes off the place. It was impressive, with a lofty central tower and elegant tracery in its Gothic windows.

'That is St Mary Overie,' mused Leigh. 'Perhaps he is going to pray for forgiveness.'

Chaloner recalled the purposeful way the villain had moved before striking, and knew remorse had no part in his plans. 'I suspect he is either going to divest himself of his killing clothes, or he is going to report to an accomplice. Either way, we need to—'

'All right,' said Leigh grimly, and began to stride towards the door before any sort of strategy could be

15

discussed. 'No one commits murder on *my* watch, not even of iconoclasts.'

Chaloner sighed, and wished the Earl employed more sensible men to serve him – or, if he did insist on populating his household with simpletons and lunatics, that he did not force him to work alongside them.

Leigh had moved fast, and was inside the church by the time Chaloner caught up with him. There was no sign of the killer, and Chaloner grabbed Leigh's arm to prevent him from storming up the aisle to look for him.

'What?' demanded the little soldier irritably, freeing himself with a scowl. 'Do you want to lay hands on this scoundrel or not? If you dally, he might escape.'

'But if we arrest him and he refuses to talk, what then?' asked Chaloner with quiet reason. 'We need to tell the Earl *why* Blue Dick is murdered. And the best way to do that is by seeing where the culprit goes and who he meets.'

Leigh stared at him for a moment. 'Very well. We shall sneak around like thieves then, if that is what you want. Follow me. I am a skilled soldier, decorated in battle. I know what I am doing.'

Chaloner refrained from remarking that if Leigh was among the best the Royalist army had to offer, then it was small wonder they had lost the civil wars.

'No, we need to separate,' he said, struggling for patience as he seized the man's wrist a second time. 'Watch him from two different angles, to ensure we do not miss anything. So you take the south side, and I will take the north.'

Leigh rolled his eyes at the need for such tactics, but obligingly strode towards the area Chaloner had indicated, booted feet slapping on the flagstones. The racket he made obviated any need for stealth, but Chaloner moved silently anyway, out of habit, as he made his way through the northern part of the church.

St Mary Overie was an attractive place, full of yellow-grey pillars that soared up to a yellow-grey roof. It smelled of damp plaster and the decorative greenery that had been placed in the windows by parishioners. Because the day was overcast, the light filtering through the soot-coated windows was dim, and the building was full of shadows.

The killer was in the north transept, and Chaloner reached him before Leigh. But the fellow was not alone. He was with six others, all clad in wide-brimmed hats and anonymous cloaks. Their lower faces were covered by the kind of scarves designed to protect the wearer from London's foul air, but which were also favoured as disguises by the criminal fraternity.

Chaloner eased closer – they were talking, and he was keen to hear what was being said. He crouched behind a chest to eavesdrop, hoping Leigh would see him and have the sense to hold back.

'—on the Bridge,' the killer was whispering. There was blood on his hands; it had been an efficient attack, but not a clean one. 'No one saw me.'

'I wish you had consulted us first,' murmured a man who was taller than his companions. He seemed to be in charge. 'This may attract unwanted attention.'

'Well, it is done now,' said the killer, oozing defiance. 'And I am not—'

He whipped around at the rattle of footsteps: Leigh had arrived. The little soldier baulked when he saw the killer had company, and started to back away, but it was too late: seven swords had been hauled from seven scabbards. Chaloner was begrudgingly impressed when Leigh

17

did not run, as most men would have done when faced with such unattractive odds, but resorted to bluster.

'I want a word with you,' he said imperiously to the killer. 'And the rest of you may as well show your faces, too, because I do not approve of disguises. Come on, unmask yourselves. I command you, by authority of the Earl of Clarendon, Lord Chancellor of England!'

The leader laughed his disbelief. '*You* order *us*? In the name of that rogue? He belongs in the Tower, and I cannot imagine why the King does not slice off his head.'

'You insolent dog!' cried Leigh. He drew his sword and prepared to do battle. 'How dare you!'

It occurred to Chaloner that if he stayed hidden until Leigh was killed, he might discover the identities of the men *and* learn why one had murdered Blue Dick – and Leigh would only have himself to blame for his predicament. But Leigh was a colleague, when all was said and done, and Chaloner supposed he owed him some support. With a sigh of resignation, he surged to his feet and had disabled two of the cloaked men before they realised that the feisty warrior was not alone.

The fighting was unexpectedly brutal, and while Chaloner took care not to inflict fatal injuries – he had no wish to kill anyone before he understood what was going on – the same was not true of his opponents. They were not particularly skilled swordsmen, but they fought with a fierce, unwavering resolve that was unnerving. It reminded him of the savage hand-to-hand combat during the civil wars, when men were protecting the things they held dear: their families and homes.

'Who are you?' Chaloner demanded, when he had managed to corner the killer and had a blade to his throat. 'Tell me your name.'

'Never!' came the hissing reply. Eyes glittered furiously above the scarf. 'I would sooner die.'

Chaloner was tempted to oblige – the man was a cold-blooded murderer, after all – but a sound behind caused him to whip around, and then he was obliged to fight three men at once. He grabbed the scarf of one who came too close and pulled it hard, intending to expose the fellow's face, but it had been tied too tightly to come off. Then there was a loud crack that echoed around the church, and set up a wild squawking of gulls outside.

'Stop!' came the commanding voice of the leader. He held a second gun, and was pointing it at Chaloner, who saw it was primed and ready to fire. Meanwhile, Leigh was lying on his back with a sword at his throat. 'And back away. I shall not miss the next time.'

The cold, angry gleam in his eyes said he meant it. Reluctantly, Chaloner did as he was told, and the leader indicated with a flick of his head that his cronies were to leave the church. They obeyed immediately.

'I will be waiting outside for the next few minutes,' the leader said, before turning to follow them. 'If you come after us, I will shoot you.'

Chaloner waited until he was out of sight, then hared after them. He wrenched open the door, then jerked backwards when there was a sharp report. It was closely followed by a second crack, and the wood near his head flew into splinters.

'Three shots fired so far,' whispered Leigh, coming to stand behind Chaloner. 'Three guns. Do they have a fourth, do you think? Shall we risk it, and run out?'

Chaloner shook his head. The last shot had come closer than was comfortable, and the chase was not worth their lives. He leaned against the door and closed his

19

eyes, wishing Leigh had not blundered in so soon, because he had heard nothing that would allow him to identify the killer and his companions.

'Lord!' breathed Leigh, wiping his forehead with his sleeve. 'What they lacked in skill they certainly made up for with mettle. I do not think I have ever met such resolute opponents.'

'I have,' said Chaloner softly. 'In the civil wars – men who believed God was on their side.'

'You mean fanatics?' asked Leigh uneasily. 'I wonder which particular brand these are: Catholics, old Roundheads, Fifth Monarchists, general rebels. How shall we go about finding out?'

'*We* shall not,' said Chaloner, deciding the time had come to dispense with Leigh's annoying company. '*You* are going to report to the Earl, while I stay here and ask a few questions.'

Chaloner rarely ventured south of the river, which meant he did not know Southwark very well. When he had first visited it, he had assumed it would be an extension of the City, but was soon disavowed of that notion. Southwark was a place like no other, with its curious combination of stately homes and hovels, its discreetly gardened brothels and lice-infested whore-houses, and its sprawling taverns and bear-baiting arenas. It was always crowded, and many of its lanes were so narrow that there was no room for carriages. It did not stop drivers from trying to use them anyway, and the result was some wicked congestion and very frayed tempers.

He headed for the main street, trying to decide which way the killer and his cronies might have gone. He was immediately mobbed – scruffy children tried to sell him cheap trinkets, prostitutes flaunted their wares, and vagrants whined for alms. His hand dropped to his sword, which led some to melt away, but not all. He supposed they were used to threats.

As there was no sign of his quarry, and enquiries among the clamouring throng yielded nothing in the way of sensible answers, Chaloner headed for the area known as St George's Fields, where there was an inn-cum-brothel named the Dog and Duck. He had been there a few weeks before, and while he did not imagine its bawds would know the men he was looking for, they might be able to provide him with a list of potential haunts – the kind of taverns known to look the other way when masked men gathered.

He reached the Dog and Duck, still pursued by one man determined to sell him a pair of used gloves, and stepped inside. His eyes smarted. It was noon, and the time when dinner was eaten – the place was full, and every patron was puffing a pipe; he could not see the opposite side of the room through the fug. He was barely through the door when a woman came to take possession of him.

'What will it be?' she asked, all business. 'Food first, and then me? Or just me?'

'Alice?' asked Chaloner, trying to see past the paints and pastes slathered on her face. She was not attractive when washed and wearing her Sunday best, but the vivid mask and sluttish clothes made her look vaguely unearthly, like the wax grave-models in Westminster Abbey. 'Is that you?'

'Tom!' she exclaimed in pleasure. 'I did not recognise you. Where have you been? We all assumed you had left the city. After all, there must be some reason why you have not been to visit.'

Chaloner could have told her that he had been in the nearby village of Wimbledon, monitoring Lord Bristol's country estate – the Earl had acquired a number of enemies through the years, but Bristol was by far one of the most dangerous. The sly nobleman had tried to topple the Earl from power the previous summer, but the plot had backfired and a warrant had been issued for his own arrest instead. Wisely, Bristol had fled the country, but there had been rumours of late that he was back. Alarmed, the Earl had demanded an investigation. However, Chaloner had watched Bristol's house for the best part of six weeks, and had seen nothing to indicate the gossip was true.

'I have been away,' he replied vaguely.

Fortunately, Alice was not interested in his travels, which was just as well, because Chaloner had been trained never to talk about himself. He believed that intelligence officers – he disliked the term 'spy', although it was how the Earl described him – should collect information rather than dispense it, and although he was no longer operating in enemy territory, it was a difficult habit to break.

'Meg died of the French pox last week,' Alice was saying. 'And Sally fell down the—'

'Meg?' interrupted Chaloner, dismayed. 'She seemed well enough in December.'

'She hid it well.' Alice grinned spitefully. 'We do not know who gave her the sickness, but she shared the gift with as many men as she could before she went. That will show them!'

'It might show you, too,' said Chaloner. He shrugged when she regarded him blankly, and explained further. 'If she infected them, they might infect you in turn.'

Alice's grin turned bitter. 'They already have. Why do you think I am covered in plaster, like an old wall? Give me a shilling, Tom. I need it for medicine.'

Chaloner passed her the coin, grateful he had declined her services when they had been offered. French pox was incurable, and the notion of explaining to his lover how he had come by it was too awful to contemplate. Hannah was a lady-in-waiting to the Queen, and the wild debauchery of the Court made her something of a free thinker – it was one of the things he liked about her – but a beau with a sexually transmitted disease would tax even her liberal principles.

'I am looking for seven men who disguise themselves and lurk in St Mary Overie,' he said, after more pleasantries had been exchanged. 'Can you think of anywhere such men might meet?'

Alice thought hard. 'There are places in Paris Garden that turn a blind eye to squalid dealings.'

'Paris Garden?' Chaloner had never heard of it.

She closed her eyes. 'It used to be a lovely park, used for bowling and gambling, but it has a bad reputation these days. Try the Beggar's Bush tavern first. But mind yourself.'

With Alice's warning ringing in his ears, Chaloner left the Dog and Duck and turned west, walking parallel to the river. The road was lined by houses that were five or six storeys high. They leaned towards each other like drunks, and in places met overhead. It made the street dark, and there were several sections that would never be touched by natural sunlight.

Children were everywhere, clamouring for money or playing games with balls and hoops. Few wore shoes,

23

and their feet and legs were covered in sores. There were a large number of dogs, too. Some were tethered outside houses and snarled at anyone who went too close; others roamed free, hunting for food among the huge piles of rubbish that lay in festering heaps at every corner.

The stench of rotting vegetables, the glistening piles of entrails outside a butcher's emporium and the reek from a nearby glueworks, not to mention the all-pervading aroma of sewage, were enough to make Chaloner light-headed. He had not thought of himself as delicate, and wondered whether life at Court, spying on treacherous noblemen for his Earl, was turning him soft.

The beggar who had followed him from St Mary Overie to the Dog and Duck, latched on to him again, waving the second-hand gloves in his face and assuring him they were the finest quality. Chaloner ignored him, then realised the fellow did not see this as a deterrent; he was used to it.

'What is your name?' he asked, turning suddenly.

The man took a step away, unnerved by the abrupt attention. 'Nat,' he replied warily.

'Do you live here?'

Nat's clothes hung loosely on his skinny frame, and he was missing most of his teeth. His skin was grey with dirt, and his hair far too oily to allow a determination of colour. All this meant it was impossible to gauge his age – he might have been twenty or fifty. He nodded back the way they had come.

'Near St Mary Overie. But look at these lovely gloves, sir. They can be yours for three pennies.'

'I will give you three pennies for some information.'

Nat's eyes gleamed, and he bared his gums in a grin.

'What do you want to know? I can tell you anything. No one knows Southwark like me.'

'Seven masked men met in St Mary Overie today. You live near there, so did you see them?'

Nat nodded eagerly. 'The masks are scarves, to protect them against smells and cold weather.'

'Who are they? And I want the truth,' warned Chaloner, predicting from Nat's sly look that he was about to be regaled with some fiction. 'I will know if you lie.'

'But I don't know their names!' cried Nat. His expression was one of acute disappointment: three pennies was a lot to lose. 'They just arrive from time to time. They look fierce, so no one bothers them. Southwark folk don't go looking for trouble, and those men—'

'How often do they come?'

Nat screwed up his face in thought. 'Maybe seven or eight times since Christmas. Of course, they take care to keep to themselves, so they *may* have come a few times without me noticing . . .'

'I do not suppose you know their business?' Chaloner was not hopeful of an answer he could trust, but there was no harm in asking.

'I tried to sell one a ring once, but he said he got no use for cheap baubles.' Nat sounded indignant. 'So, I drew me own conclusions. They are boring religious types, like the folk who stopped us from having fun when the Old Tyrant was pretending to be king.'

Chaloner rubbed his chin. He had no use for cheap baubles, either, but that did not make him a Puritan. And Blue Dick *had* been a Puritan, with his penchant for smashing churches, so surely it was unlikely that the masked men were Puritans, too? Why kill one of their own?

'But they are nothing,' said Nat with a dismissive wave of his hand when Chaloner made no reply. 'There are far more important visitors to these parts than them.'

Chaloner imagined there were, because the prostitutes of Southwark were famous for their variety, and whoring was a popular pastime among certain members of Court.

Nat began to name them. 'The Duke of Buckingham comes regular, and so does Mr Progers, who hires women to take to the King. And the Penderel brothers, who are that horrible Dowager's latest favourites. Everyone knows she's thinking about getting herself a nice young husband, and they came to London in the hope that she will pick one of them.'

Chaloner had also heard it said that the King's mother was on the prowl for a youthful spouse, but doubted it was true. The old queen was far too fond of being a widow. And there was always spiteful gossip about her, because her prickly character and arrogance meant she was unpopular.

'*She* comes here, too, you know,' Nat went on, when Chaloner still did not answer.

Chaloner raised his eyebrows, amused by the notion. The Dowager was one of his Earl's many enemies, and he had often been sent to spy on her. Although he had never met her in person, he had watched and listened to her often enough to know she was a prim, impatient snob, who would deplore the poverty and roughness of Southwark. She would never deign to set foot in such a place.

Nat became indignant when he saw he was not believed. 'She does! Not to a tavern, obviously, but to Winchester Palace, where the Bishop of Winchester stays while he is in London.'

'She visits Bishop Morley?' Chaloner did not think

that was very likely, either. The fiercely Catholic Dowager would have little to say to a high-ranking Anglican cleric.

'No, she goes there when he's out,' replied Nat.

Chaloner regarded him sceptically. 'Why would she do that?'

Nat looked furtive – he did not know. 'Perhaps she likes the view across the river.'

Chaloner supposed she must have taken a fancy to some piece of art in the Bishop's collection. Nobles were an acquisitive crowd, especially the ones who had suffered privation under Cromwell, and it was not unusual for them to covet someone else's property. And they often got it, too, because objections by the injured party tended to be met with indignant accusations of treason.

'I heard Lord Bristol was with her once,' Nat gabbled on. 'And he's a wanted man! The King ordered him arrested, but Bristol thinks he can flout the law by slinking back into our country.'

'You only heard?' asked Chaloner keenly. 'You did not actually see him?'

'No, but it is true. The Dowager will hide him in her own mansion – Somerset House. He will be safe there, because not even the King orders a raid on his mother's home.'

But Chaloner knew the Dowager would never do anything to put her son in such an invidious position. Moreover, he did not believe the rumours that said Bristol was back in England. There had been dozens of reported sightings, but when he had investigated, not one had been true. If it had, Chaloner would have hunted the man down, and Bristol would be in the Tower. Where the Earl wanted him.

* * *

27

Alice was right: Paris Gardens had once been a fine park. But now it was all bedraggled shrubs, muddy paths and overgrown copses that looked as though they would be dangerous to explore. It was populated by slovenly men, children with pinched, hard little faces, and greasy-headed slatterns. Shanty houses surrounded it – the kind that were thrown up overnight, and that seemed to be expanding at an alarming rate as folk flocked from the countryside in search of work.

The Beggar's Bush tavern overlooked an arena where bear-baiting, cock-fighting and rat-racing took place. It was an enormous place, and boasted accommodations fit for visiting aristocrats, as well as for the lower kind of customer. There were rooms for playing cards and drinking tea, there were bedchambers that could be hired by the hour, and there were nooks where men could sit quietly and drink Southwark's famous ale. It even served food, although that day's menu was limited to a choice of braised calves' brains or pickled sweetbreads.

Chaloner entered the largest of the public rooms, and found a bench in the shadows near the back. The reek of tobacco vied with that of unwashed, sweaty bodies, and the place was busy with patrons of all ages, from all walks of life. Well-dressed lawyers sat at one table, while the next was full of rowdy apprentices, all laughing about a tale from St Paul's Cathedral, where a gargoyle had dropped off the roof and killed a pigeon. Chaloner winced – he liked birds.

He looked around him, weighing up the clientele. A huddle of heavily armed men sat near a back door; they spoke in whispers, and he was under the distinct impression that they were planning a crime. Others sat alone, smoking and staring into space. It did not look like the kind of place that would yield its secrets easily, so he decided to sit for a while, to assess which patrons might be more inclined to talk – either for money, or because he was holding a knife to their throats.

He was still observing an hour later, when the door opened and two men walked in. The first wore his fashionable clothes with an elegant rakishness, and exuded the sense that he thought very highly of himself. His companion was also finely attired, but his muscular build and pronounced stoop meant he would never achieve his companion's careless élan.

The landlord regarded them warily, and as his other patrons were hardly choirboys, Chaloner's interest was piqued. The duo took a table near him, so he pretended to be asleep, in the hope that they would speak more freely than if they thought he was awake and listening.

'Mr Phillippes,' said the landlord, addressing the shorter of the two, and then turning to his friend. 'And Mr Kaltoff. I am surprised you dare show your faces here.'

Phillippes made a moue of annoyance. 'Oh, come now, sir! Can we not let bygones be bygones? We have, after all, been faithful customers for many years.'

'I suppose you have,' said the landlord begrudgingly. 'Will it be the usual, then? Rhenish wine?'

Phillippes inclined his head. 'You are most kind.'

'I heard the ghost of the old king was seen again last night,' said Kaltoff conversationally, as the landlord set about serving them. 'And did you know that the learned men in Gresham's College are planning an experiment to weigh air tomorrow?'

The landlord regarded him in mystification. 'Why would anyone want to weigh air?'

Phillippes bristled. 'I will have you know that the weighing of air is a vital scientific objective. I have written a scholarly paper on the matter, and plan to read it to the Royal Society.'

'You have been elected at last, then?' asked the landlord. He did not sound very interested.

Phillippes continued to glare. 'Not yet, no,' he said stiffly. 'But it is only a matter of time before they welcome me into their fold. I *am* the inventor of the Phillippes Tide-Ring, after all.'

'And *I* built it,' added Kaltoff proudly. '*I* turned theory into reality.'

Chaloner supposed they did look like instrument-makers – men who earned a respectable wage and who were a cut above the average merchant in terms of education and social status.

'What is a tide-ring?' asked the landlord. The distrustful expression on his face suggested he thought it might be something diabolical.

Phillippes looked pained. 'It is a device that calculates the ebb and flow of tides. The King has asked me to design one for him, because it will let him predict when the Palace of White Hall will flood. So has the Earl of Clarendon. Their patronage is a great honour.'

'Phillippes will do the designing, and I shall construct them,' elaborated Kaltoff. 'The work of both of us will grace royal eyes.'

'Is that so?' said the landlord flatly. 'Then all I can say is that you cannot test them here. You almost demolished my tavern when you tried out your last invention, and I am not having it again.'

Phillippes winced. 'How many more times must we

apologise? The experiment *should* have worked, and neither of us understands why it failed.'

Kaltoff grinned suddenly. 'But look on the bright side: no one was badly hurt, and you have made a fortune from all the people who drink your ale as they listen to you describe what happened. Besides, we told you not to stand too close.'

The landlord sniffed, indicating Kaltoff was right. 'I still have dreams, you know. You have no idea what it was like. There I was, watching you light your special fireworks one moment, then the next, I was blown clean off my feet, while my hat ended up on the roof. My nerves will never recover.'

'It should have produced a magnificent display,' said Phillippes. He shook his head in bafflement. 'It should have lifted off and filled the sky with a blossom of falling purple lights. I still do not understand why it did not work. It was a good theory.'

'If you say so,' said the landlord flatly. 'But you can find somewhere else to test the next one.'

He stamped away, leaving Kaltoff to embark upon a long and tediously detailed report about some obscure aspect of the King's new tide-dial. Phillippes listened, but looked bored, and his gaze roved aimlessly over the tavern's other occupants. It settled on Chaloner, who was still pretending to be asleep. Phillippes stiffened, studied the intelligencer intently for a moment, then jabbed Kaltoff with his elbow and whispered something in his ear.

'Are you sure?' Kaltoff asked, his voice much lower than when he had been holding forth about his work. Fortunately, Chaloner had excellent hearing.

Phillippes nodded. 'I am good with faces – he has not

been here before. Moreover, I do not like the look of him. Why does he choose to nap here?'

'Perhaps he is tired,' suggested Kaltoff.

Phillippes glared at him. 'How can you be so blasé? You know what is at stake, and what we stand to lose, should we be found out. He is a spy, sent to watch us. I feel it in my bones.'

'But we have been careful,' objected Kaltoff, while Chaloner braced himself for trouble. 'No one knows our plan. You are worrying over nothing.'

'Worrying is wise, given what we have agreed to do,' retorted Phillippes firmly. 'So I recommend we follow him when he leaves, and ask him a few questions.'

'But that will tell him there *is* something to be interested in,' Kaltoff pointed out uneasily.

Phillippes's lips set in a grim line. 'Then we shall have show him that curiosity is dangerous.'

Chaloner had no intention of being trailed home by Phillippes and Kaltoff when he left the Beggar's Bush, and nor was he inclined to spend the rest of the day pretending to be asleep in the hope that they would decide he really was just a man who had nodded off over his beer. Moreover, he wanted to know whether their enigmatic remarks pertained to the murder of Blue Dick – both looked agile and strong enough to have been the killer – but it was clear he was not going to find out by eavesdropping. Keeping his face hidden by his hat, he pretended to come awake, then stood, stretched and made for the door.

He walked briskly, and although he was occasionally aware of Kaltoff and Phillippes behind him, they were adept at keeping out of sight. He was impressed, and realised that here were no rank amateurs, but men who had some idea of what they were doing. He was loath to waste time with games, though, and had his own questions to ask. He cut down a narrow, shadowy lane to his right, and ducked into the first available doorway, so as to be hidden when they turned the corner.

But they did not appear. He frowned. Were they less able than he had surmised, and the tactic had flummoxed them? Or had they guessed his intentions, and had their own ideas about how the situation was going to evolve? If the latter, then he would have to be careful, because he did not want them knowing where he lived.

He was about to abandon the doorway and take a tortuous route that would foil even the most experienced of trackers, when he heard footsteps coming from his right. It was not the direction from which Phillippes or Kaltoff should be approaching, and the clatter indicated that several men, not two, were on their way. A second rattle told him that people were approaching from the left, too, and a quick glance into the lane showed eight men converging on him. Phillippes led one group, and Kaltoff the other. Disgusted, Chaloner saw he had allowed himself to be outmanoeuvred.

'I know you are in here,' Phillippes called softly. 'So you may as well come out. My friends here will be vexed if you put them to more trouble than is necessary.'

Seeing there was no choice, Chaloner stepped out. His hat was still pulled low over his eyes, and he kept it that way, determined that his captors should not see his face.

'What do you want?' he asked coolly. 'Or is every new patron at the Beggar's Bush provided with this sort of reception?'

Phillippes regarded him arrogantly. 'You were spying on us. We want to know why.'

'Spying on you?' asked Chaloner, feigning astonishment. 'Why would I do that?'

Phillippes shrugged. 'Perhaps you heard something about us.'

Chaloner spread his hands. 'What could I have heard? I am a stranger here.'

'Enough of these games,' said Kaltoff abruptly. 'It seems to me that you know something about our business, and that is unacceptable. Who sent you?'

'No one,' replied Chaloner truthfully. 'But perhaps we can help each other. You look like men who may know the answers to a few harmless questions.'

Kaltoff started to refuse, but Phillippes held up an imperious hand. Then he indicated with a jerk of his head that their men were to back away, out of earshot. 'What sort of questions?'

Chaloner decided to use a combination of honesty and lies. 'I am looking for seven men who meet in St Mary Overie. I may have work for them – work that pays well.'

Phillippes's expression was unreadable. 'We know of no such men.'

'No, we do not,' agreed Kaltoff. 'And we do not like strangers who eavesdrop on our private conversations, either. In other words, we have no more to say to each other.'

He turned to leave, but Phillippes had other ideas, and beckoned to the waiting louts. Chaloner knew their kind: dirty, slovenly men who hung around on street corners, and who would do anything for a few coins. It would not be a fair fight, and he did not like the odds of his winning.

When Phillippes barked the order to attack, Chaloner

charged across the lane to a gate in the opposite wall – he had noticed it ajar when he had taken refuge in his doorway. Sincerely hoping it would not lead somewhere from which there would be no escape, he shot through it, and slammed it behind him. He heard a roar of startled outrage from Phillippes, followed immediately by a thud as someone smashed into it with his shoulder. It shuddered, and although Chaloner jammed a log against it, he knew it would not keep anyone out for long.

He looked around him, aware that someone was already beginning to scale the wall – he could hear the scrape of shoes against bricks. He was in a small yard, and there was a door at the far end. He dashed towards it, then lost valuable seconds picking the lock. By the time he had it open, Kaltoff and two of his men were over the wall and dropping down into the yard.

Chaloner knew the house in which he found himself belonged to a tailor, because it was full of cloth and half-finished clothes. Pins rolled under his feet as he darted across the flagstone floor, aiming for a second door, which he hoped would open into the main road. But it was also locked, and he knew he would not be able to pick it before he was caught. He drew his sword, supposing it was time to fight. The odds were unfavourable, but there was no other alternative that he could see.

Kaltoff saw the sword and reached for his knife, but at that moment, there was the scrape of a key in a lock, and the door behind Chaloner opened. The house's owner was home.

Chaloner jigged around him and raced into the street. Behind, he heard a furious commotion as the tailor attempted to do battle with the remaining intruders. By the time Kaltoff had fought his way past the fellow,

Chaloner had taken refuge in a passing hay cart and was hidden from sight. Breathing hard and clearly disgusted when he saw his quarry gone, Kaltoff gave up the chase and began to slouch away.

Prudently, Chaloner remained in the cart until it had crossed the Bridge, and he was sure he had not been followed. As it rumbled along, he considered what had happened. Were the instrument-makers responsible for stabbing Blue Dick? Or was it some other mischief that warranted them hiring louts to attack men they did not like the look of? He supposed he would have to return to Southwark later, and make enquiries. He decided he would go that night, but not until after ten o'clock, when ale had had time to lubricate tongues.

He jumped off the cart when it reached Thames Street. The short winter day was almost over, and the streets were full of people, all going home from work. But Chaloner was too unsettled to go home – two rented rooms in Fetter Lane – and nor did he wish to inflict his agitation on Hannah, whom he knew would be tired. Hannah's mistress, Queen Katherine, took her religion seriously, and that Friday was the feast-day of one of her favourite saints. Hannah did not mind the additional duties she had been allocated for the occasion, having converted to Catholicism herself, but he did not think she would thank him for arriving full of restless energy, even so.

Feeling he should do something to make up for the fact that his enquiries into Blue Dick's murder had been rather less than successful, he decided to do a little spying on his Earl's behalf.

Somerset House, where the King's dowager mother

lived, had recently become a meeting place for anyone who hated the Earl. By listening at doors and windows, and once by breaking in, Chaloner had managed to foil three attempts to besmirch his master's reputation alone in the week since he had returned from Wimbledon. All had been spiteful little schemes that would have seen the Earl accused of dishonesty. Alarmed by his enemies' sly determination to harm him, the Earl had ordered Chaloner to monitor the place as often as his other duties allowed.

So Chaloner went to Somerset House, which was a vast Tudor palace with stately grounds and a splendid façade overlooking the Thames. It was protected by high walls, but these were no object to a spy of his skills and experience: he had identified several places with convenient hand- and footholds, the easiest route being through the gardens of neighbouring Worcester House. And as his Earl lived in Worcester House, gaining access to the enemy's stronghold was simplicity itself.

He scaled the wall and dropped over the other side, rolling as he landed, to lessen the impact on the leg that had been damaged during the Battle of Naseby some nineteen years before, and that still troubled him on occasion. Then he stood, brushed himself down, and jogged towards the house, noting that it was ablaze with lights. The Dowager was entertaining.

As he approached, a haunting melody wafted across the garden, and he smiled when he recognised the distinctive tones of the King's Private Musick. They were playing Matthew Locke, one of his favourite composers. He listened for a moment, eyes closed, but then opened them abruptly when he became aware that the exquisite harmonies were pulling him into a world of their own.

37

He could not afford to be distracted when he was prowling around a building crammed to the gills with his employer's most bitter opponents.

The Dowager's guests had gathered in the room called the Great Chamber, a cavernous, high-ceilinged hall on the ground floor. It was graced by six massive windows, and liberally decorated with gold leaf and gilt mirrors. The curtains had been drawn in an attempt to keep out the cold, but the servants had been careless, and a size-able chink allowed Chaloner to see directly inside.

The musicians were playing at one end of the room, and the Dowager and her visitors – all folk who hated the Earl – milled about at the other. As usual, the flamboyant Duke of Buckingham was the centre of attention. Tall, handsome and exquisitely attired in the very latest fashion, he stood in the midst of an admiring throng. The throng included Edward Progers, whose chief talent was said to lie in supplying prostitutes for the King. He was an exceptionally ugly man, who attempted to conceal his ill looks by wearing extra lace and an especially frilly coat.

The Duke's cousin, Lady Castlemaine, was there, too, revelling in her role as King's Mistress. She was surrounded by lesser courtiers, all of whom vied for her attention like smitten schoolboys. Her dress was cut so low that she was forced to make adjustments each time she moved, to avoid embarrassing spillages. Chaloner supposed it was the prospect of such an accident that kept the sycophantic hordes buzzing around her, because it would not be for pleasant conversation. He had only met her once, but considered her sharp tongued, devious, selfish and shallow.

The Dowager sat in a chair near the fire with a rather

hideous lapdog in her arms. She watched her frivolous guests with an expression that was difficult to read, and Chaloner supposed her dislike of the Earl must be great indeed to force her into such company – she was religious, humourless and dour, and he doubted she approved of the courtiers who cavorted around her. He studied her carefully, taking in her arrogant, haughty features and elegant black finery. She had never forgiven England for beheading her husband, and the black clothes were to remind everyone of it.

She was surrounded by Capuchin friars, grey-robed clerics who were an offshoot of the Franciscan Order. As easily identifiable Catholics, they were hated by the general populace, and Chaloner suspected the Dowager kept them near her as an act of defiance – to show Londoners that she did as she pleased and cared nothing for their opinions. This put the poor Capuchins in an invidious position, and they looked acutely uncomfortable in the presence of such ostentatious luxury, too – the three knots on their rope belts represented poverty, chastity and obedience, none of which were in any great evidence at Somerset House that evening.

Four men stood near them, raising goblets in sloppy toasts and laughing as they did so. They bore enough of a resemblance to each other to suggest they were close kin, and had the lean, hungry look of fortune-seekers. Chaloner had seen the Penderel brothers before; they rented a house on Tothill Street, where Hannah lived. The Southwark beggar had mentioned them, too – they were the men rumoured to think themselves worthy candidates for the Dowager's hand in marriage.

After a while, the Dowager clapped her hands. Immediately, the music stopped, and the players trooped out of the room; the entertainment was over, and it was time for business. The lesser courtiers were politely but firmly herded into another chamber, and the Dowager was left with her inner circle. This included Buckingham, Progers, Lady Castlemaine and the Penderels.

The Capuchins also withdrew, although a dark-haired, slender man wearing the robes of a Catholic priest remained. He looked uneasy, even when a bulky fellow with an enormous moustache came to grip his shoulder reassuringly. Unfortunately, Chaloner could not hear what was being said, and knew he had to get inside if he wanted to learn anything useful.

Stealthily, Chaloner made his way to the back of Somerset House, and fiddled with the shutter on a window until it came loose, exactly as it had done the last time he had broken in. Then he climbed inside, and crept along a service corridor until he reached the Great Chamber.

There were two ways into the room. One was through the grand entrance used by the nobility; the other was via a servants' door that was set behind a sheet of brocade, an arrangement designed to ensure the great and the good would not be distracted by the comings and goings of minions. Chaloner opened the servants' door carefully and stepped through it, taking care to remain hidden behind the curtain.

'—will be coming,' Buckingham was saying. 'Soon.'

'How soon?' demanded Lady Castlemaine. 'I *hate* the notion of that vile Earl sitting next door, enjoying his ill-gotten powers. Incidentally, did you hear he has invited every bishop in the country to dine with him on Shrove Tuesday? He wants to stuff them full of fine food before all the fasting and self-denial of Lent.'

'Of course,' replied the Dowager. She spoke French, a language Chaloner knew from time spent spying there. 'That is why I have decided to throw a soiree of my own the same day – one that will outshine his in every respect.'

Lady Castlemaine clapped her hands in spiteful delight. 'Will there be fireworks? We could cause a good deal of irritation with those! And there is nothing he will be able to do about it!'

The Dowager nodded, eyes glittering with malice. 'That has already occurred to me, I assure you. However, Shrove Tuesday is almost two weeks away. It is a long time to wait.'

'You must be patient, ma'am,' said Buckingham soothingly. 'We must not—'

'I *have* been patient,' the Dowager snapped, rounding on him. 'However, I have decided that Shrove Tuesday is my limit. And if we do not have results by then, there will be trouble.'

'But that may not be practical,' objected Progers uneasily. 'And we do not want to risk—'

'Do not talk to me of risk,' snarled the Dowager. 'You know nothing of risk. And do not fob me off with talk of time and patience, either, because I am tired of it. I *shall* have what I want.'

'Yes, ma'am,' said Buckingham soothingly. 'And Lord Bristol will help. But he cannot show his face yet, because the King will have him arrested and thrown into prison.'

'Is he at Wimbledon?' asked the priest. His voice trembled when he spoke, and his hands were clenched into fists at his sides, apparently to prevent them from shaking. 'Only I heard rumours—'

'Of course he is not at Wimbledon,' said Buckingham

irritably, causing the priest to step back in alarm. 'He is reckless, but not a complete fool.'

Lady Castlemaine rested her hand on the priest's arm. It was intended to be a comforting gesture, but he shrank away from it as though it held poison. The Lady's eyes narrowed at the rebuff, and she immediately set about draping one elegant, smooth-skinned arm around his shoulders in a spitefully transparent attempt to fluster. She grinned her triumph when the hapless cleric flushed such a deep red that Chaloner wondered whether he might have a seizure.

'Father Stephen only repeats what is being said at Court,' she crooned, pulling her horrified victim closer towards her. Her bodice threatened to release its contents into his unwilling hands.

'I have heard those tales, too,' said the man with the moustache, reaching out to pull the priest away from her. She scowled, but let her victim go. 'Apparently, Thomas Luckin, Wimbledon's vicar, has been arrested for giving Bristol holy communion.'

'But Bristol is Catholic,' said Progers, sounding puzzled. 'And Luckin is Anglican. Why would Bristol deign to receive holy communion from such a man?'

'To ingratiate himself with the King,' explained Buckingham impatiently. 'By renouncing the Pope and asking Luckin to accept him back into the Anglican Church, he hopes His Majesty's heart will soften, and the arrest warrant will be revoked. However, while Luckin may well have obliged with a communion ceremony, the business certainly did not take place in Wimbledon.'

Chaloner tensed suddenly when he heard a sound behind him. Someone was coming! He was going to be caught, trapped between whoever was approaching and the Dowager's gathering. He ducked farther behind the curtain, desperately hoping the servant would be so engrossed in his duties that he would not look in the shadows to his right.

'Here come Doucett and Martin at last,' said Buckingham, cocking his head when he also heard the briskly tapping footsteps. 'Perhaps they have news to report.'

The first of two rough, soldierly men strode past Chaloner without noticing him, but he caused a draught as he went, and the curtain moved.

'*Gêneur*!' shouted the second furiously, immediately reaching for his sword. '*Larron*!'

Chaloner rushed at him, bowling him from his feet before turning to race back along the corridor. His companion had fast reactions, though, because Chaloner could hear him hot on his heels, howling in French as he went. Meanwhile, Buckingham was bawling for re-inforcements, Progers was calling for guns, and the Dowager's lapdog was yapping frantically. Chaloner scrambled through his window and tore towards the river, aiming to hide in the shrubs at the end of the garden. It was cold outside, and he did not anticipate the hunt would last long.

But he was wrong. The notion of a spy in her house had enraged the Dowager, and she was shrieking that no one was to be allowed back inside until they had laid hold of him. Every servant was rousted out to help, even the scullery maids, and there was soon an army of people beating the bushes in search of the invader. With a grimace, Chaloner saw he was going to have to revise his plans.

He broke cover, aiming for the gate that led to the river, hoping there would be a boat he could use. He found his way barred by the two French soldiers. He felled one with a punch, but the other's sword was at the ready, and he and Chaloner exchanged a series of brief but brutal ripostes.

Meanwhile, Buckingham had seen what was happening, and was running to their assistance. Resorting to gutter tactics, Chaloner hurled a handful of dirt into his opponent's face, blinding him, then bolted through the gate.

He found himself on a slippery pier that reeked of seaweed. A skiff was tethered, and he jumped into it, landing so hard that it almost capsized. Then he seized the oars and pulled away. It was difficult to see much in the velvety blackness of night, but he was aware of the pier filling with people. They bombarded him with missiles – stones, knives, pieces of wood, and even an uprooted plant – but he rowed steadily, and it was not many moments before he was invisible on the dark waters of the Thames.

Chapter 2

The Palace of White Hall was a sprawling affair that boasted more than two thousand rooms. It was the London residence of the King, his Queen and a number of high-ranking nobles, and comprised manicured gardens, sumptuous apartments, bakeries, laundries, steam rooms, cellars, breweries, butteries, pantries and galleries. It had been built piecemeal over the centuries, as and when money had been available, and the result was a chaotic jumble of buildings connected by irrationally winding corridors, oddly shaped yards and narrow alleys. It had taken Chaloner weeks to find his way around, and even now there were pockets with which he was still unfamiliar.

He was very familiar with the suite of first-floor offices overlooking the Privy Gardens, though, because it was here that the Earl of Clarendon, currently Lord Chancellor of England and the man who employed him, did business.

Just after dawn the following morning, Chaloner climbed the marble staircase that led to the Earl's office. He did so slowly, not looking forward to the impending interview, because he was going to be in trouble on three counts: for failing to prevent the murder of Blue Dick Culmer, for neglecting to lay hold of the killer, and for coming so close to capture at Somerset House the previous night. The last crime was likely to be regarded as especially heinous, because his arrest would have been embarrassing for the Earl.

At the top of the stairs was a tiny, cupboard-like chamber, which was the domain of the Earl's secretary. John Bulteel was a slight, nervous man whose clothes always fitted him poorly, no matter how much he spent on tailors. He was unpopular among his colleagues, because he was socially inept, and when he revealed his decayed teeth in a smile, it was the sort of expression that made most men want to secure their purses, despite his reputation for honesty. He liked to bake in his spare time, and often shared his cakes with Chaloner – and as espionage was not an occupation conducive to making friends, this was appreciated more than Bulteel would ever know.

'I was worried about you,' said Bulteel, when Chaloner poked his head around the door. 'Leigh told me about your desperate battle in St Mary Overie yesterday, during which firearms were discharged. Then he said you went off alone to search for the culprits. That was reckless.'

'It was like looking for a needle in a haystack,' said Chaloner gloomily, declining to comment on Leigh's penchant for exaggeration. 'I have no idea who those men were, or how I might find them again. All I know is that they have met in that church before.'

Bulteel jerked his head towards the Earl's office. 'You had better not keep him waiting. He is in a foul mood today.'

'Gout?' The Earl was a martyr to the condition, which sometimes kept him in bed for weeks.

'No. He is furious because the Dowager has booked all the best musicians for Shrove Tuesday. This morning we heard that she intends to host a ball on the same day that the Earl has invited all the bishops to dine with him, and she has wasted no time in recruiting entertainers. The King's Private Musick sent a note saying they were sorry to cancel, but the Dowager offered them more money.'

Chaloner shrugged. 'There are other performers in London. She cannot have hired them all.'

'Actually, she has – or all the best ones, at least. Personally, I suspect she does not need so many, and only wants to be sure there are none left for him. You know how she hates him. And she hates his Anglican prelates even more.'

'Yes, but . . .' Chaloner trailed off. Bulteel was right: stealing all the top musicians was the kind of petty tactic the Dowager might employ to spite the Earl.

'She is having fireworks, too,' Bulteel went on grimly. 'Lots of them. She promises a spectacular show, but I hate fireworks – all gaudy colours, nasty smells and loud bangs. Did we not have enough explosions during the wars?'

Chaloner certainly had: it had been an exploding cannon that had given him his lame leg. 'I imagine any display commissioned by the Dowager will be properly controlled,' he said, hoping it was true. 'Professional men will light them, and—'

'The professional man is dead,' interrupted Bulteel. 'He was murdered last Bonfire Night, when he was walking home late. The Court has not yet appointed a replacement Green Man.'

The royal firework master was called the Green Man,

possibly because he covered himself with green leaves – partly to protect himself from sparks, but mostly to make sure spectators did not see him lighting his fuses.

'Why is the post left empty? Does no one want to take it?' asked Chaloner.

'One man is desperate for the honour. Sir John Winter knows more about gunpowder than any man alive, and he is a long-serving, deeply loyal Royalist. But he will never be appointed.'

'Why not?'

'Because he is Catholic, and the government does not want one of those in charge of large quantities of gunpowder. Why do you think they encourage people to celebrate Guy Fawkes Night? To remind us all of what might happen should papists get hold of explosives.'

Chaloner laughed, thinking he was joking, but Bulteel's expression remained grave. 'But the plot to blow up parliament was more than fifty years ago!' he objected, shocked by his friend's bigotry.

'So what?' argued Bulteel. 'There is nothing to say they will not try it again, and I can tell you now that Winter will never be trusted with that post.'

'That is ridiculous,' declared Chaloner, although he could see he was wasting his time by trying to reason with Bulteel – the secretary had an unfortunate and irrational tendency to believe the government could do no wrong. He changed the subject before they could argue; he did not want to lose one of his few friends to a petty quarrel, and Bulteel was a very good cook. 'Is this all that has annoyed the Earl this morning? The Dowager poaching the King's Private Musick?'

'No. He is also vexed with you for letting that iconoclast die. The body has been taken to the Westminster charnel house, by the way. I doubt it will yield much in the way of clues, but you had better inspect it, anyway. Surgeon Wiseman has been instructed to do the same.'

Chaloner did not think that was necessary. 'I saw Culmer stabbed. An examination is unlikely to yield anything useful, so tell Wiseman not to waste his—'

'I shall do no such thing! Besides, he will do as the Earl asks, because he is obedient. I advise you to be the same – work started on the Earl's fine new mansion over in Piccadilly last week, and it is transpiring to be more expensive than he anticipated.'

'So?' asked Chaloner, failing to see the connection.

'So he will be looking to make cuts among his staff to finance it. And he will pay above the odds for Clarendon House to be finished as soon as possible, because he hates his current residence with a passion. And who can blame him? It does stand next door to the Dowager's lair.'

'Clarendon House!' spat Chaloner in disgust. 'It is too grand, and will make him unpopular. And so will his rigid stance on any form of religion that is not devised by Anglican bishops—'

'Hush!' hissed Bulteel, looking around in alarm. 'He will hear you.'

'I wish he would: it might save him from disaster. Incidentally, do you know a man named Phillippes? He is designing some sort of scientific instrument – a tide-ring – for the Earl.'

Bulteel nodded. 'He is what is known as a dial-maker, although I cannot say I took to him. Or to his associate, Casper Kaltoff. They came here to discuss measurements and prices, and I suspect they are overcharging the Earl

49

because he does not really understand what a tide-ring does.'

'Then why does he want one?' asked Chaloner, baffled.

'Because the King has commissioned one, and that means they will soon become fashionable.'

Chaloner supposed he should not be surprised: appearances were important in Restoration London. 'What can you tell me about Phillippes and Kaltoff?'

'Not much,' said Bulteel apologetically. 'Both are Catholic, and eager to join the Royal Society. Mr Williamson had them investigated when the King began to invite them to his private quarters for scientific chats, but there was no suggestion of anything untoward.'

Williamson was currently Spymaster General, a sly, aloof man who ran the country's intelligence network. In an ideal world, Williamson would have recruited Chaloner, and would have been delighted to secure the services of a man who had more than a decade's experience in espionage. But the reality was that Williamson hated Chaloner, partly because Chaloner had spent most of his adult life employed by Oliver Cromwell's regime, and partly because he blamed him – unfairly – for the death of a friend.

'How do you know what Williamson's investigations found?' Chaloner asked curiously.

Bulteel shrugged. 'He told me over dinner last night.'

'You had dinner with Williamson?' Chaloner was appalled. He could not imagine why a decent, honest man like Bulteel should elect to keep such unsavoury company.

Bulteel nodded happily. 'He often talks to me about his work. He talks about you, too.'

'He does?' Chaloner was acutely uneasy. What game

was the Spymaster playing? 'What does he tell you? His dreams of having me assassinated? We both know he wants me dead.'

Bulteel looked horrified. 'No! He would never resort to that sort of thing. At least, not to you.'

Chaloner regarded him suspiciously. 'You seem very sure.'

'I *am* sure. You are aware that he makes me provide him with information about the Earl – you once said it is his job to recruit spies in White Hall, and that I do the Earl no disservice by reporting details of his business, just as long as I reveal nothing harmful. Well, he often asks about you, and I know for a fact that he wants you alive. He says you might be useful one day.'

'He wants me for his intelligence service?' Chaloner was filled with a sudden hope that he might be forgiven at last. He spoke several languages, had a good grasp of Dutch politics, and there was nothing he would like more than to be posted back to The Hague. Spying on hostile foreign governments was what he was good at – far more so than hunting killers and absconded barons.

'No, he does not trust you enough for that. But he says one can never be sure of what one might need in the future, and you may prove to be a useful asset one day.'

Chaloner supposed it was better than hearing that the Spymaster still wanted his blood. But not by much.

With a sense of foreboding, Chaloner tapped on the door and entered his employer's office. It was sumptuous, with thick rugs on the floors, paintings by Great Masters on the walls and lavishly upholstered furniture. The Earl of Clarendon was sitting behind his desk, surrounded by

51

paper. He was short, fat and prim, with a penchant for fancy clothes and large wigs. He also liked ridiculously narrow shoes that could not possibly be good for his gout, although no one had the nerve to tell him so, not even Surgeon Wiseman, who was notorious for his bold opinions and blunt tongue.

Chaloner's feelings towards the Earl were ambiguous. On the one hand, his master possessed moral courage and was comparatively honest – at least, by White Hall standards. On the other, he was bad-tempered, secretive and unpredictable. Meanwhile, the Earl's attitude towards his spy was equally ambivalent. He was abusive, contemptuous and critical, yet only a few weeks before, he had put himself in danger to save Chaloner's life. Chaloner did not understand him or their relationship, but suspected the Earl's lingering mistrust was because of his past.

After finishing his studies at Cambridge – interrupted when his regicide uncle had dragged him away to fight for Cromwell in the civil wars – Chaloner had gone to Lincoln's Inn to study law. There he had met a man named John Thurloe, who had later become Cromwell's Secretary of State and Spymaster General. Thurloe had recruited Chaloner as an intelligencer, sending him off to spy in France, Spain and Holland. But then Cromwell had died, Thurloe had been dismissed, and a second Charles had been invited to take the throne. Chaloner had expected to continue his work – the new King needed accurate reports on unfriendly foreign regimes just as urgently as Cromwell had – but Spymaster Williamson had made it perfectly clear that no ex-Parliamentarians were going to be employed in *his* intelligence service.

For a while, Chaloner had been destitute, but then he had met the Earl, who had agreed, albeit reluctantly, to overlook his past loyalties. However, while the Earl appreciated being able to tap into Chaloner's arsenal of specialist skills, the fact that they had taken opposite sides during a series of very bitter wars would always be something of a barrier between them.

'There you are,' said the Earl icily. Chaloner felt like an errant schoolboy when his master glared at him, hands folded across his ample paunch. 'I expected you sooner. It is almost eight o'clock.'

'I am sorry, sir. I spent most of last night in Southwark, trying to find the men who killed Blue Dick Culmer, and I was still trawling through taverns, alehouses and brothels at dawn. I had no idea there were so many of them.'

'Two hundred and thirty eight,' replied the Earl promptly. 'Of course, that is only taverns and alehouses. I would not know about the other places.' He pursed his lips prudishly.

Chaloner wondered how he came by such a precise number. Perhaps it was something to do with how much they could be taxed – the Court's expensive tastes had to be financed somehow.

The Earl eyed him balefully when he made no reply. 'You owe me a number of explanations. Let us start with Blue Dick. Why was he killed when you were supposed to be watching him?'

Chaloner was tempted to say he might have had some answers to give if Leigh had not charged into the situation like a wild bull, but it went against the grain to tell tales. 'It happened very fast,' he said instead. He gave a terse account of Blue Dick's death and the subsequent battle in St Mary Overie, finishing, 'and no one told us his life was in danger. If they had, we might have been able to save it.'

The Earl gaped at him. 'Is this your way of blaming *me*? You think I withheld information?'

'Do you know anything that might allow the killer to be identified?' Once the question was out, Chaloner realised it implied that he *did* believe the Earl had been less than honest with him. He braced himself for a tantrum, but the Earl only glowered.

'One day, you will push me too far, Chaloner. But the answer to your question is no. I heard – from a source I decline to divulge – that Blue Dick was in the city, and I was keen to know why. I cannot say I am sorry he is dead, given what he did to Canterbury Cathedral.'

'Do you have any idea who might want to kill him?'

The Earl nodded vigorously. 'Just about any right-thinking man and woman in the country. He despoiled priceless works of art, not to mention urinating on the shrine of St Thomas Becket.'

'I thought Becket's shrine – and its contents – was destroyed during the Reformation.'

'It was rebuilt, *sans* bones. But that is beside the point, which is that Blue Dick was a loathsome specimen. I do not know who killed him, but I suppose we had better look into the matter. We cannot have private citizens murdered all over the place. Where would it end?'

'Very well, sir.' Chaloner knew, with every fibre of his being, that he was not being told the whole truth. He also knew there was nothing he could do about it, and it was at times like these that he wished he still worked for Thurloe. Thurloe had been a professional in every sense of the word, and would never have sent his people into dangerous situations with only half a story. Moreover, he was a friend, something the Earl would never be.

'Now let us turn to another matter,' said the Earl.

'Namely the complaint I received pertaining to an intruder in Somerset House. The Dowager has accused me of sending a spy last night. Is it true?'

Chaloner was not sure what he was expected to say. Surely, the Earl remembered telling him to watch Somerset House as often as possible? Or was he distancing himself from the instruction, so he could claim the idea had been Chaloner's own?

'You did not order me there last night *specifically* . . .' he began.

'You know what I am asking,' snapped the Earl. 'Did you climb through a window, eavesdrop on a conversation in the Great Chamber, and then escape by stealing a boat?'

'I did not *steal* it,' objected Chaloner. He might be many things, but a thief was not one of them. 'It can be collected from the Milford Stairs, just a short distance from—'

'You really are a reckless scoundrel,' said the Earl, shaking his head in disbelief. 'Do you not understand what would have happened to you, had you been caught? *I* could not have helped – it would have been tantamount to admitting that I sent you there.'

'Then it is fortunate that I escaped,' said Chaloner coolly.

'Fortunate for both of us,' agreed the Earl blithely. 'So what did you learn during this perilous escapade? I hope you have something useful to report after taking such a risk.'

'They are planning something for Shrove Tuesday—'

'I am already aware of that. The Dowager will host a ball designed to disrupt my Bishops' Dinner – the occasion I have been organising for weeks. Tell me something I do *not* know.'

'I have a feeling there is more to it than a ball. And I think it might involve Lord Bristol. There is a report that he has renounced his Catholicism, in the hope that the King will forgive him for—'

'Never!' cried the Earl furiously. 'He will *never* be allowed to return to this country – not as long as I am alive. Are you sure he is not in Wimbledon?'

'Certain. He *might* be in his Great Queen Street mansion, though, and—'

'Rubbish! He would not dare come to London. I know he is brazen, but hiding not a mile from White Hall would be wildly stupid, even for him. If you visit Great Queen Street, you will be wasting your time, and I forbid you to do it.'

Chaloner nodded acquiescence, although he thought the Earl a fool to tie his hands so. The Earl scowled when he made no other reply.

'What else did you hear at Somerset House?' he demanded.

'Is that not enough?' asked Chaloner uneasily. 'That your enemies plan to make a concerted move against you on Shrove Tuesday, and that it probably involves Lord Bristol?'

'I suppose it is useful intelligence,' conceded the Earl ungraciously. 'But you must learn more. Meanwhile, I am late for a Privy Council meeting. It is to be held in the King's Presence Chamber today, because His Majesty wants to play cards while we discuss affairs of state.'

Chaloner regarded him askance, not sure if he was joking. But the Earl was not noted for his sense of humour, and it seemed unlikely that he would jest about the King. 'Play cards with whom?'

'The Lady,' replied the Earl through gritted teeth. So

deep was his dislike of the King's mistress that he could never bring himself to utter Lady Castlemaine's name: she was always just 'the Lady'. 'And Buckingham, Progers and that revolting little Chiffinch.'

Chaloner was horrified to think that such feckless, hedonistic people should be in a position to listen to Privy Council debates. It was hardly good for national security. But it was not for him to criticise the King, especially to his Lord Chancellor. He changed the subject.

'I will return to Somerset House tonight,' he began, 'to see if the servants have—'

'Not tonight,' interrupted the Earl. 'They will have posted additional guards, and your capture would be embarrassing so soon after last night's debacle. Leave it for a day or two.'

Chaloner inclined his head, and turned to another matter. 'I met two men named Phillippes and Kaltoff yesterday. They are—'

'They are making me a ring-dial,' interrupted the Earl. He frowned. 'Or is it a tide-dial? I cannot remember now, but it is a scientific instrument that deals with tides and dials and rings. I will not bore you with an explanation of its function, because you would not understand it anyway.'

'Right,' said Chaloner. 'Do you know anything about these men? Such as whether they knew Blue Dick or—'

'Of course they did not know Blue Dick!' cried the Earl. 'What wild idea is this? They are scientific fellows, who discuss mathematics with the King. By contrast, Blue Dick was a fanatic who smashed cathedrals and who was clearly in London to cause trouble. They never met.'

'You seem very sure of that, sir,' said Chaloner. 'How—'

57

'Because it is obvious!' snapped the Earl. 'What can dial-makers and iconoclasts have in common? The very idea is preposterous, and you will dismiss it from your mind immediately. You will not catch the real killer if you hold silly preconceptions, and I order you to forget them.'

'Very well, sir,' said Chaloner, bemused by the vehemence. He bowed a farewell and turned to leave, not sure what to think. He knew the Earl was withholding information from him, but did it pertain to Phillippes and Kaltoff? Or did his master genuinely believe that the two men had nothing to do with Blue Dick's stabbing?

'Where do you think you are going?' demanded the Earl, before Chaloner could take more than two or three steps towards the door. 'I have not said you can go.'

Chaloner regarded him in confusion. 'I thought you wanted me to find Blue Dick's killer. And listen to rumours about what the Dowager might be planning for Shrove Tuesday.'

The Earl looked annoyed. 'I do, but you will escort me to the Presence Chamber first. Leigh has gone to Piccadilly to solve a problem with my new house, and it would not do for me to arrive unescorted. And I can hardly ask Bulteel, who does not know one end of a sword from another. You must do the honour.'

As the crow flew, it was not far to the King's Presence Chamber from the Earl's offices – just a few rooms away, and on the same floor. But White Hall was a contrary place, and Chaloner and Clarendon were obliged to walk down the stairs, across the chilly, windblown expanse of His Majesty's private gardens, then climb the grand steps that led to the Privy Gallery. This was a long hall that was always full of people who wanted an audience with His Majesty, although, given the 'early' hour, it was not as crowded as it would be during the late afternoon and evening. The King's Presence Chamber lay at the far end.

Chaloner did not enjoy walking the length of the Privy Gallery with the Earl at his side. The Earl was hated by the younger members of Court, because he frowned on any activities they deemed to be fun – their wild revelries, lewd plays, duels and debauchery. They glowered at him as he passed, and the only person who smiled was the Bishop of Hereford, with whom the Earl shared some inflexible views on religion.

'Do not worry, Chaloner,' whispered the Earl. 'I am used to this sort of thing, and it no longer bothers me.'

It bothered Chaloner, though. He had known his employer was not the best loved member of Court, but was appalled by how brazen the antipathy had become. He wondered how much longer the Earl would be able to cling to power, especially if the King decided he had had enough of his first minister's prim ways and nagging tongue. And then what would happen to Chaloner himself?

Eventually, the Earl stopped outside a door, and indicated that the man on duty was to open it. Chaloner was surprised to recognise the guard as someone who had been in the Dowager's mansion the previous night – one of the four brothers who were thought to be courting her. He was a burly fellow with a wind-burned face, and his clothes were new enough to look stiff and uncomfortable. He was older than Chaloner, with wisps of grey hair poking from beneath his wig.

'What do you want?' the fellow demanded. 'Stand back at once! Both of you.'

'The Lord Chancellor has an audience with the King,' said Chaloner curtly, somewhat taken aback by the impudent greeting. 'Let him pass.'

'The King is not ready for him.' Suddenly, the Privy Gallery was silent as everyone stopped talking to listen, and the man's three kinsmen appeared from nowhere to stand encouragingly at his side. 'I have been charged to protect His Majesty's privacy, and that is what I intend to do.'

'And who are you, pray?' demanded the Earl, looking him up and down with unconcealed disdain. The man bristled, and Chaloner saw the Earl had just added someone else to his already impressive list of enemies.

'I am Rupert Penderel,' replied the man. He nodded to the fellows at his side. 'And these are my brothers Oliver, Neville and Edward. We are newly appointed Yeomen of the Presence Chamber.'

'Penderel,' mused the Earl, while Chaloner thought that here was a title which did not exist – the Penderels had been fobbed off with an office that held no legitimate standing. Of course, given that all four carried swords and looked as though they were ready to use them, legal niceties were hardly relevant. 'In the last civil war, five brave Penderels helped the King to escape after the Royalist defeat at the Battle of Worcester, but their names were Richard, John—'

'They are our cousins,' interrupted Rupert briskly. 'But we are just as devoted to his cause. Cromwell stole our estates during his reign of terror, so we came to London to throw ourselves on the King's mercy. He has been very generous.'

Yet more scavengers, using the wars as an excuse to gain something for nothing, thought Chaloner in disgust. It was

60

easy to descend on White Hall, declaring penury due to Royalist-held convictions, and people flocked to do it in droves. And most of the claims were bogus: if Cromwell really had acquired all he was accused of stealing, he would have been the richest man in the world by an enormous margin – and he had been nothing of the kind.

'Are you Catholic?' demanded the Earl, somewhat out of the blue. 'Like your cousins?'

Rupert regarded him with dislike. 'Yes, we are. What of it?'

'Catholics are not permitted to hold positions at Court,' the Earl declared triumphantly. Chaloner winced; this was hardly a statement to calm troubled waters. 'So your appointments are unlawful.'

'They are not!' declared Rupert hotly. 'His Majesty made an exception for us.'

'It is a stupid rule, anyway,' said Oliver sullenly. He was smaller than his brother, but the scars on his knuckles indicated a penchant for brawling. 'We four are the most loyal men in the country. Why should we not serve His Majesty at Court?'

'Oliver speaks the truth,' said Rupert. 'And you would not *have* a king, were it not for Catholics – it was not Anglicans who risked life and limb to spirit him to safety after Cromwell won the wars. And with no king, there would be no lord chancellor, either.'

'Open the door,' ordered the Earl, tiring of the debate. 'I shall speak to His Majesty as and when I choose. No *Catholic* has the right to interfere with that.'

'Well, these Catholics do,' countered Rupert. 'The King is playing blind-man's buff with Lady Castlemaine, and I will send for you only when he is finished. Wait over there.'

Chaloner could see there was no point in arguing, and all four brothers were fingering their swords meaningfully. He flailed around for an excuse that would allow his master to leave without acknowledging that the Penderels had won the confrontation.

'You cannot wait, sir – you have an urgent appointment with the Bishop of Winchester,' he said, referring to one of the Earl's closest friends. 'We should go, and return later to see the King.'

The Earl was not a fool, and knew when it was wise to beat a retreat. 'Very well,' he said, turning on his heel and beginning to waddle away. 'I am a busy man, and cannot afford to waste valuable time. Council business must wait.'

There were a number of smirks as he retraced his steps, although no one spoke, and he and Chaloner walked the entire length of the Privy Gallery in a ringing silence. Once outside, the Earl heaved a sigh of relief.

'Thank you,' he said unsteadily. 'Those ruffians might have assaulted me if you had not invented that excuse for us to leave. Perhaps I should not have mentioned the illegality of their offices.'

'Perhaps not,' agreed Chaloner.

The Earl sighed again. 'They provoked me with their insolence, but I should not have risen to the bait. I have seen many Penderels pass through Court – greedy parasites, whose true colours will soon be exposed, at which point they will be dismissed. Summon my carriage, if you please.'

'Where are you going?'

The Earl grimaced. 'I have no idea, but we had better go somewhere, or my enemies will say I lied about seeing the bishop. How about St James's Park?

It is pleasant there of a morning, and we can discuss your investigation into the murder of Blue Dick.'

St James's Park was indeed pleasant of a morning, because it was too early to be crowded with courtiers tearing up and down its paths, showing off their equestrian skills to their mistresses. It was a large area enclosed by high walls that afforded it privacy, although certain members of the public were allowed inside. Chaloner saw the navy clerk Samuel Pepys there, strolling along with cronies from the Admiralty. Pepys bowed a greeting to Chaloner, but only because he was with the Earl. Usually, he snubbed him, deeming him as someone insufficiently lofty to warrant recognition.

'There are Scarlet and Hussey,' said the Earl, peering out of the carriage window to see if there was anyone to whom *he* could wave. He ducked hastily back inside. 'I do not like them.'

Chaloner looked to where he pointed, and saw an ill-matched pair. One was tall and fat, and the other short and wiry. Both wore the kind of clothes that said they were men of substance, but weathered skin suggested they spent time outside. The smaller of the two was sobbing, and his companion was trying to comfort him.

'Who are they?' asked Chaloner.

'Wardens of the Bridge.' The Earl saw Chaloner's blank look and grimaced. 'It is about time you learned these things. How can you serve me, if you do not know the first thing about London?'

Chaloner was tempted to point out that he might learn them faster if Clarendon did not keep sending him on missions away from the capital – Ireland, Spain and Portugal, Oxford, and most recently, Wimbledon – but he managed to hold his tongue. 'What do they do, exactly?'

'They are responsible for the Bridge – they supervise the carpenters and masons who maintain it, collect rent from the folk who live in its houses, and hire guards to patrol it. Fat Robert Hussey is the Senior Warden, while his junior is little Anthony Scarlet. I shall send you to spy on them soon, because there is something odd going on with that Bridge, and you are the man to find out what.'

'What sort of something?' asked Chaloner. It sounded a much more interesting assignment than the death of an unpopular iconoclast.

'Well, the Dowager has taken to frequenting it for a start, whereas she always used to travel by water. But speak of the Devil and he will appear, because there she is and her henchmen with her – Buckingham, Winter, Progers, the whole cabal. *And* the vicar of Wimbledon – Luckin is his name. He was recently arrested, you know.'

'For allegedly witnessing Lord Bristol's conversion back to Anglicanism, and giving him holy communion,' said Chaloner, recalling what he had overheard at Somerset House the night before.

'It was not *alleged*,' countered the Earl testily. 'It happened. I visited Luckin in the Tower myself, and he made no effort to deny it. Indeed, he had the audacity to gloat at me – to claim that Bristol's public renouncing of his religion is the first stage in his regaining favour with the King.'

'So Bristol *is* in England?' asked Chaloner, wondering why the Earl had not mentioned it before.

The Earl grimaced. 'I do not know, because Luckin refused to say where this curious event took place.

64

Spymaster Williamson offered to find out, but the King does not want the Church clamouring at him for maltreating its vicars, so he ordered Luckin set free. And where did Luckin go afterwards? Straight to Somerset House!'

'Why would he do that? If Bristol is no longer Catholic, then the Dowager will see him as a traitor to her faith, and Luckin as the facilitator of that treachery.'

'On the contrary. If the ploy sees Bristol restored to the King's good graces, she will consider Luckin a friend. And they certainly seem comfortable in each other's presence, because he has been entrusted with her lapdog – and I do not refer to Progers. I mean that nasty yapping creature.'

Chaloner looked towards the Dowager's entourage, and saw one man holding a bundle of black and white fur. The fellow had been in Somerset House the previous night, suggesting the Earl was right about him being in the Dowager's favour. He was a lean, sharp-eyed specimen, with a large purple nose and the look of someone who found a great deal to displease him.

'He is talking to Sir John Winter,' the Earl went on disapprovingly. 'Do you know him?'

Chaloner recognised the enormous moustache from the previous night, too – Winter had also been at the Dowager's gathering in Somerset House.

'He knows a lot about gunpowder, and wants to be the next Green Man,' he said, recalling what Bulteel had told him about the man called Sir John Winter.

The Earl nodded. 'His Majesty is resisting his petitions, though. And I thank God for it, or we would all be blown up in our beds. Winter is Catholic, you see.'

Chaloner itched to point out that *all* Catholics did not

harbour murderous designs on members of the government, but knew there was no point: the Earl was not reasonable where religion was concerned. He nodded noncommittally, and tuned out the bigoted diatribe that followed.

The Earl was still holding forth when they reached St James's Park's newly dug canal, which was prettily dappled with swans and geese. The air was clean and fresh outside the city, and smelled of damp grass and frost. The day was a fine, crisp, winter one, with the sun shining in a clear blue sky.

'I like this place,' said Chaloner, to change the subject from Catholics. He took a deep, appreciative breath. 'It is peaceful.'

'It is,' agreed the Earl. 'And when it is built, Clarendon House will have fine views across it.'

'Really?' asked Chaloner unhappily.

The Earl scowled at him. 'I know you think my new mansion too grand, but I am Lord Chancellor of England, so I *should* have somewhere palatial to live. And why not? I suffered with the King all the years he was in exile, so why should I not be rewarded for my discomfort?'

'Because it is going to be funded by public money, so its opulence will cause resentment.'

'You mean I might lose the respect of apprentices and traders?' asked the Earl unpleasantly. 'Why should I care about them?'

'Because they are on your side, sir,' explained Chaloner, struggling for patience. It was not the first time they had covered this particular topic. 'They favour you over your enemies, because they see you as a moral man in a corrupt government. But Clarendon House will turn them against you.'

'According to you, they are against me anyway, because of my stance on religious dissenters,' said the Earl tartly. 'The Clarendon Code – the new laws that suppress all those aggravating non-Anglicans – bears my name, and while I did not write these edicts, it is common knowledge that I support them to the hilt. So what do I have to lose by invoking the wrath of grubby Londoners?'

'Your post as Lord Chancellor? The life you have built for yourself in London? The City holds the Court's purse-strings, and if its people bay for your head, the King may well give it to them.'

'You have a blunt tongue,' said the Earl, regarding Chaloner with wide eyes. 'But at least you are honest. You are wrong, of course, but that is to be expected, given that you seem more foreigner than Englishman, especially regarding religion. How is Hannah Cotton, by the way?'

'She is well, thank you.' Chaloner was not sure he liked the juxtaposition of remarks. 'Why?'

'I am just making polite conversation – there is no need to look suspicious. I understand you and she have been . . . *walking out* for some weeks now.' The Earl leaned back in his seat and let the pale winter sun touch his face. 'You should marry her. It is a good match, because she is the daughter of a gentleman, and you are the son of one. I shall give the union my blessing.'

The thought had crossed Chaloner's mind to turn his relationship with Hannah into something more perma-nent, but spies did not make for good husbands: their occupation was hazardous, and Hannah had been

67

widowed once already. He said nothing, thinking it was none of the Earl's affair.

'Of course, she is old for bearing children,' the Earl went on. 'But you may be lucky.'

Chaloner was not sure he wanted children, for the same reason that he was not sure he wanted a wife. Besides, he had had them once, and had lost them to the plague. It was not an experience he was keen to repeat.

'Did you say you wanted to discuss the murder of Blue Dick Culmer?' he asked, to bring an end to a discussion that was becoming uncomfortable for him.

The Earl looked hurt when he saw his fatherly advice was not appreciated. 'Yes, I suppose we had better,' he said, with a wounded sniff. 'He was a zealot, like his colleagues Dowsing and Herring. They went about their work with a fervour that was sickening, and dozens of our finest churches will never be the same again.'

'I do not know Herring,' said Chaloner, although everyone had heard of Dowsing, the man famous for smashing his way through the religious buildings of East Anglia.

'These days, he is the churchwarden of St Mary Woolchurch, here in London. But during Cromwell's ascendancy, he did a lot of damage to chapels in Essex. Such fanatics *must* be silenced, and everyone made to worship God as the Anglican Church sees fit.'

'I see,' said Chaloner flatly.

'Stephen Goff told me that Herring and Blue Dick were girding their loins for mischief and . . .' The Earl trailed off, looking pained. He had let slip something that he had meant to keep to himself.

'Stephen Goff?' pounced Chaloner. 'Who is he?'

'No one you know.' The Earl rubbed his hands together briskly, trying to gloss over his blunder. 'Just a friend in the Dowager's household. But to return to our dead icon-oclast—'

'Not *Father* Stephen?' asked Chaloner, recalling the nervous, dark-haired priest who had been at Somerset House the previous night. If the Earl had recruited *him* to spy, then it was small wonder the poor fellow was uneasy!

The Earl looked annoyed. 'You are too sharp for your own good. But yes: Stephen Goff is the Dowager's chap-lain, and supplies me with information from time to time. However, his position is a precarious one, and I prom-ised him I would keep his identity a secret.'

'Why would he help you?' asked Chaloner suspiciously. 'You make no secret of your dislike of Catholics, so why has *he* allied himself to your camp?'

'Because he is a decent soul who is appalled by the Dowager's plots to harm me,' snapped the Earl. 'And because we became friends when we were in exile together. We have known each other for years, and I trust him completely. He may be a papist, but he is a good man.'

Chaloner was unconvinced, but knew better than to argue. He changed tack. 'How does Stephen Goff know that Blue Dick and Herring were "girding their loins for mischief"?'

The Earl shrugged. 'He has his own set of inform-ants, I imagine.'

Chaloner frowned as something else occurred to him. 'There was a Goff who signed the old king's death warrant . . .'

'That was *Will* Goff,' supplied the Earl. 'He fled to

New England when he realised he was going to be executed for his crimes, although we have dispatched agents to hunt him down.'

Unbidden, a sudden, vivid memory of Will Goff flashed into Chaloner's mind, one that had lain dormant for years. Goff had visited the Chaloner estates in Buckinghamshire, when Chaloner had been a child – a lean, unsmiling man with dark, almost foreign features. He had made a nuisance of himself with demands for music. It had been high summer, and Chaloner recalled his resentment at being forced to remain indoors all day, to entertain the guest with his bass viol.

'I met him once,' he said, sufficiently startled by the clarity of the recollection to blurt it out.

The Earl eyed him balefully. 'I suppose I should not be surprised, given your family's political leanings, but it is not something you should admit to anyone else. Stephen is Will's brother. Perhaps that is why he passes me information – he wants to distance himself from his treacherous sibling, just as *you* prefer not to be associated with *your* regicide uncle.'

'Do you want me to find Herring?' asked Chaloner, deftly turning the conversation back to iconoclasts. His flamboyant kinsman was far too uncomfortable a subject to air with one of His Majesty's most powerful ministers.

'I suppose you had better,' said the Earl unenthusiastically. 'Do you think Herring could have been one of the men you fought in St Mary Overie?'

Chaloner considered the question carefully. 'It is possible – a falling out among fanatics. Are you sure you want me to look into this, sir? You may not like what I find.'

'You are afraid the culprits will be decent men, who abhorred what happened to Canterbury's cathedral, and I will be angry with you,' surmised the Earl, although it was not his ire Chaloner was worried about, so much as being ordered to look the other way once he had his answers. He had never approved of selective justice. 'But we should locate the villains before worrying what to do with them. Do you not agree?'

'Yes, sir. Is there anything else I should know?' Chaloner was acutely aware that the Earl was still holding something back from him.

The Earl hesitated, but then shook his head. 'No. Just find some answers. You can begin by inspecting Blue Dick's corpse in the Westminster charnel house. Surgeon Wiseman has agreed to meet you there at five o'clock.'

The Earl took Chaloner with him to view the site of his Piccadilly mansion when they had finished driving around the canal. It stood on the northern edge of St James's Park. His Sergeant at Arms, Humphrey Leigh, was there, arguing with workmen, and Chaloner was dispatched to find out what was happening – the sun had gone in, and the Earl did not want to leave his warm carriage to stand around in the cold.

'They say metal is more expensive now than when the plans were first drawn up, so we will have to pay double for whatever silly device they are constructing,' explained Leigh irritably, indicating two artisans with an angry jab of his finger. 'It is brazen robbery!'

With a start, Chaloner saw he was referring to Phillippes and Kaltoff, although he supposed he should not be surprised to see them at Clarendon House: they were building the Earl a tide-ring, after all. Phillippes was studying a pile of diagrams, his brow furrowed in concentration, while Kaltoff was packing up some tools.

'I will talk to them,' he offered, seeing an opportunity to ask some questions – assuming they did not recognise him from the Beggar's Bush and run him through, of course. But he had kept his face hidden, and he had been wearing different clothes – he was fairly sure they would not associate him with the shabby stranger they had tried to trounce. 'You can escort the Earl back to White Hall.'

Leigh brightened. 'Really? You do not mind?'

Chaloner indicated he should go, and the little soldier marched towards the Earl's carriage with open relief. Phillippes watched him leave, standing with his hands on his hips. Then his gaze turned to Chaloner, but there was no hint of recognition in it. Meanwhile, Kaltoff was more interested in his instruments than in emissaries from the Earl.

'Leigh is a fool,' Phillippes declared uncompromisingly. 'He has no understanding of scientific matters. And his master is no better. Why does Clarendon want a tide-ring here, so far from the river? It will be of no use to him on dry ground!'

'Perhaps he will take it to White Hall,' suggested Chaloner, tactfully refraining from explaining that the tide-ring had only been commissioned because the King was having one. 'His offices overlook the river.'

'You may be right,' conceded Phillippes. Then he gave a courtly bow. 'But I am forgetting my manners. I am Henry Phillippes, soon to be admitted to the Royal Society. And you are?'

'Thomas Chaloner, in the service of the Earl of Clarendon.'

'I shall soon be admitted to the Royal Society, too,' said Kaltoff, looking up from his tools. 'My name is Casper Kaltoff, although do not assume from it that I am foreign. I am as English as you are, and there is no reason at all for my learned colleagues to exclude me on the basis of my heritage. I cannot help it if my mother had a penchant for the exotic.'

'Right,' said Chaloner, bemused. He smiled pleasantly, and addressed them both. 'I have heard of you, of course. My friend Will Leybourn often praises your work when I visit him in Uxbridge.'

'You know Leybourn?' asked Phillippes eagerly. Leybourn was Chaloner's friend, although he did not recall him ever mentioning the dial-makers. 'I am flattered that he should talk about me. He is one of the giants of mathematics and surveying, and a man I greatly admire.'

'He told me you were creating a tide-ring to be used in Southwark,' said Chaloner, to lead the discussion to matters south of the river. 'It is a—'

'Then he is mistaken,' interrupted Kaltoff. 'We are only engaged in two projects at the moment – one for the Earl of Clarendon, and the other for the King. Neither involves Southwark.'

'Was he wrong when he said he saw you in the Beggar's Bush, then?' asked Chaloner, adding artfully, 'Perhaps it was someone else's scientific theories that so impressed him.'

'Oh, he may have heard us pontificating in the Bush,' said Phillippes carelessly. 'We like it there, because the landlord lends us his yard to conduct our experiments in. Or he used to, at least. We live on the Bridge, you see, where there is no space to do anything.'

'In Nonesuch House?' asked Chaloner, deliberately pandering to their vanity by making the assumption that they could afford the finest house available.

Phillippes looked pained. 'Unfortunately not. We live with Tyus the bookseller, who rents his upper storeys to professional men wanting lodgings. It is poky, but convenient for monitoring the tides. I shall write a treatise about them soon, which will have the Royal Society wondering why I was not invited to be one of their founder members.'

'Have they set a date for your enrolment?' asked Chaloner.

Phillippes waved an airy hand. 'Not yet, but it will not be long. Then they will see what they have been missing all these years.'

'I am sure they will,' said Chaloner. He changed the subject. 'I do not suppose Tyus has any vacancies, does he? I might be looking for rooms myself soon.'

Unfortunately, this was true. Fifteen months before, the house next to the one where he lodged had caught fire, resulting in major subsidence in the adjoining properties. His landlord refused to accept that anything was wrong, but a leaking roof, slanting floors and buckling walls suggested otherwise. The place was ripe for collapse, and Chaloner did not want to be in it when it fell.

'He is full at the moment,' replied Phillippes. 'There *were* some free rooms, but Kaltoff here moved into them last month. I am sorry to disappoint you, especially as you are a friend of Will Leybourn's. What else did he say about me?'

'That he would like to hear more of your ideas,' lied Chaloner. 'Whatever you expounded in the Beggar's Bush clearly caught his fancy. Do you ever discuss anything other than science?'

74

It was a little blunt, but neither Phillippes nor Kaltoff seemed to notice. Both hastened to answer.

'*I* hold forth on all manner of subjects,' declared Phillippes proudly. 'In fact, there is very little upon which I do not hold an opinion.'

'And no one can tell *me* anything I do not already know about mathematics,' bragged Kaltoff.

'What about iconoclasm?' asked Chaloner baldly. 'Leybourn is very interested in that.'

'Is he?' Phillippes regarded him askance. 'Well, each to his own, I suppose.'

'I do not like it,' said Kaltoff, wrinkling his nose. 'Smashing churches is not a very nice thing to do. But here comes the blacksmith with our new samples. We have better get to work, Phillippes, or Clarendon and the King will never have their tide-rings.'

They left before Chaloner could ask more, although he felt he had pushed the discussion as far as he could without giving himself away. He had learned one useful fact, though: they lived on the Bridge – the place where Blue Dick had been murdered. Later that day, he decided, he would visit their lodgings and search them for evidence of other connections.

It was noon, and the time when men went to taverns, cookhouses and 'ordinaries' for their midday victuals. Hannah had given Chaloner something she claimed was cake that morning, but it had been hard and salty, and he had tossed it on the fire the moment she had turned her back. She had many talents, but cooking was not one of them.

Hungry now, he decided to dine at Rider's Coffee House on Chancery Lane. It was a long way from

Piccadilly, and the food was hardly worth the journey, but he was not going for his stomach alone. When he arrived, he opened the door, blinking at its dim, smoky interior, and looked around.

The man he wanted to see was slightly built, with blue eyes and brown hair. His clothes were simple but well made, and showed him to be a man of comfortable means. John Thurloe, once Cromwell's Secretary of State and Spymaster General, was softly spoken, with mild, almost diffident manners. But there was a core of steel in him that had led more than one traitor to underestimate him – and spend the rest of his life regretting it.

Rider's was Thurloe's favourite coffee house, where he liked to keep abreast of current affairs by reading the many newsbooks, newsletters and pamphlets to which the landlord subscribed. Usually, he sat alone, preferring his own company to the cross-section of men – never women – who came to drink Rider's dubious brews and enjoy the occasionally erudite conversation. That day, however, he was the centre of attention. It was so odd to see the reticent ex-Spymaster holding forth to the world at large that Chaloner stopped dead in his tracks and listened.

'It is ridiculous,' Thurloe was saying in an uncharacteristically strident voice. 'The government has no right to tell people how they might commune with God, and the Clarendon Code is an absurd and wicked piece of legislation that should be challenged until it is overturned.'

Chaloner was horrified. Thurloe was likely to get himself arrested if he went around making that sort of statement. And it was peculiar behaviour, to say the least: Thurloe was normally the soul of discretion, and rarely ventured opinions about politics, even to his closest friends. Chaloner regarded him in concern.

The ex-Spymaster had not long returned from his family home in Oxfordshire, and looked fit and well. Chaloner had been delighted to see him back, because Thurloe was his only real friend in London and he had missed him – although if Thurloe was going to start making perfidious speeches in public places, then Chaloner might wish he had stayed away longer. He grabbed the ex-Spymaster's arm before he could add anything else, and escorted him politely but firmly to a table at the back of the room, mumbling something about an urgent private consultation.

'What in God's name are you doing?' Chaloner hissed when they were safely out of earshot. 'Have you taken leave of your senses?'

Thurloe regarded him coolly. 'I might ask you the same question. Coffee houses are commonly accepted forums for expressing opinions. I am within my rights to say what I think.'

'*You* are not,' argued Chaloner. 'As you know perfectly well. You are not an ordinary citizen, and your criticisms will be seen as treason. Do you want to be hanged?'

'You are overreacting,' said Thurloe impatiently. He clicked his fingers at a serving-boy, who brought a dish of coffee for Chaloner, and a bowl of something that smelled of rotting vegetation for him. Chaloner winced when Thurloe downed it in one. The ex-Spymaster was something of a hypochondriac, and was always dosing himself with some new remedy that promised vitality and health. Perhaps, Chaloner thought worriedly, one had caused him to lose his wits.

'Are you ill?' he asked, rather more gently. 'Tell me what is wrong.'

'Nothing,' replied Thurloe. 'I am as well as any man with a delicate constitution.'

77

'Perhaps you should return to Oxfordshire.' Chaloner sipped the coffee. As usual, it was unpleasantly acrid, and he was glad he had not acquired a taste for it, because he suspected it would dissolve his teeth if he drank it every day.

Thurloe ignored the suggestion. 'Try one of these pills, Tom. They promise to cleanse the head of foul vapours.'

Chaloner brushed the proffered tin aside, and looked hard at his friend. 'Something is amiss, but it has nothing to do with foul vapours. What can I do to help?'

'I never could deceive you, could I?' Thurloe shot Chaloner a rueful grin. 'But I am afraid it is something I cannot discuss with you, so please do not press me. In fact, I would rather you were not seen with me at all. You have at last risen in favour with Clarendon, and it would be a pity to jeopardise that by hobnobbing with outspoken Parliamentarians.'

Chaloner raised his eyebrows. 'Risen in favour? I do not think so!'

'You are wrong,' said Thurloe quietly. 'The Earl relies heavily on you now.'

Chaloner knew Thurloe was leading the discussion away from his curious and uncharacteristic rant against the Clarendon Code – the laws that had been passed during the Earl of Clarendon's Lord Chancellorship, so bore his name – but he also knew he had pushed him as far as he could. Thurloe was stubborn, and it would take a far more devious mind than Chaloner's to bend him. So, he allowed the conversation to turn to his own problems instead.

'Clarendon neither trusts me nor likes me,' he said, rather bitterly. 'But he needs me to deal with the more unsavoury aspects of his existence. Today is a good

78

example. He has ordered me to investigate the murder of an iconoclast called Blue Dick Culmer, and to learn what another iconoclast called Herring plans to do in the future. But he will not tell me why.'

'Cromwell and I quarrelled about that,' said Thurloe distantly. 'Did I ever tell you? We did not disagree often, but we almost came to blows over Dowsing, Blue Dick and Herring. They despoiled several places I loved, and I have not been able to visit them since. Cromwell appreciated fine things, and I still do not understand why he let those louts loose on our beautiful churches.'

'You do not seem surprised by what the Earl has asked me to do,' remarked Chaloner, who knew an evasive answer when he heard one.

Thurloe shrugged. 'A number of my former spies keep me supplied with news and gossip. They told me Blue Dick was assassinated by an unknown assailant on the Bridge.'

'And Herring? Have they told you anything about him?'

'Only that when the Royalists returned to power, he accepted that Puritans no longer had the upper hand, so he slipped into anonymity like all sensible men. He lives quietly now, as churchwarden of St Mary Woolchurch.'

'What does he look like?' Chaloner wondered whether he had seen the man and not realised it.

'Barrel chest, short legs, and when he walks, it is as though he wants to batter his way forward with his head. Cromwell was keen for me to hire him as a spy, but he has crossed eyes, which would have made him too distinctive for disguises, so I refused. He is deeply religious, of course . . .'

'Why would Cromwell press a fanatic on the intelligence

services?' Chaloner hated working with zealots, because their single-mindedness tended to make them dangerous allies.

'It was at a time when we exposed a lot of traitors, and Herring's loyalty was unwavering, which was refreshing and appreciated. But here comes Rider, to ask what you will eat. I recommend the bread and cheese. Between you and me, the creation he calls haggis is rather nasty.'

The bread was surprisingly fresh, and was made from fine white flour. But when Chaloner glanced around, he saw the other patrons had been supplied with much coarser fare: Thurloe, as a special customer, had been furnished with something better.

'Herring,' prompted Chaloner, when the landlord had gone.

Thurloe was silent for a moment, and when he spoke, his voice was low. 'You would be wise to walk away from this particular assignment, Tom. It will almost certainly end badly.'

'What makes you say that?'

Thurloe set down the knife with which he had been cutting his cheese. 'Many good men deplore the excesses of Court – its drunkenness, debauchery and unruliness. They think it is time something was done, something to bring our country back into sober, God-fearing hands.'

Chaloner stared at him, a knot of alarm tightening in his stomach. 'You mean there is another rebellion in the making? We are going to be plunged into more civil war?'

Thurloe looked him in the eye. 'And if we were, where would you stand? With the King and his band of empty-headed fools, who play cards when they should be attending affairs of state? Or with your honest friends, with whom you fought the last time?'

Chaloner shook his head in disbelief. 'I cannot believe I am hearing this! You swore you would never dabble in politics again, and—'

'I gave the best years of my life to a cause I believed to be just and good. The country was stable and prosperous under our military dictatorship, whereas now it is wild and unsettled. Did you hear what happened in Turnstile the other day? A woman was in bed with her husband, when masked men broke in and raped her. Then they abused her with a torch, which was said to be lit.'

Chaloner winced. 'It is horrible, but your military dictatorship was no haven of peace and justice, either. Dreadful crimes were still committed, and a lot of people were dissatisfied with the regime. Why do you think they embraced the King's return so eagerly? They were tired of despots.'

Thurloe regarded him balefully. 'Cromwell was *not* a despot, and those who disagreed with his rule tended to be rakes and debauchees. I had not numbered you among them, Thomas.'

Chaloner declined to rise to the bait. 'If your rebellion involves associating with one-time iconoclasts, then you should withdraw while you still have your head.'

'You are missing the point,' snapped Thurloe. 'Which is that the Court's antics have encouraged a large number of discontented folk to flock to the capital – of all political and religious persuasions. We are not talking about an eccentric sect here, but a displeased majority.'

'I do not care,' objected Chaloner, becoming more alarmed by the minute. 'When the uprising fails – which it will – they will go home. But you will be tried for treason, as your enemies think you should have been more than three years ago, when the King first returned.'

Thurloe's expression was suddenly sad. 'I am glad you think we will fail, because it means you will not join us. It is better that way – safer for you.'

Chaloner was bewildered, not sure what to make of such enigmatic remarks. He sat back in his chair and studied Thurloe hard, but he had never been good at reading the ex-Spymaster, and he knew he could stare at him all day and learn nothing.

'Please,' he said eventually. 'What you are suggesting is madness. Leave London. Go home to Ann and the children before it is too late.'

'I cannot, Tom,' said Thurloe softly. 'I wish I could, believe me. But I cannot.'

There was something in his friend's low whisper that turned the blood in Chaloner's veins to ice, and made him wonder what new turmoil was about to overtake London.

Chapter 3

When Thurloe stood to leave the coffee house, Chaloner accompanied him across the road to Lincoln's Inn, where the ex-Spymaster lived while in London. The porter waved them through the great front gate. The day's clear skies had brought with them a cracking cold, so the courtyard beyond was empty. It meant there was no one to hear them talk, except the porter, who was back inside his lodge with the door firmly closed against the winter chill.

'I wish you would reconsider,' said Chaloner, regarding his friend sombrely. 'I walked under the Stone Gate on the Bridge yesterday. Some of the severed heads on display there belong to men who thought rebellion was a good idea. I do not want yours to join them.'

Thurloe was silent. He had liked and respected most of the men whose grisly remains were exhibited for all to jeer at, and some had even been friends. For a brief, hopeful moment, Chaloner thought he was going to agree to withdraw from whatever he had embroiled himself in, but then his expression hardened, and he changed the subject.

'Why did you come today, Tom? Was it to tell me that you are ordered to investigate the murder of Blue Dick

Culmer? Or to ask whether I have heard anything to help you solve the crime?'

'Actually, it was just to see an old friend,' replied Chaloner. Then he regarded the ex-Spymaster searchingly. 'Why? *Have* you heard something?'

The ghost of a smile touched Thurloe's lips. 'I am afraid not, and although Blue Dick was the kind of fanatic who gave us Puritans a bad name, I do not condone cold-blooded slaughter. I shall be interested to know the name of his killer, when you have it.'

'Have you heard of a man called Henry Phillippes?' asked Chaloner. Thurloe was one of the best informed men in London, and if he was of a mind to be helpful, then Chaloner knew he should take advantage of it. 'Or his associate, Casper Kaltoff?'

Thurloe frowned. 'Do you mean the Catholic dial-makers? Our mutual friend Will Leybourn mentions them on occasion, usually rather scathingly. Phillippes designed something called a tide-ring, which Will informs me is extremely inaccurate. He provided a lot of arithmetic to prove his point, but I am afraid he lost me after the first page of calculations.'

'Is that all you know about them? That their tide-ring is not all Phillippes claims?'

Thurloe frowned at him. 'Why? Surely, you cannot suspect *them* of killing Blue Dick?'

'Why is that so incredible? They live on the Bridge, not far from where Blue Dick was stabbed, and shortly after the murder, I overheard them discussing some dark business that they wanted kept secret.' Chaloner repeated verbatim what he had heard. 'They followed me into a lane afterwards, to ask why I was spying on them.'

'But you *were* spying on them,' Thurloe pointed out.

'So you cannot blame them for wanting to know what you were doing. Is there any other evidence to connect them to the murder?'

Chaloner shook his head. 'But I might have some after I have searched their rooms.'

Thurloe looked thoughtful. 'Then do it now. The learned men at Gresham College plan to weigh air this afternoon, and Phillippes and Kaltoff will certainly be in the audience. Their lodgings will be empty, and you can rummage through their possessions without fear of being caught.'

'Thank you. Perhaps I will find something that will allow them to be arrested and questioned for Blue Dick's stabbing.'

Thurloe regarded him uneasily. 'The link between them and the murder is tenuous, to say the least, Tom. I imagine a great many men conduct dubious business in the Beggar's Bush, and the conversation, as you reported it to me, held absolutely nothing to say it was Blue Dick's death they were discussing. You cannot arrest them with what you have.'

'Then I will have to find more,' said Chaloner, loath to abandon his only suspects. 'Besides, even if they are innocent of murder, it was clear they are involved in something untoward, and they are making a tide-ring for the Earl. It is my duty to investigate them, to make sure that whatever it is does not rebound on him. Is there anything else I should know about them?'

Thurloe thought about it. 'Well, both are ardent Royalists, and they are sometimes invited to Somerset House, but so are dozens of other folk. However, I did hear one snippet of gossip, although I doubt it is significant: Phillippes sometimes visits Sir John Winter.'

'The Catholic gunpowder expert, who wants to be the next Green Man?'

Thurloe raised his eyebrows at the description. 'Yes, although he is better known for being rich. He owns a fortune in timber and lead, and is so wealthy that he can afford to rent Nonesuch House – that great Tudor mansion on the Bridge.'

'I know Nonesuch House.' Chaloner's thoughts tumbled. How many more times was the Bridge going to feature in the various mysteries that confronted him?

'Do not read too much into it, though,' warned Thurloe. 'The connection between Winter and Phillippes could be innocent – they are near-neighbours, after all. Moreover, they share political and religious views, in that both are devoted Royalists who are also Catholic.'

But Chaloner was inclined to be suspicious. 'Perhaps their association arises from this brewing discontent you have mentioned – they meet to chat about the laws that are strangling their religious freedoms. You are insane to become embroiled in whatever is hatching. It has a bad feel to it.'

'I must do as my conscience dictates,' said Thurloe stiffly. 'But I refuse to discuss it with you, Tom. You are safer not knowing.'

'I disagree,' argued Chaloner. 'Being in the dark has never been better than being informed. How can I work efficiently when I do not understand the dangers and—'

'Enough!' barked Thurloe. His voice was uncharacteristically sharp, but he lowered it when he saw Chaloner's shock, and forced a smile. 'We must not quarrel. It is difficult to know one's friends in these uncertain times, but I have never doubted you. And you should never doubt me. But come to my chambers, let me prepare you a tonic. You look tired.'

'I am tired,' admitted Chaloner, rubbing his eyes. 'I did not sleep last night, and my wits are like mud. And I have been bombarded with so much peculiar and contradictory information today that I am not sure what to believe about anything.'

'I have not been contradictory,' objected Thurloe, stung. 'I may have refused you information about my business, but I would never lie to you.'

'Not you – Clarendon. For example, he says he befriended a priest named Stephen Goff during his exile. But Stephen Goff is the Dowager's chaplain, and the Dowager is Clarendon's sworn enemy. Moreover, Stephen is the brother of Will Goff the regicide, a committed Puritan. I do not understand how a Puritan regicide comes to have a brother who is a Catholic priest, or how Stephen can maintain his friendship with Clarendon while still working for the Dowager.'

'Clarendon is telling the truth: he and Stephen *did* become close when the King was in exile. I heard about their friendship from several of my spies. And Stephen *converted* to Catholicism, probably because he spent so much time in France. Indeed, I am surprised you did not do the same. I imagine Hannah would prefer you papist.'

'I am sure she would. But I do not feel strongly enough about any denomination to warrant making a public statement about it.'

Thurloe grimaced. As a religious man himself, he did not understand Chaloner's indifference towards matters of faith. He glanced up at the sky.

'These clear winter days may be lovely, but they are

brutally cold, and I am chilled to the bone. Do not keep me talking out here any longer – my feet are in desperate need of thawing.'

Chaloner took his leave, but the encounter had left him distinctly uneasy, so he lurked near the Rolls Chapel opposite, until a coach rattled out of Lincoln's Inn. He was not surprised to glimpse Thurloe inside it. The fact that the ex-Spymaster had not spent long defrosting his toes indicated he had not been as cold as he had claimed, and it had been a ploy to escape his friend's company.

Chaloner rubbed his chin unhappily. Should he try harder to prevent Thurloe from falling face-first into disaster? But Thurloe was a man of principle, and would do what he thought was right, regardless of the risk to himself. He would not be easy to dissuade. With a heavy heart, and the sense that something was about to go very badly wrong, Chaloner set off towards the Bridge.

The streets were busy that afternoon, and it took him some time to reach his destination. When he arrived, the Bridge was teeming with carts, pedestrians and a veritable Noah's ark of animals – cows, geese, sheep, horses, pigs and mules. He paused at the open area called the Square, and glanced over the parapet to the river below. The tide was in full spate, roaring through the arches in frothy brown jets. Spray rose in a misty pall, carrying with it the dank aroma of dirty water.

Chaloner was still gazing at the spectacle when he became aware of a commotion up ahead. It was centred around the scaffolding-swathed Chapel House, which Blue Dick had visited before he had been stabbed. A carriage had parked outside it, bringing north-bound traffic to a standstill. Furious drivers were yelling at the coachman to move, and the coachman was bawling pithily worded refusals. Chaloner was surprised no one had hauled him from his seat and shifted the offending vehicle themselves, but soon saw why: he was being protected by two men with guns. He recognised them immediately: they were the Frenchmen, Doucett and Martin – the pair who had almost caught him spying in Somerset House the previous night.

Curious to know what was going on, Chaloner slipped into the haberdashery shop opposite, and settled down to watch, anonymous among several other customers. He did not have to feign an interest in buttons for long, because there was soon some action.

Seeing the carriage was not going to be moved by threats or force, one of the carters had gone to fetch someone in authority. He returned with two men the Earl had pointed out in St James's Park that morning. The diminutive Junior Warden Scarlet was white-faced and red-eyed, and took no part in the ensuing discussion; Chaloner wondered whether he was ill. And Senior Warden Hussey was accompanied by four of the fattest children Chaloner had ever seen. They could barely walk, and when they stood in a row side by side, they represented a formidable obstruction all on their own.

'What is going on?' Hussey demanded of the offending coach. 'You know the rules: traffic keeps moving on the Bridge, and deliveries can only be made at night.'

'The Dowager is visiting Chapel House,' replied the Frenchman who Chaloner thought was called Doucett. His English was thickly accented. 'And she stops where she pleases.'

'Oh,' said Hussey, the wind taken out of his sails at

the mention of such an august personage. 'I see. Well, in her case, we must make an exception, but—'

Fortunately for Hussey – those trapped in the traffic did not see why the King's mother should be treated differently to anyone else – the Dowager chose that particular moment to conclude her sightseeing. She strode out of Chapel House and stepped into her carriage without so much as a glance towards the simmering crowd. Clearly, there was to be no apology for the inconvenience she had caused.

Three of her cronies followed. The moustachioed Winter was deep in discussion with the purple-nosed vicar of Wimbledon, while trailing unhappily after them was Father Stephen. When they had all clambered into the carriage, Doucett and Martin jumped on to the footplates at the back, and the vehicle began to move away. It was followed by a hail of missiles, most derived from animal dung. One hit Martin, staining his fine coat, and for one awful moment, Chaloner thought he was going to discharge his firearm into the crowd, but Doucett said something that stopped him. Hussey breathed a sigh of relief when the coach was out of sight, and turned to his junior.

'I wish she would not do that. It is damned inconsiderate.'

'Write to her,' suggested Scarlet. His voice was flat, as if he was speaking automatically and the matter did not have his full attention. 'Tell her not to do it again.'

Hussey released a sharp bark of laughter, which was eerily echoed by the four fat children. 'You do not issue orders to the Dowager, Scarlet! It would be more than your job is worth.'

'I do not like this post anyway,' said Scarlet. 'I should never have accepted it.'

'Now, then, lad,' said Hussey briskly. 'There is no need for that sort of talk. Come home with me to Bridge House, where we shall fortify your spirits with a glass of wine. And perhaps we shall have cake, too, if my children have not eaten it all.'

They set off towards the Southwark end of the Bridge, the four fat boys waddling behind them, although the lads' oily cheeks and the crumbs on their coats made Chaloner suspect Scarlet was likely to go hungry. Meanwhile, the haberdasher, whose name was Armitage, had joined Chaloner at the window, and had also been watching the scene unfold.

'The Dowager has taken an interest in Chapel House,' he confided, polishing a smear from one of his panes with the sleeve of his coat. 'It is not the first time she has visited.'

'Why?' asked Chaloner. The building in question did not look any different from its neighbours – four storeys high, plus a cellar, the latter of which was built into the stone of the starling below. It was shabby and old, and he would have said there was nothing about it to excite interest.

'I have no idea,' replied Armitage. 'And I am not alone in thinking it is strange, either.'

Chaloner considered the place's name. 'Chapel House. Does that mean there is an oratory inside it?' He supposed the deeply religious Dowager might be interested in one of those.

'No, it is called that because a church once stood there,' explained Armitage. 'Dedicated to St Thomas Becket, apparently. But it was demolished when the last King Henry broke with Rome, and was rebuilt as a private lodging. It has been secular for hundreds of years.'

91

'I see,' said Chaloner, declining to point out that the monarch in question had only been dead for a little more than a century.

'The Dowager has taken to visiting Winchester Palace, too,' Armitage went on, clearly in the mood to gossip. 'Do you know it? It is where the Bishop of Winchester stays when he visits London, and is in Southwark, not far from the end of the Bridge. But she only goes there when he is out. It is damned suspicious, if you ask me.'

'Perhaps she likes the view across the river,' suggested Chaloner, thinking of what Nat had said.

'Have you heard about the ball she is planning for Shrove Tuesday?' asked Armitage, getting into his stride. 'It will be attended by Catholics and rakes. Someone should take the opportunity to blow them all up, because England will be a better country without the likes of *them* running it.'

Chaloner headed for the door. He did not want to be having such a conversation, because to disagree might lead to a fight, while to concur might see him arrested – Spymaster Williamson was notorious for ordering his agents to encourage seditious discussions.

'Personally, I wish the old hag would go back to France,' Armitage called after him. 'And take her brat and her Capuchins with her. London was much nicer under Cromwell.'

As he left, Chaloner saw the haberdasher's customers nodding agreement, emphasising how far the King had fallen from favour with his wild ways and dissolute friends. In Chaloner's opinion, there was little to choose between Cromwell and the monarchy, because both systems had their faults. But he did wonder how long the King would be able to hang on to his throne in the face of such strong public disapproval – and whether he himself would be able to change his allegiance to yet another regime, should the King follow in his father's footsteps and end his life on the scaffold.

It did not take Chaloner long to reach the place where Phillippes and Kaltoff lodged, because Tyus the book-seller's premises were a mere two doors from Chapel House. Before he went in, he took a moment to survey their lair.

It was a very tall building, and seemed taller still because it was unusually narrow – Chaloner had bought books there in the past, and recalled that he could almost touch both walls simultaneously by stretching out his arms. It was extraordinarily deep, though, so not only did Tyus have a shop at ground level, but a counting house and a sitting room, too. This was possible because the house jutted a long way out over the river, a notion that made Chaloner uneasy – he disliked the thought of being suspended above the raging Thames by a few floor-boards.

He was not permitted to study the bookshop for long, however, because a cart was bearing down on him, and he had the distinct impression that it was not about to stop for anyone. He fumbled with the handle to Tyus's door, and stumbled inside an instant before the thundering wheels would have crushed him. An agonised cry from outside suggested someone else had been less fortunate.

'Lord!' exclaimed Tyus, going to peer out of his window. 'I swear drivers are getting worse.'

Charles Tyus was a neat man with a silver beard. He was assisted in his business by his wife Sarah, a raven-haired beauty two decades his junior. She was famous for making male customers feel very welcome, which she achieved with a battery of come-hither smiles and suggestive winks.

'It must make people reluctant to shop here,' said Chaloner, brushing himself down. 'I imagine most prefer somewhere they can reach without dicing with death.'

'Lots of *men* come here,' said Sarah, coming to lay a convivial hand on Chaloner's arm. 'They think we are worth the risk.'

'Business is booming,' agreed Tyus cheerfully. '*And* I have two lodgers on my upper floors. It means Sarah and I are a little cramped, but the extra income is well worth the inconvenience.'

'Have you come to purchase Will Leybourn's latest book?' asked Sarah, adjusting her neckline so it revealed more frontage. 'We can have it printed for you in less than a week.'

Leybourn's latest book was not high on Chaloner's future reading list. All the mathematician–surveyor's works were characterised by complex language and incomprehensible terminology, which made about as much sense to Chaloner as the speech of the Moors.

'Or perhaps you came for a copy of the Clarendon Code,' suggested Tyus. 'It makes for fascinating reading, and it is high time these fanatics were suppressed.'

'Oh, piffle!' declared Sarah. 'Most of these so-called dissenters are doing no harm, and I do not see why we cannot put aside our differences and learn to live in peace. And love,' she added, fixing Chaloner with an eye that glistened.

'It is not *most* dissenters I am worried about,' argued Tyus. 'It is the ones who are prepared to make a nuisance of themselves until they get their own way. Have we not had enough of civil strife? I say we have, and the Clarendon Code is the best way to ensure a peaceful future.'

'Actually, I came to see whether you have any rooms to rent,' said Chaloner, when Sarah opened her mouth to argue her point further. He was loath to be caught in the middle of a domestic dispute.

'Unfortunately, we do not,' said Tyus apologetically. 'Had you asked two weeks ago, I would have been able to oblige, but I have just leased them to Casper Kaltoff, Henry Phillippes's associate. Meanwhile, Mr Phillippes himself has the top chamber.'

'Then let us oust Mr Kaltoff to make room for this gentleman,' suggested Sarah eagerly. 'Mr Kaltoff is not a very attractive specimen, and he has habits.'

'Habits?' asked Chaloner, bemused.

'Habits,' repeated Sarah firmly, but declined to elaborate. She turned to her husband. 'Well? What do you say, Charles? We do not want it said that we condone what Mr Kaltoff does up there.'

Tyus considered the suggestion, but then shook his head reluctantly. 'We signed a rental agreement with him. I do not like his habits, either, but they do not break the terms of the lease, so we are bound by the law to keep him.'

'Might I see the rooms anyway?' asked Chaloner. He smiled encouragingly when Tyus hesitated. 'Perhaps his habits will require more space in time, and he will move out. Why not have an interested replacement standing by?'

'True,' agreed Tyus, smiling back. 'And you do not look like a man with habits.'

'At least, not unpleasant ones,' said Sarah, with one of her meaningful leers.

*　　*　　*

While Tyus served his other customers, Sarah escorted Chaloner to the rooms that had been let to Kaltoff. They were larger than the chambers on the ground floor, because the walls were not so thick, but they were narrow, even so. There were two of them, both Spartan in their décor. Not surprisingly, there was nothing lying around that indicated Kaltoff was involved in murdering iconoclasts. Or that he owned any disturbing habits, for that matter. But Sarah walked to the table, on which were piled several books, and a number of loose papers.

'Look,' she said, her voice dripping disapproval as she picked up a tome between thumb and forefinger. 'This is what he does when he is up here alone of an evening. I am sure you will agree that it is not nice.'

Chaloner took it from her, and saw it was full of drawings of people. They were not classical sketches, which portrayed a person's features accurately, but ones that distorted them to the point where they were grotesque. Yet even so, the folk they depicted were recognisable. There was one of his Earl, concentrating on the double chins, gouty feet and ridiculously tiny shoes, and one of Lady Castlemaine with an improbably large bust and calculating eyes. Chaloner had never seen anything quite like them, and was inclined to think they were more clever than 'not nice'.

'This is his habit?' he asked, flicking through the pages to see dozens more people he recognised, along with many he did not. Clearly, Kaltoff liked to caricature anyone he met.

Sarah nodded, pouting. 'He did a horrible one of me. He made me look like a whore.'

'He is a dial-maker,' mused Chaloner, looking at a very skilful depiction of the Dowager, all black veils, pinched mouth and disdainful eyes. 'He will be used to producing precise drawings, and these are merely an extension of—'

'They are cruel!' declared Sarah. 'Except the one of that horrible Earl of Clarendon, which is rather good. You can see immediately who it is. Mr Kaltoff has captured the jowls perfectly.'

Chaloner barely heard her. He had been rifling through some of the loose pages, and one image had leapt out at him. The drawing was in pen and ink, so there was no colour to give clues, but the little figure was busily poking glass from a church window. It had a fierce face, thin legs and an exaggerated paunch. Was this the evidence he had been looking for? Did it prove Kaltoff knew Blue Dick, and disapproved of what he had done? Or was it a generic depiction, illustrating what Kaltoff thought of iconoclasts as a whole? When Sarah looked the other way, Chaloner slipped the sketch into his pocket.

'May I see Phillippes's rooms, too?' he asked. 'I heard him say he might take a post at the University in Cambridge, so who knows how much longer he will be here?'

Sarah regarded him dubiously. 'I doubt they will hire him at Cambridge – their mathematicians are said to be the best in the world, and Will Leybourn thinks Mr Phillippes is not the genius he claims. Perhaps you misheard, and he was talking about Oxford. I understand they take anyone.'

'That must have been it.'

'I hope you are right, and he *is* leaving,' said Sarah, leading the way up a tiny staircase. 'I used to like him, but he has started to go out at strange times. He says it is because he is making tide-rings for the King and the Lord Chancellor, but I am not so sure.'

'What do you think he might be doing?'

Sarah pursed her lips. 'Some people find Mr Kaltoff's drawings amusing, so perhaps he is selling them. He has certainly come by extra money of late – he bought himself a lot of nice new clothes.'

Chaloner stared at her. Was this evidence that Phillippes and his associate had been paid to commit murder? He followed Sarah up the stairs, his thoughts whirling.

Phillippes's chambers were crammed to the gills with books, papers and mathematical instruments. He also had something hanging out of the window on a long piece of rope; Chaloner supposed it was a device for recording the tides. The place was chaotic and untidy, and very different from Kaltoff's neat lair.

He tried to search the place without Sarah guessing what he was doing, but she hampered him by coming to stand very close each time he stopped moving. At first, he assumed she did not want him to touch any of Phillippes's belongings, but hastily revised his opinion when she began to slip out of her bodice. However, while it might have been pleasant to accept what was being freely offered, it was hardly prudent to do it with her husband downstairs. Chaloner eased away.

'Are you sure?' whispered Sarah in a low, husky voice. 'You will not regret it.'

'I might, if Tyus comes looking for you.' Or Phillippes, he thought, not liking the notion of being caught in such a vulnerable position by a man who might be dangerous. He indicated Sarah was to precede him down the stairs, which she did with some reluctance.

'You were a long time,' said Tyus genially, when they arrived. 'Did you like what you saw?'

98

'He declined to look at much,' replied Sarah, pouting as she adjusted her bodice. 'But perhaps he will find more to his liking when Mr Phillippes moves to Oxford.'

'Mind the scaffolding when you go,' warned Tyus, as Chaloner aimed for the door. 'There was nothing wrong with Chapel House, but a major restoration is in progress anyway. It is a shameful waste of money, because Bridge funds could be much better spent elsewhere. For example, the starlings under Nonesuch House need replacing, while the gutters on the Stone Gate are a disgrace.'

'Then why are they doing it?' asked Chaloner, pausing. London was a practical city, and no one wasted money on repairs that were unnecessary.

'God knows,' replied Tyus. 'Traditionally, it is the home of the Junior Warden, but Scarlet does not seem like the kind of man who would use Bridge revenues to benefit himself. Yet who knows? He and his wife have gone to live in Turnstile until the work is finished, and I do not blame them. The workmen have ripped the heart out of the place.'

'I see,' said Chaloner, wondering whether the infor-mation was significant. Had Blue Dick slipped into Chapel House because he knew it was empty, and so available to use as a vantage point to see whether he was being followed? Chaloner supposed he would have to visit it and find out. But not that day. It was past four o'clock, and nearing the time when the Earl had ordered him to go to the Westminster charnel house, to look at Blue Dick's corpse with Surgeon Wiseman.

It was dark when Chaloner left the Bridge and began to make his way west. The streets were busy with coaches and hackney carriages, as those who could afford them rode home. He joined the flow of pedestrians, stepping over and around the rutted piles of manure that had been left by horses, cattle and donkeys. He walked along Thames Street, then crossed the Fleet River by the gloomy prison of Bridewell. He glanced up at its barred windows and dismal façade, and shuddered. He hated gaols, and one of his darkest fears was that his spying would see him incarcerated in one.

Fleet Street and The Strand were reasonably well lit, so it was not necessary to hire a linkman with a torch to light his way. Lamps gleamed in the houses of the rich merchants and nobles on the south side of the road, although the northern one was darker, on the grounds that these were owned by less-affluent traders – fuel was expensive, and was used sparingly by poorer households.

Chaloner shivered as a keen breeze cut through his clothes, and was sorry for the beggars who huddled in the porch of St Dunstan-in-the-West. Then the door opened, and the rector, looking around furtively to ensure he was not being watched, beckoned them inside. Chaloner was sure the wealthy congregation would not approve of vagrants sleeping in their fine church, but Joseph Thompson had a kind heart, and Chaloner applauded his covert charity. He stopped for a few moments, to make sure none of the recipients were the sort of men to cut their benefactor's throat in exchange for the contents of the poor box, then continued on his way.

Eventually, he reached the great open space around Charing Cross. That evening, two puppeteers were putting on a show for the homeward-bound. He was disturbed to note that the theme of their display was the Court, and that their string-controlled hero was an apprentice who set White Hall alight, thus ridding the country of an unnecessary financial burden. Most of the crowd were cheering, although there were a few shaken heads and frowns around the fringes.

Then Spymaster Williamson's men arrived, and the entertainment came to an abrupt end. Mallets were used to smash the little stage and the painted dolls, although the puppeteers themselves managed to escape – the size of the crowd had made it impossible for the soldiers to lay hold of them. The multitude stood silent and resentful as the officers vented their spleen on the hapless marionettes, and when people eventually dispersed, it was with angry mutters.

However, one man stood near the front of the gathering and applauded loudly as the puppets were crushed, either careless or oblivious of the fact that he was putting himself in danger from lobbed rocks – or worse. Chaloner might have dismissed him as someone not quite in control of his wits, had he not glanced at the fellow's face and noticed the crossed eyes.

'Michael Herring,' supplied a butcher's apprentice in response to Chaloner's whispered question. 'One-time despoiler of churches, and currently churchwarden of St Mary Woolchurch. Personally, I think the King should have hanged the lot of them. There is no place for fanatics in London.'

On the contrary, Chaloner thought to himself, London seemed to attract them in droves, because he did not think he had ever known a place that was quite so well-endowed with lunatic opinions. He regarded Herring with interest, taking care to do so in a way that ensured the iconoclast-turned-churchwarden did not see him.

Herring was a sturdy, angry-faced individual who wore

brazenly Puritan clothes. Indeed, he looked as though he had stepped directly from the civil wars, because he had made no concession to the changing times with his attire – no lace or coloured thread, and he had donned an old 'sugarloaf' hat that had been unfashionable a decade before. Chaloner recalled that Thurloe had described him as a man who walked as if he wanted to batter his way forward with his head. It was an astute observation, and captured the man's open belligerence perfectly.

Only when the soldiers had reduced the puppets to sawdust did Herring leave. Chaloner hesitated. Should he whisk the fellow down one of the many alleys that radiated from Charing Cross, and demand to know his future plans, as the Earl would no doubt recommend? Or should he follow him, to see where he went and who he met? It did not take Chaloner long to reach a decision. He could tell from Herring's savage demeanour that he would not be an easy nut to crack, and suspected knives at throats were unlikely to loosen his tongue. Chaloner would learn more by watching.

Herring strode towards St Martin's Lane, then turned down an alley to the left. Chaloner followed as quickly as he dared, not wanting to get close enough to be spotted, but aware that it would be easy to lose his quarry once away from the larger roads.

It was much darker in the alley, and he could barely see where he was putting his feet. Then he became aware that someone was behind him, and the hair on the back of his neck rose when the footsteps kept pace with his own. He turned a corner, and swore under his breath when he saw Herring had disappeared. He faltered for a moment, but then kept walking, acutely aware of the danger looming behind. Was it Phillippes or Kaltoff? If so, then he needed to shake them off quickly, because he doubted they would let him escape from a second confrontation.

He began to run, hurtling around a corner so fast that he stood no chance of avoiding the cudgel that swung towards him. He managed to protect his head, but the blow caught him on the shoulder and knocked him clean off his feet. His senses reeled – it had been like running into a stone wall – and when his vision finally cleared, it was to find himself flat on his back while someone pinned him to the ground by kneeling on his chest. Herring was standing to one side, swinging a thick piece of wood in a way that suggested he would dearly like to use it a second time.

'Who are you?' demanded Herring's companion. Chaloner could not see his face, because the lane was too dark, but it was someone strong and heavy – he could barely breathe. It was not Kaltoff, because he was the wrong shape, and it was too large to be Phillippes.

'I could ask you the same thing,' Chaloner countered, shifting slightly in an attempt to ease some of the weight from his chest.

His captor gave a grunt, and pressed down so hard that Chaloner thought his ribs were going to break. 'You are not in a position to make demands. Tell me your name, or I will cut your throat.'

Chaloner saw the glint of metal in the gloom, and suspected it would be cut anyway – or an attempt made, at least. He twisted his arm, so the dagger he always carried in his sleeve slid into the palm of his hand.

'Casper Kaltoff,' he gasped, using the first name that came into his head. 'Now let me go.'

The man glanced up at Herring. 'Is it true? It is too dark to see his face.'

But Herring had questions of his own. 'Why were you following me? Who sent you?'

'What makes you think I was sent by anyone?' Chaloner managed to wheeze. 'Perhaps I admired your courage . . . in standing against the mood of the mob.'

'Did you?' asked Herring. He sounded flattered. 'It was a—'

'He is lying,' snarled his companion. He pushed the dagger against Chaloner's throat. 'Who are you working for?'

The blade began to bite, so Chaloner drove his own knife into the man's leg, as hard as he could. His captor howled and jerked away, enabling Chaloner to squirm free and stagger to his feet. Immediately, Herring came at him with the cudgel, but Chaloner ducked, and pieces of wood flew when it struck a wall. Herring swore under his breath when he found himself left with a stump.

Then the other man began to fumble with something jammed in his belt, and Chaloner knew he was going to produce a gun. He turned and fled, stumbling over piles of rubbish, pieces of masonry, old wood, and something that felt suspiciously like a dead pig.

He did not go far. Finding an abandoned warehouse, he picked the lock and slid inside, fighting to silence his laboured breathing. Behind him, there were rats – claws skittered on stone, and there was a thick, rank smell, as though something large had died there.

He peered through a hole in a wall, and saw Herring and his companion tear past, the latter limping. After a moment, Chaloner slipped out and began to follow. But they knew the alleys and he did not, so, despite his best efforts, it was not many moments before he lost them. He searched for a while, but it was hopeless. With a grimace of exasperation, he accepted defeat.

Rubbing his shoulder, angry with himself for being so easily overcome, Chaloner retraced his steps to Charing Cross, then walked down King Street. Eventually, he reached the Palace of Westminster, which adjoined White Hall, and was where several government departments had their offices. Even though the evening was wearing on, the streets were busy with clerks and lawyers, some aiming for home, and others setting out for one of the many eating houses in the neighbourhood.

But Chaloner's business was at the end of a dingy lane that led to the river, where a man named Kersey operated. The charnel house had originally been established to house bodies dredged from the river – a distressingly high number, because the Thames was deep, strong and swift. It had expanded since then, and now anyone who died a suspicious or unexpected death in Westminster or White Hall was delivered into Kersey's care.

From the outside, Kersey's domain did not look very big, but this was a deception. Immediately on the right as the visitor entered, was a handsome antechamber in which the charnel-house keeper entertained bereaved friends and family, and on the left was the sumptuous office in which he counted his takings. And beyond these was the mortuary itself, a large, low-ceilinged affair that was full of tables, each either occupied by a blanket-covered body, or carefully scrubbed ready to receive its next visitor.

Kersey was a wealthy man, not only because he was paid to look after his charges, but because he was entitled to keep anything not claimed by the next-of-kin.

105

And people were curious about corpses, so he made a fortune in spectators' fees, too. Moreover, he had recently opened an exhibition of the most interesting artefacts he had recovered over the years. It was a popular tourist attraction, and visitors flocked to it in droves.

Chaloner knocked on the door, and a servant conducted him to the visitors' room. Kersey was not alone, and Chaloner braced himself for trouble when he recognised the vast frame, scarlet robes and red hair of Richard Wiseman. The escapade with Herring meant it was much later than the appointed five o'clock, and he knew the Court Surgeon was unlikely to be very understanding about his tardiness. In fact, he had hoped the man would have given up on him and gone home.

Wiseman was an impossible person – arrogant, opinionated and overbearing, and was highly unpopular at Court. He was rarely invited out, mostly due to his unappealing personality, but also because he liked to describe grisly surgical techniques while people were eating. It meant he had plenty of time on his hands, which he filled by devising new and bizarre medical theories, and honing his already-powerful frame with a regime of lifting heavy weights. Given the number of enemies his acid tongue had earned him, Chaloner supposed it was not surprising that Wiseman needed to be able to defend himself, and the exercises had turned him into a formidable opponent.

'You are late, Chaloner,' declared Wiseman, speaking from Kersey's most comfortable chair. 'Or did you hope to avoid me by coming after dark?'

He roared with laughter at the notion, although Chaloner was sure he would not find it quite so amusing if he knew it was true. Most people who had met Wiseman were prepared to go to considerable lengths to dodge an encounter with him.

'Traffic is heavy at this time of night,' Chaloner replied evasively. 'It was a bad time to choose.'

'It was Clarendon's idea,' said Wiseman, slightly dangerously. For some inexplicable reason, he had decided the Earl was worthy of his devotion, and his unwavering loyalty was his one redeeming feature, as far as Chaloner was concerned. 'And I shall thank you not to question his judgement.'

Hastily, Chaloner bowed an apology. He was cold, tired, his shoulder hurt and he was not equal to exchanging hostile words with the likes of Wiseman. He shook his head when Kersey offered him wine, because Wiseman was in the habit of using Kersey's goblets when he performed some of his dubious – and certainly illegal – anatomical examinations of those victims not claimed by kin.

'Wiseman has been telling me about the charming ladies he knows in Hercules' Pillars Alley,' said Kersey amiably. 'He has offered to introduce me to them.'

'You mean Temperance North's brothel?' asked Chaloner, hoping to put the charnel-house keeper off with his blunt description. Temperance was a friend, and he did not like the notion of her establishment being frequented by the likes of Wiseman and Kersey. He knew she entertained worse – the rakes from Court, for example – but for reasons he could not explain, they seemed more acceptable, somehow.

'It is a *gentleman's club*,' corrected Wiseman curtly. 'A place where a fellow can relax and enjoy pleasant female company in an atmosphere of genteel hospitality. Half the Court's musicians are paid to play there, so the entertainment is very fine. And there is not much fighting.'

'I had not taken you for a bawdy-house man,' said Chaloner, somewhat baldly. He knew the surgeon was lonely, but he was surprised to learn he sought solace in bordellos.

'It is *not* a bawdy-house,' snapped Wiseman irritably. 'There is a world of difference between the brothels of Fleet Alley and Temperance's concern. She is a lovely lady, and I like visiting her and her entertaining friends.'

That was one way of describing them, thought Chaloner, but he held his tongue.

'Is she beautiful, then?' asked Kersey, rather wistfully. 'This Temperance?'

Chaloner loved Temperance like a sister, but even to his fond eyes she was plain and fat. He decided it was more tactful to say nothing.

'She is perfect,' declared Wiseman. Chaloner looked at him sharply, wondering if he was making a joke, but the surgeon appeared to be perfectly serious. 'Her fine eyes, lovely body—'

'You are enamoured with *Temperance*?' blurted Chaloner, seeing the oddly dreamy expression on the surgeon's face. He could scarcely believe it, because while she had some excellent qualities as a person, she was hardly someone who should have sane men swooning.

The surgeon blushed. 'Let us say I enjoy her company.'

Chaloner was tempted to tease him about it, in revenge for several inconvenient medical experiments that had been conducted on him in the past, but found he could not do it. If Wiseman felt for Temperance what Chaloner was beginning to feel for Hannah, then it was not something to be mocked.

'Have you looked at Blue Dick?' he asked, hoping the answer would be yes, so he could listen to the report and then spend the rest of the evening with the woman who was becoming so important to him.

'No – I have been waiting for you,' came the disappointing reply. 'There is no point in examining a corpse if no one is around to appreciate my expertise.'

Stifling a sigh of resignation, Chaloner watched Wiseman finish his wine and begin to prepare himself for his work by rolling up his sleeves and donning a leather apron, like the ones worn by fishmongers. It already bore ominous stains.

'An apron is a good idea,' said Kersey approvingly. 'Blood is difficult to remove from one's clothes. Even yours, which are all red anyway.'

'I know,' said Wiseman. 'And Temperance told me she did not like it.'

With the sense that he was about to be subjected to an experience he could well do without, Chaloner followed Wiseman and Kersey into the mortuary. Ever thrifty, Kersey lit only one lamp. It sent eerie shadows into the deeper recesses of the room, and for one unnerving moment, Chaloner thought he saw one of the bodies move.

'I heard you have been in Wimbledon these last few weeks,' said Wiseman conversationally. 'In the hope that the villainous Lord Bristol will show his face.'

'It was a waste of time,' said Chaloner tiredly. 'However, I am beginning to suspect that there might be some truth in the rumours after all – that he has indeed returned to England. I would like to visit his Great Queen Street house, but the Earl has forbidden me to go.'

'The Earl is right – Lord Bristol is not in Great Queen Street,' said Wiseman with great conviction. He saw

Chaloner's raised eyebrows and went on to explain. 'I thought he might be there, too, so I went along and hammered on his door. No one answered.'

Chaloner would not have answered *his* door, if *he* had looked out of his window to see the likes of Wiseman waiting to come in. And Bristol was not a fool: he knew Wiseman was one of the Earl's supporters, and would make every effort to avoid him. Thus the lack of a reply meant nothing one way or the other.

'I have never had an iconoclast in my care before,' said Kersey, pulling the cover from one of his charges to expose Blue Dick's body. 'I cannot say I approve of what they did.'

'I thought they had the right idea,' countered Wiseman, always argumentative. 'Some of our churches are very cluttered, and they looked better once they had been cleared out a bit.'

'But the iconoclasts did not "clear them out a bit",' Kersey pointed out. 'They knocked statues into dust, threw paint over pictures, ripped the pages out of Bibles, and pissed on shrines. It all made a terrible mess, and most chapels look the worse for their attentions.'

Wiseman sniffed, and did not deign to discuss the matter. He had already stripped off the dead man's clothes, and stood back for a moment, inspecting the naked corpse through gleaming eyes. Chaloner watched him in distaste, not sure how he could take such obvious enjoyment in his work.

'What do you think about that rape, which occurred over Turnstile way?' asked Kersey, averting his eyes quickly as Wiseman produced a small knife. Chaloner looked away, too, never comfortable with what the surgeon did in the name of science. 'I heard a torch was used – a lighted one.'

'It is true,' said Wiseman grimly. 'And her husband

was bound hand and foot, and made to watch. I was summoned to tend them. Sometimes I wonder what sort of monsters walk our streets.'

'Will she die?' asked Kersey.

'I hope not,' said Wiseman. His voice was gruff, and Chaloner was surprised to see the incident had upset him. As the surgeon rarely empathised with the plight of his patients, Chaloner could only assume the attack had been unusually disturbing.

'I heard the old king's ghost has been walking along Fleet Street,' said Kersey, after a moment's silence, changing the topic again. 'And the river's tides have been wrong for weeks now. It is an omen, you know.'

'An omen for what?' asked Chaloner.

'For bad things to come. Everyone says it is the Court's fault, because it is so debauched. But when you have crimes like the one committed against that poor woman, you must wonder whether there is not a greater evil prowling our city.'

Chaloner was not particularly sensitive to atmospheres, but Kersey's words sent a shiver down his spine. Perhaps it was the fact that he was in a dark mortuary with two men he considered rather sinister, and Wiseman's knife was making unpleasant squelching sounds as he probed his victim's innards. Or perhaps he was still shaken from his encounter with Herring. Regardless, he wished he was at home with Hannah.

'What can you tell me?' he asked briskly, wanting the business over, so he could be on his way.

'Culmer was stabbed in the heart,' replied Wiseman, 'which is not an easy thing to do, because bone tends to get in the way. Of course, I imagine you know how to avoid that particular problem.'

111

'Was it a professional strike or a lucky hit?' asked Chaloner, deciding to ignore the remark.

'There is no way to know. But the Earl tells me you witnessed the attack, so what do *you* think?'

'Professional,' replied Chaloner, recalling the confident way the killer had moved. Yet again, it occurred to him that Phillippes or Kaltoff were perfect candidates – not only were they the right size to have been the cloaked man, but their pursuit of Chaloner outside the Beggar's Bush indicated they were skilled at clandestine man-oeuvres, too.

'Death was instant,' Wiseman went on. 'And that is all I can tell you, I am afraid. Unless you want to know what he ate for his last meal?'

Chaloner regarded him in horror. 'You mean to examine the contents of his stomach?'

Wiseman nodded gleefully. 'I am becoming quite skilled at identifying half-digested slime in—'

'Are you going to search his garments, Chaloner?' interrupted Kersey, indicating that even the robust charnel-house keeper was unsettled by Wiseman's grisly suggestion.

With relief, Chaloner turned his attention to the task. As he would have expected from a man who liked destroying great works of art, the iconoclast's clothes were almost crude in their simplicity. And every item was blue. The only exception was his white 'falling band' – a square of material that hung from the neck like a bib.

'There is something hidden here,' said Chaloner, feeling a slight irregularity in the falling band's hem. He took his knife and cut some tiny stitches to reveal a scrap of paper. It was about the size of his little finger, and

112

was covered in minuscule writing. Kersey brought the lamp closer, but it was still a struggle to read.

'It is cipher,' Chaloner said eventually. 'I shall have to take it home, and examine it properly.'

'You understand such things?' asked Kersey. He sounded more dubious than impressed.

Chaloner shrugged. 'If it is a simple code, I should be able to break it, but if it is based on some book known only to the writer and recipient, then the chances of unravelling it are slim.'

'Well, I am glad *I* do not have to deal with it,' said Wiseman, rolling down his sleeves and brushing himself down. 'I have more interesting things to do. I am going to see Temperance.'

Despite feeling tired and out of sorts, Chaloner decided to go with Wiseman when he visited Hercules' Pillars Alley. He had not seen Temperance since he had returned from Wimbledon, and did not want her to feel slighted. He knew Hannah would be waiting in her little cottage on Tothill Street, but the excursion would not take more than an hour, and then he could go to bed with a clear conscience – he wanted to ensure that Temperance did not mind Wiseman foisting himself on her, and that she did not need help escaping an unwelcome admirer. He had been the one to introduce them to each other, so he felt a certain responsibility for the situation.

They hired a hackney carriage, which rattled along at a furious lick towards its destination. Chaloner did not mind, because the rocking and bucking prevented Wiseman from regaling him with too vivid a description of the latest Public Anatomy he had performed. Apparently, the King had come to watch him slice up some hapless cadaver, and Wiseman was still riding high on the royal praise that had been lavished on him afterwards.

Hercules' Pillars Alley was a small lane off Fleet Street, named for the tavern that stood on the corner. The inn was a disreputable place, famous for gambling and serving large portions of meat. Loud voices emanated from within, followed by a piercing squeal. Chaloner grimaced in distaste, suspecting a game involving rats was in progress.

By contrast, Temperance's establishment was a model of discretion. Railings and a small courtyard separated it from the street, and elegant music wafted out. It was a piece composed by Matthew Locke, and because it was being played by members of the King's Private Musick, it was exquisite. Chaloner stopped to listen, closing his eyes to appreciate the harmonies. He opened them abruptly when Wiseman shoved him hard enough to make him stagger.

'I want to see Temperance,' the surgeon declared robustly. 'Come with me if you will, but do not stand blocking my path.'

Chaloner followed him inside. It was still early, so the guests were not too unruly, although he knew it was only a matter of time before that changed – the club was patronised by courtiers, and any place containing *them* was unlikely to remain genteel for long. However, as Temperance hired a doorman to exclude any obvious undesirables – essentially anyone who could not pay her inflated prices – her neighbours could rest assured that their slumbers were going to be disturbed only by members of the aristocratic elite. In other words, by a higher class of lout.

The doorman's name was Preacher Hill, a nonconformist

fanatic who bawled rabid sermons about sin in the day, and earned his bread at the brothel during the night. Chaloner was amazed that the man never seemed to realise that this made him something of a hypocrite.

'What do *you* want?' Hill snarled. He had never liked Chaloner, and the spy was seldom allowed past without some sort of insult being hurled. 'You have not been here in weeks, and I was beginning to hope you had met an unpleasant end.'

Chaloner regarded him coolly. He had never understood why Temperance insisted on employing such a surly brute, although he had been told that Hill was exceptionally skilled at identifying trouble-makers. He wondered what that said about him, given the preacher's repeated and dogged attempts to keep him out. He opened his mouth to reply in kind, but Wiseman was there before him.

'Now, now,' admonished the surgeon. 'Is that any way to speak to your mistress's friend? Let us past, or you and I will have a falling out.'

Wiseman represented a formidable figure with his rippling muscles and impressive height, and Hill gulped in alarm as he stood aside. The surgeon thrust past him, into the house beyond.

'Temperance!' he cried, surging towards the object of his desire like a great red galleon.

Customers and working girls alike were knocked out of his way, and Chaloner was astonished when Temperance flung away the handful of cards she had been holding, and rushed to meet him. She did not forsake games for Chaloner, obliging him to wait until she had finished before deigning to greet him. He watched in amazement as they flew into each others' arms. Temperance's expression was

115

one of unbridled delight, and it was clear that Wiseman's affections were fully reciprocated. So, Chaloner thought, wondering what they saw in each other, his brotherly protection was not required after all.

Temperance had gained more weight since Chaloner had last seen her, and her dress did nothing to disguise the fact. It did not suit her, and made her look sluttish. Her cheeks had been slathered with some sort of paste to give them a fashionable pallor, and the black 'face patches' currently popular at Court were stark against it. She gave Chaloner a cool, disinterested wave, then took Wiseman's arm and led him to her table.

'You are not in as high favour as you once were,' said Hill, watching the scene with a spiteful smirk. 'It is only a matter of time before she lets me eject you.'

Chaloner suspected that was true. It was barely a year since the demure teenager had shocked everyone by opening her club, and she had been drifting away from him ever since.

'What do you think about Dowsing and his associates?' Chaloner asked the preacher, mostly to change the subject from one that was hurtful, but also because it was an opportunity to quiz a man who had made religion the centre of his life. 'Blue Dick Culmer and Herring?'

Hill's eyes glittered. 'They are great men, who understand that chapels stuffed with papist trinkets are bad for the soul. They did the work of God when they smashed those statues.'

'Have you heard any rumours that they plan to— to *cleanse* any more churches?' Chaloner asked, stopping himself from saying 'despoil' at the last minute.

'No, why? Have you?' asked Hill eagerly. 'Because if so, I would like to join them.'

116

Chaloner was sure he would. 'Herring is probably plotting something. If I agree to tell you what I learn about him, will you reciprocate? Pass me anything you happen to hear?'

'No,' said Hill firmly. 'Because *your* intention will be to stop his holy work. So, I shall not pass you anything. And that is a pity for you, because I have a snippet of information that you would probably find *very* interesting. But I am not going to give it to you.'

Casually, Chaloner drew his dagger from its sheath, and began to inspect the blade. 'No?'

Hill regarded it uneasily. 'You would not stab me. Not in here.'

'You will remain in all night, will you? You will not go outside during the course of your duties?'

The preacher regarded him with a glittering hatred, but there was something in Chaloner's quiet words that convinced him that it would be better to comply.

'All right, there is no need for that sort of talk. My news is that there is something momentous in the offing. And the reason I know is because of omens – the old king's ghost seen walking along Fleet Street, parts of St Paul's Cathedral falling down, changes in the tides. These all mean one thing: that a great catastrophe is about to befall the city.'

Chaloner was disappointed. 'I have been listening to this kind of speculation all week. It is the talk of the coffee houses.'

'You interrupted me, I had not finished.' Hill pursed his lips, then leaned forward confidentially. 'When you are a doorman, people tend to ignore you, and you hear things. I learned last night that Lord Bristol has been seen visiting the Dowager Queen at Somerset House.'

117

This was a piece of intelligence Chaloner *was* interested to hear. 'When?'

'It is because he is Catholic,' Hill went on, ignoring the question, almost certainly because he did not know the answer. 'And so is she. It is obvious that the papists are planning something terrible, and brave men like Herring are flocking to London to prevent it.'

He scuttled away when Chaloner made no reply, apparently nervous that his information might be insufficient to prevent him from being speared. Chaloner watched him go. Was he right? Was Thurloe's 'dissatisfied majority' part of the same rebellion, or was the city in such a turmoil of discontent that revolts and plots were springing up like mushrooms?

And where should Chaloner stand on the issue? With the Earl who paid his wages, lending his sword to protect the inept, dissolute band of hedonists who ran the country? Or with decent, honourable men like Thurloe? Chaloner rubbed his head wearily, and hoped to God that folk came to their senses before the situation went that far.

Chapter 4

While he waited for Temperance to finish her game of cards, Chaloner passed the time by listening to the King's Private Musick, although the performers had been given too much wine and the bowing of the bass violist was beginning to deteriorate. Chaloner played the bass viol, or viola da gamba, himself, and music was important to him. It cleared his mind when he was anxious, helped him to think clearly, and gave him more pleasure than he could express. One of the things he liked about Hannah was that she – and he by extension – was often invited to soirees where there were creditable amateur ensembles for him to join.

When he could no longer bear the sour notes, he moved to the other end of the room, and took up station in the shadows cast by a large statue. The lacklustre performance was making him itch to upbraid the musicians – he knew for a fact that they could do better – but that would have attracted attention to himself, and he was glad he had exercised restraint when he saw several people he recognised, all from his spying mission to Somerset House the previous night.

The Dowager's Frenchmen – Doucett and Martin – were pawing a couple of Temperance's ladies near the wine fountain. Chaloner listened to their banter for a while, but they said nothing of substance, and their sole concern seemed to be which of the two women had the biggest bust. They were drinking heavily, and Chaloner imagined it would not be long before there was trouble.

A short distance away was Winter, the Catholic gunpowder expert, his enormous moustache carefully waxed for the occasion. He was with the four Penderel brothers, who were bellowing with laughter. The source of their amusement was Father Stephen, who had evidently been coaxed into the place as a practical joke. The poor man was mortified, and sat rigidly in his chair, staring fixedly at his feet. He looked to be on the verge of tears. Winter was not smiling, either.

'You should be ashamed of yourselves,' he snapped, taking Father Stephen's arm and hauling him to his feet. 'The man is a Catholic priest, for God's sake. What is wrong with you?'

The brother Chaloner thought was called Edward drew his dagger, sudden anger suffusing his face at the reprimand, but Rupert stepped forward to lay a calming hand on his arm. Winter shot them both a sneer of disdain, then escorted Father Stephen to the door. Chaloner heard the priest informing his rescuer exactly what he thought of men who played low tricks on hapless clerics.

'Let me escort you home, Father,' Winter said quietly. 'It was a cruel jape, and I apologise on their behalf. They will be sorry tomorrow, when wine is not befuddling their senses.'

Stephen sniffed. 'I doubt it. They are horrible men,

and I fail to understand why the Dowager tolerates them. And do not tell me it is because she might take one as a husband. She will never remarry – she told me so herself.'

'I suppose they must have their uses,' said Winter with a sigh. 'Although I cannot imagine what they might be. But here is the carriage. Let me help you inside.'

'If you take me home, you will miss the revelries.' The priest looked pointedly at Winter's pristine moustache and fine clothes. 'And I suspect you planned to enjoy yourself tonight.'

'Then I shall see it as penance. Come, Father. Let us get you away from this place.'

When Chaloner turned his attention back to the Penderels, they were looking for someone else to torment. For a brief moment, he thought they were going to pick on him. Did they recognise him, he wondered, from their encounter at White Hall earlier that day, and considered one of the Earl's retainers fair game for their teasing? But if they did recall him, they did not deem him worthy of attention, because they soon moved on.

They descended on Wiseman in the end, asking him silly, impertinent questions about his Public Anatomy. Chaloner smirked when Wiseman began to answer in gory detail, gratified to see Edward pale suddenly, obliging his brothers to sit him down and press his head between his knees.

He was on the verge of leaving – there was only so long he was prepared to wait for Temperance – when the brothel-mistress finished her card game and came towards him.

'Have you been away, Thomas?' she asked coolly. 'I do not think I have seen you for a while.'

121

'You cannot remember?' he asked, a little hurt.

Temperance shrugged. 'I am always so busy these days, especially since you introduced me to Mr Wiseman.' She turned, saw the surgeon looking at her, and waved. He waved back, a coquettish little gesture that was grotesque on a man of his bulk. 'He is such a dear man.'

'Oh,' said Chaloner weakly. He changed the subject. 'I have been in Wimbledon these last—'

She rounded on him before he could finish. 'I hope you were not after poor Lord Bristol. Your horrible old Earl is determined to see him in the Tower, because he is afraid Bristol will rally support against these nasty religious laws he supports so vigorously – the Clarendon Code. Well, if Bristol does manage to do it, then good luck to him.'

'Is it true that Lord Bristol is back in the country, then?' asked Chaloner casually.

Temperance's clients often gossiped, and as her club was patronised by men from Somerset House, he was hopeful she might have heard something useful. And there was no point trying to defend the Earl's enthusiasm for the Clarendon Code, when Chaloner was unhappy with it himself.

'Oh, yes, although no one knows where, precisely.' Temperance smiled suddenly, and pointed at the floor. 'What do you think of my new rugs? I made so much money last month that I decided to get rid of all the old ones.'

She must be earning a fortune, Chaloner thought in amazement, if she could afford to squander her profits so carelessly. Perhaps Hill was right, and the place *would* soon be too exclusive for him.

'How much does one of your ladies cost?' he asked, purely from idle curiosity.

She regarded him in surprise. 'You want one? I thought you had a sweetheart in Tothill Street – a lady you have never introduced to me, incidentally.'

Chaloner was not sure what to say. Hannah was liberal-minded, but he imagined that even she would baulk at being presented to a brothel-keeper. 'I have only been back a few days,' he mumbled awkwardly.

But Temperance was not listening to him anyway. 'Does she make you happy?' she asked, looking wistfully in Wiseman's direction.

Chaloner regarded her uneasily. 'What do you mean by "happy"?'

'It is time I met her,' said Temperance, abruptly turning to face him. 'You must invite me to dine with you both. I shall bring Richard, too.'

'Richard? You mean *Wiseman*?' Chaloner was horri-fied. It would be bad enough managing Hannah and Temperance, and he could not cope with the irascible surgeon being added to the mix, too. It would be the soiree from Hell.

Temperance's expression was belligerent. 'Yes, Wiseman! I want him with me when I meet this paragon of virtue who has captured your heart. So, when shall we come? How about tomorrow?'

Chaloner saw he was trapped. 'How about a week next Wednesday?'

That was in eleven days time, when, hopefully, he would have thwarted whatever the Dowager and her cronies were planning for Shrove Tuesday, arrested Blue Dick's killer and persuaded Thurloe against joining the pending rebellion. And if past experience was anything to go by, the Earl would then send him out of the city on some errand, and he would be able to cancel.

123

'Ash Wednesday,' mused Temperance. 'The first day of Lent, and the day after the Dowager's ball and your Earl's ecclesiastical dinner. Well, why not? It is as good a time as any.'

It was bitterly cold when Chaloner left Hercules' Pillars Alley, and he walked at a rapid clip, hoping the brisk pace would warm him. He maintained a fairly comfortable temperature along The Strand and King Street, but once into the more open area around Hannah's home, the wind cut through him like a knife – Tothill Street was bordered by St James's Park to the north and open fields to the south, and although it had a pleasantly rural feel in summer, it could be bleak in winter.

He paused as he passed the house rented by the Penderels. He was very tired, and ached to be in Hannah's warm bed, but as the brothers were currently enjoying Temperance's hospitality, it seemed a good opportunity to investigate four men who were hostile to his Earl. He looked around carefully. The street was deserted, so he picked the lock to their front door and let himself inside.

He was surprised to discover the house was almost identical to Hannah's – a short corridor with doors opening to sitting room, parlour and kitchen on the ground floor, and narrow stairs leading to bedrooms above. But unlike Hannah's home, the Penderel lair was a pigsty. Unwashed clothes were strewn across the floor, and the whole place reeked of stale food, dirty feet and pipe smoke.

Chaloner looked around in distaste, then rifled unenthusiastically through some papers in a chest. He was disappointed to find they were mostly receipts for the clothes that had been bought since the brothers' arrival in London, along with demands for payment from exasperated tailors. Then he went upstairs, where there was plenty of evidence that the Penderels liked to entertain women, and a pool of something dark and sticky that he assumed was spilled wine.

The largest bedroom was marginally tidier than the others, and contained several items that told him it was occupied by Rupert, the eldest. Among them was a family Bible, in which someone had painstakingly drawn a family tree. Chaloner found the names of the five brothers who had helped the King escape after the Battle of Worcester, and saw that their relationship to the men currently in London was rather more distant than 'cousin'. As he had suspected, the London Penderels were fortune-seekers, aiming to capitalise on the courage of remote kin. There was nothing else to find, though, so he left the house, taking care to secure the door behind him.

When he arrived at Hannah's home, he was dismayed to find her entertaining. Lamps blazed in her parlour, and the sounds of merriment were loud enough to make him wonder whether she had invited half the Court. Someone was playing a trumpet, and the laughter was boisterous. He winced when he recognised Buckingham's guffaw. Hannah was fond of the Duke, although Chaloner could not imagine why, and it was one of several things about which they disagreed vehemently.

He hesitated before going in. He had only known Hannah for a few months, and they still had a lot to learn about each other. There were occasions – and this night was one of them – when he wondered what it was that drew them together. She was lively, sociable and popular, while he was reticent with few real friends. Reviewing their relationship dispassionately, he suspected it had evolved because they were both lonely. He often asked himself whether it would last, and was always surprised to find himself hoping it would, although he could not have said why, other than the fact that he liked her. Perhaps that would be enough, and the differences in their characters would serve to unite, rather than divide them. But he wished she had not chosen that evening to have visitors, when all he wanted was to sleep. Taking a deep breath, he opened the door.

'There you are,' said Hannah, smiling as she came to meet him. She took his hand in hers. 'You are freezing! Come and sit by the fire.'

'There does not appear to be room,' said Chaloner, pulling away because he was loath to be thrust into the midst of such a gay throng when he was tired and his shoulder hurt.

She grabbed his hand a second time. 'Do not be silly, Tom! The Duke will not mind moving for you. I keep telling you that he is a lovely man.'

Chaloner was sure Buckingham *would* mind being asked to give up his fireside chair for one of his enemy's retainers, and then there would be a scene. He disengaged himself again.

'I cannot stay,' he said apologetically. 'There is something I must do. For Clarendon.'

Hannah rolled her eyes. She was small, with a face that was more striking than pretty. Like all the Queen's ladies-in-waiting, she was dressed in the height of fashion, with a tight-boned bodice that accentuated her slender figure, and long, full skirts that brushed the floor. Her fair hair was curled into ringlets, pressed flat across the top of her head and falling in coils at the sides.

'Your Earl is a miserable old killjoy,' she said crossly.

126

'How can he order you to work so late? But at least come in for a glass of wine. There is music,' she added, playing on his love for the viol.

'Yes,' said Chaloner, tactfully declining to remark that it was not very good music. 'But I really cannot stay. I just came to see if all was well with you.'

'Actually,' she said, easing him towards the door, so they could talk without being overheard, 'it is not. Did you hear what happened to Jane Scarlet?'

'Who is Jane Scarlet?'

'The wife of Anthony Scarlet, Warden of the Bridge. Men broke into her house and raped her, forcing her husband to watch. And there was talk of a lighted torch . . .' Hannah looked slightly sick.

Connections began to form in Chaloner's mind. He recalled being told that the victim of the horrific assault lived in Turnstile, and that Scarlet and his wife had moved there from Chapel House while it was being renovated. Furthermore, Scarlet had been crying in St James's Park that morning, and had looked ill and in low spirits later, when he and Senior Warden Hussey had arrived to sort out the traffic jam caused by the selfish Dowager. Now Chaloner understood why.

'Jane and I have been friends for years,' Hannah went on. 'Why would anyone harm her?'

'Perhaps because of her husband's work?' suggested Chaloner. There it was: the Bridge again.

Hannah wiped away the tears that had pooled in the corners of her eyes. 'I doubt it! What can be contentious about being Warden of the Bridge?'

Chaloner had no reply.

'Poor Jane!' Hannah sniffed. 'I could not bear the thought of being alone tonight, so I invited these friends

127

over. I would not have done it, had I known you were certain to visit.'

He heard the admonition in her voice, but there was nothing he could do about the hours he was obliged to keep. He shot her a remorseful glance. 'Do you want me to come back later?'

She stood on tiptoe to kiss him. 'I doubt they will be gone before dawn, not if the Duke is here. Will you explore what happened to Jane? Whoever ordered the attack *must* be brought to justice.'

'Ordered the attack?' echoed Chaloner. 'How do you know it was not a random act of violence, committed by men in their cups? You just said it can have nothing to do with her husband's work.'

'Because common robbers would have stolen something, but these villains did not,' replied Hannah promptly, indicating that she had been mulling the matter over in her mind. 'They broke into the house, assaulted Jane, and left. It was *not* a random act of violence. It was premeditated.'

'Then do you think they wanted information from Scarlet, and used Jane to make him speak?'

Hannah regarded him soberly. 'That is an unpleasant notion. Do you think that will happen to me one day, because of the work *you* do?'

It was something all spies dreaded. 'My Earl's most deadly enemy is in your parlour,' Chaloner said with a smile, hoping to reassure her. It was not entirely true – Lady Castlemaine and Lord Bristol were just as dangerous, and so was the Dowager. 'He will not let anything happen to you.'

Hannah forced a smile. 'The Duke *is* fond of me. But will you look into the assault on Jane? Spymaster

Williamson has promised to investigate, but I am not sure I trust him to do it properly.'

Chaloner was surprised. 'Why not? It is an outrage committed against the wife of a city official. It is his responsibility *and* his duty to catch the culprits.'

Hannah lowered her voice. 'Yes, but I did not like the expression in his eyes when he told the Duke he would do his best. It was not . . . *honest*. Do you know what I mean?'

Chaloner knew exactly what she meant. But the Spymaster would be furious if Chaloner meddled in one of his cases, and he had more than enough to do with his own enquiries.

'Please,' begged Hannah. 'I want justice for Jane. Besides, you will not be doing it for her, but for all men whose occupations put their friends and families at risk. Ultimately, it will protect *me*.'

It was a sly argument, but one that had some merit. Perhaps catching and making an example of Jane's attackers would make the point that such tactics were unacceptable, and would make London a safer place for Hannah. Reluctantly, Chaloner nodded that he would try.

'You will need to interview her,' she said. 'But Surgeon Wiseman said she cannot have visitors until at least next Sunday. You had better not question her before then, lest it makes her more ill.'

'Her husband might be a better source of information, anyway,' said Chaloner. 'He witnessed the attack, after all. Do you know where in Turnstile they live?'

'In one of those small alleys that run between Holborn and Lincoln's Inn Fields. I do not know which one precisely, but you will find it.'

Chaloner was touched by her confidence. 'I understand

Scarlet and Jane moved there because their home on the Bridge is being renovated.'

Hannah nodded. 'The Dowager wanted Chapel House repaired, despite the fact that there is nothing wrong with it. She has taken quite an interest in the place, although no one is sure why.'

'Do you think Jane's rape and the renovation are connected?' Chaloner could not see how, but it had to be more than coincidence that Chapel House was the focus of so many puzzling incidents.

Hannah shrugged. 'I do not know. But *you* will find out if they are, and I feel much happier now I know you are looking into the matter. Safer, too.'

Chaloner kissed her, then slipped away into the night.

Bells were ringing when Chaloner awoke the next day, summoning people to their Sunday devotions. He yawned as he rose, aware of a slight stiffness in his lame leg – he had spent too much of the previous night prowling the damp, narrow lanes known as Turnstile, watching the Scarlet house and asking questions of late-night revellers as they returned to their homes.

Unfortunately, he had learned nothing to help him solve the crime. He had been too tired for such activities really, but the notion that Jane had been attacked because of her husband's connection to the Bridge had lent a sense of urgency to the matter, and Chaloner had not returned to his rooms in Fetter Lane until well after two o'clock.

It had not taken him long to identify the Scarlet residence, because it had a new lock on the door. He had picked it with ease, and padded upstairs. A lamp was lit in one bedroom, and he had heard the Junior Warden talking to his wife within. The door to the other was firmly closed, and when Chaloner stepped inside, there was blood on the sheets and muddy footprints where a succession of people had tramped – not just the rapists, but the officials who had come to investigate afterwards.

His first task should have been to interview Scarlet, but he had heard Jane's bitter weeping, and had felt her husband should not be dragged away from the business of comforting her. Instead, he had lit a candle and conducted a methodical search of the room where the atrocity had occurred.

He had uncovered two interesting facts. First, a crucifix nailed to the wall indicated the Scarlets were Catholic. And second, a strongbox under the bed contained legal documents, jewellery and, right at the very bottom, a small piece of paper covered in tiny writing. It was in cipher, and appeared to be identical to the note he had found in Blue Dick Culmer's clothing.

He pondered the messages as he dressed the following morning. What could an iconoclast and a Warden of the Bridge have in common? It would not be religion, because they were at opposite ends of a spectrum – Blue Dick had destroyed the 'papist images' the Scarlets would revere.

Chaloner put the two papers on the table in the window, and studied them while he ate a breakfast of bread and salted fish. His cat, drawn by the smell, began to wind around his legs. He fed it, but it took only a mouthful before losing interest. He was not very good at providing it with regular meals, but it was sturdy and sleek, suggesting it was perfectly capable of fending for itself – the building's ongoing battle with gravity meant the gap between the window and the wall was now so large that it could leave to hunt whenever it pleased.

As the sun rose, touching the rooftops with its wintry rays, the house began to make noises. Chaloner jumped when there was an especially loud creak, and found himself reaching for his sword. He glanced up, sure there were more cracks in the ceiling than there had been before he had gone to Wimbledon. There was more dust on the floor, too, and he wondered how long it would be before the place tumbled about his ears. As a precaution, he had taken his best viol and some clothes to Hannah's house, and there was not much else he possessed of any value.

He glanced at his second-best viol, tempted to spare a few moments for music, but the day was wearing on, and he was apt to lose himself once he started playing. And he could not afford to squander time if he was to find out who killed Blue Dick, learn Herring's plans, discover what the Dowager had in mind for Shrove Tuesday, and look into the assault on Jane Scarlet.

He turned his attention back to the two pieces of paper, then fetched pen and ink. Years ago, Thurloe had taught him the order of frequency in which letters appeared in the English language, and the list was indelibly imprinted on his mind. The most common was E, so he went through both messages, and discovered the letter most often used in them was R. Then he repeated the process for T, and so on. Unfortunately, what emerged was gibberish. Not a simple code, then, he thought, and decided to take them to Thurloe, who had a lot more experience in such matters.

When the bell in St Dunstan-in-the-West stopped chiming, Chaloner knew it was time to leave. The religious laws established by the Clarendon Code had resulted in a register being taken on Sundays, and any parishioner who absented himself was presumed to be Catholic or nonconformist. To Chaloner, who liked to keep a low profile and went to some trouble to stay off such lists, it was a nuisance. To others, it was an outrage – the state imposing its own brand of religion on citizens.

As he walked down the stairs, he wondered whether the Clarendon Code's unpopularity would force the bishops to repeal some of its edicts. Perhaps naïvely, he was hoping the matter would be aired when the prelates came to the Earl's dinner, and the moderate ones would persuade the extremists that they were doing the Church no favours with their uncompromising decrees.

When he reached St Dunstan's, he sat at the back and used the time to work on the cipher, although with no success. Fortunately, Rector Thompson had lost the notes for his sermon, and the homily he mumbled without them was mercifully brief. Afterwards, Chaloner made sure his name was in the roster, explained that a sojourn to Wimbledon had caused him to miss the last five Sundays, and left with some relief.

Thurloe was about to attend his own devotions in Lincoln's Inn's chapel when Chaloner arrived. The ex-Spymaster had the look of a man who had slept badly. He was taking some small blue pills, and Chaloner wondered whether it was his penchant for dubious medicine or his involvement with rebels that was adversely affecting his health.

'I wish you would go back to Oxfordshire,' he said, regarding his friend with fresh concern.

Thurloe grimaced. 'I cannot, not yet. And please do not besiege me with questions again, because I do not want you involved in my affairs.'

'But I am already involved. I am charged with solving Blue Dick's murder, and I am sure his presence in London had something to do with your "displeased majority". I am also ordered to learn what Herring plans to do, and I imagine rumours of rebellion have drawn him into the open, too.'

'Nonsense,' said Thurloe. 'That is pure conjecture on your part – you have not a shred of evidence to make such assertions. Besides, as I told you yesterday, you would be wise to stay away from this particular enquiry. Tell Clarendon you have taken both matters as far as you can, and offer to concentrate on ensuring his Bishops' Dinner goes according to plan instead.'

'He will dismiss me if I say I am giving up on a case after a day. Besides, your warning is suspicious in itself: it makes me even more certain that there is something I should know about.'

Thurloe sighed. 'Well, I cannot confide in you, and that is that. However, if you must insist on meddling, then I strongly recommend you be on your guard.'

'I am always on my guard,' said Chaloner shortly, exasperated and annoyed with him.

Unexpectedly, Thurloe smiled. 'Yes, just as I have trained you to be, although *I* find constant vigilance wearing. I think I may retire permanently to Oxfordshire when this current affair is over.'

Chaloner did not know whether to be relieved or sorry. On the one hand, he would be happier with Thurloe away from London's simmering intrigues; on the other, he would miss him badly.

'Did you search Phillippes's and Kaltoff's homes yesterday?' asked Thurloe, when Chaloner made no reply. 'If so, I assume you found nothing to link them with

Blue Dick, because you would have mentioned it by now. I told you they were not the right culprits.'

'I found this,' said Chaloner defensively, handing him the caricature he had found in Kaltoff's room. 'It is Blue Dick.'

Thurloe studied it carefully. 'It *might* be Blue Dick. However, it also looks like several other iconoclasts I could name.' He handed the sketch back. 'It it is interesting, but proves nothing one way or the other. If this is all you found, you wasted your time.'

'Then what do you suggest?' demanded Chaloner, becoming disheartened.

'Not a direct confrontation with them, that is for sure,' said Thurloe. 'From what I know of their characters, neither is the kind of man to throw up his hands and confess. I am not sure what to advise, except one thing: do not be too convinced they are your culprits, because it will blind you to alternatives. Perhaps you should ignore them for a while, and investigate other avenues.'

'What other avenues?' asked Chaloner disconsolately. 'Phillippes and Kaltoff are all I have.'

'Yes, but that does not make them guilty,' Thurloe pointed out. 'Incidentally, I have reflected on the conversation you overheard in the Beggar's Bush – that Phillippes reminded Kaltoff what was at stake, and what they stood to lose should they be discovered. Perhaps he was just alluding to the fact that their tide-ring is not all they claim. In other words, maybe they are just cheats.'

'It is possible,' acknowledged Chaloner reluctantly. 'They do seem to be charging a vast amount for the one they are making for the Earl. But what about the fact that they live on the Bridge?'

'They live on the Bridge because they monitor the

135

tides,' said Thurloe with a shrug. 'It is an integral part of their profession, regardless of whether or not they are good at it.'

Chaloner supposed he might be right, although there was something about the pair that made him determined to keep them in his sights until he was sure they were harmless. He watched Thurloe remove a small phial from his pocket and sip from it. Even from a distance, it smelled rank.

'Where did you go yesterday?' he asked curiously. 'You left in a carriage when you said you would be warming your icy feet by the fire.'

Thurloe stared at him, and the expression was not a genial one. 'You were watching me? Please do not do it again, Thomas. It is not seemly between friends.'

'Neither is lying. You claimed you were cold, but it was an excuse to be elsewhere.'

Thurloe closed his eyes. 'This matter will drive a wedge between us if we let it, so I recommend we discuss something else before things are said that will later be regretted. We shall talk about Blue Dick's murder instead. Have you learned anything new?'

Acknowledging that perhaps he had overstepped the mark when he had spied on his old mentor, Chaloner passed Thurloe the ciphers he had recovered. 'Can you decode these? One came from Blue Dick, and the other was in the house of Anthony and Jane Scarlet.'

Thurloe frowned as he looked at the tiny pieces of paper. 'But they are virtually identical! What can a murdered iconoclast and the wife of a respectable official have in common?'

'Well, there is the Bridge – Scarlet is one of its wardens, and Blue Dick died on it. And there is the fact that both are victims of violent crimes. But perhaps these papers will give us the answer. Will you decipher them yourself, or ask one of your old cryptographers to do it?'

'I shall see to it myself. I am trying to reduce contact with old acquaintances at the moment – the fewer people who are associated with me, the better. And that includes you.'

The chapel bell began to chime at that point, and Thurloe excused himself. Chaloner watched him go, and experienced a wave of exasperation. Why was Thurloe declining to confide, and how could he stop him from walking headlong into disaster? With a sigh, Chaloner turned to leave.

He had not taken many steps before a familiar figure materialised in front of him. William Prynne was one of London's least attractive characters, a venomous Puritan pamphleteer who railed against everything, from politics and religion, to playhouses, dancing and maypoles. His views on Quakers, Jews and Baptists were deeply repugnant, and Chaloner usually walked the other way when he saw him coming. Unfortunately, his preoccupation with Thurloe meant he had not noticed Prynne until it was too late, and now an encounter was unavoidable.

'Any news from Court?' Prynne asked casually, as their paths crossed.

From anyone else, this might have been an attempt at polite conversation, but Chaloner knew Prynne was fishing for gossip to use in one of his nasty tirades. As usual, Prynne wore a frayed black cloak and a quilted cap that served to hide the fact that his ears were missing – they had been lopped off in retribution for some acerbic tract he had composed in the past. He had been branded on the cheek, too, and imprisoned and fined heavily, but none of these punishments had succeeded in stemming the stream of vitriol that gushed unrepentantly from his pen.

'No,' said Chaloner shortly, making to step around him.

'There probably is, but you do not want to share it with me.' Prynne sighed ruefully. 'So you can answer another question instead. Is it true that Blue Dick Culmer has been murdered?'

Chaloner saw no reason not to confirm the tale. It was hardly a secret. 'Yes, on Friday.'

'Then I have something to tell *you*. You are the Earl of Clarendon's man, and I like him. He is not one of those perverse, wretched sinners who gives himself to lewd, ungodly and heathenish—'

'What did you want to say to me?' interrupted Chaloner, before the man could get started on his opinions regarding the Court.

The rabid old lawyer shot him a resentful look. 'You youngsters are all the same – all hurry and no patience. But let me ask you a question before I begin. The rumour I heard was that Blue Dick was killed on the Bridge by a man who then dashed into St Mary Overie. Is this correct?'

Chaloner nodded cautiously. 'Why do you want to know?'

'Because Sir John Winter is a resident on that Bridge. He lives in Nonesuch House, and is a devious popeling, whose pedigree originates with the Devil himself, to whose honour and service all papists are devoted—'

'I know where Winter lives,' said Chaloner tersely. Thurloe had already mentioned it, along with the fact that the moustachioed gunpowder expert had been visited by Phillippes.

Prynne looked triumphant. 'But did you know that Winter was friends with Blue Dick?'

Chaloner did not believe him. A respectable Catholic merchant was highly unlikely to develop a relationship with a Puritan iconoclast.

'It is true,' insisted Prynne, seeing the scepticism in Chaloner's face. 'And how do I know? Because they had a common acquaintance in Will Goff.'

'Will Goff the regicide, who escaped to New England when the Commonwealth fell?' asked Chaloner dubiously. Now he was sure Prynne was mistaken, because that was even less likely than Winter befriending Blue Dick. 'And whose brother Stephen is chaplain to the Dowager?'

'The very same,' averred Prynne, beady eyes gleaming. 'Will Goff fled to Connecticut, where he lives in a cave to avoid the Royalist agents sent to murder him. He is a Puritan, but a fanatical one – the kind that gives the rest of us a bad name.'

Chaloner smothered a smirk, thinking that even a regicide would have a long way to go before reaching the dizzying standards of zeal set by the poisonous Prynne.

'Will Goff applauded the iconoclasts, and even funded some of their work,' Prynne went on. 'He loved Blue Dick. And he was a friend of your family. Your uncle knew him well.'

'My dead uncle,' Chaloner reminded him, wishing, not for the first time, that his kinsman had not played such a prominent role in murdering a king. He tried to make sense of what Prynne was saying. 'I understand how shared religious convictions link Will Goff to Blue Dick, but what about Winter? Few Catholics approve of statue smashing, so how did Goff come into contact with *him*?'

'A shared passion for *music*.' Prynne put sinister emphasis on the last word, and Chaloner recalled that music was one of the many things the lawyer considered sinful and unnecessary. 'Will Goff and Winter have unusually fine voices, and belonged to an elite choir that performed in St Mary Overie. Will Goff invited Blue Dick to join, too. He was a tenor.'

'I know Goff liked music,' said Chaloner, recalling the summer he had been obliged to remain indoors to accommodate the man's insatiable demand for a viol. 'But I cannot see him – or Blue Dick, for that matter – singing with Winter, whose political and religious convictions diverge so fundamentally from his own. They would argue, and all pleasure from the exercise would be lost.'

'Sinful men cleave to worldly pleasures,' began Prynne. 'And the Devil clamours at them to abandon their convictions in order to taste these vile depravities. The common nurseries of villainy and wickedness, where sinners are seduced by the pomps and vanities of carnal desire to—'

Chaloner stopped him with a raised hand. 'I really have no idea what you are talking about.'

Prynne grimaced his annoyance, but returned to less flowery language. 'Music is a great leveller. You play your viol with some of the greatest rakes in the country, but you overlook their failings in exchange for good entertainment. Will Goff, Blue Dick and Winter did the same.'

'I see.' Chaloner was not sure whether he believed it.

'Winter will make music with anyone, even those scoundrels Scarlet and Hussey.'

'Why do you call them scoundrels?'

'Because they tax any book sold on the Bridge, and I object. Why should I contribute to the upkeep of that preposterous and misguided structure? It is a festering sore, abominable in the eyes of God. And anyone who says otherwise is a heathen!'

Chaloner could not imagine why the Bridge should have excited the old Puritan's animosity, but was unwilling to ask for an explanation that would probably be incomprehensible anyway.

'Thank you,' was all he said. 'I will tell the Earl you helped him.'

Prynne grinned. 'That is very civil of you. And there is something else I should mention, too, although knowing your affection for that Cromwell-loving Thurloe, I do not think you will like it. But honour and duty force me to speak out.'

'What?' asked Chaloner coldly, wondering if the man was about to spin a yarn to see Thurloe in trouble. Thurloe had always treated Prynne with compassion and respect, but Prynne was far too steeped in his own bigotry to reciprocate in kind.

'I happened to spot Blue Dick in a Southwark tavern a few days ago. He was in company with that fanatical Herring and several other iconoclasts, and I did not like the notion of such a gathering, so I followed Herring when he came out.'

'And?' prompted Chaloner, when Prynne paused for dramatic effect. The expression on the old man's face could only be described as malevolent.

'And he went to Rider's Coffee House in Chancery Lane, where he met Thurloe.'

'I do not believe you,' said Chaloner, although his stomach churned, and he suspected the tale was true, because even Prynne would not fabricate such a tale and repeat it to Thurloe's friends.

'They did not talk long,' Prynne went on smugly. 'Then Herring left. It may have been an innocent encounter – both worked for the Commonwealth, after all, and may have been friends. Or it may have been sinister. That is for you to decide.'

If Prynne had been a younger man, Chaloner would have grabbed him by the throat and threatened him with all manner of reprisals if he told anyone else what he claimed to have seen. Prynne seemed to sense his thoughts, because he took a step away and wagged his finger.

'Do not worry, I will not blab to anyone else. Thurloe may be a reprobate, but he is a fellow member of Lincoln's Inn, so I owe him the benefit of the doubt. But my eyes and ears will be open, and I will not stand by while treason is done. You can tell him that.'

'Thurloe is no traitor,' declared Chaloner vehemently.

'I am glad to hear it.' Prynne grinned again. 'But it seems a visit to the Bridge is in order for you. Do it tomorrow, though. It will be more crowded then than on a Sunday, which will give you more cover. But be careful. I would not like the Earl of Clarendon to lose a faithful servant.'

Chaloner had every intention of being careful.

The rest of the day was spent trying to learn more about the choir in which an iconoclast, a regicide and a Royalist gunpowder expert had sung. Chaloner managed to track down several other members of the ensemble, but they all said the consort had broken up when Will Goff had fled for his life at the Restoration, and had not met since. He was surprised to learn that Prynne had been right:

all three *had* set aside their religious and political convictions for music, and although they had not been friends, there was no hint of any unpleasantness between them.

Eventually, he walked across the Bridge to St Mary Overie, intending to talk to its vicar. When he arrived, he found the cleric in a state of high agitation, because three prelates had descended unannounced on his Sunday service. The bishops of Hereford, Salisbury and Rochester were in London for the Earl's dinner, and were apparently amusing themselves by picking random churches and sitting in the front row together in full ecclesiastical regalia.

'Rochester took notes all through my sermon,' the vicar wailed. He was a plump, red-faced fellow by the name of John Feake. 'Salisbury fell asleep, and Hereford kept shaking his head.'

Chaloner struggled to keep a straight face. 'Would you have given a different homily, had you known they were coming?'

'Well, I certainly would not have tackled the Book of Revelation, which I have never really understood anyway. Damn Clarendon and his Bishops' Dinner!'

'Are many prelates coming to this repast, then?' The Earl had talked about little else since Chaloner had arrived back from Wimbledon, but, bored with it, Chaloner had stopped listening.

'All of them, except Gloucester and Oxford – and I am told they are desperately trying to worm their way out of previous engagements, so as not to miss it.'

'Why are they so keen?' asked Chaloner, puzzled. 'It is only a meal.'

'The Bishop of London told me last year that it was the best event he had ever attended. And Clarendon promised it will be even better this year. I assure you, it is far more than just a meal.'

It was all very interesting, but not relevant to the choir that had contained Blue Dick, Winter and Will Goff. Unfortunately, Feake could tell Chaloner nothing about the ensemble that had practised in his church, other than that it had been good enough to perform at several state occasions, and that there was never trouble between its members. They left politics and religion at the door, he said, and although the three men had not been close, they had treated each other with courtesy and respect.

'So this choir really has been disbanded,' concluded Chaloner.

'Yes, when Will Goff fled to New England, to avoid being executed for king-killing.'

'Then what do you know about the armed men who use your church for covert meetings?'

Feake regarded Chaloner askance. 'I have no idea what you are talking about.'

'Oh, I think you do. They seemed quite at home when I encountered them here, and I am told they gather on a regular basis. They are unlikely to do that without your consent.'

Feake was indignant and angry. 'How dare you make such accusations! I know nothing about any masked men. And you must leave now, because I am about to lock up.' He rattled his keys.

'I never said they were masked,' pounced Chaloner. 'I said they were armed.'

Feake became flustered. 'Armed, masked, it is all the same. I cannot help you.'

'The Earl of Clarendon does not take kindly to men who hinder his investigations.'

144

Feake regarded him in horror. 'Clarendon sent you? But I do not *know* anything! They keep their faces covered, and I have no idea who they are. Then on Friday evening, just after Blue Dick died, their leader gave me a bag of coins for the poor, and said I would not be seeing them again.'

'Damn!' murmured Chaloner. 'So they paid you to be here?'

'They provided funds for the poor,' corrected Feake stiffly. 'I saw no harm in letting them use the place. They were always respectful, which is more than can be said for some of our visitors.'

'You must have some idea of their—'

'Well, I do not,' snapped Feake. 'You may think me incurious, but it is safer that way in these uncertain times. The poor were grateful for the money, and that is all I care about. I do not know their names. I do not know what they discussed. I do not even know how many of them there were, because I cannot be certain it was the same men who came each time.'

'Then what reason did they give for wanting to be here?' pressed Chaloner. 'Surely, a tavern would have served them better?'

'They met mostly at night,' said Feake, elbowing him out of the door and jabbing one of his keys in the lock. 'Southwark taverns tend to be crowded then, and there is always a danger that Spymaster Williamson's men might be watching. My church is usually empty after dark, and it is safe, quiet and has back doors for easy escapes.'

Chaloner raised his eyebrows. 'All that suggests you think their business was not legal.'

Feake began to walk away, calling over his shoulder. 'I was not paid enough to think.'

* * *

Chaloner left Southwark feeling as though he had wasted a whole day. It was already dark, and a persistent drizzle made the wheels of carts swish as they drove along the streets. He trudged back across the Bridge, and paused outside Chapel House, wondering whether it might be a good time to explore it. But the door opened and Hussey stepped out. He was with Scarlet and several workmen, and they were talking about tasks to be completed the following day. Scarlet looked as though he did not care, but Hussey was arguing furiously. The debate looked set to continue for some time, and Chaloner did not feel like waiting in the wet, so he turned towards home.

He arrived to find rain coming through the roof. He set bowls to catch the drips, covered his second-best viol with the tarpaulin he kept for such a purpose, and set out for the greater comfort of Hannah's house. He took a hackney carriage, and when he alighted, the first thing he saw was an enormous pile of rubbish that had been put outside her door for the laystall men to collect. It included four wine kegs, and he could only assume that an excellent time had been had by all.

He knocked, to let her know he was coming, then made his way inside. He was a little surprised to find two men asleep on the floor, and even more startled by the chaos – goblets and crockery strewn all about, not all of it in one piece, and discarded food everywhere. There was even, he noted with distaste, some adhering to the ceiling. He found Hannah in the kitchen.

'You should move house,' he recommended. 'It will be easier than cleaning this one.'

Hannah laughed. 'The Duke said it was one of the best soirees he has ever attended.'

'Was that before or after he started breaking pots and lobbing syllabub?'

'After, I think. He is always a man for fun, bless him. It is a pity you did not arrive ten minutes earlier, because you would have met him. He has only just left.'

Chaloner regarded her warily. 'You mean he has been here since yesterday – he stayed last night and all of today?'

'Everyone did. I slipped out to attend mass this morning, but when I came back the party was still in full swing.' Hannah smiled fondly. 'The Duke knows how to have a good time.'

'Christ!' Chaloner wondered whether the man took some sort of medicine to keep him going. He also wondered about Hannah, unsettled that he had not appreciated her to be the kind of woman who was willing and able to host a soiree of such uncommon length. It underlined to him yet again that they did not know each other very well. But then he looked at her humorous blue eyes, and the way her mouth had quirked upwards into a smile, and found his doubts evaporating. Did it really matter that they were so different, as long as she induced in him a warm feeling of contentment and an accompanying desire to cherish her?

Hannah cocked her head as bells began to chime. 'Is it really that late? I had better go. I promised to accompany Her Majesty to church again tonight, because her own chaplain is unwell and the Dowager is lending hers. The Queen is shy with strangers, and wants me to be there.'

'The Dowager's chaplain?' asked Chaloner, dragging his thoughts away from romance and its attendant complications. 'You mean Stephen Goff?'

'You know him?'

Chaloner shook his head, but Father Stephen was on his list of people to interview. He wanted to ask whether the priest had heard anything more about Herring's plans, and about his brother's musical relationship with Winter and Blue Dick.

'I will come with you,' he offered. 'The streets had an unsafe feel to them tonight.'

She smiled as she grabbed her winter coat. 'Thank you, Tom. That is very thoughtful.'

Chaloner experienced a twinge of guilt. It was hardly fair to use Hannah to gain access to witnesses. But then he recalled his wasted day, and reminded himself that he needed answers if he was to solve his mysteries. He winced when she began to extol his gallantry further.

'Temperance and Wiseman want to meet you,' he said, hastily changing the subject. Of course, it was not one that was any more comfortable for him – an evening with three such disparate personalities promised to be taxing, to say the least.

To his surprise, Hannah seemed pleased. 'I like Wiseman. He is kind and gentle.'

Chaloner would not have used words like 'kind' or 'gentle' to describe the surgeon, when 'arrogant' and 'prickly' sprung more readily to mind. It reminded him that Hannah was capable of forming her own opinions, and rarely let the views of others influence her. It was something he admired, although he had a bad feeling it would lead to arguments between them in the future.

'I am sure I shall like Temperance, too,' Hannah went on, as they stepped over the recumbent forms of the last two revellers, and began to walk towards White Hall. 'But you cannot entertain them in your rooms, Tom – I fed your cat when you were in Wimbledon, and plaster kept dropping off the ceiling. It would be a pity if one of us was brained as we dined.'

'It is not that bad,' objected Chaloner. 'And I can—'

'So they must come to me instead. I shall arrange for something to be cooked in the palace kitchens. Unless you think they might like a pickled ling pie? It is my speciality, as you know.'

Chaloner was all too familiar with that particular creation, but doubted whether Temperance, who was used to fine food, would be impressed, while Wiseman might well deem it a health hazard. Hannah continued to make plans, and he supposed her long hours in the company of Buckingham and his cronies had dulled the shock of Jane Scarlet's assault, because she seemed her usual self again. But when they reached White Hall, she stopped and took his arm.

'I have been thinking. Perhaps you should *not* look into what happened to Jane. It occurs to me that it might be dangerous, and I do not want you hurt on my account.'

'I can look after myself.'

She touched his cheek. 'I know, but it is not worth the risk. Not to me. Perhaps I was wrong to distrust Spymaster Williamson. As you said last night, it *is* his duty to catch the culprits.'

'Did Buckingham tell you that?' he asked, not sure what to make of her change of heart.

She looked vaguely offended. 'No, he did not – although he did say that whoever carried out the attack must be exceptionally ruthless. And he said he was grateful *he* was not obliged to investigate, which made

149

me realise I was wrong to have asked you. I would like you to forget the matter.'

Chaloner followed Hannah across White Hall's Great Court, and then up the wide marble staircase to the Queen's private apartments. These comprised a suite of rooms that overlooked the river, and were pleasant in summer. During the winter, they were damp and miserable.

One of the smaller chambers had been converted into a chapel, to allow Queen Katherine to practise her faith in private. She spent a lot of time in it, mostly praying for a son – it had been two years since she had married, and although Lady Castlemaine had produced a pair of royal brats in that time, the Queen remained childless. There were rumours that she was barren, or was part of a Catholic plot to deprive England of a legitimate heir. Her bewildered loneliness tore at Chaloner's heart every time he saw her.

The mass had already started when he and Hannah slipped in at the back. Father Stephen had a good voice, and performed the rites with a deft confidence that was quite unlike the nervous, fumbling fellow Chaloner had seen at Somerset House and Temperance's brothel.

When the service was over, Hannah went to join the other ladies-in-waiting, who were talking about Jane Scarlet. Chaloner overheard one say that Wiseman had announced an improvement, but Jane was still allowed no visitors, lest overexertion should disturb her humours.

Meanwhile, her devotions completed, the Queen stood to leave. Unfortunately, her ladies were more interested in their discussion than their obligations, and did not notice. Hannah was usually dutiful in that respect, but her back was to the door. Then Katherine saw Chaloner, and her forlorn, haunted face broke into a smile. It transformed her, and Chaloner looked around uneasily, afraid someone else would see the expression and assume something inappropriate was going on.

'Thomas Chaloner,' she said, beckoning him forward. 'Where is your Earl these days? He used to visit me regularly, but I have barely seen him in weeks.'

She spoke Portuguese, a language Chaloner knew from his duties overseas, and he suspected her pleasure at seeing him was largely because he represented a respite from her struggles with English.

'He is busy organising his Bishops' Dinner, ma'am,' he explained. 'He thinks of little else.'

'He thinks about these horrible religious laws – the Clarendon Code,' said the Queen unhappily. 'I wish he would distance himself from them and refuse the villains who devise them permission to use his name. Not only do they suppress my fellow Catholics, but they are causing division among Anglicans – between those who think they are too harsh, and those who think they are not harsh enough. The whole business will end in tears, I fear, and he will be blamed.'

Chaloner was acutely uncomfortable with the discussion. While he liked the Queen, it was not a good idea to criticise government policy with her. Not for either of them.

The Queen saw his unease, and tactfully changed the subject. She nodded towards her ladies. 'They are chatting about Jane Scarlet, although they speak too fast for me to understand. Is she ill?'

'She was attacked by men who broke into her house.' Chaloner was unsure how much detail to provide; the

Queen was easily distressed, and Hannah would be furious if he said anything to give her nightmares. 'Her husband was unable to fend them off.'

The Queen's hands flew to her mouth. 'Oh, how terrible! I did not know her well, but I met her at Somerset House on several occasions. She was with her husband, the Junior Warden.'

'You visit Somerset House?' Chaloner could not imagine why, because it was likely to be full of people who would not be very nice to her, such as Buckingham and Lady Castlemaine.

'The Dowager invites me there. I sit in a corner, ignored, while her cronies chat to each other. They think I cannot understand them, but I do. I know Lord Bristol is not in France, for example.'

'He is in London?' Katherine's English was improving slowly, so Chaloner supposed she might have caught something the Dowager's friends would rather have kept secret. Then he realised he was interrogating her like one of his suspects. Fortunately, she did not seem to notice.

'I am not sure whether he is actually in *London*, because they gabbled that part. However, I think they said that when he appears, they will mark his return by holding a celebration on the Bridge.'

'What sort of celebration?' asked Chaloner, surmising it would be at Nonesuch House. Winter, like Bristol, was Catholic, and the pair might well be friends.

'A religious one, something to do with St Thomas Becket. They mentioned his bones.'

'His bones?' asked Chaloner sceptically. Perhaps her English was not as good as she thought.

She nodded fervently. 'Holy relics.'

Chaloner frowned. Becket's remains had been destroyed during the Reformation. Of course, the Bridge's old oratory – demolished and rebuilt as Chapel House – had been dedicated to the saint, so he supposed that lay at the root of the Queen's misunderstanding.

'Sir John Winter is going to make some fireworks for the occasion,' she went on when he made no reply. 'He is something of an expert on them, apparently.'

'You should be careful, ma'am,' warned Chaloner. While he doubted the Somerset House folk had let her overhear anything overtly seditious, it was unwise for a Catholic queen to be party to discussions involving things that exploded. 'You might learn something you wish you had not – something that may be dangerous for you. Perhaps you should decline these invitations in future.'

'But they are the only ones I ever receive!' cried Katherine. 'A barren queen is not someone people rush to befriend, you know.'

Chaloner winced. 'Can you not ask the Dowager to visit you instead?'

Katherine looked as if she might cry. 'Yes, but then I will never leave White Hall!'

Chaloner did not know what to say, and his heart bled for her as she walked away. Her ladies were still chatting, but broke off when he announced in a ringing voice that the Queen was leaving. Hannah ran to catch up with her mistress, but the others followed at their own pace.

Chaloner lingered in the chapel when the royal entourage had gone, waiting for Father Stephen to emerge from the vestry. He wondered whether he should have kept his advice to himself, but on reflection, he knew he had done the right thing. Katherine was an innocent where Court politics were concerned, and was in an acutely vulnerable position. It was not safe for her to go around reporting half-understood conversations about explosives.

It was not long before Father Stephen appeared. He was flanked by the Dowager's henchmen, Doucett and Martin, and when Chaloner stepped forward to speak, Doucett shoved him away.

'Piss off,' he said in his highly accented English. He rounded on Stephen when the priest started to object. 'We promised to take you back to the Dowager as soon as the Queen's mass was over. There is no time for chatting with . . .' He flicked a dismissive hand at Chaloner.

Fortunately, there was no recognition in his pugilistic features, and Chaloner supposed it had been too dark for the pair to know he was the intruder they had chased two nights before.

'I need to speak to Father Stephen,' he said. 'On a personal matter. It will not take long.'

'I told you to piss off,' snarled Doucett shoving him again, harder this time. Martin began to draw his sword. 'Or do you *want* to die?'

With a sigh of resignation, because he had no desire to resort to violence, Chaloner leapt forward and slammed Doucett's head into Martin's before either realised what he was going to do. Both dropped to the floor, stunned. Father Stephen gaped at him.

'Are you here to murder me?' The priest looked terrified, but made no effort to run. 'Because I am Catholic and in the service of an unpopular woman? I suppose I should not be surprised. People hate me – they are always yelling abuse and throwing things at me in the streets.'

'I just want to talk.' Chaloner raised his hands to show he meant no harm. 'A friend sent me.'

Stephen did not look reassured. 'What did you want to talk about?' he asked shakily. 'But before you start, I swear I have already passed on all there is to know about the gunpowder.'

'What gunpowder?' asked Chaloner. Perhaps the Queen had not misheard after all.

Stephen became flustered. 'The gunpowder I have already discussed with Spymaster Williamson. You *are* one of his men?' His hands flew to his mouth. 'You are not! Oh, Lord!'

'I am in the Lord Chancellor's retinue. My name is Thomas Chaloner.'

Stephen gaped at him, then closed his eyes and crossed himself in relief. 'Chaloner? Thank God! The Earl told me about you and your fighting skills. I should have known it was you by the way you dealt with Doucett and Martin.'

Chaloner was not amused. How could he operate as an intelligencer, if the Earl discussed him with strangers? 'You mentioned gunpowder,' he prompted, a little curtly.

'I mentioned there is no more to learn about it. You see, the Earl found out that Winter had acquired some from the Master of Ordnance, but it is just for fireworks. The Dowager is holding a ball on Shrove Tuesday, and these fireworks will form part of her celebrations.'

'I heard they were going to be ignited on the Bridge.'

Stephen regarded him askance. 'I sincerely doubt it! Its houses are made of wood, and they would catch fire. Besides, the wardens would never agree to it, and rightly so.'

'You told the Earl about the iconoclasts gathering, too,'

said Chaloner, turning to another matter. Doucett and Martin were stirring, and he wanted to be gone before they regained their senses.

Father Stephen lowered his voice and began to speak quickly, pulling Chaloner away from the groaning bodyguards. 'I spotted Blue Dick Culmer, Herring and several other one-time church-smashers in Southwark a few days ago. I *had* to inform someone about the matter, because if they intend to make trouble, they must be stopped.'

'Why choose the Earl?'

'Because we have been friends for years, and I trust him. Besides, who else is there? People will say I am trying to make trouble for Anglicans if I report that sort of thing to just anyone.'

'But you are taking an enormous risk, passing intelligence to the Dowager's enemy. Then there is the fact that you are Catholic – the Earl is busily trying to suppress your religion.'

Stephen fixed him with agonised eyes. 'Do you think I do not know all that? I live in constant fear of being caught, and the Clarendon Code is one of the most wicked pieces of legislation ever to be written. But I cannot sit by while my poor country is plunged into yet more civil unrest.'

'Civil unrest that may see Catholics emerge with greater freedom,' Chaloner pointed out.

'No freedom is worth death and violence,' argued Stephen passionately. 'Moreover, I love my Church, and do not want it stained with the loss of a single life. If there is a way to prevent bloodshed, then I shall do my utmost to pursue it.'

It was a noble stance, and one Chaloner applauded, but it was clear that it was costing Stephen dear – his nails were bitten to the quick, and his hands shook even as he stood talking. Chaloner hoped the priest would not snap under the very considerable strain.

'One more question,' said Chaloner urgently, glancing at the Frenchmen. 'Your brother Will—'

'My brother no more,' interrupted Stephen sadly but firmly. 'What Will did was unconscionable, and he brought shame to our family. He fled to New England when he realised his misdeeds were about to catch up with him, and I hope he stays there for ever. I bear him no malice – he had his own twisted reasons for murdering God's anointed – but I am finished with him.'

'Perhaps so, but have you heard whether he is—'

'I have heard nothing about him, and nor will I,' declared Stephen. 'As far as I am concerned, he is dead. Now, we shall say no more on the matter, if you do not mind. The subject is too painful.'

'I am sorry, I—'

'Go,' urged Stephen, when Doucett started to sit up. 'I will tell this pair that you wanted to confide your sins, and they will not press me about it – they are Catholic, and appreciate the sanctity of confession. If I have more information for the Earl, I will find a way to send it. But please do not approach me yourself. It is too dangerous – for both of us.'

Chapter 5

The next day was bright and clear, and London sparkled, as if the rain had washed away some of its grime. Chaloner woke when his cat jumped on his bed, and the creature was lucky not to be skewered when his dagger slipped into his hand before he was properly cognisant.

He stood, stretched, and walked to the window. The dawn sky was tinged pink and orange, and he recalled his friend Will Leybourn once telling him that such hues were caused by light reflecting off dust particles in the atmosphere. Chaloner had not been sure whether to believe him – science under Charles II was being given rather a free rein, and all sorts of eccentric theories were being aired. He heard one shortly thereafter, when he went to the Rainbow Coffee House.

'What news?' called the owner, James Farr, as he entered. It was the traditional coffee-house greeting, but Chaloner was spared from having to reply, because someone was behind him. It was Joseph Thompson, the gentle rector of St Dunstan-in-the-West.

'The men at Gresham College weighed London's air on Saturday,' Thompson announced. He sounded impressed. 'And now they are going to Tenerife, which we all know is the highest point on Earth, where they will repeat the experiment. They expect the two airs to weigh different amounts.'

'Of course they will be different,' declared Farr scornfully. 'London's will be heavier because it is full of soot. What news?'

The last remark was addressed to the next patron through his door, a man Chaloner recognised from previous visits to the Rainbow as a cheerful young printer named Fabian Stedman.

'A pinnacle dropped off St Paul's Cathedral last night,' replied Stedman, wedging himself on the bench between Chaloner and Thompson. 'It caused a horse to bolt, throwing the rider.'

'We already know that,' said Farr, setting three dishes on the table and pouring a dense black sludge into them. Chaloner regarded it without enthusiasm, wondering what it was about the beverage that was so popular. 'The rider was Progers, the King's procurer of whores and one of the Dowager's creatures. But he was unharmed, more is the pity.'

'Now, now,' admonished Thompson sternly. 'That is not a Christian thing to say.'

'Progers is not a Christian,' countered Farr. 'He is Catholic. And rumour has it that the papists are planning something terrible for our city. They resent the sensible laws in the Clarendon Code, you see, and are determined to have their revenge on us.'

'Stop,' ordered Thompson sharply. 'That kind of talk does no one any good.'

'It does *me* good,' countered Farr. 'I am tired of turning a blind eye to the danger they represent. And something

159

bad *is* about to happen, because there have been omens. The old king's ghost was seen outside the Banqueting House last night, weeping for his lost crown. And Phillippes, who invented the tide-ring, says something peculiar is happening to the Thames. It is disturbed.'

'Disturbed?' queried Chaloner warily.

'Troubled, unstable,' elaborated Farr. 'It ebbs when it is supposed to flow, and flows when it is supposed to ebb. In other words, it is warning us that Catholics are planning an attack.'

'Then there is the fact that bits keep dropping off the cathedral,' added Stedman. 'That is an omen, too. Why else would it be falling to pieces, unless it is God showing His displeasure?'

'Because it is old, and nothing has been spent on its upkeep for years?' suggested Chaloner.

Thompson shot him a grateful look. 'Quite. But the Clarendon Code is far too contentious a topic for me this morning, so let us discuss something else instead. What does *The Newes* say today?'

The government provided its people with two news-books each week – *The Newes* on Mondays, and *The Intelligencer* on Thursdays. *The Newes* was hot off the press that morning.

'It says the Swedish ambassador has a chill,' said Stedman, flinging a copy on the table. 'And that the King's House theatre is being measured for new curtains. And very little else.'

But it transpired that Farr had strong opinions about curtains, too, so that even a discussion about draperies turned acrimonious. Chaloner tuned out the bickering, and read the newsbook instead.

As usual, it contained no domestic intelligence, on the

grounds that the government preferred its people not to know what it was up to. There was not much in the way of foreign news, either, although Chaloner read with growing despair an editorial that urged war with the Dutch Republic. He knew diplomats could avert the crisis, because Hollanders had no wish to squander money on needless conflict, but hawks like Buckingham wanted a fight, and their braying, insistent voices were going to prevail over the moderates.

When the conversation turned to his Earl's mansion – and on this, everyone agreed: it was too grand and a wicked waste of taxpayers' money – Chaloner left. He did not want Thompson to recall that *he* worked for the Earl, and demand justification for the project.

Once outside, he walked to Chancery Lane. Thurloe was a man of habit, and just after dawn each day, he strolled in Lincoln's Inn's fine gardens. But he was not there that morning, and his manservant did not know where he had gone or how long he would be.

Chaloner experienced a twinge of unease, and wondered whether Thurloe's atypical behaviour had something to do with Herring. Since Prynne had told him what he had seen in Rider's Coffee House, Chaloner had been telling himself that either the poisonous old pamphleteer was mistaken, or that Thurloe had just forgotten to mention his meeting with the iconoclast. But in his heart he knew both were unlikely. He waited a while, but the ex-Spymaster might be gone for hours, and Chaloner could not afford to waste time when he had so much to do.

He returned to his rooms, where he donned a brown wig, a fashionable long-coat with lace down the front, and shoes with red heels. By the time he was ready, he looked like a courtier, which he hoped would be enough to disguise him from the people with whom he had fought recently – the Dowager's Frenchmen, the masked men in St Mary Overie, and Phillippes and Kaltoff. They would recognise him at close quarters, but he did not intend going near any of them that day.

He headed for the Bridge, intending to spend a few hours watching it and its various inhabitants. But first, he went to Black Friars Stairs, near where the greasy grey smear of the Fleet River emptied into the Thames, and hired a boat. He knew what the Bridge looked like from the road, but he wanted to see it from the river, to gain a different perspective.

He gazed up at it as the little craft bobbed about on the water. It stretched across the Thames in a long ribbon of uneven rooftops and bristling chimneypots. Smoke poured from them, adding their own pall to the fog that hung over the water. The tide was coming in, so the boatman was hauling hard on his oars, fighting the current. The vigorous exercise did not stop him from talking, though, and he was more than happy to answer questions.

'The starling under Chapel House is larger than the others,' said Chaloner. He had never noticed this feature before, although it was an obvious one. 'Do you know why?'

The man nodded, pleased to display his superior knowledge. 'To support the church that once stood on it. It was pulled down years ago, but its cellar is left. A crypt, I suppose you would call it.'

'Are we going through one of the arches now?' asked Chaloner uneasily. The Bridge formed a sizeable barrier to the river's natural flow, and when the tide was in full spate, the water on one side could be more than six feet higher than on the other. It roared between the starlings at a colossal rate, and reports of drownings while people 'shot' the Bridge were distressingly common.

The boatman laughed. 'Not when we are upstream and the tide is coming in. No man in the world could row against that. If we were going in the other direction I might risk it, because old Father Thames is oddly sluggish today, and I believe we could make it.'

'Sluggish?' Chaloner thought about Phillippes's contention that the river was playing odd tricks.

The boatman lowered his voice. 'The river has not been itself these past few weeks. It is an omen – the King is allowing Catholics to gain favour in his Court, and this is God's way of showing us that He does not like it.'

Chaloner suppressed a sigh, but did not argue lest the boatman tried to tip him overboard. He turned his attention back to the Bridge. It towered above them, its great piers dark with weed and slime. He wondered what secrets it held – and whether it would relinquish them to him.

Chaloner asked to be let off at the Old Swan Stairs, then walked up the narrow alley that led to Thames Street, to join the stream of traffic that was moving towards the Bridge. It was unusually busy, and carts and carriages had been forced to a standstill. Pedestrians were able to weave their way forward, but anything on wheels was out of luck.

He wondered whether the Dowager had decided to visit Chapel House again, selfishly deciding that the rest of London could wait. Then he smiled to himself when he saw her carriage was one of those caught in the jam. He eased towards it, although when he spotted Doucett and Martin sitting with the driver, he was careful to keep his face shadowed by his hat.

Her coach was accompanied by three horsemen, all Penderels. He looked for the fourth, but he was not there. Chaloner edged closer. The brothers were trying to keep their voices down, but the Bridge was noisy, and they needed to speak at a reasonable volume to make themselves heard.

'—do not know where Edward might be,' said Rupert, the oldest and biggest.

'But *someone* must know,' said the youngest – Neville. 'A man cannot simply disappear.'

'We will find him,' said scar-knuckled Oliver with grim determination. 'And if I learn our dear brother has been whoring these last two days, I will skin him alive.'

'He has not,' said Rupert firmly. 'Edward knows better than to worry us like this.'

'We should be looking for him,' said Neville unhappily. 'Not jaunting off to Winchester Palace again. Personally, I am getting a bit tired of all this homage to St Thomas Becket.'

'Hush,' said Rupert urgently, nodding towards the Dowager's carriage. 'She will hear you.'

At that point, the coach door opened, and Progers stepped out. The King's pimp jerked his thumb towards the inside of the vehicle, and addressed the Penderel brothers, lowering his voice as he did so. They craned forward to listen, and so did Chaloner.

'She is getting impatient. She wanted these prayers finished by noon, because she has cooks coming to discuss the food for her ball. She aims to poach the Earl of Clarendon's baker.'

Oliver grinned, delighted. 'The old goat will be livid

164

when he finds himself deprived of the best chef in London. He will have to send out to a cookshop for his bishops' bread!'

They began to discuss other ways to spoil the Earl's plans, although Chaloner doubted they would manage to block his chimneys, exchange sugar for salt, or rub lard on his dining room chairs. The Earl's servants were used to thwarting those kinds of tricks. He edged to the other side of the carriage, where a window had been cracked open for air. It was ridiculously easy to eavesdrop on what was being said inside.

'England will not be whole again until she is a *Catholic* country,' came the Dowager's harsh, uncompromising voice. 'And I do not care who needs to die for that to happen.'

'Yes, ma'am.' Chaloner recognised the calm, conciliatory tones of Father Stephen. 'But this is not the place to express such views, because the Bridge is crowded, and who knows—'

'I do not care who hears! I care nothing for the opinions of shopkeepers and ruffians. Indeed, I have asked St Thomas Becket to send a plague, to rid us of every last Anglican among them.'

'My Lady!' Stephen sounded shocked, and so was Chaloner.

'The saint will listen to my petitions,' the Dowager went on, unmoved by her chaplain's horror. 'I feel a kinship to him like no other saint, and I know he will do as I demand.'

'Then I hope he only strikes down *sinful* Anglicans.' When the speaker leaned forward to tweak the curtains for more air, Chaloner recognised Luckin, the purplenosed vicar of Wimbledon. 'The rest of us do not deserve such a fate.'

The carriage was full, because two Capuchin friars were in it, too. They were exchanging uncomfortable glances at the nature of the conversation, but made no attempt to stop it.

'*You* are acceptable to us, Luckin,' acknowledged the Dowager loftily. 'But the rest of Anglican London deserves a pestilence. It is full of grasping Puritans and unscrupulous merchants, who—'

'Here come the wardens, ma'am,' called Rupert, unwittingly interrupting her tirade. Chaloner saw the Capuchins exchange a glance of relief. 'They want to apologise for the inconvenience.'

'A fish-cart overturned,' explained Hussey. Next to him, Scarlet walked like a man in a dream, his face pale and drawn. Chaloner wondered whether Jane had taken a turn for the worse.

'It is unforgivable,' snapped the Dowager. 'Fish-carts will be banned from the Bridge from now on. I order it. And anyone who ignores my edict will be hanged.'

'But the city will grind to a halt without the fish-mongers, ma'am,' said Hussey uneasily.

'And, more to the point, we do not want to antagonise them when we have ordered three loads of sole for your ball next Tuesday,' added Progers reasonably. 'They may send us rotten wares in retaliation. Perhaps it is wiser to let the incident pass.'

The carriage began to move off at last, and Chaloner stared after it unhappily. Could his Earl really survive long-term when he had enemies like the Dowager? If she prayed for plagues to wipe out London, then to what other depths would she sink? He thought about the gunpowder that Sir John Winter had obtained for her fireworks. Could she be trusted to use it innocently?

He decided she could not, and that a visit to Nonesuch House was in order.

Nonesuch House, so named because there was 'nonesuch' like it anywhere else, was indeed an unusual place. It had four turrets topped by green onion domes that had been striped white by seagulls and pigeons, and more glass than Chaloner had ever seen in a single building; he could only imagine it must be very cold to live in, exposed as it was to the full brunt of the wind.

He knocked at the door, and asked to see Winter. A servant conducted him to a large chamber on the first floor that had a stunning view down the river. When he opened a window and peered out, he could see white water foaming between the piers below.

'If you want yet *another* report, you must tell her to wait,' came a voice. Chaloner turned, and saw a look of confusion immediately cross Winter's face. His mammoth moustache quivered in consternation. 'Forgive me. I mistook you for someone else.'

'Who?' asked Chaloner curiously.

Winter waved a dismissive hand. 'How may I help you? Do you want to buy lead or timber?'

Up close, Winter was large, and looked as if he knew how to handle the blade that hung at his waist. It was not an ornamental 'town sword', like those favoured by gentlemen of fashion, but a functional weapon that was ready for action, like Chaloner's own. Chaloner thought he would be a formidable opponent, especially when his knowledge of explosives was taken into account. But his brown eyes were kindly, and the laughter lines around them indicated a sense of humour.

'How about gunpowder?' asked Chaloner.

Winter's eyebrows shot up. 'No one knows more about gunpowder than me, but my interest is strictly civilian these days – I use it for fireworks only. Indeed, I have been asked to make some for the Dowager's Shrove Tuesday ball, and when I first saw you standing there, I thought you were someone from her retinue, demanding yet another update on my progress.'

'Such a commission is a great honour,' said Chaloner, hoping flattery might encourage Winter to talk.

Winter beamed at him. 'Well, yes, it is, and I intend to produce a display so delightful that the King will appoint me Green Man on the spot. No one can create a Purple Fountain like me.'

'Where do you buy the powder you will need?' Chaloner asked curiously.

Winter regarded him askance. 'One does not *buy* powder. One *applies* for it from the Master of Ordnance. It comes from government supplies, you see, and is strictly controlled.'

'You do not manufacture your own?'

Winter looked shocked. 'I do not! Fireworks cannot be made from any old stuff, such as might be shoved in cannons and muskets. It needs to be pure. But why do you want to know? If you are in the market for rebellion, you have come to the wrong place. I have no truck with traitors, or the kind of fanatic who is always itching to blow something up.'

'I do not want anything blown up,' said Chaloner sincerely. The exploding cannon at Naseby had taught him to stay well away from anything that might ignite or combust. 'But I heard you are planning a firework display on the Bridge, and—'

'Then you heard wrong!' cried Winter, clearly appalled

by the notion. 'It would be far too dangerous. One stray spark would see the whole thing ignite, and then where would we be? Besides, the wardens would never allow it. But why did you come, Mr . . . ?'

'Chaloner,' supplied the spy, supposing the Queen had misunderstood what she had heard, which was not surprising given her poor English. 'And I came because we have a mutual acquaintance – I once played my viol to Will Goff's singing.'

He did not mention that he had been ten years old at the time, or that Goff would almost certainly not remember him.

Winter's expression went from suspicion to open pleasure. 'Did you? Then you are a lucky man, because he was the best bass in London. I make no comment on his politics, but his singing . . .'

'Fit for angels,' said Chaloner, hoping the regicide's talents had not been exaggerated.

Winter beamed. 'If you played for him, then you must be good, because he was very particular.'

Chaloner shrugged modestly. 'I practise a lot.'

Winter looked wistful. 'Decent accompaniment is difficult to come by for voices these days, because instrumentalists will insist on showing off their own skills, which detracts from *our* performances. Are you one of those?'

'I would like to think not.'

Winter smiled craftily. 'Perhaps I should be the judge of that. I have a viol upstairs, and I am in the mood for a little entertainment. Come.'

Chaloner was taken back. *He* would not have been so blithely trusting of a stranger who called unannounced and started chatting about gunpowder and past acquaintances who were wanted for high treason. But then he recalled Prynne's words about people being prepared to overlook a great deal for music – and Winter was obviously passionate about his muse.

He followed the man up some stairs to another grand room, this one on the top floor. The view was magnificent, with St Paul's dominating the chaos of smaller buildings around its feet. The cathedral seemed so vast and permanent that it was difficult to believe it was falling to pieces.

'How about a little Dowland?' asked Winter, handing Chaloner a viol that was as fine as any he had played. 'I adore Dowland, but I have not sung him in weeks.'

Chaloner nodded, spent a moment tuning the instrument, then indicated he was ready. Winter began to sing, and his voice transpired to be a pure, sweet countertenor, which was unexpected in so hefty a man. His high notes wrapped around the deeper, richer tones of the viol in a manner that was exquisite, and Chaloner soon realised he was in the presence of a master, a man whose skills far exceeded his own. As often happened with good music, he lost track of time, and when he glanced outside, he was horrified to see it was well into the afternoon. He stood abruptly.

'Must you go?' asked Winter, full of disappointment. 'I have not enjoyed myself so much since Will Goff fled to New England, and our little choir was disbanded.'

'Surely you still meet some of the other members for duets and trios?' asked Chaloner innocently. 'I recall Blue Dick Culmer also possessed a fine voice.'

'Tenor,' agreed Winter sadly. 'But he is dead, I am sorry to say. Murdered, on this very Bridge.'

Chaloner feigned shock. 'Who would do such a thing?'

'No one with a love of music, that is for sure. It was

a terrible waste! I had no idea he was in London, which is a pity, because I would have leapt at the chance to sing with him again.'

'Why did he return, then, if not for music?' asked Chaloner, setting his bow on the table.

'I have no idea. We were not friends, and rarely discussed anything other than singing – with men like him, it was better to avoid politics and religion. What do *you* want?'

The last question was directed at a maid, who came to murmur in his ear. He listened for a moment, then asked Chaloner to excuse him. Chaloner made the most of the opportunity by going to the desk in the window and beginning to rummage. He was somewhat startled when his random prying revealed a note written in cipher – most people tended to be more careful with such things. It was not the same complex code used in the other two messages he had found, and Winter had already deciphered it – he had taken a pen and written the letters underneath. It read:

Meet Goff at the Beare, Brigge Foote, at Noone Monday before Lent. Herring.

Chaloner stared at it. Why would Herring set up a meeting between Winter and Father Stephen when the paths of the two probably crossed in Somerset House, anyway? Or had Winter intercepted the message, and it was actually intended for someone else? If so, then did it mean Winter was a spy, working to learn what the iconoclasts intended to do in London? Or was it not *Stephen* Goff who would be in the Bear tavern, but *Will* Goff, his regicide brother? After all, the tales that said

171

he was living in a cave in New England were only that: rumours. No one could prove them.

Chaloner frowned as he stared at the missive. There were two more interesting points to note, too: the time and the place of the assignation. The time was the day before Shrove Tuesday, when the Dowager intended to hold her ball and the Earl his Bishops' Dinner. And the place was the Bear at the Southwark 'foot' of the Bridge. Why did everything revolve around the Bridge?

'I am afraid business calls, but you must come again,' said Winter, arriving a few moments later to find his guest standing at the window watching a ship arrive at the Customs House. 'Will Goff knew what he was doing when he chose to sing with you, because you are very good. Perhaps you might consider attending a soiree I am holding later this week? Saturday at one o'clock.'

'I do not suppose Mr Phillippes is coming, is he?' asked Chaloner, feeling he should at least *try* to prise something useful from the man with whom he had spent such a large part of the day. The query was somewhat out of the blue, but Winter was obviously busy, so there was no time for a more circuitous approach. And the question needed to be put: Thurloe did not think the association between the two men was significant, but Chaloner wanted to make up his own mind about it.

Winter regarded him askance. 'My guest list is not yet complete. Why do you ask?'

Chaloner shrugged. 'He is your neighbour, and I understand he likes music.'

'Does he?' asked Winter doubtfully, leading the way down the stairs. 'He has never mentioned it to me, and we have conversed several times of late.'

'About what, if not music?' asked Chaloner, rather desperately.

'Other matters,' replied Winter vaguely, although Chaloner did not blame him for being reticent. He was, after all, talking to a stranger.

'With Kaltoff, too?' pressed Chaloner, aware that they had nearly reached the ground floor.

'No. I dislike him. He is a mechanic, in essence, building instruments to the designs Phillippes gives him, yet he has ideas above his station. He thinks his association with Phillippes is sufficient reason for him to be admitted to the Royal Society.'

'And it is not?'

'Of course not! Any monkey can shove a few moving parts together. But will you come on Saturday? I can promise you a memorable afternoon.'

'I will,' said Chaloner, thinking Winter was probably wrong to belittle Kaltoff's skills. His friend Will Leybourn had told him that instrument making was a fine art.

'Good,' said Winter, beaming as he opened the door.

'I wish Will Goff could join us,' said Chaloner. In an effort to prolong the discussion, he became inventive. 'I heard a rumour that he has left New England, and is currently back in London.'

Winter regarded him silently for a moment, then lowered his voice. 'The rumour is true. And New England has not blunted his voice, because it is still as exquisite as ever.'

Chaloner regarded him in astonishment, as surprised by the fact that Winter was willing to confide, as he was by the admission that a famous regicide was in the city. He had not for a moment expected his careless remark to be confirmed.

'You met with him?' he asked in disbelief. He could

not see the Dowager being very pleased to learn that her firework-maker was dallying with one of the men who had killed her husband.

'Just the once. I did the ethical thing, and urged him to leave the country – it would be a crime for that rich bass to be silenced by execution. You understand, given that you have heard him.'

'When was this?'

Winter smoothed down his moustache as he considered his answer. 'Let me think . . . two, perhaps three, weeks ago.'

'Christ!' muttered Chaloner. Did it mean Goff was still in the city? 'Do you know why he came back in the first place?'

'Lord, no!' exclaimed Winter. 'As I said, I never discuss politics or religion with men who are likely to disagree with me. I did not ask, and Goff did not tell. We met by chance in Southwark, and he accepted an invitation to come for music. And that was the sole extent of our encounter.'

Chaloner was bemused by Winter, who seemed far too naïve to be a successful businessman. Or was it unreasonable to assume that anyone who had made a lot of money was by necessity devious? Chaloner had liked him – his friendly brown eyes, his open, bluff manner, and his passion for music – and found he was looking forward to meeting him again. Moreover, he had enjoyed being judged on his skill with the viol, rather than on his friends, family or choice of employer. There was something refreshingly egalitarian about it.

But what about the coded message? Was Winter the intended recipient, or had he intercepted a letter intended for someone else? Chaloner grimaced. If Winter *was* a spy, then he would not be one for very long – he was too willing to trust strangers, not only with information that would have been best kept to himself, but by leaving them unattended in rooms that contained ciphered missives.

Chaloner turned his thoughts from Winter, and considered Will Goff. Clearly, he would have to find out whether the regicide was still in the city, because he represented a significant threat to the government. There was no point in asking his brother: Father Stephen had made it perfectly clear that he wanted nothing to do with his sibling, and had rebuffed Chaloner's attempts to talk about him. Or was it a front, and the priest knew exactly where he was? But Chaloner did not think so – Stephen's rejection had seemed genuine to him.

He decided to ask Thurloe instead, but then he saw that was no good, either. Thurloe and Will Goff had been colleagues during the Commonwealth, and Thurloe was not the kind of man to betray old friends, not even regicides. Moreover, there was also the possibility that Goff had come to London to assist with the simmering rebellion – the one Thurloe considered justified.

His mind teeming with questions, Chaloner began to walk towards Southwark. It was time to visit Bridge House, to see whether its Senior Warden knew what manner of mischief seemed to be unfolding on the place of which he was in charge.

He reached the end of the Bridge, and was pondering whether to turn left or right, when he saw a familiar figure. It was Nat the beggar, trying to sell gloves to a portly merchant. Angered by his persistence, the merchant gave him a shove that sent him sprawling. Chaloner went to help him up.

'Have you come to pay me for more gossip?' Nat asked eagerly, wizened face breaking into a smile. 'I been lurking around St Mary Overie, to see whether them men you asked about would come back.'

'And have they?'

Nat stuck out his hand. 'Money first, then I tells. Or maybe you can buy me a hat instead? I lost mine, and I been chilled to the bone ever since.'

Chaloner handed him several coins and an old grey cap that happened to be in his pocket. It was not so long ago that he had been penniless himself, and he knew what it was like to be cold and hungry. Nat grinned in pleasure as he jammed the hat on his head, then looked sheepish.

'They've not been back. And I asked around, but no one else has seen them, either.' He clutched the money hard, as if he was afraid Chaloner might demand its return.

'I am looking for Bridge House,' said Chaloner, not surprised by the answer: the vicar of Southwark had already told him that the masked men were not coming back. 'Do you know it?'

'Of course. It's by St Olave's Church. Follow me, and I'll show you. The Senior Warden always lives *near* the Bridge, see, but not *on* it, in case it falls down.'

Chaloner laughed. 'That cannot be very reassuring for his tenants.'

'*I* would not sleep on it for a kingdom. And there's something odd going on there, anyway – everyone in Southwark senses it. Ask the wardens why Chapel House is being pulled about, when there's nothing wrong with it. And why men like Phillippes and Kaltoff have taken rooms nearby.'

'I intend to,' muttered Chaloner.

Nat scampered ahead, then stopped outside St Olave's Church. Next to it, so clearly marked that Chaloner was disgusted with himself for not noticing it sooner, was Bridge House.

The Senior Warden's residence was a sizeable place, comprising living accommodation for him and his family, plus a long hall and several offices in which his clerks conducted Bridge business. Chaloner did not have to knock at the door, because it was open, and people thronged in and out. There was a guard to ensure the likes of Nat could not enter, but anyone who looked affluent was allowed past without question. Chaloner, in his Court clothes, did not warrant a second glance.

Inside was a large chamber, with desks all around the edges. Clerks hunched over them, counting and recording the Bridge's revenues. In the open space at the centre were a number of obviously wealthy merchants, all talking about money at the tops of their voices. There was no sign of Senior Warden Hussey or his junior, so Chaloner was obliged to ask where they might be.

Assuming from his dress that he had legitimate business, a clerk conducted him to Hussey's private parlour. It was full of fat children, and when they saw Chaloner, they swarmed towards him. The eldest looked to be about twelve, a portly lad whose face was sticky with the sweet-meat he had been scoffing; the youngest was kicking and gurgling in a crib. The rest were impossible to count, because they did not keep still long enough, but Chaloner estimated there were at least ten. They clamoured at him, grabbing his clothes and urging him to join them in a game.

177

'Now, now, children,' said Hussey, scrambling out from beneath a table. His wig was askew, and the mask he hauled off suggested he had been pretending to be a lion. 'Do not besiege our visitor like Dutchmen after territory. Give him time to announce himself.'

Playfully, Chaloner picked up one of the brats and swung him around, eliciting a squeal of delight. It was a mistake, because then they all wanted a turn, even the larger ones. By the time he had complied, Chaloner was gasping for breath, and some time had passed. He realised he was not making very good progress with his investigations that day, what with playing the viol for Winter and fooling around with Hussey's youngsters.

Eventually, a servant brought a plate of biscuits, and the children abandoned him to mob her, their chubby fingers reaching for the treats before the plate was even set on the table. Chaloner did not think he had ever seen food disappear so quickly. Hussey chuckled at the sight.

'I like to see a decent appetite, and my brood is the fattest and sleekest in Southwark. I have eighteen in all. The older ones are away serving their apprenticeships, while the younger ones live here. My good wife has presented me with a new baby almost every year for the past two decades.'

'Christ!' muttered Chaloner, sorry for her. His own mother thought she had done more than her share when she had had produced seven.

'If you want to discuss business, you had better take advantage of the lull,' advised Hussey. 'They will be after you again the moment they have finished eating, and that will not be long.'

Chaloner was sure it would not, given the rate at which the treats were disappearing. 'Do you not have a nurse?'

he asked, sure a senior warden should be able to afford one.

'She left because of what happened to Jane Scarlet – she said she did not want to be the next victim. I am sure you heard about the attack. It has been the talk of all the coffee houses.'

'It has,' agreed Chaloner. 'I hope your wife—'

'Safely in the country, about to produce Number Nineteen. What did you say you name was?'

'Chaloner.' Seeing the food almost gone, he began to speak more quickly, fabricating a tale that would allow him to bring the subject around to Chapel House. 'The Dowager would like to—'

'The Dowager is an interfering old busybody,' interrupted Hussey. He lowered his voice, so the children would not hear. 'And I am tired of her. She ordered the renovation of Scarlet's house, because she said it was shabby – we disagreed, but did as she ordered – and now she meddles in *every* aspect of the work. What is the place to her? She has never shown any interest in it before.'

Chaloner frowned. 'It was the Dowager who ordered the—'

'Yes!' snapped Hussey. His face was red, and it was clearly a subject that vexed him. 'She said she wants it to look pretty for when the French court visits her in the summer.'

Chaloner was bemused. Most of the Bridge's buildings were 'shabby' because they were coated with soot, and many had suffered some sort of damage from passing carts, whether it was scratches, dents or bits knocked off. Why had she picked Chapel House as exceptional?

'Scarlet has been obliged to move out until the work is finished,' Hussey went on, his voice thick with disapproval.

'Because the Dowager wants it virtually gutted and rebuilt. It will be very nice when it is done, but it is a wretched inconvenience. Scarlet rented a cottage in Turnstile, and it was there that Jane was attacked. I thought the area was safe, and I am shocked to learn it is not.'

'Was much stolen?' asked Chaloner innocently.

'Not a single thing. Spymaster Williamson believes the culprits took fright before they could search the place properly, but I am not so sure. There have been so many odd incidents of late . . .'

'The tides have certainly been strange,' agreed Chaloner encouragingly.

Hussey nodded fervently. 'Yes! And the Dowager and her friends have recently taken to using the Bridge, whereas they always used to travel by boat. And to top it all, the old king's ghost rode across it at the witching hour last night, with his head tucked under his arm.'

Chaloner regarded him askance, wondering whether he was joking, but the Senior Warden's face held no trace of humour. 'Did you see him?'

'Not personally, no,' admitted Hussey. 'I was asleep – looking after children is very tiring. But three apprentices came out of the Bear, and saw him quite distinctly.'

Chaloner imagined the apprentices were either drunk or had invented the tale for attention. Regardless, he was astonished that Hussey should take it seriously. 'Do you and Scarlet ever use cipher to communicate?' he asked, changing the subject. 'When I send messages to—'

'Of course we do not!' exclaimed Hussey. 'Why would we, when we see each other every day? Besides, we have no secrets at Bridge House – anyone can inspect our accounts at any time. It is the way we assure folk that we are trustworthy.'

Chaloner would have been surprised if that were true, given the revenues that were changing hands in the hall below, because they represented too great a temptation. Or was he maligning honest men – had he spent too long at Court, and now assumed everyone was corrupt?

He took his leave when the children began to waddle towards him. He did not want his arms to be so fatigued that he could not draw his sword, and he had the feeling he might need it that night, because he had decided to break in to Chapel House, to find out why the Dowager had taken such an interest in the place. And while he was there, he would try to establish why Blue Dick Culmer should have slipped into it just moments before he was killed, too.

It was almost dark when Chaloner left Hussey. The Bridge was crowded with people going home, and traffic was so slow that it was almost at a standstill. Chapel House was causing its usual obstruction, and he saw some of the scaffolding was askew, where a cart had hit it. He grabbed the door-handle as he passed, but it was locked, and the place was in darkness. Next to the door was a window, mostly shielded from view by a piece of tarpaulin. Chaloner crossed to the haberdasher's shop opposite, spent a few moments ensuring he had not been followed, then retraced his steps.

He was lucky. A cart had been forced to stop outside Chapel House, because a large vehicle was trundling the other way. It concealed him while he slipped behind the tarpaulin and fiddled with the window latch. Moments later, he was standing in a spacious parlour on the ground floor. It was in darkness, but, in accordance with the dictates of the City Fathers, a lamp had been left burning above the door outside. It allowed some illumination of the interior, albeit not much.

Chaloner stood for a moment, letting his eyes become accustomed to the gloom and his ears to the sounds of the house – the creak of timber as the temperature dropped, the ever-present rumble of rushing water, and traffic. But there was another noise, too: a faint but rhythmic banging. It was coming from downstairs, and he supposed some conscientious craftsman must be working late.

He decided to search the upper floors first. There were three of them, each larger than the one below, as it over-jettied the street or the river. But there was nothing to find, because every chamber had been stripped bare for the renovation. He returned to the main parlour.

A flight of stairs led to the lower floor, from which still came the sound of knocking. Curious as to why workmen should consider cellars worthy of beautifica-tion, he headed towards them.

Unlike the rest of the building, the cellar was made of stone. It was low-ceilinged, barely high enough for a man to stand, and was, in effect, little more than a space hollowed out of the starling. It felt damp, and the roar of the river was louder than in the upper storeys.

It was empty, though, and the thudding was coming from an even deeper room – one that was more like a vault, and that was accessed via a trapdoor and a ladder. Chaloner supposed someone was effecting repairs to the foundations. He approached and peered down. One man was hacking at the floor with a pickaxe, while another watched. As Chaloner bent to look more closely, a few particles of grit pattered to the floor below. Suddenly, there was a gun in the watching man's hand.

Chaloner registered it was being held by Phillippes at exactly the same moment as the dial-maker squeezed the trigger. The crack was deafening, and wood flew as the ball grazed the trapdoor. Cursing when he saw he had missed, Phillippes started to scramble up the ladder. He paused briefly, to grab a second loaded dag from Kaltoff, giving Chaloner just enough time to whip around and bolt back up the cellar steps – the spy had his sword, but blades were no match for firearms.

When Chaloner reached the top of the stairs, he turned, intending to bar the door, but he had reckoned without the renovation. The door had been removed from its hinges and was leaning against the wall. He took a moment to twist it around, so Phillippes would be forced to move it, but knew it would not slow him down for long.

He aimed for the front door, but when he hauled it open, he was met by the side of a cart: the Bridge was in the grip of one of its traffic jams, and the vehicle was so close to the house that a cat could not have squeezed between the gap. He dropped to his hands and knees, intending to crawl beneath it, but it was too low. He was trapped inside the house.

With no alternative, he raced up the stairs to the upper floors. He could hear Phillippes behind him, and Kaltoff's agitated cries. He reached the top storey and locked himself inside one of the bedrooms, knowing it was only a matter of moments before they realised where he had gone – and as soon as they did, they would batter down the door and shoot him. But he had faced worse odds in his life, and there was a window. He ran towards it and tugged it open.

Below, in the darkness, he could just make out the

boat-shaped starling, with frothy white water roaring along either side of it. The tide was in full spate, and jumping into the maelstrom was out of the question. He would drown. He glanced upwards, but clambering over the outside of the building would be a dangerous strategy, because it would make him a sitting duck.

He peered back down at the starling and saw it had a platform, presumably for unloading supplies that could then be winched directly inside the house – a sort of private wharf. He would be exposed to gunfire if he stood on it, but the platform continued in a narrow ledge that disappeared under the Bridge. If he could reach it, he would be out of sight. It was not an ideal solution to his predicament, but it was better than any other option available.

He had to work quickly, because Phillippes and Kaltoff were already outside the door, and were beginning to kick it. Fortunately, the workmen had left plenty of rope lying around. He knotted several lengths together, then tied one end around a ceiling beam, and dropped the rest out of the window. He worked coolly, his training preventing him from panicking as the door slowly disintegrated under the increasingly furious assault.

He scrambled on to the windowsill, grabbed the rope and started to slither down it. He had not gone far when he heard the door fly open and footsteps hammer across the wooden floor. They would see the rope and know where he had gone, so he had only seconds to reach safety.

His hands burned as friction scorched them. Above, he could see two heads etched against the darkening sky. Then the rope jerked. They were cutting it, so he would fall to his death. He increased his downward pace, and had perhaps ten feet to go when the rope gave way. He landed with a thud that drove the breath from his body.

The starling was slick with spray, and his momentum carried him towards the roaring water. Desperately, he clawed at the slippery stones, coming to a halt at the very edge of the platform, so close to the water that spray all but blinded him. Then there was a sharp crack and he felt something punch through the lace on his sleeve. The second shot came so close to his head that shards of stone grazed his cheek.

He glanced up. Phillippes and Kaltoff had gone, and he supposed they were reloading. Sure they would not miss the next time, he struggled towards the narrow ledge that disappeared under the arch. It was treacherous going, and when he reached it, he found it was smaller than he had anticipated, barely wide enough for his feet. Moreover, a profusion of algae meant it was like standing on ice, and one false move would see him skid into the raging river.

The next shot made him jump, a movement that caused his foot to slip, sending him to one knee. He flailed with his hands, relieved when his fingers encountered metal. It was a mooring ring. He used it to haul himself to safety. Unfortunately, it was ancient, rusty and on the verge of tearing away from its fastenings, but he gripped it gratefully, and took stock of his situation.

He was out of sight from above, but his feet threatened to lose purchase each time he tried to ease into a more comfortable position, and unnerving grating sounds from the ring indicated it was unlikely to hold him for long. How was he going to escape from what was essentially an island in the middle of the Thames? Should he let himself drop into the water, and hope he would survive

185

what would be a very turbulent ride? But then what? The river was powerful, and he doubted he could break free of the midstream current to swim ashore.

He leaned towards the wall, to ease the weight on the ring. His feet skidded, but eventually he found a position that was, if not comfortable, then relatively secure. If he kept still, he might stay there until low tide the following morning, when he could summon help from a passing skiff.

Of course, the night was bitterly cold, and he was not sure he could hold on for another hour, let alone eight or nine. Reluctantly, Chaloner began to accept that here was a position he could not escape by cunning, strength or sheer determination. It was the river he was up against this time, not a human enemy, and he found he was over-matched.

Bit by bit, the city grew darker as lights were doused and people retired to bed. Idly, Chaloner wondered whether Phillippes and Kaltoff would slide down another rope, to pick him off at their leisure. Or had they assumed he had either been hit or had fallen in the river? However, he was certain they would continue to watch for a while, just to be sure, so he could not return to the wider part of the starling just yet.

To distract himself from the growing ache in his shoulders, he reviewed his investigations. What did Phillippes and Kaltoff expect to find in Chapel House? Had Blue Dick hidden something there, perhaps something stolen from one of the churches he had despoiled? Chaloner smiled grimly. If so, then Thurloe had been wrong to dismiss his theory that Phillippes and Kaltoff were connected to the iconoclast's murder.

The night grew colder as time ticked past, and when he snapped out of a peculiar half-doze to find himself sliding backwards, Chaloner knew he could no longer stay where he was. Surely, Phillippes and Kaltoff would have given up their vigil and gone home by now? He decided that even if they had not, then being shot was preferable to death from drowning or exposure.

With infinite care, he began to inch towards the wider part of the starling, but did not get far. All manner of objects were washed downstream when the Thames ebbed, and that night, a mass of silt-clogged branches had fetched up on the area for which he was aiming. They were too precariously lodged for him to climb over, but too heavy to be tipped into the water. He was trapped.

Suddenly, his lame leg gave a monstrous twinge, causing him to flinch. The ring squealed in protest, and he felt its rusty moorings begin to tear free. Balancing on his good leg, he leaned on the ring, to push it back into the wall. It went, but it was a temporary measure at best, and he knew it would not survive him jerking it a second time. That meant he either had to stand on one leg for what remained of the night, or admit defeat and take his chances in the water. But when he glanced behind him, at the dense black spume that was thundering past, he knew it would kill him.

When he first heard voices, he thought it was his imagination. Then he saw several boats being propelled towards him. The yells grew louder, mixed with wild laughter and screams. It took a moment for him to realise what was happening, but then he understood: some lunatics were going to try to shoot the Bridge while the tide was in full spate. They sounded drunk, and their competitive howls suggested some sort of race was in progress.

One of the little crafts was lining up to pass through his arch.

Could he leap into it as it passed? And if he succeeded, would his weight throw it off balance and capsize it? But there was no time for debate, because the boat was already moving his way. He could hear the whoops and shrieks of the passengers as it was caught in the current, and the oarsman struggled to keep it midflow. Fortunately for Chaloner, the fellow could not manage, and it began to veer towards his starling. The oarsman's white, terror-filled face said he knew his craft was going to be dashed against the stone and destroyed.

The fact that Chaloner timed his jump perfectly owed more to luck than to skill. His frozen limbs refused to obey him when he tried to turn, so he ended up flopping backwards in as ungainly a manoeuvre as he had ever performed. And his weight jerked the boat away from the pier just far enough to prevent it from being smashed into pieces. Then there was some alarming lurching, during which Chaloner could see nothing but darkness and feel nothing but flying spray. Then all was calm again, and his fellow travellers were screeching their victory.

There were four people in the boat: the oarsman and three fares. Two of the passengers were strapping lads with the short hair and clean-shaven faces of apprentices. The third was Fabian Stedman, the printer who liked to engage in lively arguments at the Rainbow Coffee House. The waterman leaned on his oars and looked as if he might be sick, aware that he had just done something very stupid and was lucky to be alive. He regarded Chaloner balefully.

'That was a reckless thing to have done. You might have killed us all.'

Chaloner tried to shrug, but was far too cold and stiff for any such coordinated gestures. 'You would have drowned had I *not* jumped. I did you a favour.'

'Chaloner?' asked Stedman, peering at him in the darkness. His cheerful face was flushed from drink, and his voice was slurred. 'Where did you come from?'

'He jumped off the Bridge,' supplied the oarsman venomously. 'Damned madman!'

'You mean suicide?' asked Stedman, wide-eyed. 'That is illegal!'

'So is playing the fool on the river,' said Chaloner coolly.

'Did the others make it?' asked one of Stedman's cronies, peering backwards into the darkness. 'I can see the bakers, but not the butchers. And I think the fish-mongers are aiming for the wharf.'

'We had better hurry, then,' said Stedman to the oarsman. 'It would be a pity to lose the bet now we have done the dangerous bit. You will get nothing if we arrive second.'

The oarsman began pulling towards the shore for all he was worth, and when they reached Botolph's Wharf, he and the two lads raced towards the nearest tavern. A large number of people were there to cheer them on, and Chaloner gathered from the jubilant shouting that the printers were currently in the lead. He alighted rather more slowly, trying to move in a way that did not make him appear drunk. Stedman watched with arched eyebrows.

'Do you make a habit of shooting the Bridge at full tide?' Chaloner asked, feeling the printer was hardly in a position to regard him with such censure.

Stedman hiccupped. 'No, this is my first time. And my

last. I had to swallow two pints of claret before I felt ready to try it, and now I feel a bit queasy.'

Chaloner nodded towards the tavern. 'Go, or your friends will celebrate without you.'

Stedman winced. 'The stench of ale would make me vomit, and that would be embarrassing. Shall we share a carriage home? It will be safer to travel as a pair – hackneymen have a reputation for robbing those they consider easy prey.'

'Neither of us is easy prey.' Although Chaloner was not so sure about Stedman.

'No? Neither of us can stand upright. I would say we both represent attractive targets.'

Chaloner conceded he was right when he tried to walk up Botolph Lane, and found he could not do it – he needed Stedman's shoulder. He was not sure who was supporting whom as they lurched towards Thames Street, where carriages could usually be found for hire, even at night.

'Where to?' asked Stedman. 'You live in Fetter Lane, do you not?'

But Chaloner did not want his cold, cheerless garret. 'Tothill Street,' he told the driver, thinking longingly of Hannah's cosy home, blazing fire and warm body.

It felt like an age before they reached their destination, and every jolt and lurch hurt. When they arrived, Chaloner climbed out slowly, relieved when Hannah opened the door to his knock.

'He tried to kill himself by jumping off London Bridge,' called Stedman from the carriage, when it did not occur to Chaloner to offer her an explanation for his bedraggled state. 'But he landed in my boat instead.'

'It is not true,' said Chaloner tiredly, seeing Hannah's shock. 'I will explain tomorrow.'

But he knew he would do no such thing, because it was not safe for her to know about the Bridge or any of the other mysteries currently confronting him. He staggered towards the chair by the kitchen fire, and it was not long before sleep overtook him.

Chapter 6

When Chaloner woke the following day, the sun was high in the sky, and he estimated it was at least ten o'clock. He was in Hannah's fireside chair, covered by several heavy blankets, and the flames that leapt in the hearth were high enough to risk setting the chimney alight. He was hot, and realised it was discomfort that had woken him.

He sat forward and rested his elbows on his knees. He was stiff all over, and when he felt his face with his fingers, there was a scratch on one cheek from where splinters had flown from one of Phillippes's missiles. His hands were tender from sliding down the rope, and his lame leg gave a protesting twinge when he stood up. It did not stop him from hobbling towards his viol, though.

He set the bow to the strings, pleased when his fingers lost their soreness after a few moments, allowing him to play with his customary skill. It was not an inspired performance, but it was passable. He had not been playing long when Hannah came in. She regarded him warily.

'How are you?'

'Hungry,' replied Chaloner, hoping she would not offer him anything she had cooked herself.

'I thought you would never wake,' she went on, coming to sit next to him. 'I was on the verge of sending for Mr Wiseman.'

'Promise me you will never do that,' said Chaloner, alarmed. 'I was only sleeping.'

'Like the dead, whereas normally you wake at the slightest sound. You did not even stir when Sergeant Leigh came to visit. And that Mr Stedman told me you had jumped off the Bridge.'

'Stedman was drunk,' replied Chaloner, aware that self-murder was considered a mortal sin for Catholics, so Hannah would certainly disapprove. He struggled to think of a credible explanation. 'I was exploring one of the starlings for the Earl, but became trapped by the rising tide. I *did* leap into Stedman's boat as it passed, but suicide was never my intention.'

She did not look convinced. 'Well, you were playing your viol prettily enough just now, so whatever black demons plagued you must have gone now. I shall make some breakfast while you change into clothes that are not matted with slime.'

He saw with distaste that she was right, and went to wash in a bucket of warm water. The water was filthy by the time he had finished, and he checked the street very carefully before he tipped it out of the window, not wanting it to land on anyone.

Hannah had sharpened the knife he used for shaving, and clean clothes had been laid out on the bed, ready for him. He smiled. It was many years since his wife had died, and he had forgotten what it was like to be looked after. It was pleasant, and he experienced a surge of affection for Hannah. Was it love, he wondered? And if so, did it mean he should ask her to marry him? Or was the

193

question precipitous, and would destroy the precious thing they had been building?

And was she really the one for him, anyway? Ruefully, he reminded himself that his history with women was hardly radiant with success – he nearly always chose the wrong ones. Even his wife had not been a particularly wise selection, and although he had loved her at the time, he was honest enough with himself to know that their relationship would have cooled, had she lived.

But could it be different with Hannah? They had little in common, and she was as unlike him as it was possible to be. Yet there was much to admire – her integrity, optimism and humour. But would it be enough that he liked her company, even when she was tired or irritable, and that the sight of her brightened his day? Or would their disparate personalities drive them apart in time?

And would she chafe when he preferred to stay home rather than attend some wild event in White Hall? Would she tire of his reticence, and long for someone more open and lively? Moreover, what did he have to offer her? The Earl had not threatened to dismiss him for some time now, but that did not mean his job was secure, and, as the youngest son of a large family, there was no inheritance coming. All told, marriage to him was not a particularly attractive proposition, and Hannah would have to be insane to accept.

He pushed such thoughts from his mind as he walked down the stairs, where he saw the parlour had been cleansed of the soiree's ravages, and one wall given a new coat of paint. At least two rugs were missing, though, and he supposed they were still being cleaned, probably by professionals who had substances for dealing with the kind of stubborn stains members of the Court tended to generate while celebrating.

Hannah presented him with a plate of something he assumed were cakes, but that might equally well have been ballast for ships. They were fist-sized, extremely dense and tasted of vinegar. He ate one with difficulty, and hoped he was not expected to consume them all. He was halfway through the second and struggling, when there was a knock at the door.

Chaloner had no weapons on him, but he had the cakes. He grabbed one, ready to hurl, should the caller prove to be someone who meant him harm. But it was only Leigh, his small, military frame clad in an eye-catching purple coat.

'Chaloner!' he barked, reaching out to grip the spy's hand. He withdrew it hastily when the gesture saw him provided with a fistful of crushed cake. 'Hannah has been worried about you, and so have I. There really is no need to dispatch yourself over your failure to solve your various cases.'

Chaloner blinked. 'You think that is what happened?'

Leigh patted his shoulder. 'It is only natural that you should deny it, but your secret is safe with me. And the Earl and Bulteel. And I may have mentioned it to—'

'Christ!' groaned Chaloner, supposing Hannah must have repeated Stedman's story, and the rumour had taken a life of its own, as such tales were always wont to do. It occurred to him that it was his own fault – if he had bothered to provide her with an explanation the previous night, she might not have been inclined to listen to drunken printers with lurid imaginations.

Leigh smiled with a false cheer he probably always inflicted on those he perceived as invalids. 'I came to tell you that the Earl wants you to spend today recovering. To be honest, he is more concerned with his prelates' dinner than Blue Dick's murder at the moment. He heard yesterday that the Bishop of Oxford can come, which only leaves Gloucester uncertain now.'

'He must be pleased.'

'Delighted,' agreed Leigh. 'But I have been busy. The Dowager is buying up all the supplies of oysters – not for her ball, but because she wants to make sure none are available for the prelates.'

'She will try to poach his baker, too,' said Chaloner, recalling what he had overheard on the Bridge. It felt like an age ago, and seemed almost too petty to mention.

Leigh was appalled. 'Really? Then I shall lock him inside Worcester House, to make sure her agents cannot reach him. Thank you, Chaloner: the Earl will appreciate the warning. Incidentally, the old king's ghost was seen again last night, and people are beginning to be afraid.'

'Afraid of what?'

'They see his appearances as a sign that something awful is about to happen. A new crack was found in St Paul's this morning, too, while the Thames's tides have become inexplicably erratic. These omens may mean the old order is about to topple. Perhaps the Clarendon Code *is* too harsh.'

'Do not let the Earl hear you say that,' warned Chaloner. 'They may not be laws he wrote, but he supports every letter to the hilt.'

'I know,' said Leigh grimly. He shook his head, worried. 'But I wish his Bishops' Dinner was not so soon – that we could postpone it until we understand what all these portents mean.'

*　　*　　*

Leigh left the house still trying to wipe the cake from his hand. It clung like glue, and Chaloner told Hannah he was full when she tried to press another on him. Her face fell.

'It is that horrible Earl's fault,' she cried in sudden distress. 'He is responsible for you losing your appetite. I hate the way he keeps sending you on dangerous missions. He does not care if you die, and you would be better off with a master who has some scruples. Would you like me to put in a word with the Duke? I am sure he could use a man with your skills.'

'Christ, no!' Chaloner was genuinely appalled by the notion of working for Buckingham – and seriously doubted the Duke would be interested in hiring a man who had been employed by one of his enemies, anyway. Then he saw Hannah's hurt expression, and relented. 'I am not ready to abandon the Earl yet. Not in the middle of an investigation.'

'An investigation that drove you to despair,' she said bitterly.

'Hannah, I did *not* attempt suicide,' said Chaloner firmly. 'Surely, you know me better than to think I would kill myself over some paltry enquiry?'

Hannah regarded him soberly. 'I imagine that depends on the sort of thing you are discovering. Incidentally, Father Stephen asked me to pass you a message, but I am not sure I shall. I want you to withdraw from this business, not give you intelligence that will encourage you to delve deeper into it.'

'If you do not tell me, I will have to ask him myself. And I would rather spend the day with you.'

She stared at him, eyes full of hope. 'You mean it? You will stay with me all day?'

197

'I will not even go to the cookshop,' he promised, although this was a serious concession because it meant he might have to eat more of her cakes. However, even that could not detract from the pleasurable prospect of a whole day with her. He could not remember the last time he had done it, and was grateful to the Earl for giving him licence to malinger.

She smiled, won over. 'Then can we go to see *The Indian Queen* in Drury Lane?'

Chaloner smiled back. 'If you like.'

'Well, as you are being so amenable, I shall tell you Father Stephen's message,' Hannah decided. 'It was that the King's dial-designer might know something about Chapel House, although Father Stephen does not know what. He says judicial questions may yield answers, whatever that means.'

Chaloner decided to interview Phillippes as soon as he could the following day.

'I have been invited to a reception in Somerset House on Saturday,' Hannah chattered on. 'Normally, I would take you with me, but not this time. A lot of people who dislike Clarendon will be there, so it will be too uncomfortable for you.'

Chaloner supposed he would have to attend without an invitation, then, because a gathering of the Earl's enemies so close to the Bishops' Dinner was something that needed to be watched.

'Did I tell you that the Dowager has asked me to her Shrove Tuesday ball, too?' asked Hannah, when he still said nothing. 'You could accompany me to that, but I suspect your Earl will force you to be at Worcester House, listening to the bishops hold forth about politics and religion.'

'I imagine politics and religion might feature in discussions at Somerset House, too,' remarked Chaloner. 'The company will be full of Catholics and other dissenters.'

Hannah's cool expression told him she had taken umbrage, reminding him that religion was one of the many subjects upon which they held diverging views. As a practising Catholic, she took her faith seriously, whereas Chaloner rarely gave his much thought.

'Perhaps, but *we* will not be inventing laws that deny a person's right to pray as his conscience dictates,' she retorted acidly. '*We* are not tyrants.'

Sorry his thoughtless remark had offended her, Chaloner took Hannah to the play in Drury Lane within the hour. The King and Lady Castlemaine were there, although they were more interested in each other than in anything the actors were doing, and canoodled brazenly throughout.

In an adjacent box were several friends of the Dowager – the ugly Progers and three Penderels. The brothers sat silently, and did not give the impression that they were enjoying themselves. Meanwhile, Progers wrote continuously on a piece of paper, and barely looked at the stage. Chaloner wondered why any of them had bothered to come.

Another friend of the Dowager joined them during Act Two. The vicar of Wimbledon's nose was especially purple that day, as if he had been drinking. He began whispering to Progers, loudly enough to disturb those trying to watch the play. Eventually, it even penetrated the King's consciousness. His Majesty tore his attention away from the Lady to glare. Rashly, Luckin scowled back, and the Penderel brothers were obliged to haul him outside before he could be arrested for insolence.

During the interval, Hannah began to chat to some people she knew from Court. They were James Carkesse, a navy clerk who described himself as a poet, and his wife Susan. The discussion soon turned to the Clarendon Code. Carkesse thought it was a very good idea, because it allowed the state to identify potential fanatics; his wife disagreed, and declared it unnecessarily suppressive.

'Even Spymaster Williamson has been heard expressing reservations,' Susan said, to underline her point. 'And he is a member of the government!'

'He is just daunted by the amount of work the Clarendon Code represents for his intelligence service,' said Carkesse dismissively. 'It is laziness speaking, not his conscience.'

'Regardless of his motives, he is right,' said Hannah, never one to hold her tongue when there were issues about which she felt strongly. 'The Clarendon Code is a nasty collection of laws, and people should refuse to obey them.'

'The only people who would do that are Catholics and nonconformists,' Carkesse pointed out. 'The rest of us follow these edicts anyway.'

Chaloner changed the subject at that point, afraid Hannah would make a declaration about her own faith. Catholicism was not illegal, but it was not something to be announced to virtual strangers, either. Hannah glared at him, to let him know that she had not appreciated the interruption.

Also among the audience was Sir John Winter. He was with Phillippes and Kaltoff, laughing at some anecdote Phillippes was telling. Phillippes was elegant, handsome and graceful in his finery, but although Kaltoff's clothes were obviously expensive, he was not the right shape to achieve the stylish insouciance for which he was aiming, and the result was vaguely comical.

When Winter spotted Chaloner, he broke away from the dial-makers and strode towards him, moustache quivering with pleasure as he launched into a description of a performance of the King's Private Musick the previous evening. Chaloner looked for a way to escape when he saw Phillippes and Kaltoff prepare to leave the theatre, intending to follow them, but Hannah was clinging to his arm and Winter was disinclined to stop talking. With resignation, Chaloner watched the dial-makers climb into a carriage. Had they recognised him from the encounter in Chapel House, or was it some other business that called them away in the middle of the performance?

'It pulled at the heart-strings,' Winter was declaring, dabbing at the corner of one eye with his sleeve. 'Even today, the memory of those haunting melodies has the power to move me.'

'I wish I had been there,' said Chaloner, politely masking his frustration.

'You should be proud of your husband, madam,' said Winter, turning to Hannah and still struggling with his emotions. 'It is rare to see such talent among amateurs.'

'I am proud,' agreed Hannah, squeezing Chaloner's hand. 'And *I* play the flageolet.'

Few real musicians took that particular instrument seriously, but Winter was a gentleman. 'Then I should like to hear you sometime,' he said graciously. He frowned suddenly, and when Chaloner followed the direction of his gaze, he saw several of the Dowager's grey-robed Capuchins.

'It is unusual to see friars at the theatre,' remarked Hannah, also staring at them.

'Yes, it is,' muttered Winter. 'Damn! I thought I had persuaded the Dowager to excuse them from today's performance. It is the Feast Day of St Juliana, you see, and they wanted to spend the time in private devotion.'

Hannah frowned. 'The Dowager makes her priests watch plays?'

'She likes all her court to be well-versed in contemporary arts,' explained Winter. 'The Capuchins do not mind attending musical events, but I doubt they enjoy the stage.'

'I doubt it, too,' said Hannah. 'And they should not be here – people are glaring at them.'

They were doing a good deal more than glaring. A number of patrons, who had imbibed rather too liberally of the intermission wine, had surrounded the hapless clerics, and were clamouring insults at them. Among the unmannerly mob was Carkesse, who began to bawl acid remarks about the undesirability of Catholics frequenting public places.

Chaloner watched in distaste, and when the abuse turned to actual jostling, he went with Winter to escort the Capuchins out, placing himself between the friars and those who were being rather free with shoulders and elbows.

'Thank you,' said Winter quietly, when the friars had been packed into a coach and sent out of harm's way. 'I could not have managed alone – at least, not without drawing my sword, and that would not have been wise. I am Catholic myself, and people know it. I might have been lynched.'

There was a troubled expression on Hannah's face when Chaloner returned to her. 'The Penderels are Catholic,' she whispered unhappily. 'And so is Progers.

Why did *they* not rescue the Capuchins? Instead, they skulked in a corner and let you and Winter take the risks.'

But Chaloner understood. 'They are vulnerable, too, and dashing into such situations might see them targeted in future. They are wise to maintain a low profile.'

'You did not,' Hannah pointed out. 'Does that mean you are at risk from bigots from now on?'

Chaloner glanced at Carkesse, and saw him muttering venomously to his cronies. He could best any of them with one hand tied behind his back, so they did not worry him, but he was unsettled to see how much hatred the Clarendon Code was engendering. Where would it end?

The second half of the play was dull, and Chaloner used the time to think about his various mysteries. He still had no idea why Blue Dick had been murdered, what the other iconoclasts planned to do, why Jane Scarlet had been assaulted, or who the masked men were that he had fought in St Mary Overie. Nor was he any further forward with learning what the Dowager and her cronies had in mind for Shrove Tuesday, except that it would probably involve fireworks and would certainly inconvenience the Earl.

He frowned suddenly. Fireworks. The Dowager was having some at her ball, made by Winter, who had procured gunpowder from government supplies. But Phillippes and Kaltoff were also associated with fireworks: Chaloner had heard them himself in the Beggar's Bush, discussing one that had exploded. Was it relevant? For the life of him, he could not see how, but decided to keep it in the back of his mind when he questioned them about what they had been doing in Chapel House.

He turned his mind to the fact that Will Goff and

Lord Bristol were in the country. Bristol represented a considerable threat to Clarendon, while Goff represented a considerable threat to the government, so both needed to be caught before any plans could be realised. And then there were the iconoclasts who were said to be gathering. Thoughts of Herring reminded Chaloner of Thurloe, and he wondered why his friend should have been hobnobbing with the man. He sighed unhappily when it occurred to him that it might have been unwise to pass the ciphers he had discovered to Thurloe for decoding – Thurloe might know their contents all too well.

Because it was not far, he suggested that he and Hannah visit Lincoln's Inn on the way home. Hannah liked Thurloe, and agreed happily to the diversion, but they arrived to find him out. The fire had been banked, suggesting he intended to return at some point, but his manservant did not know when. Chaloner took the opportunity to look quickly around the rooms, but Thurloe was not a man to leave incriminating evidence lying around for spies to find. Chaloner did not expect to discover anything to tell him what his friend was embroiled in, and nor did he.

He took Hannah home, and spent the evening trying to teach her how to make bread that would not serve as a viable alternative to cannonballs. He was not a particularly good cook, but he could produce an edible meal when necessary, and his guests were usually in possession of all their teeth at the end of it. The same could not be said for Hannah, and by bedtime, he had reached the conclusion that she was a lost cause.

'When we are married, I shall hire a cook-maid,' she declared, somewhat out of the blue as she banged her loaf on the table to test its hardness. 'Then we shall not have to worry about bread.'

Chaloner gaped at her. 'You mean when you are married to me?'

It was her turn for raised eyebrows. 'Of course. Or are you saying that you never intend to make an honest woman of me? I should like our union sanctified by God, Tom. The Duke says such scruples are nonsense, but I disagree.'

'You have discussed marriage with the Duke?'

'Yes. He is a very dear friend, and always ready with advice, although not all of it is very sound. However, he did say one sensible thing: that I should snare you while I can.'

Chaloner stared at her. 'You will take me? But I have so little to offer.'

Hannah laughed, and the sound was music in his ears. 'Well, you have modesty in abundance, which is not a virtue often encountered at Court. I never thought I would love another man after my husband died, but you have grown special very quickly. I know we share little in terms of interests and acquaintances, but I do not think that matters.'

'Perhaps not.'

Hannah's face fell. 'You do not sound very sure.'

Chaloner hastened to make amends. He had not meant to seem uncertain, but the truth was that his mind was in a turmoil of confusion. He *did* want to marry Hannah, but there was a small, rational voice at the back of his mind that whispered simple affection might not be enough to keep them together for the rest of their lives. They needed more.

'I *am* sure,' he insisted. 'But we have never talked . . . I did not imagine . . .'

Hannah regarded him soberly. 'You can say no, if you would rather we maintained our current arrangement. Or has this discussion frightened you away from even that?'

'No! I will marry you tomorrow, if you like.' There, it was out, and there was no going back now. Perhaps it was not the right decision, but time would tell. And it was infinitely preferable to spending the rest of his life wondering what he had lost.

Hannah smiled at last. 'If we did that, tongues would wag. Everyone would assume I was with child! Besides, we need time to make the arrangements. How about a date in the summer?'

'Spring,' said Chaloner firmly. Now the decision was taken, he found himself eager to act on it. Was it because he was afraid he might change his mind? 'I do not want to wait too long.'

Hannah flung her arms around his neck. 'Then spring it shall be.'

Chaloner woke the following morning with the sense that his life had been irrevocably changed. The pleasure – and relief that his own feelings were reciprocated – he had experienced the previous day had faded, and unease had taken its place. Hannah had mentioned their differences, indicating he was not the only one who had wondered about their long-term compatibility. He took a deep breath and rolled over to look at her as she lay sleeping.

In repose, there were lines around her eyes and mouth that he had never noticed before, and her fair curls were a chaotic jumble around her head. Careful not to wake her, he reached out to touch them. They were soft and warm, and he found himself hoping that she would not regret the step she had taken. But lying in bed pondering the terrors of marriage was doing no one any good, so he rose, aware that he had a lot to do, and left while she was still asleep.

It had been several days since he had reported to the Earl, so he decided to visit White Hall first. The day was crisp and clear, with a sharp breeze blowing in from the north. The rooftops were brushed white with frost, and glittered in the sunlight. White Hall looked pretty, with its jumble of gables and chimneys, slightly shrouded in smoke from the huge fires in the kitchens.

The Great Court was treacherously slippery, though, and Chaloner went to the assistance of one man who took a tumble. It was Progers. The three Penderel brothers were with him, but they were more interested in jeering than helping him up. They were all drunk, and Chaloner could tell by the way they were dressed that they had been out all night, and were just returning home. Progers looked particularly disreputable, his ugly face smeared with powder from the cheeks of a whore.

'I have broken my leg,' he howled, rolling on the ground as he clutched his knee.

'You have not,' said Chaloner firmly. 'Let me help you stand, and then you can—'

'This is more my domain than yours,' boomed a familiar voice.

Chaloner turned to see Wiseman bearing down on them, all flowing red hair, scarlet robes and finely honed muscles. His heart sank: he was not in the mood for the surgeon's irritating arrogance that morning.

'I need a drink,' Progers gasped, as the surgeon examined the afflicted limb. 'Wine.'

'You need my unique cure for drunkenness,' countered Wiseman, waving a bottle at him. 'And then a decent nap. Stand up, man. You are not hurt. And you owe me two shillings.'

'For what?' demanded Progers, shocked. 'I am not buying your cure, because I know it contains vinegar and slug juice – Buckingham told me. And you have not done anything else to earn a fee.'

'I inspected you and pronounced you fit,' argued Wiseman, holding out his hand. 'So give, or you will be sorry the next time you are laid low with some embarrassing pox.'

Resentfully, Progers began to count out the money, while the Penderel brothers sniggered at the spectacle. Chaloner took the opportunity to talk to them, sensing they were too tipsy to recognise him as one of the Earl's retainers.

'I thought there were four of you,' he began pleasantly. 'Where is Edward?'

'Why?' demanded Oliver belligerently, humour evaporating fast as he clenched his scarred fists.

Chaloner raised his hands defensively. 'It was just a polite enquiry.'

'Please stop snarling at everyone, Oliver,' chided Rupert wearily. 'It is only natural for people to ask, given that we are usually all four together.' He turned to Chaloner. 'We do not know where he is. He has been missing since Sunday. Personally, I think he tired of London and went home.'

'He would not have gone without telling us,' countered Neville worriedly. 'Something has happened, I am sure of it. This is a dangerous place, and I wish we had not come.'

'On the contrary,' argued Oliver. 'Our fortunes are rising – we have a place at Court, a decent home, and the Dowager trusts us. It is a good place, and we are going to stay for as long as we can.'

They all looked around at the sound of hurrying footsteps. It was Luckin and Father Stephen, their clerical robes flying as they ran. Stephen looked agitated, but then he always looked agitated, and neither the Penderels nor Progers seemed unduly concerned by his alarm.

'There you are!' he cried, skidding to a standstill and almost suffering the same fate as Progers as he slipped on a patch of frost. 'The Dowager wants you all.'

'What, now?' asked Progers. He belched, then put his hand over his mouth, as if he thought he might be sick. 'We were about to go to bed. Not together, of course. I have a nice young whore waiting for me – one of the actresses from *The Indian Queen*.'

'Which one?' demanded Oliver. 'It had better not be the fair-headed wench, because I want her.'

'The Dowager intends to visit Winchester Palace, and demands your company,' said Luckin sharply, before Progers could reply. His nose was very purple from the cold. 'So, I advise you to splash some water on your faces and attend her immediately, because you know what she is like when she does not get what she wants.'

The notion of losing the favour of a powerful patron was enough to drive Progers and the Penderels to the nearest fountain, although nothing would have induced Chaloner to put *his* face in it. He had seen courtiers urinating there in the past, and it was a repository for all manner of filth. Luckin went with them to supervise, grimacing his disapproval at the state they were in.

'Thank you for sending me the message about the

King's dial-maker,' said Chaloner to Stephen in an under-
tone. 'I shall visit him as soon as I can. What do you
think he might know?'

The priest looked around uneasily. 'I overheard
Phillippes say something about digging for gold. I have
no idea what he was talking about, but I sensed something deeply untoward.'

Chaloner groaned. There was something about gold
that always brought out the worst in people, and he hated
cases that involved treasure.

'Luckin is coming back!' hissed Stephen urgently. 'We
must talk about something else.' He cleared his throat
and spoke rather loudly. 'Is it true that you jumped off
the Bridge on Monday night? Because if so, it is my
sacred duty to warn you that self-murder is a mortal sin,
and—'

'It is not true,' Chaloner snapped. 'I was at home on
Monday night.'

'Did I hear mention of suicide?' demanded Luckin.
'It *is* a sin, but not as great as some I could name. Like
injustice, for instance. Did you hear that I was arrested
and held in the Tower, just because Lord Bristol chose
to tell me he was no longer Catholic? *That* is injustice at
its worst.'

'Are you saying Lord Bristol is currently in the country?'
pounced Chaloner.

'I doubt he is here now, having seen what happened to
me,' replied Luckin grimly. 'He hoped for a reconciliation
with his King, and instead all he got was an innocent
vicar clapped in irons. They said he was an outlaw, and
that I should have arrested him. But how ridiculous! He
had a sword, for a start, and I was unarmed. The whole
episode was disgraceful!'

'Yes, it was,' said Stephen soothingly. 'But we must go, or the Dowager will be angry. Are the brothers and Progers respectable? Let me rephrase that: are they ready? Yes? Then let us be off.'

Chaloner watched them scurry away. He had rarely seen a more unprepossessing rabble, and wondered why the Dowager wanted their company. Surely, there were better companions available?

'How is Jane Scarlet?' he asked, when Wiseman came to stand next to him.

'Not making as rapid a recovery as I would have hoped. Meanwhile, her husband does nothing but weep, and I had to order him back to work lest he turned himself mad with grief. It is a sorry situation, and Spymaster Williamson tells me he has made no headway with catching the villains responsible.'

'Does he have any clues?'

'None he shared with me. Why? Are you thinking of launching your own enquiry?'

'No,' lied Chaloner. 'I am just concerned that the culprits may do it again.'

'You are worried about Hannah,' surmised Wiseman. 'I can understand that – I am concerned for Temperance, and I told Preacher Hill to abandon his door-keeping duties and guard her full-time. It is a bad business, and if you do decide to dispense your own justice, then there is not a man in London who would not shake your hand for it.'

Chaloner regarded him askance. 'You, a Court surgeon, advocates vigilantism?'

Wiseman met his gaze. 'Of course, when it serves to protect the innocent.'

*   *   *

Chaloner resumed his journey to the Earl. White Hall was comparatively empty, because it was too early for most courtiers to be up – with the obvious exception of those who had not yet gone to bed. He saw the Queen taking her morning exercise in the Shield Gallery, but her retinue was noticeably reduced; Lady Castlemaine was among those who would not put in an appearance until at least noon.

Secretary Bulteel intercepted him before he could reach Clarendon's offices. 'I hoped you would come today,' he said, offering Chaloner one of a batch of aniseed-flavoured knot biscuits he had baked. 'I have something important to tell you.'

'Good,' said Chaloner. 'Because I still have no idea who killed Blue Dick, what the Dowager's cronies plan to do on Shrove Tuesday, or what those iconoclasts discuss when they meet.'

Bulteel grinned. To anyone who did not know him, it was a sinister expression, and explained why he did not have many friends. 'I may be able to help you with some of that. *And* I know why the Earl ordered you to investigate Blue Dick's death, when most of us think you would be better placed monitoring our enemies.'

'Yes?' prompted Chaloner, when the secretary paused, presumably for dramatic effect.

'All these things are connected.' Bulteel smiled again. 'I learned it from Spymaster Williamson, when I dined at his house last night.'

Chaloner blinked. 'Williamson asked you to his home *again*? Why?'

He had not meant to be rude, but Williamson was an elitist snob who despised anyone he considered his intellectual or social inferior – and he would see Bulteel as both. And why two invitations in a week? It was down-right suspicious! Moreover, Chaloner was disappointed in Bulteel for accepting them, thinking him too good for such sly company.

Bulteel looked hurt. 'He likes me. I supply him with information – something you told me was an acceptable thing to do – and we have become friends.'

'You have?' Chaloner's disappointment intensified, and he saw he would have to watch what he said in future. He doubted Bulteel would say anything to harm him deliberately, but the man was a novice in the world of espionage, and might let something slip inadvertently. It was a blow, because he liked Bulteel, and was beginning to trust him.

'*You* said it is natural for a Spymaster to have inform-ants in all government departments,' said Bulteel, distressed by Chaloner's obvious disapproval. 'And you said I should not worry about it.'

'Yes, but I did not recommend *fraternising* with him,' said Chaloner in distaste. 'You will never know if he is asking you friendly questions or plying you for information.'

'Well, he did not ply me last night,' said Bulteel defen-sively. 'Indeed, he was more interested in dispensing intelligence than getting it.'

And why would Williamson confide in Bulteel, thought Chaloner suspiciously, when he knew perfectly well what Bulteel would do with it? It made no sense. Unless . . .

'I do not suppose he wants Blue Dick's murder solved without being obliged to squander his own resources, does he? Or perhaps without soiling his hands? Some very influential people seem to be involved, ones he will not want as enemies.'

213

'You do him a disservice!' cried Bulteel, stung. 'He is not the villain you think, not once you come to know him.'

Chaloner doubted he would ever find out, because neither he nor Williamson had the slightest desire to become more closely acquainted.

'Tell me what Williamson said,' he suggested with a placatory smile. It was clear they were not going to agree, and he did not want to quarrel.

But Bulteel was seriously piqued, and for a moment, Chaloner thought he was going to refuse. Fortunately, the desire to share what he had learned was strong, and he began to speak eventually, albeit reluctantly.

'He believes that Blue Dick's murder and the Dowager's Shrove Tuesday plans are all part of the same case,' he began. 'You see, Lady Castlemaine, the Penderel brothers, Progers and Lord Bristol – all members of the Dowager's cabal – are Catholic. And they all hate the Earl, and have vowed to see him fall from grace.'

This was not news. 'I know. He has given them plenty of cause by supporting laws that make their religion all but illegal. However, I do not see what it has to do with Blue Dick.'

Bulteel smiled triumphantly. 'But Williamson and I do! You see, Blue Dick was murdered by the Dowager's cronies. As an iconoclast, he smashed their sacred images, which incurred their wrath. So they took measures to ensure he would never do it again.'

Chaloner regarded him doubtfully. The iconoclasts' time had come and gone, and there was nothing to suggest Blue Dick had intended to resume his activities.

'Do you have evidence for this, or is it supposition?' he asked.

214

'We have evidence,' said Bulteel. His expression was smug now he saw he had Chaloner's complete attention. 'Because there is a witness to Blue Dick's murder.'

'More than one,' muttered Chaloner, thinking *he* had been a witness, too, but had seen nothing to allow him to identify the killer.

'This witness saw the culprit lurking *before* the crime,' Bulteel went on. 'He watched him, because he thought his behaviour odd. He saw him approach Blue Dick, stab him and run away. He also saw a man – you, although he does not know it and neither does Williamson – give chase.'

'Do you or Williamson have a name for this witness?' asked Chaloner hopefully.

'Yes, we do. It is the dial-maker called Henry Phillippes.'

'I see,' mused Chaloner. Was it true, or was this Phillippes's way of deflecting suspicion from himself? Reluctantly – he was not happy about losing his prime suspect – Chaloner conceded that there *may* be truth in the tale. Phillippes lived on the Bridge, so perhaps he *had* noticed the masked assassin lurking as he gazed out of his window. However, it was curious that he had not mentioned it to anyone else. 'And who does he say is the murderer?'

Bulteel's smile verged on the gloating. 'A Penderel. But he cannot be sure which one.'

Chaloner thought about it. The man he saw stab Blue Dick *might* have been one of the brothers. It was not Rupert, who was too large, but it could have been Oliver, Neville or Edward.

'I see,' he said noncommittally, unwilling to let Bulteel – and by extension Williamson – know the intelligence might be useful; he did not want to be in the Spymaster's debt.

Bulteel grimaced at his lack of enthusiasm. 'Do you want me to tell you why the Earl ordered the murder investigated, when he should be more concerned with the arrangements for his Bishops' Dinner? I did not get *that* from Williamson – it is something I discovered all on my own.'

'I assume someone told him what Phillippes saw,' surmised Chaloner. 'Leigh, perhaps.'

Bulteel looked scornful. 'All Leigh cares about is the security arrangements for the Bishops' Dinner. *He* did not tell the Earl about the Penderel connection.'

'Then who did?' demanded Chaloner.

'No one,' said Bulteel, aggravatingly obtuse. 'The Earl saw something himself. Namely Edward Penderel just an hour after the murder, with blood on his hands.'

'He did not mention this to me,' said Chaloner, not sure whether to believe Bulteel.

'He did not mention it to me, either – I overheard him telling his wife. He was saying he wanted you to identify the culprit *independently* of his own testimony for two reasons. First, because he does not fancy being called as a witness in any trial that might ensue. And second, because his silence about what he saw means he cannot be accused of pointing you towards his enemies, thus blinding you to other possibilities.'

'Those are inane reasons!' Chaloner exploded. 'And I seriously doubt this will ever come to trial, anyway. Edward is the Dowager's man, and we all know the matter will be quietly swept under the carpet. The Court will not want people to know that some of its members are killers.'

Bulteel raised his hands defensively. 'Do not snap at me. I am merely passing you facts – that Phillippes has tentatively identified a Penderel as the murderer, and that the Earl saw a Penderel with blood on his hands not long after the crime. You can make of them what you will.'

Edward was missing, thought Chaloner, and his kinsmen did not know where he had gone. Had he committed murder and fled? Chaloner swore under his breath. Why did the Earl insist on playing these games? The case might have been solved days ago, had he deigned to confide.

Angry and frustrated, Chaloner knocked on Clarendon's door and entered his office. It was baking hot, as usual, and the Earl was sitting with one foot resting on a stool, a sure sign that the weather was exacerbating his gout. It was also a warning that he was likely to be irritable, and needed to be treated with additional care. Aware that telling him he was a blithering idiot whose absurd decisions had wasted time and put lives in danger would not be taken kindly, Chaloner reined in his temper.

'I hope you are not unwell, sir,' he said politely, gesturing to the foot.

The Earl grimaced. 'Gout is a terrible condition, and I would not wish it on my worst enemy. Well, I might make an exception for Bristol. I do not suppose you have learned his whereabouts, have you? I do not feel safe, thinking he might be close.'

'There are rumours that he is in England. You ordered me not to visit his London house in Great Queen Street, but it may be worth—'

'He will not be there! He is not stupid, and I forbid you to waste time watching it. There are far more important things for you to be doing. For example, my Bishops' Dinner is in less than a week, and I heard this morning that Gloucester can come. That means all of them will be here.'

'What do you want me to do?' asked Chaloner, supposing the Earl intended to pull him away from Blue Dick's murder and join Leigh in ensuring the event ran as smoothly as possible.

'I want you to do your job,' snapped the Earl. 'To foil any attempts to ruin the occasion. To watch Somerset House and expose any plots that are hatching. To locate Bristol. And to catch whoever murdered that wretched iconoclast. In that order. So far, you have done nothing useful.'

'I have made some headway on the latter, sir,' said Chaloner coolly. 'For example, I know a witness has identified a Penderel brother as the killer. Meanwhile, another witness claims to have seen Edward washing his blood-stained hands shortly after the crime was committed.'

The Earl regarded him warily. 'Good. Interview this first witness, but do not bother with the second. Edward will have an excuse for the state he was in, and the testimony will be irrelevant.'

'If you had mentioned earlier that you saw him smothered in blood not long after Blue Dick was killed, it would have saved a lot of time,' said Chaloner, unable to help himself. 'Now he is missing – fled probably – and it will be difficult to track him down.'

He knew he had spoken bluntly, and braced himself for a cutting reprimand. But it did not come, and for a long time, the Earl did nothing but stare at him. Uncomfortably, Chaloner wondered whether he had been insolent once too often, and the Earl was entertaining himself by devising different ways of telling him he was dismissed.

'I did not confide in you, because I wanted you to discover his guilt for yourself – independently of what I saw,' the Earl said eventually. 'He is the Dowager's creature, and everyone knows I loathe the lot of them, and would love to see them accused of a serious crime. *Ergo*, it was better for me to distance myself from it, to let you find evidence that did not include my testimony.'

Chaloner stared back at him. Was he telling the truth? He was usually good at knowing when people were lying, but the Earl was a politician, and so was almost impossible to read.

'So what do *you* believe, sir? *Did* Edward Penderel stab Blue Dick?'

The Earl nodded slowly. 'Yes, I think so. He is Catholic, with an open hatred of iconoclasts, and I saw him skulking with bloody hands within an hour of the murder. But no one would have believed me if I had announced what I saw – it would have been seen as an accusation made from spite.'

It was a sorry state of affairs, Chaloner thought, when politics prevented a senior member of a government from speaking out against a capital crime.

'You ordered me to start watching Blue Dick several days before he was killed,' he observed. 'Did you suspect there might be an attack of this nature, and—'

'That is a dreadful thing of which to accuse me!' interrupted the Earl indignantly. 'You think I predicted a man's life was in danger, but did nothing to warn him?'

Chaloner supposed he did think that. 'I am only wondering what led you to order him followed.'

The Earl's expression was cold. 'I ordered him followed because I am weary of fanatics. So, when Father Stephen told me that Blue Dick was meeting other like-minded

219

men, I was worried. I wanted to know what, if anything, they were planning.'

Chaloner supposed the explanation was plausible. Just. 'Who else knows you witnessed Edward with bloody hands?'

'No one!' The Earl was appalled by the notion. 'The only person I have told is my wife. I cannot imagine how *you* come to be party to it, and I am shocked that you are.'

Chaloner was not about to tell him that Bulteel was responsible for that. 'Will you describe what you saw?'

The Earl took a deep, shuddering breath. 'I went to visit my friend Bishop Morley in Winchester Palace. Unfortunately, he was out, but his manservant insisted that I rest by the fire before going home again. I accepted the hospitality, and was gazing idly out into the courtyard, when I saw Edward, cleaning his hands in the fountain there.'

'Edward was washing in a prelate's garden?' asked Chaloner warily. It did not sound very likely.

'The fountain runs with clean water,' explained the Earl. 'And it is secluded, especially if you know the owner of the house is out. It is the perfect place to scrub off. He did not see me, and I hid behind the curtains the moment I realised what he was doing.'

Chaloner suspected he had been wise to stay out of sight. He considered the tale. Winchester Palace was not far from the Bridge, so it was certainly possible that Edward had stabbed Blue Dick, run to his associates in St Mary Overie, then stopped to scour his hands after he and his cronies had escaped from their encounter with him and Leigh. He thought about the masked men: did they include the other Penderel brothers, or had Edward acted independently? But no matter how carefully he reviewed the brief but intense battle in the church, there was nothing to provide him with answers regarding the warriors' identity.

The Earl rubbed his eyes. 'I hope what I saw does not become common gossip, because his brothers might take umbrage. You had better send for Leigh, to protect me.'

'I will stay with you,' offered Chaloner.

'No. I need you to pursue your other enquiries.'

Chaloner nodded, then turned to another matter. 'I understand you discovered that Sir John Winter has asked the Master of Ordnance for some gunpowder – although the request is innocent, because he wants it to make the Dowager's fireworks. But would you mind telling me how you came by the information?'

'God's blood, Chaloner!' cried the Earl. 'Is nothing I do secret from you? And yes, I *do* mind revealing my sources. It will be safer for them if I keep the matter to myself.'

'As you wish, sir,' said Chaloner stiffly, wishing the man was a better judge of what should be kept private and what should be shared. He supposed it came of the Earl hiring an intelligencer he did not really trust. The Earl glared at him for a moment, but then the expression softened a little.

'Incidentally, I did not believe Leigh's tale,' he said.

'What tale, sir?'

'About you throwing yourself off the Bridge. Hannah told me today that you will be married soon, so I imagine you are the happiest man alive. You have no reason to kill yourself.'

'No,' agreed Chaloner.

'I want you to go to Somerset House on Saturday night,' said the Earl, when Chaloner made no other comment. 'The Dowager is holding a soiree, and I have a feeling they intend to discuss their plans to spoil my Bishops' Dinner. You will have to break in, as you did last time, although please take care not to be caught. If you are, you must lie – say you work for someone else.'

Chaloner regarded him askance. Most of the Dowager's friends knew exactly who he was, so lying would be futile. Moreover, Somerset House would have tightened its security after the last incident, and breaking in would not be easy. He could do it, but the risk of capture – and subsequent embarrassment for the Earl – would be enormous. Then he recalled Hannah telling him she had been asked to Somerset House on Saturday night, and relaxed. Hannah was not going to be invited to take part in plots to spoil ecclesiastical repasts.

'I do not think that particular gathering will—' he began.

'I do not care what you think,' snapped the Earl peevishly. 'You will go.'

Chaloner frowned. He accepted that the Earl had good reason to be concerned about Somerset House soirees so close to his dinner, but that was no excuse for recklessness. 'It is a bad idea to—'

'*You will go*,' repeated the Earl vehemently. 'That is a direct order. If you disobey it, you can look for a new post. And the moment you have finished your duties in Somerset House, you will come to tell me what you have learned. Do you understand?'

Chaloner nodded, wondering why he should be so insistent. But the Earl waved a hand to indicate he was dismissed, so he turned and walked away, unhappy and full of questions.

*   *   *

Chaloner had two people to interview as a matter of urgency: Phillippes and Edward Penderel. He was distinctly more uneasy about Phillippes, lest he was recognised as the man who had been chased out of Chapel House. He did not think the dial-maker had seen his face, but decided to take a gun with him when he went, anyway. He disliked firearms, because they were heavy and unpredictable, but not carrying one would put him at a serious disadvantage.

To postpone what would probably be a trying confrontation, he decided to tackle Edward first.

He knew Rupert, Neville and Oliver would not be at their Tothill Street home, because they were taking the Dowager to Winchester Palace, so he picked the lock on their front door, and let himself in. He did not seriously expect to find Edward hiding there, but it would be remiss not to check.

The house was even more unkempt than the last time he had broken in, and he was disgusted by the squalor. He was not the most assiduous of housekeepers himself, but he did not leave dirty dishes until they turned hairy with mould, or toss soiled laundry into corners until it reeked.

He found several notes the brothers had left for each other, which told him they had been searching hard for Edward. Oliver had been trawling taverns, Neville had looked in brothels, while Rupert made enquires at Court. The scribbled messages told Chaloner that they genuinely had no idea where he might have gone.

Disappointed, he left, stopping at Fetter Lane to collect a handgun he had acquired during a previous investigation. It was not a very good one, and he had not used it in weeks, so he spent a few moments with an oily rag, cleaning its moving parts. Then he loaded it and tucked it into his belt, hoping the thing would not go off of its own accord and emasculate him.

He walked to the Bridge, and found Phillippes not in his rooms, but fiddling with a box that was attached to some wooden railings outside. Several wires emerged from the bottom of it, disappearing into the water below. Hussey was watching him, accompanied by five of his fat children. Chaloner edged closer. The brats were making a nuisance of themselves by poking the mechanism, and Phillippes was distracted by them. This was good, because it meant Chaloner was less likely to be noticed as he eavesdropped.

'I told Scarlet to be here,' Hussey was saying irritably. 'But he did not arrive for work again this morning. Still, I suppose it is understandable, under the circumstances. What can you tell me?'

'Yesterday's tide was unusually low,' replied Phillippes, studying his equipment. 'But the one on Monday was peculiarly high. Perhaps the rumours are right, and they *are* an omen of evil to come.'

'Never mind that,' declared Hussey worriedly. 'What about shipping?'

'Shipping?' echoed Phillippes, swivelling around to regard him askance.

'Yes, shipping. Boats' captains might lose control in turbulent water, and collide with the Bridge. It could cause untold damage. Robert! Stop that at once! It is not genteel.'

The last remarks were bellowed at a volume that brought the entire street to a standstill, and caused the hapless Robert to blush to the roots of his hair. Then Hussey strode away, his face full of concern over Phillippes's news, leaving his brats to waddle after him.

'When I see his brood, it makes me glad I am childless,' remarked Phillippes to Chaloner, who was pretending to stroll past. The dial-maker did not seem to recognise him as an adversary, so Chaloner stopped to talk. He kept his hand firmly on the gun, though, ready to pull it out.

'He does have rather a lot of them.'

'Dozens,' agreed Phillippes. 'All extremely large. Are you here to ask about the Lord Chancellor's tide-ring? If so, you can tell him it will be ready in a week. The extra money he gave me made all the difference.'

'Extra money?' Could this be the source of the sudden wealth Sarah Tyus had talked about?

Phillippes nodded. 'It served to focus my mind, and allowed me to bribe certain craftsmen.'

'I am sure he will be pleased. But I wonder if you might help him another way.' Chaloner took a deep breath and plunged on, deciding the time for games was over. 'He has asked me to look into Blue Dick Culmer's murder, and wonders whether you might know anything about the culprit. He will be very grateful for any intelligence. And he has connections to the Royal Society.'

Phillippes eyed him intently. 'You think he might get me elected?'

'He is an influential man.' Chaloner leaned against the railing and looked at the swirling brown water below. A drowned cat had been washed up, and gulls were squabbling over the carcass.

'I saw the crime with my own eyes,' declared Phillippes. 'And I reported it to Spymaster Williamson, who ordered me not to discuss it with anyone else. However, if the Earl can arrange my membership of the Royal Society, I shall tell you anything he wants to know.'

'How did you come to witness the attack?'

'I was reading in my rooms, when I happened to glance out of the window. I saw a man lurking near the cockle stall. His hat and face-scarf told me he meant to disguise himself, and that aroused my suspicions. So I stopped work and watched him.'

'Did you think he might commit murder?'

'Of course not, or I would have stopped him. To be honest, I thought he was just going to steal some cockles. He hovered for about an hour. Unfortunately for him, the wind took his hat off at one point, and I saw part of his face. He was a Penderel brother.'

'Which one?'

'Now there I cannot help you, because they all look the same to me. Anyway, suddenly, he became taut and watchful. Then, in the flash of an eye, he had leapt forward and driven his knife into Blue Dick Culmer. I saw a fellow give chase, but Penderel had too great a lead on him.'

'How did you recognise Blue Dick? Did you know him?'

'I most certainly did not! I only learned later that he was the iconoclast who had ravaged Canterbury Cathedral. Personally, I cannot find it in my heart to feel sorry for him, but murder is murder, and the culprit should answer for his crime.'

'Indeed,' said Chaloner, noting that Phillippes looked away when he spoke his sanctimonious words. 'I heard Blue Dick visited Chapel House shortly before—'

'I doubt it,' said Phillippes briskly. 'It is empty at the moment, because it is being renovated. But that is all I can tell you about the murder, I am afraid. Is it enough to satisfy Clarendon? When can I expect my invitation from the Royal Society?'

'Why is the house being restored?' asked Chaloner. 'It does not look shabbier than—'

'I have no idea,' said Phillippes impatiently. 'Perhaps it suffers from dry rot or rising damp. I would not know, because I have never been inside.'

'Have you not?' asked Chaloner, sensing he was going too far but persisting anyway. 'I wish I had. There is a tale that gold is buried in its cellars. Do you think it is true?'

Phillippes's head came up sharply. 'Who told you that?'

Chaloner shrugged. 'White Hall is always full of rumours.'

'Of course,' said Phillippes, although there was a glitter of suspicion in his eyes, and Chaloner knew he would get no more out of the man. At least, not without coercion. But a busy thoroughfare was no place to shove a knife against the dial-maker's throat and demand to know what he had been doing in Chapel House two nights before.

Chapter 7

Frustrated that he had been unable to exact more information from Phillippes, Chaloner went to the Bear tavern to consider what he *had* learned. He was inclined to believe Phillippes's testimony regarding Blue Dick, because his description of the killer's clothing and demeanour matched what he has witnessed himself. So that, combined with what the Earl had seen, meant Edward probably had stabbed Blue Dick. And Thurloe had been right about Kaltoff's drawing – even if it did depict Blue Dick, it meant nothing other than that Kaltoff had thought him a good subject to caricature.

He rubbed his chin. So Phillippes – and Kaltoff by extension – were innocent of Blue Dick's murder, and it was for some other business that they had not wanted to be watched in the Beggar's Bush. Was it the gold in Chapel House? He recalled Phillippes's words to Kaltoff: 'you know what is at stake' and 'you know what we stand to lose, should we be found out'. He might well have been referring to the discovery of a fortune, and his nervousness derived from that fact that the Dowager was probably after the same thing. In other words, he did not want her to know that he and Kaltoff intended to have it first.

Thoughts of Chapel House led Chaloner to consider Junior Warden Scarlet and Jane. Was treasure the reason the Dowager had ordered the building's refurbishment, obliging them to take lodgings elsewhere? Did the couple know what was in their home, and Jane had been assaulted because they refused to share the secret?

Knowing he had been remiss in not speaking to Scarlet sooner, Chaloner left the tavern, and headed for Bridge House. But his journey was in vain, because not only was Scarlet not at his place of work, he was not at home, either – Hussey had sent a servant to find out why he had failed to arrive that morning. No one knew where he was, although Chaloner learned from the Bridge clerks that the hapless man had taken to wandering off alone since the attack on his wife.

Feeling the need to discuss the case with someone whose opinion he valued more than any other, Chaloner headed for Lincoln's Inn and Thurloe. He nodded a friendly greeting to the porter on the gate, then made his way to Chamber XIII.

He loved the ex-Spymaster's rooms. They overlooked a pretty yard called Dial Court, and had a familiar, comforting odour of beeswax and wood smoke. Full of oak panels, sturdy furniture and books, they were the one place in London that Chaloner felt truly safe.

He knocked on the door, but Thurloe took a long time to answer, and when he did, he opened it only a crack. The ex-Spymaster's face was flushed, and he had abandoned his customary sober browns for a suit of pale blue. Usually, he preferred the simpler styles of the Commonwealth, but that day, his falling band boasted an impressive amount of frill, and the lace at his cuffs was pure elegance. Chaloner had never seen him looking so debonair, and found himself at a loss for words.

'Have you come to tell me who killed Blue Dick?' whispered Thurloe, glancing furtively behind him. 'Or the identities of the masked men you fought in St Mary Overie?'

'No,' replied Chaloner, rather taken aback by the bald questions. 'I came to ask—'

'Then not now, Tom,' interrupted Thurloe softly. 'I am indisposed.'

Chaloner frowned. 'You mean you are unwell?'

Thurloe lowered his voice further still. 'I mean I am unavailable.'

He started to close the door, but Chaloner stopped him, alarmed. 'What is wrong?'

'Please go,' said Thurloe in a low but firm voice. 'I am busy.'

'You can spare me a moment,' insisted Chaloner, easing to one side to see whether someone had a knife to Thurloe's ribs. He could not think of another reason why his friend should refuse to let him in. But no one was there. 'I need to know whether you have decoded those ciphers.'

'Not yet,' replied Thurloe, trying to close the door a second time. He sighed when Chaloner inserted his foot. 'I will send word when I have something. But now you must excuse—'

Chaloner took the bull by the horns. 'You met Herring the iconoclast in Rider's Coffee House, where you were seen by a reliable witness. Are you insane?'

Thurloe regarded him coolly. 'We have already discussed

230

this, Thomas. I told you: I shall do as my conscience dictates. Besides, I decline to talk about it with you.'

Chaloner was dismayed that the ex-Spymaster had not immediately offered an explanation that would justify what he had done. 'I cannot stand by while you indulge yourself in a rebellion that will almost certainly fail,' he cried. 'And that may see you executed as a traitor.'

Thurloe winced at the volume of his voice. 'Please, Thomas! There is no need to bawl. And while I appreciate your care for my wellbeing, I assure you, it is quite unnecessary.'

Chaloner had excellent hearing, and he stiffened when he detected a rustle from within. Someone *was* there! Was it Herring, or someone else associated with the upsurge of Thurloe's 'displeased majority'? Or had the ex-Spymaster's chambers been invaded by enemies, who had ordered him to be rid of whoever came knocking so inconveniently?

Before Thurloe could stop him, Chaloner shoved open the door and dashed into the room, sword in one hand and dag in the other. And then he stopped dead in his tracks. There was a visitor, and she was sitting by the fire.

Chaloner gaped in astonishment. Lady Castlemaine was the last person he would have expected to see in Thurloe's chambers. As a Puritan, the ex-Spymaster deplored the immorality the King's mistress brought to the Court, while she would have no time for disgraced Commonwealth ministers. She squealed her alarm when she found herself looking down the barrel of a gun. Chaloner glanced around quickly, ascertained she was alone, and lowered his weapons, thoughts reeling in utter confusion.

When she saw she was not going to be shot, the Lady leaned back in her chair, laced her fingers together and looked Chaloner up and down. She had made some effort to disguise herself, by donning a thick cloak and a veil, but even these unflattering garments could not hide the fact that she was a very beautiful woman. Loyally, though, Chaloner decided she could not hold a candle to Hannah, especially when the hard eyes and sly mouth were taken into account.

'I have seen you before,' she said, licking her lips. 'At White Hall. Who are you?'

'I work in the Accompting House,' lied Chaloner, selecting the most tedious occupation he could think of, in the hope that it would prevent her from asking questions about it.

'Is that so? Do all accompters burst into the rooms of ex-spymasters with drawn weapons, then?'

'Like many dutiful Royalists, he likes to amuse himself at the expense of hapless old Roundheads,' explained Thurloe tightly. He turned to Chaloner with a pained expression, making it clear that his friend had seriously overstepped the mark. 'Now please leave.'

'Please stay,' countered Lady Castlemaine, eyeing Chaloner from under her lashes. It made her look wanton. 'John and I are discussing the Clarendon Code, a most wicked piece of mischief.'

'*John?*' echoed Chaloner, scarcely believing his ears. Even he did not address Thurloe with such familiarity. 'And the Clarendon Code is hardly a suitable subject for—'

'John makes no secret of his disdain for it,' interrupted Lady Castlemaine, clearly enjoying his discomfiture. 'He denounces it in coffee houses and—'

'He does not,' declared Chaloner hotly. 'He gave up

232

politics when the Commonwealth fell, and spends his time . . .' How *did* Thurloe spend his time? Chaloner realised he was not exactly sure.

'No one gives up politics in London,' said the Lady, favouring him with a slow, lazy smirk. 'It would be like giving up air. But join us by the fire, and prepare to have your eyes opened in a way you never imagined possible.'

Chaloner was not sure he liked the sound of that, and saw there was nothing for it but to bow to her and take his leave. Thurloe accompanied him to the door.

'I am sorry,' Chaloner said, as he was ushered out. 'I thought there was someone inside with a gun to your head. I was trying to—'

'If there had been, your dramatics would have seen my brains spattered across half of Lincoln's Inn,' Thurloe remarked drily. 'Besides, do I *look* as if I need your help?'

'Well, no,' admitted Chaloner uncomfortably. 'Are you . . .'

He hesitated, not sure how to phrase the question. He had always assumed Thurloe was faithful to his wife, not only because of his religious principles, but because he loved her. And yet Chaloner had always been surprised that he should spend so much time in London while Ann stayed in Oxfordshire. However, to pick the King's mistress for a dalliance was rash, to say the least.

'Hurry up, John,' came Lady Castlemaine's sultry voice. 'I am bored on my own. Either send the fellow away, or let him come back and entertain me. He looks like a man who—'

'Go,' ordered Thurloe, elbowing Chaloner through the door. 'And the next time you come, perhaps you might wait for an invitation before bursting in.'

* * *

Mind reeling, Chaloner left Lincoln's Inn. It was dusk, and he wanted nothing more than to be with Hannah. As he passed the Penderel brothers' house, he heard raised voices, although the words were too muffled to make out. He was tempted to keep walking – he had had enough for one day – but his sense of duty prevailed. He knocked on the door, thinking that although he had already ascertained that they did not know Edward's whereabouts, they still might be able to tell him *why* their brother had killed Blue Dick. And whether they were among the masked men at St Mary Overie.

He jumped back smartly when the door was whipped open. Rupert, the oldest and biggest, held a sword in one hand and a dagger in the other. He peered at Chaloner.

'The Earl of Clarendon's henchman,' he said in distaste. 'My brothers and I did not recognise you earlier today when Progers took a tumble, or we might have run you through for your poor choice of masters. What do you want?'

'Edward was seen with bloodstained hands shortly after a murder,' said Chaloner, deciding on a blunt approach. 'In the gardens of Winchester Palace. And there is a witness who saw him commit the crime. I would like to hear Edward's side of the story.'

For a moment, Rupert did nothing but stare. Then he stood aside, and indicated Chaloner was to enter the house. Chaloner hesitated, although he understood why Rupert was loath to discuss such a matter in the street. Reluctantly, he stepped inside, then watched uneasily as Oliver and Neville approached from the kitchen, trapping him between them. He rested his hand on the butt of his gun, but did not draw it, preferring to see what he could learn peaceably before resorting to violence.

'You want Edward's side of the story?' demanded Oliver, scarred hands clenched into angry fists at his sides. 'Well, here it is: he is innocent.'

'Right,' said Chaloner. 'But I think the courts will need a little more than that to convince them.'

'Spymaster Williamson sent one of his creatures to see us last night,' snarled Oliver. 'Swaddell. He told us there was a witness in the form of Phillippes the dial-maker. But Phillippes is lying.'

'Why would he do that?' asked Chaloner quietly.

'For many reasons,' replied Rupert, gesturing that Oliver was to leave him to do the talking. 'Perhaps he was paid to lie – the Dowager likes us, because our brave cousins helped the King escape all those years ago, but some folk are jealous of her affection for us. Then there is a tale that one of us intends to marry her, which we cannot do if the family is discredited. Take your pick.'

But Neville was more astute than his older brothers. He narrowed his eyes as he considered what Chaloner had said. 'Swaddell did not mention that Edward was seen with bloodstained hands. That means there is a *second* witness. Who is it?'

'Yes, who?' demanded Oliver, drawing a knife. 'Then we can pay *him* a visit, and teach *him* what happens to those who fabricate nasty tales about the Penderels.'

'Wait,' ordered Rupert, raising a hand to prevent Oliver from lunging. 'Our visitor might volunteer the information willingly – there may be no need for further bloodshed.'

'*Further* bloodshed?' echoed Chaloner. The dagger from his sleeve was in the palm of one hand, while the fingers

235

of the other gripped the dag. Oliver would come nowhere near him.

'Swaddell,' explained Rupert. '*He* will make no more vile, spiteful accusations to slander Edward's good name. Oliver saw to that. He trounced him thoroughly.'

Chaloner was astounded. Swaddell was Williamson's best agent, a vicious, efficient assassin, who would not have been easy to overcome.

'If you did assault Swaddell, there will be trouble,' he said warningly. 'Williamson has a long memory, and access to criminals who will kill anyone for a shilling.'

'We can best any of them,' bragged Oliver confidently.

'No, we cannot,' said young Neville. He shrugged when Oliver regarded him in surprise. 'We know how to wield an honest sword, but we are no match for the kind of villain *he* is talking about. We should leave London, as I have been telling you this last hour. I said from the start that it was not a good idea to come here, and I was right. Let us go, while we still can.'

'Not without Edward,' said Rupert. 'Besides, there is more to be had from White Hall yet.'

Chaloner was disgusted by his brazen rapacity. 'If your brother is innocent, he will not prove it by hiding. He needs to tell the authorities his version—'

'He has been missing since Sunday,' interrupted Neville shortly. 'We do not know where he is. I only wish we did, because we are worried sick!'

'So we shall have the name of your second witness,' said Oliver, fingering his dagger threateningly. 'Perhaps he knows Edward's whereabouts.'

'He does not, because it is me,' said Chaloner, loath for them to guess it was the Earl. 'I saw Blue Dick murdered, and I followed the culprit to St Mary Overie,

236

where he met with six others. I fought them, but they escaped.'

'Well, it was not us,' said Oliver dangerously.

'Then help me find the truth,' urged Chaloner. 'Tell me who might benefit from seeing Edward – and perhaps the rest of you, too – implicated in a capital crime.'

There was an uncomfortable exchange of glances, then Rupert indicated Oliver was to sheath his dagger. Oliver glowered, making it clear he thought his brothers were making a mistake by talking to the Earl's man, but he lowered the weapon. He did not put it away, however.

'We have so many enemies that I barely know where to start,' Neville began, and the expression on his face said he was appalled by the situation in which he found himself. 'We are hated for our Catholicism *and* for the favour the Dowager shows us.'

'Then who are your friends?' asked Chaloner, coming at the problem from another angle. In White Hall, not everyone who smiled was an ally, something the brothers had yet to learn.

'We have lots,' declared Oliver sullenly. 'The most important being the King.'

But Neville shook his head. 'He found us amusing at first, because he likes to recount the tale of his escape after the Battle of Worcester. But we were not the ones who helped him, and he is disappointed when we cannot supply the details he has forgotten.'

'Perhaps so,' acknowledged Rupert reluctantly. 'But what about Buckingham, Progers and Lady Castlemaine? They are great companions, and we are always carousing with them.'

'They tolerate us,' said Neville flatly. 'But I think it is time we cut our losses and left. God only knows what has happened to Edward, but I do not want to be the next to disappear.'

'He will turn up,' said Oliver, although he did not sound convinced. 'And why should we leave when our pockets are only half-full? If we go now, we will spend the rest of our lives regretting it.'

'Besides,' added Rupert, 'we are not going anywhere until we find Edward.'

'Find him *where*?' cried Neville, exasperated. 'He would not go away without sending us word, so something terrible has happened to him. It pains me to say it, but he is dead. They needed a scapegoat for Blue Dick, and he fitted the bill.'

'But what about his bloody hands?' asked Chaloner. 'What explanation can you offer for that?'

'Perhaps he had been cockfighting,' suggested Rupert lamely. 'Or he cut himself. There are all kinds of explanations.'

Oliver bristled when he saw Chaloner's doubtful expression. 'You are not here to help Edward! You are here to damage him – and damage us, too. And I will not let that happen.'

Chaloner drew his gun before the man could reach him. 'You had better stand back.'

Unfortunately, Oliver was too stupid to know when he was overmatched. He lurched forward anyway, and Chaloner was obliged to resort to gutter tactics to avoid shooting him. He waited until Oliver had closed, then kicked him in the shins, cracking the butt of the gun on his head when he doubled over. Oliver dropped to the floor, stunned.

'If you have any sense, you will do what Neville recommends,' said Chaloner, backing away before the other two could come at him. 'And leave London before you are dragged any deeper into whatever is fermenting here.'

Once outside, Chaloner resumed his journey to Hannah's house. He had learned little from his confrontation with the Penderels, although he suspected that he had probably just increased the number of men who meant him harm. He thought about their claims as he walked. Their explanation for Edward's bloody hands was feeble, to say the least, and he was much more inclined to believe the testimonies of Phillippes and the Earl. Had Edward acted independently of his brothers, then, and killed Blue Dick without telling them? Chaloner sighed: he really had no idea.

When he arrived at Hannah's house, he found her reading poetry by the fire. The book was one of his own – one of two mementos he had from his dead wife. The other was a cracked mirror he could not bring himself to throw away.

'John Donne,' explained Hannah, indicating the tome. 'The Duke suggested I might like it.'

'And do you?' asked Chaloner. He was not sure how he felt about her using Aletta's book. It caused a sudden surge of emotions that he could not begin to understand.

Hannah grimaced. 'Not really. It is rather turgid, to be frank. But never mind that. You sneaked out this morning without saying a word. Why?'

Her voice had turned accusing, and the way she folded her arms told Chaloner that he was in trouble. He frowned in confusion. Sneaking out was something he did on a regular basis, because of the odd hours he kept.

'You expected me to wake you? But I left very early.'

'Very early on the day after we had agreed to marry,'

retorted Hannah coolly. 'I expected to see you when I opened my eyes.'

'Oh.' Chaloner was not sure why this should make any difference. He smiled, in an effort to placate her. 'Then tomorrow, I shall wake you long before dawn.'

He winced. It was not quite what he had intended to say, and had sounded rather threatening. He opened his mouth to rephrase it, to assure her that he would not leave without saying goodbye in future if that was what she wanted, but she chose that moment to toss the book on the floor, and the words did not come.

'You plan to leave before dawn?' she demanded, hands on hips. 'Why? What can possibly be happening at such an hour? Most people – normal, sane, decent people – are in bed then.'

'Exactly,' said Chaloner. 'I do not deal with "normal, sane, decent people" much of the time.'

'Well, you will not tonight, and that is for sure,' said Hannah grimly. 'Because you must go to Somerset House.'

Chaloner frowned. 'Must I? I was hoping to spend the evening with you. Did the Earl send—'

'No,' said Hannah, cutting him off. 'That villain knows better than to leave messages with me ordering you on dubious assignments. This is something *I* have decided you must do.'

Chaloner stared at her. 'I do not understand. You know Somerset House is full of the Earl's enemies. Why would you encourage me to visit a place that might be dangerous?'

Hannah flinched. 'Your Earl assures me that you have a unique talent for entering perilous places and escaping unscathed. I let myself believe him, because otherwise

I would spend all my time worrying. Please do not tell me he is wrong.'

'He is not wrong. But why do you want me to go to Somerset House?'

'Because today, I overheard those Penderel louts telling Lady Castlemaine that there was to be a meeting there tonight, to discuss the Dowager's plans for Shrove Tuesday.' Hannah swallowed hard and looked away. 'When the Lady informed them that she was not interested in which bakers and musicians they had poached from the Earl, Rupert told her he meant the *other* plans.'

'What other plans?'

'He did not need to elaborate, because she understood his meaning immediately. But there was an expression on her face, Tom!' Hannah came to take his hands, and he saw tears glittering. 'It was sly and vengeful, and I *know* it bodes ill. And Catholics will be blamed for whatever she is doing, because it will come from Somerset House – from the home of the King's papist mother.'

'That is probably true, but—'

'Can you not see what will happen?' The tears began to fall in earnest. 'If they perpetrate some mischief that sees your Earl and his bishops insulted, there will be a terrible backlash. But it will not be the Somerset House Catholics who will bear the brunt of the mob's fury. It will be normal folk – like your tailor, the family who live by the King's Theatre, and the man who bakes our bread.'

'And you have no idea what these "other plans" might be? You have heard no rumours?'

'Not specifically. But there are tales of iconoclasts gathering, and that White Hall's wild ways are beginning to cause resentment among the people. I fear rebellion, Tom.

And if that happens, we will all be the losers. None of us want more civil war.'

'No,' agreed Chaloner, coils of unease writhing in his stomach when he recalled that it was not only iconoclasts who were massing, but dangerous men like Will Goff and Lord Bristol. 'Did the Penderels give a time for this gathering?'

Hannah nodded. 'Ten o'clock. I was about to write a note to the Duke, warning him to stay away. He is a good man, and if he is involved in this matter, it will be because he does not understand the consequences.'

'If you do that, it will warn them that they are discovered, and it will be virtually impossible to learn what they intend to do. Send no letters. Buckingham knows how to look after himself.'

And, Chaloner thought but did not say as he took his leave, the Duke would know *exactly* what he was doing. He applauded her loyalty to a man she liked, but if there was mischief afoot in Somerset House, then it could be guaranteed that Buckingham would be at the heart of it.

Somerset House was ablaze with lights when Chaloner reached it, and the gardens were full of men carrying pitch torches. He swore under his breath when he saw the level to which security had been increased following his invasion five nights before. It would not make slipping inside easy, although he knew he could do it. He had, after all, invaded far more secure places in the past.

He was just reviewing his options when a carriage arrived, and every guard paid it minute attention when it transpired to carry a rather scantily clad Lady Castlemaine. Buckingham was with her, and was drunk enough to stagger when he handed her down the coach steps. The lurch caused her bodice to slip, and while the guards gazed admiringly at the resulting display, Chaloner took the opportunity to slip through the gate and dart towards the house.

Fortunately, an ancient oak threw its shadows across one of the windows overlooking the Great Chamber, and they concealed him nicely. Through a chink in the curtains, he could see inside, although listening was more difficult. He was reluctant to break in though, especially as he was under orders to do it again on Saturday, so he resigned himself to learning what he could from outside.

He could see the Dowager pacing back and forth, her lapdog scurrying at her heels. Progers, Luckin and Father Stephen were doing the same, and Chaloner grinned, thinking the sight an amusing one. The Dowager was agitated, and her cronies were trying to calm her. The Capuchin friars stood in a grey-robed huddle nearby, looking acutely uncomfortable. She was shouting very loudly, and he soon learned that the reason for her vexation was that they had failed to poach the Earl's baker.

Then the Penderel brothers arrived. They were still minus Edward, and Oliver was in a foul mood. He swore at one of the guards, then aimed a kick at the Dowager's pooch. Immediately, the two Frenchmen appeared and wrestled him against a wall. He nodded sullenly to their muttered warnings, and tried to shake himself free. They let him go eventually, although they continued to watch him for some time after. Meanwhile, Neville was pale and anxious-eyed, while Rupert's expression was impassive. Chaloner tensed when Rupert and Luckin abandoned the main party and strolled towards his window.

'It will be worth the wait,' he heard Luckin say to

Rupert as they sat down together. 'The Dowager grumbles and groans at the passing time, but when our plans come to fruition, all England will reel with the enormity of it. Shrove Tuesday will be remembered for centuries to come.'

'If you say so,' Rupert replied. He looked sullen. 'Will you tell me what you mean to do, exactly? All this secrecy is beginning to be annoying.'

Luckin laughed. 'You are better off in the dark. But all will be revealed in time. Our enemies will not know what has hit them, and they will crumble away like old bones.'

At that moment, Winter exploded into the company like one of his fireworks, moustache bristling with good humour. Behind him were Phillippes and Kaltoff. Phillippes looked completely at home, elegant in a fashionable silk jacket, while Kaltoff wore a long-coat with far too much lace, and his wig was overly ostentatious.

The Dowager beckoned the dial-makers towards her, and engaged them in conversation. Phillippes began muttering in her ear, but it was clear that she did not like what she was hearing. Her face hardened, and her eyes took on the quality of gimlets. Kaltoff backed away, although Phillippes held his ground. He continued speaking, and eventually, he seemed to have mollified her. When she finally smiled, Kaltoff mopped his forehead with his sleeve, clearly relieved.

Meanwhile, Winter set about entertaining the company with a lute he had brought with him. He played for a while, then Luckin was called upon to take over. The vicar demurred, purple nose flushed with embarrassment, but capitulated when the Dowager appeared to inform him that he would oblige or experience her displeasure. Chaloner could hear Winter sing, because the man had a strong voice, but he could not hear the lute. However, judging by the rapturous applause that followed, he supposed it must have been good. Encouraged, Luckin began another piece.

After a while, the party settled down to supper. The Dowager sat at one table, with Buckingham, Progers, the Lady and Father Stephen. The Penderels and a number of lesser courtiers, including Winter, Luckin, Phillippes and Kaltoff, were at another. Once they began eating, the outside guards relaxed. They gathered together in small knots, and little flames flared as pipes were lit.

Chaloner did his best to follow the ensuing conversations by reading the diners' lips, but no one seemed to be discussing anything contentious. The Dowager continued to hold forth about her minions' failure to steal Clarendon's baker, and Luckin dominated the other table with a detailed and indignant account of his time in the Tower. Lady Castlemaine, who had been alert and excited when she had arrived, had settled into a sullen slouch that indicated boredom, and the glances she kept shooting at the Penderels said she thought she had been misled. At one point, Rupert shrugged helplessly at her.

Chaloner was growing exasperated when he heard a sharp snap followed by a muffled curse. He tensed. Someone was creeping towards his tree. The person wore a black cloak and a large hat – clearly a disguise – and moved clumsily, like a pig trying to tiptoe. Was it an enemy of the Dowager, which might mean a friend to the Earl? Silently, Chaloner eased behind the oak, and watched as the fellow reached the window and put his eye to the chink in the curtain. Chaloner waited for a few moments, then stepped forward, wrapping one arm around the newcomer's neck and putting the other across his mouth to prevent him from shouting out.

His captive struggled violently, and Chaloner was hard-pressed to keep hold of him. The man was not tall, but he was powerful, with wide shoulders and muscular arms, and he flailed furiously. Chaloner began to worry that he might give them both away to the guards.

'Quiet!' he hissed angrily. 'Or I will cut your throat.'

Something in his voice convinced his prisoner that the threat was genuine, because he went rigid. When Chaloner was sure he was under control, he removed his hand from the man's mouth.

'What do you want?' the fellow whispered immediately. 'Who are you?'

'Who are *you*?' countered Chaloner. He shifted his grip, so he could see the man's face in the faint light from the window. He recognised the crossed eyes instantly.

'I am the churchwarden of St Mary Woolchurch,' replied Herring. 'And a loyal servant of the King.'

'And an iconoclast,' added Chaloner tartly.

'I may have been one of those in my youth,' acknowledged Herring. 'But maturity has moderated my opinions. I am a different man now.'

'A different man who invades the King's mother's garden in the dead of night?'

'My activities are none of your affair. But we have met before, because I recognise your voice. You are the one who followed me after that puppet show in Charing Cross. My colleague caught you, but you managed to escape. What are you doing here?'

'Who was he? Your colleague?'

246

Herring's head went up defiantly. 'I shall never reveal that.'

'Then tell me about Blue Dick instead. He was a friend of yours. And now he is dead.'

'Murdered,' agreed Herring. 'But he was not my friend, because he was an extremist who continued to believe that smashing statues was a good thing. His death is no tragedy.'

'Did you kill him?'

Herring tried to turn and look at him, but Chaloner made sure his face remained in shadow.

'No, I did not,' Herring snapped, annoyed that he could not identify his captor. 'I have not taken a life in a very long time. However, that will change if you do not release me.'

'When were you last at St Mary Overie?' Chaloner was grasping at straws – he had no idea whether Herring had been one of the masked men in Southwark, but there was no harm in asking.

'I am saying nothing else,' declared Herring haughtily. 'Kill me if you must, but bear in mind that my murder *will* be avenged. You will never sleep soundly again, because my friends will find you.'

'Tell me why are you here,' ordered Chaloner. 'And then I will let you go.'

'I shall tell you nothing,' hissed Herring. 'Our discussion is over.'

Chaloner could tell by the rigid set of Herring's body that he meant it, and that he expected to be knifed for his lack of cooperation. That he was prepared to throw away his life for whatever cause he was currently embracing told Chaloner he was not as moderate as he claimed – he was still a fanatic.

He was about to devise a way of arresting Herring

– the Earl would want him questioned properly – without being caught by the Dowager's guards, when several of the soldiers started to stroll towards them. All were armed with muskets. Herring released a small, vengeful laugh, delighted by the notion that Chaloner was about to be captured, too.

But Chaloner had other ideas. He shoved Herring as hard as he could, so the iconoclast stumbled forward on to his hands and knees. Herring gave a sharp, involuntary cry as he landed. The guards homed in on the sound. Seizing the unexpected chance to escape, Herring picked himself up and began to run.

'There!' yelled one of the guards, stabbing a finger. 'After him!'

Chaloner watched the chase for a moment, then left unnoticed through the front gate.

Chaloner lingered for some time outside Somerset House, watching it from the shadows of a doorway. Eventually, the commotion died down, and the guards returned to their patrols. They were empty handed, so he supposed that either Herring had managed to elude them, or he had been quietly dispatched.

He did not have the energy to walk all the way to Hannah's house, so he went to his own lodgings on Fetter Lane instead. His rooms were cold, damp and uninviting, and when he lay on the bed, he found he was too tense for sleep. He played his second-best viol for a while, but even music failed to soothe him, and when he did manage to doze off, it was to dream that the Earl had murdered Blue Dick, and washed the blood from his hands in Chapel House while Lady Castlemaine and Thurloe frolicked in the background.

When he woke, it was pouring with rain. Within moments, the instrument-maker who lived in the rooms below – a man named John Spong – came to hammer on his door, because water was gushing through his ceiling. There was a veritable flood across Chaloner's floor, and it was unpleasant sloshing through it in bare feet.

'I am leaving this place,' Spong declared, when he saw Chaloner's home was in a far worse state than his own. 'Landlord Ellis says there is nothing wrong, but he is mistaken.'

Chaloner agreed. 'Where will you go?'

'Near St Paul's.' Spong shot Chaloner a rueful grin. 'The cathedral is falling to pieces, so it will be a veritable home from home. What about you? You cannot stay here, either.'

'I am to be married soon.' Saying the words felt awkward. 'My wife-to-be has a house.'

'Congratulations!' exclaimed Spong. 'But I hope you are not planning a summer wedding, because this place will not survive that long. Neither will you if you stay here.'

He turned and walked away, leaving Chaloner concerned for the safety of his second-best viol.

There was a scratching at the window, so he went to let his cat in. It mewed demandingly at him from a dry perch on a chest, well away from the flood on the floor. He gave it some salted fish, which it ate quickly then disappeared the way it had come. Did it sense something was wrong with the building, and declined to be in it longer than necessary? The animal certainly spent very little time there. Of course, neither did Chaloner. He looked around, and saw it was an unprepossessing place, with little to say about its occupant. There was a small jug his mother had given him, which sat on the mantel-piece, and the cracked mirror from his dead wife, but nothing else of a personal nature.

It was depressing, and he stayed just long enough to wash in a bowl of icy water and put on a clean shirt. In view of the inclement weather, he donned a military-style jerkin and thick boots. Then he made sure all his weapons were in good working order: sword at his waist, dagger in his left boot, dagger in his sleeve, and dagger in his belt. The gun he left behind. He would not be able to keep the powder dry in the rain, and it would almost certainly be an encumbrance.

His first call was to the Rainbow Coffee House, because he thought a hot drink might serve to warm him. *The Intelligencer* was hot off the press, full of talk about the looming Dutch war. It also contained a report about the old king's ghost, along with the editor's opinion that the dead monarch was haunting London because he was uneasy about the number of Catholics who lived there. Chaloner flung the publication away in disgust, wishing he had not soiled his hands with it.

'There is no need for that!' cried Stedman, leaping to his feet as the hurled newsbook swept a dish of coffee into his lap. 'I know the grammar is poor, but that is hardly my fault.'

'My apologies,' said Chaloner, insincerely. He had still not forgiven the young printer for starting the rumour about his attempted suicide.

'Did you hear the old king rode across the Bridge last night?' asked Stedman brightly. He seemed unaware of Chaloner's antipathy towards him. 'He was spotted by some of the Dowager's Capuchins, which must have given the sly old devils a turn.' He laughed uproariously.

Chaloner did not share his amusement. 'I see.'

Stedman's humour faded. 'Do not tell me *you* are a Catholic?'

'No,' replied Chaloner shortly, aware that several other men were listening to the discussion.

'Good,' said Stedman. 'So tell us what you think of the Clarendon Code. You listen to us debate the subject, but you never join in.'

Chaloner shrugged. 'That is because I know very little about it.'

'So?' demanded Stedman. 'A lack of knowledge does not stop the rest of us from holding forth.'

'No, but it should.' Rector Thompson of St Dunstan-in-the-West came to sit at their table. 'Do you *really* think the old king has risen from his grave to go wandering about London, Stedman?'

'I do,' said Stedman, quite seriously. 'Clearly, he is concerned for his city, and is warning us to be on our guard against those who mean it harm – Catholics, dissenters and the like.'

'I heard he carries his head under his arm,' added Landlord Farr. 'Perhaps that means he cannot see very well, and he is not so much wandering as lost.'

Chaloner left when the discussion began to range towards the ridiculous, wondering how intelligent men could believe such nonsense. He supposed the old king's appearances had been given more credibility for being put in print, and wished the newsbooks' editor had not done it.

It was still early, but Chaloner walked briskly to Tothill Street to wake Hannah, as he had promised. Then, before she had properly gathered her wits – she was not a morning person – he told her what had transpired at Somerset House the previous night.

'So I was right to be worried,' she said unhappily, blinking sleep from her eyes. 'They *are* planning something, and that purple-nosed Luckin is at the heart of it.'

Chaloner nodded. 'Yes, but I was unable to find out what.'

'I will help you.' Hannah reached out her hand to Chaloner's lips when he immediately began to object. 'I do not mean by breaking into houses and listening at windows. Or even by interviewing dangerous men like Luckin, Progers and the Penderel brothers. But I can listen for rumours, and I can inveigle invitations – for both of us – to venues where they are likely to be.'

'No,' said Chaloner firmly. 'That is out of the question. I do not want you involved.'

'Then that is too bad,' she said quietly but firmly. 'Because my conscience will not allow me to sit back while some great evil is perpetrated. And that means you have two choices. You can let me work with you in the way I have suggested. Or I can operate alone. I assume you will be happier with the former?'

Chaloner could see her mind was made up and admired her courage. Perhaps they were more alike than he had thought, because he would have given the same alternatives, had the situation been reversed. He was not happy about it, however.

'Very well. But only if you promise to do no more than listen, even if a situation arises that provides a perfect opportunity for you to interrogate someone. Will you swear to me that you will resist?'

She scowled. 'You drive a hard bargain, but I agree

to your terms. However, in return, you must tell me all you have learned so far. You mentioned yesterday that Mr Thurloe is too busy for discussions, so perhaps you can use me to test your theories.'

Chaloner started to say no. Hannah was not Thurloe, and he doubted she would be able to throw light on the muddle of facts he had uncovered. But he saw an angry light come into her eyes when she thought he was going to refuse, so he hastened to oblige.

He was unused to sharing information with people, and did not find it easy, but he persisted, and furnished her with a clear, if somewhat condensed analysis of his findings – that Edward Penderel had murdered Blue Dick for reasons unknown; that Phillippes, Kaltoff and the Dowager were hunting for gold in Chapel House; and that some very dangerous men were gathering in London and might be readying themselves for an uprising. He also included what the Queen thought she had heard – that Lord Bristol's return was going to be celebrated with some sort of religious ceremony on the Bridge, perhaps involving St Thomas Becket, but that Winter had denied the possibility of using fireworks there. When he had finished, Hannah was thoughtful.

'It seems to me that the best way forward is to iden- tify the masked men you fought at St Mary Overie,' she said. 'Edward fled to them after the murder, and they sound well organised and dangerous. Perhaps they are the ·ones who will actually carry out whatever mischief Somerset House is plotting.'

Chaloner regarded her doubtfully. 'There is no evidence to support that.'

And, he thought to himself, Luckin had given the impression that he intended something a lot more serious than 'mischief'. It sounded to him as though the vicar of Wimbledon had an atrocity in mind. He did not tell Hannah, but interviewing Luckin would be his main objective that day.

'No, but it stands to reason,' she argued. 'Will Goff and Blue Dick sang in a choir that practised in St Mary Overie, and now you have these masked men meeting in the same place. Moreover, the Penderels are at least peripherally involved in the Somerset House plot, and one of them murdered Blue Dick. These are connections you cannot ignore.'

Chaloner supposed they were not, and saw that time spent in Southwark was as good a way as any to further his investigations. He kissed Hannah briefly, and was gone before she could make him breakfast.

Marching up to Somerset House and demanding an audience with Luckin was unlikely to be very fruitful, so Chaloner decided to waylay the vicar outside. He was just settling down for what might be a lengthy vigil, when the Penderel brothers emerged. They were pale and heavy eyed, and even though his hiding place put him some distance from them, Chaloner could still smell the stale wine on their breath. He could only suppose that the Dowager's party had turned wild after she had retired to bed, and that a good night had been enjoyed by all.

'I *did* ask,' Rupert was saying in response to a question from Neville. 'And I thought he was going to tell us last night, but he changed his mind at the last minute.'

'He does not trust us,' said Oliver, clenching his scarred fists resentfully. 'Oh, we are fine to do his dirty work – the running around and all – but Luckin does not trust us. He never has.'

'Well, I do not trust him either,' declared Neville. 'And I continue to think we should leave London while we still have our heads. Why should we risk ourselves, when Luckin will not even explain what he has in mind? And where is he this morning, anyway?'

'He left the city on some errand, but will be back for the Banqueting House reception this evening,' replied Rupert. 'Do not ask me what he is doing, Neville, because I do not know.'

Their voices faded away, and Chaloner saw his confrontation with the vicar would have to be postponed. He abandoned his doorway, and headed for Southwark, deciding to do as Hannah had suggested, and pursue his enquiries into the masked men.

St Mary Overie was a busy church, and a good many parishioners drifted in and out. All waxed lyrical about the choir that had contained Winter, Blue Dick and Will Goff, but no one knew anything about the masked men. Evidently, the warriors who had paid the vicar for the use of his church had taken care to keep a low profile.

'I thought *I* had answered all your questions,' grumbled Feake resentfully, when he saw what Chaloner was doing. 'I told you – these fellows said they would not be back. You are wasting your time.'

Chaloner suspected that was true, but Hannah was right to recommend looking into the masked men more carefully, and St Mary Overie was the only lead he had on them. Or was it? He went to find Nat, to see if the beggar had learned anything new. But Nat, still wearing Chaloner's cap, sported a black eye, and informed Chaloner that he had decided against a career in espionage. The masked men had heard that he had been asking questions about them, and had objected with their fists.

'As soon as I got enough money for the coach, I'm going to live with me sister in Manchester,' he whispered, sniffing wetly. 'I don't like Southwark no more.'

Chaloner gave him the necessary coins, sympathetic to a man who considered the city too dangerous. He was beginning to think the same himself. 'You should leave as soon as poss—'

'God reward you for your kindness, sir!' cried Nat, grabbing Chaloner's hand and kissing it. Chaloner tugged it away, embarrassed. 'And because you been good to me, I shall tell you one thing that might help, although they'll kill me for certain if they find out I blathered. The coach leaves on Sunday, so promise me not to use it 'til then.'

Chaloner nodded assent. Nat took a deep breath, and for a moment, Chaloner thought he had reconsidered his offer – that he had decided it was not worth the risk. But then he began to speak.

'They rent a cottage near Winchester Palace, I know, because I seen them going in and out. But it's a little house, shabby and poor, so I don't think they actually *live* there.'

Chaloner was puzzled. 'Do they keep women there, then?' he asked. 'Mistresses, perhaps, that they do not want their wives to know about?'

'None that I ever seen. I think they use it to spy on Winchester Palace.'

'That makes no sense. The bishop spends most of his time in his See, and is rarely in London.'

Chaloner knew this for a fact, because the prelate was the Earl of Clarendon's friend, and visited him whenever he was in the city. It did not happen very often.

'Then I have no idea what they are doing,' said Nat,

pulling his hat down further over his ears. 'But don't try to find out until Sunday. Swear to me, sir.'

Chaloner promised again.

His enquiries in Southwark at a dead end, Chaloner went to White Hall, where he spent the rest of the day listening for rumours about the murder of Blue Dick, Edward Penderel's disappearance or anything that was planned for Shrove Tuesday. He learned nothing useful, but did discover that the old king's ghost had visited Cheapside, that more of St Paul's Cathedral had crumbled the previous evening, and that most folk smelled rebellion in the air. Unsettled, Chaloner headed for the Banqueting House when afternoon faded to evening, intending to tackle Luckin there.

The event to which the Court's most influential members – and its many hangers on – were flocking was a reception for the French ambassador. The event was a grand one, comprising plenty of pomp and ceremony. The Dowager and her entourage were among the first to arrive, and she made a fuss until she was given the chair that had been reserved for the Queen. Katherine's face fell when she saw she had been ousted, but she was used to being treated shabbily and knew better than to make a scene. She sat near the back, small, lonely and unnoticed.

The Earl of Clarendon had been invited, too, and Leigh asked Chaloner to keep an eye on the Dowager's entourage, because there was a rumour that they had been stockpiling bad eggs. When Chaloner glanced at Progers, and saw the gleefully expectant expression on his ugly face, he was sure the tale was true. Unfortunately, Luckin was not among the Dowager's party, and Chaloner heard Progers mutter to the Penderels that the vicar had been delayed, but was expected later.

The event began with a long and rather tedious speech in Latin by Father Stephen, which was lofty enough that even Chaloner struggled to follow its arguments – and he had enjoyed a university education. Then there were a number of toasts in French, followed by a sumptuous meal. Afterwards, the tables were cleared, the King's Private Musick arrived, and there was dancing. The Queen watched longingly as the King swept Lady Castlemaine around the room. Her feet tapped to the rhythm, and Chaloner wished someone would invite her on to the floor. No one did.

'I dislike all this stupid prancing around,' grumbled Clarendon, sitting with his gouty ankle propped on a stool in front of him. 'Moreover, I have eaten too much, and it has made me queasy. Incidentally, are those Penderel devils scowling at me or you? I cannot tell.'

They were glaring at Chaloner. Fortunately, the Dowager had ordered them to stay by her side, so they were not at liberty to wreak vengeance on the man who had knocked one of them senseless. It did not stop them from looking as though they wanted to try, though. Then Progers approached, and the glowering turned to smirks. The fact that they all then studiously avoided looking at the Earl made Chaloner sure some plan was about to swing into action.

'You should leave, sir,' he said urgently. 'Now, if possible.'

He was surprised when the Earl held out his hand to be helped to his feet. Clarendon did not often listen to his retainers' advice.

'I would much rather be working on the arrangements

for my Bishops' Dinner, anyway,' he said snappishly. 'I shall inform His Majesty that I am unwell and must lie down.'

Leigh escorted him to the King, and Chaloner saw the flash of disappointment in Progers's eyes when he saw his victim was leaving. The Earl hobbled through the door, leaning heavily on Leigh's arm, although the limp eased dramatically the moment he was outside the main hall and in the vestibule. Chaloner bundled him quickly into his carriage when he saw Progers make his way to the door, too. The ugly courtier was not alone – Luckin had arrived at some point, and was with him. The vicar's clothes were mud-splattered, suggesting he had spent his day riding.

'Where did Clarendon go?' demanded Progers, looking around in dismay. He was tipsy, and Chaloner suspected that the bulging bag he carried so carefully might be full of the bad eggs. Progers' eyes narrowed when he spotted the spy, and he jabbed an imperious finger. 'You! Take me to your master.'

Chaloner bowed obligingly, and started to walk down the stairs that led to the undercroft. Progers sniggered as he and Luckin followed, but his mirth did not last long. Chaloner pretended to stumble, knocking into him so he dropped his bag. There was a dull cracking sound. Progers squeaked in alarm, and stumbled back up the steps. Within moments, a foul stench began to pervade the air. Gagging, Luckin turned to leave, too, but Chaloner grabbed his arm and kept him there.

'I understand you have something in mind for Shrove Tuesday,' Chaloner said softly. 'So you have two choices: you can tell me what it is now, or you can die as a traitor later. The government is not very sympathetic to rebels, so I strongly recommend confession.'

Luckin shook himself free; he was stronger than he looked. 'I am no traitor,' he spat. 'Unlike you, who works for a man whose laws are plunging our country into bitter turmoil. Moreover, the King trusts *me*, because his mother tells him he can. Who will tell His Majesty that he can trust you? The Earl of Clarendon, who is fast losing royal favour?'

'The King will believe me,' Chaloner blustered, unwilling to admit that Luckin had a good point. 'And he will not allow you to—'

'The Dowager is holding a ball,' snarled Luckin, pushing his face close to Chaloner's. 'I do not hold with such occasions personally, but she is a wealthy woman, and wants to entertain her friends. *That* is what is being planned for Shrove Tuesday. Organising balls is not treason.'

'I have evidence to say there is more to your—'

'You have nothing,' hissed Luckin furiously. 'Because there is nothing to find. Our activities are innocent, and if you persist with these outrageous claims, you will be sorry. The Dowager has many powerful friends, and it would be a pity if you had an accident.'

He turned and stalked away, his sleeve over his nose against the poisonous reek of the eggs. Chaloner followed, painfully aware that the interview had not gone exactly according to plan. While he had not expected Luckin to confess all, he had anticipated that the threat of treason would shake something loose. As it was, he had learned nothing, except for the fact that Luckin was not an easy man to intimidate. Worse, the vicar had been warned to be on his guard from now on.

Chaloner walked outside, taking deep breaths to clear the stench from his lungs. After a few moments, one of the Capuchins approached. His name was Brother Pascal, and he had spoken to Chaloner before.

'I am glad Clarendon escaped with his dignity intact today,' he said quietly.

'Are you?' asked Chaloner coldly. He was angry with himself for handling Luckin so badly, and not in the mood for chatter. 'I thought everyone at Somerset House hated him.'

'I despise what he stands for,' acknowledged Pascal. 'Intolerance is not an attractive trait, and unworthy in any Christian. But I mean him no harm, and I am glad Progers's trick was foiled.'

'*This* one was foiled,' said Chaloner acidly. 'But what about the next? And what about whatever is planned for Shrove Tuesday? I imagine that involves more than just bad eggs.'

Pascal regarded him in confusion. 'I doubt the Dowager will have any of those at her ball! She intends it to be a glittering occasion, where her guests will be provided with the best of everything. It will be noisy, though, and Progers, the Penderels and Luckin will try to ensure it disturbs the erudite conversation at the bishops' table next door. But that is the full extent of their schemes.'

'It will be more than that,' persisted Chaloner sullenly. 'There are rumours of rebellion.'

'Well, yes, there are,' agreed Pascal. 'But they have nothing to do with the Dowager's ball. She would never embroil herself in anything that would harm the King.'

'It is not the King she is aiming to harm,' Chaloner pointed out. 'It is the Earl.'

'You are muddling two completely separate issues,' stated Pascal firmly. 'The Dowager's ball has nothing

261

– *nothing* – to do with whatever insurgency is bubbling. I will stake my life on it.'

'But Lord Bristol is rumoured to be in the country, and the Dowager is planning some sort of celebration with him. Perhaps with fireworks, which are made from gunpowder, and—'

'There will be fireworks at her ball,' interrupted Pascal. 'Sir John Winter has been asked to make them. And yes, they will contain gunpowder – they would not go off without it, which would defeat the purpose somewhat. But the rumours about Bristol are just that: rumours. No one has actually *seen* him – and I am not sure I believe these tales about his so-called conversion back to Anglicanism. We Catholics do not take our religion lightly.'

Chaloner was not sure what to believe. He had known, with every fibre of his being, that Luckin's denials were lies, but Pascal was much harder to read.

'It must be difficult for you, living here,' he said eventually, feeling some sort of response was necessary. 'The Dowager's friends are hardly suitable company for priests.'

Pascal smiled. 'It is God's will. And good men hurry to help us when matters turn nasty, as you did at the theatre the other day.'

'How long do you think you will stay in London?'

Pascal shrugged. 'For as long as the Dowager demands. But we *are* doing some good. We urge her wilder followers to moderation, and while we do not succeed every time, we have some impact. So does Father Stephen, who is a sane and sensible man. Between us, we shall prevail, never fear.'

But Chaloner did fear, and it was with a heavy heart that he watched the Capuchin leave.

Chapter 8

Brother Pascal's claims had left Chaloner confused and uncertain. Desperate for more information, he spent the rest of the evening at the Banqueting House, eavesdropping on anyone who frequented the Dowager's home. But he heard nothing useful and, frustrated and tired, he took his leave when the clocks chimed nine. It was time to go to Chapel House and hunt for buried treasure – he had been trained to locate things that had been hidden, and was confident that he would be better at it than Phillippes, Kaltoff or the Dowager. He met the Queen near the door.

'My guards have disappeared,' she said in Portuguese. 'Will you escort me home?'

Chaloner nodded, so she indicated he was to fall into step at her side. Hannah followed, but the other ladies-in-waiting were enjoying themselves far too much for such an early night, and were nowhere to be seen.

'Have you made use of that information I gave you?' the Queen whispered, taking his arm for balance when they reached the cobbled courtyard. 'The business about fireworks on the Bridge?'

'We should not discuss it, ma'am. It is not safe for you.' Chaloner flailed around for a tactful way to change the subject. 'Do you like dancing?'

'Oh, yes!' He was startled by the sudden passion in her voice – he had never heard her so animated. 'My husband the King hired me a dancing tutor last year, and he says I have quite an aptitude for it.'

Then it was a pity, thought Chaloner sourly, that His Majesty had not invited her to partner him in a jig. It would have cost him nothing, and the pleasure to the Queen would have been immeasurable. She chattered on as they walked, listing the various dances she had learned since her lessons had started. When they reached her chambers, she was reluctant to stop, and it was only the chill of the night that eventually drove her indoors.

'What did you learn today?' whispered Hannah, before she followed her mistress.

'Nothing important.' Chaloner's mind was spinning from descriptions of gavottes, sarabandes and gigues. 'Luckin was uncooperative, and I could not trace the masked men.'

Hannah's eyes shone in the lamplight. 'Well, *I* have had a very successful day. Something is definitely brewing at Somerset House, and I have been told that details of it will be given to a select few on Saturday night – at the soiree to which I have already been invited. We shall discuss tomorrow how best to get you inside.'

'Why not tonight?' asked Chaloner uneasily.

'Because it will take me an age to settle the Queen now you have started her off talking about dancing. Besides, you look exhausted. Go home and get some sleep.'

But Chaloner could not afford to rest, and took a

hackney to the Bridge. It was late enough that the streets were empty, and most homes were in darkness. He picked the lock on Chapel House's front door and let himself in. Then he stood still and listened intently. He heard the river roaring beneath his feet, and the night was cold enough to make the timbers creak as they contracted.

When he was satisfied he was alone, he lit a lamp and made for the cellar. The vault where Phillippes and Kaltoff had been digging was covered by a rectangular trapdoor. He pulled it open, and saw a ladder leading to a small, stone-sided chamber. It looked like a bottle-dungeon, and he baulked. He hated prisons, and the notion of climbing into one made his blood run cold. In an effort to avoid doing so, he tied his lamp to a piece of rope, and let it down. He saw pits in the floor where Kaltoff had been hacking, but it was not enough – he needed to inspect the place more closely.

He set his foot on the uppermost rung of the ladder, and forced himself to descend, gritting his teeth and breathing deeply to control his rising revulsion. His hands were shaking when he reached the bottom, and when the house gave one of its periodic creaks, it took every ounce of his self-control not to bolt.

The chamber was not very wide, but it was long, with enormously thick walls. He thought it an odd place, until he recalled that it had once been part of a chapel. Then it began to make sense. He saw lancet windows, now bricked in, and the ceiling was vaulted. It looked like a crypt. A grave.

To take his mind off such bleak thoughts, he concentrated on his search. The vault contained several barrels and a number of wooden crates. The barrels had been sealed with lead, and his knife was unequal to prising them open. They looked as though they would contain salted fish – he had seen similar casks on ships when he had spied on the Dutch navy.

The crates were more easy to search, because their lids were only held in place by nails. He prised them off, then frowned in bemusement when he found them full of religious statues, all carefully packed in straw. Some of the statues were broken, and he wondered whether iconoclasts had been responsible. Was this the reason Blue Dick had visited Chapel House before he had been killed – he had heard a rumour that popish works of art were being stored there, and he wanted to know whether his destructive services were required?

When the house creaked again, Chaloner's resolve crumbled, and he told himself that if one of the barrels did contain gold, then he was not going to recover it that night. He would inform the Earl the following morning, and then Leigh could investigate, hopefully armed with the right kind of tools for cracking lead seals. He shot up the ladder in relief.

By the time he stepped into the street, his heart-rate had slowed and his breathing had returned to normal. His legs felt rubbery, though, and he walked unsteadily towards Thames Street. He was just skirting St Paul's Cathedral when he became aware of a grating sound above his head. He flung himself backwards instinctively.

A moment later, there was a crash that made the ground tremble. Dust rose in a cloud, and through it, he saw a heavy stone gargoyle, now reduced to rubble. He stared upwards, stomach churning, but could see nothing in the darkness. Had it dropped by chance, or had it been pushed? He found it was impossible to tell.

*   *   *

The narrow miss with the gargoyle had put Chaloner on his guard, so when he heard his name being called from a passing carriage a few moments later, his hand went instinctively to his sword. Was it Luckin, intent on ensuring he had the 'accident' he had threatened earlier? The coach rattled to a standstill, and Chaloner was relieved when it was only Wiseman who leaned out.

'Jane Scarlet has summoned me,' the surgeon said, opening the door and indicating Chaloner should climb in beside him. 'As it is on my way, I shall give you a ride home. What are you doing out so late, anyway? Do you not know it is dangerous to walk about on your own at such an hour?'

Chaloner sheathed his weapon. 'May I come with you? I should like to speak to Jane.'

'You may escort me,' consented Wiseman pompously. 'But you cannot see Jane, because she is not yet well enough. You can talk to Scarlet, though: it is high time that someone took this vile attack seriously. Incidentally, I understand Temperance and I are to dine with you next week. The invitation arrived today.'

Hannah must have sent it, thought Chaloner, and wished she had not. 'I have just discovered a hoard of old religious carvings,' he said, to avoid the subject of the dinner party. He knew it was not sensible to discuss his investigations with a man he neither liked nor trusted, but he was tired enough to feel reckless. 'Can you imagine why anyone should keep such things?'

Wiseman considered the question carefully, gratified to be asked for an opinion. 'For their artistic merit,' he suggested. 'Or maybe because they are held to be sacred. Or perhaps they have been gathered together for safe-keeping.'

Chaloner thought of the gargoyle that had come close to flattening him. Had the crated statues come from the cathedral, to prevent them from falling down and killing anyone? But why store them in Chapel House? It had not been a place of worship for more than a century, and there were dozens of real churches in London that would make far more suitable repositories. Or were they going to be used for Chapel House's refurbishment? Perhaps the Scarlets had an affinity for religious décor. Or, more likely, the Dowager did.

Receiving no comment on his suggestions, Wiseman began talking about the recent irregularity in London's tides instead, and Chaloner settled back to listen as the carriage rocked along. He was surprised when they stopped outside a house on Wych Street, tucked between a lawyers' foundation called Lyons Inn, and a tavern with a reputation for literary talk named the Shakespeare's Head. He regarded Wiseman with raised eyebrows.

'Jane was not recovering in Turnstile, so I brought her and Scarlet here,' explained the surgeon. 'It belongs to a colleague, who is away at the moment.'

He opened the door, and Chaloner followed him into a spacious parlour. Scarlet stood there, wringing his hands. He was pale, and dark rings under his eyes told of the torment he was suffering.

'She is in pain,' he whispered. 'It is unfair to summon you in middle of the night, but . . .'

Wiseman patted his shoulder, awkwardly compassionate. 'You may call me any time you please. Now, sit down and talk to Tom Chaloner here, while I see to her. He may look like a scoundrel, but he works for the Earl of Clarendon, and has offered to hunt down your attackers.'

Obediently, Scarlet sank on to a bench like a man in

a dream. There was a jug of wine on a table, so Chaloner poured him a cup. Scarlet's hands were shaking so badly that he could not hold it, and Chaloner was obliged to help him drink. After a few mouthfuls, colour drifted back into his cheeks.

'It is all my fault!' he said wretchedly. 'Jane did not want me to be a Warden of the Bridge, but I was flattered when Hussey asked me. Had I refused the honour, she would not have been hurt.'

'Are you saying she was assaulted because you are Junior Warden?'

Scarlet nodded miserably. 'It thrust us into too prominent a position. I was a successful merchant, and I should have been content with that. But no! I had to be vain and greedy, and accept an important public office, too. It is all my fault.' He began to cry again.

'It is not,' said Chaloner firmly. 'And feeling sorry for yourself will not help Jane.'

Scarlet sniffed, and summoned a feeble smile. 'That is what Wiseman said. It is obvious that you two are friends, because you are so alike.'

Chaloner sincerely hoped that was not true – and Wiseman was one of the last men in London he would consider a friend. 'I appreciate you must be tired of answering questions, but—'

'It was awful,' interrupted Scarlet unsteadily. 'They were only two men, but they came in so fast that I could do nothing to stop them. They tied me up, and forced me to watch while Jane . . . I will never sleep easy in my bed again. That Earl has a lot to answer for, the horrible old tyrant!'

'Which Earl?'

'*Your* Earl,' gulped Scarlet. 'Clarendon. I am sorry if

I offend, but it is true. He is openly supporting those rigid laws against anyone who is not Anglican, and we are . . .'

'Catholic,' finished Chaloner, recalling the crucifix in the Turnstile home. He waved away Scarlet's alarm, not wanting to tell how he knew. 'My lady is Catholic,' he added, to soothe him.

'Is she? Then you had better hope Clarendon does not find out, or he will dismiss you.'

'Tell me about the attack. How did they get in?'

'They just appeared in our bedchamber,' replied Scarlet, shuddering at the memory. 'We are conscientious about locking doors, so they must have forced a window. There were two of them, and they wore veils over their faces, to prevent us from seeing who they were. One had dark hair, and the other wore a wig. I cannot remember more.'

Chaloner changed the subject to one that was less painful. 'Before you left Chapel House, did you notice anyone taking an unusual interest in the place? Or in its cellar?'

'Well, there was the Dowager. She visited one day, and told us our home needed to be renovated. We declined, but she is a forceful lady, and overrode us. Her cronies – do not ask which ones, because they all look the same to me – went into the cellar, but she kept us talking in the parlour, so I do not know what they did down there.'

'What is it used for?' asked Chaloner, thinking about the statues. 'Storage?'

'We keep some lead-sealed barrels of salted fish, but it is too damp for anything else.'

'Then has anyone sent you coded messages that—'

'No!' cried Scarlet appalled. 'I am a simple man. I do not dabble in such matters.'

He began to sob. Wiseman, returning a few moments later, grimaced when he saw the Junior Warden in floods of tears and Chaloner kneeling in front of him.

'Jane is asleep now,' the surgeon said. 'But she will recover a lot more quickly if she is not worried about you. In other words, you *must* pull yourself together. Can you manage that? For her?'

Scarlet nodded, but the tears continued to slide down his cheeks.

After witnessing Scarlet's distress, Chaloner did not feel like going to his lonely garret, so when Wiseman said he was off to visit Temperance, he decided to go with him. The gentlemen's club was a good source of gossip, and he was willing to take information from wherever he could find it. Wiseman was delighted.

'Temperance will be pleased to see you,' he declared, traversing the short distance between Wych Street and Hercules' Pillars Alley at an impressive lick. Chaloner was hard-pressed to keep up with him, and realised yet again that the surgeon was a very fit and powerful man.

'I doubt it. But she will be pleased to see *you*. She says you are a dear friend.'

'Does she?' Wiseman stopped dead in his tracks, his haughtiness replaced by a sudden and uncharacteristic insecurity. 'Do you think she might consider me . . . Do you think she might . . .'

'Might what?' asked Chaloner, enjoying the man's disquiet. It was usually Wiseman disconcerting him, and it felt good for the boot to be on the other foot. 'Agree to become your patient? It is possible, although she is rarely ill.'

'I was thinking of a more intimate arrangement. One

in which the relationship between *medicus* and patient would be transcendent. Do you think she would consent to become my . . .'

'Wife?' asked Chaloner, finally taking pity on him.

'Actually, I was thinking more along the lines of mistress. I already have a wife.'

Chaloner gaped at him. He had known Wiseman for more than a year, and not once during that time had he ever mentioned a spouse. He had assumed Wiseman was one of those men doomed to perpetual bachelorhood, because no woman in her right mind would take him.

'I doubt it,' he managed to say eventually. 'She has her principles.'

'Does she? Damn!'

'Where is your wife? Why does she not live in London?'

'She *does* live in London. In the Hospital of St Mary Bethlehem, to be precise.'

Chaloner gaped again. 'You mean *Bedlam*? She is insane?'

'She was not mad when I married her,' replied Wiseman stiffly. 'It was only later that she started to chew carpets and tell people she was a parrot. When she tried to fly out of the window with one of my apprentices under her arm, I felt compelled to move her to a place of safety. Do you think I should confide all this to Temperance, or will she think less of me for it?'

'I really have no idea.' Chaloner was struggling to come to terms with the tale himself.

'I do not suppose you would ask her for me, would you? Tell her I have admired her from the first time I saw her, and would like to bed her.'

'Absolutely not,' declared Chaloner with finality, as they turned into Hercules' Pillars Alley and headed for the house that was full of lights. It was late, but Temperance's club was rocking. 'I am no Progers, organising other men's amours.'

Wiseman looked crushed, but made no further attempt to persuade. Inside, the music was loud, and the air so full of pipe smoke that it was poisonous. It made Chaloner's eyes smart, and he almost turned around and walked out again. It was no place for a man who was tired.

'Would you like a pie, Tom?' asked Temperance's helpmeet, a large, comfortable matron named Maude. She sat at a table at the bottom of the stairs, ready to prevent patrons from storming up them and getting in among the women. In Temperance's club, a man put in a request for a lady, and was only conducted to a bedroom when she had finished with her previous client and was ready to receive him with the proper decorum. 'I made them myself.'

Chaloner accepted gratefully. It looked delicious, with golden-brown pastry and oozing juices. He bit into it. And then only just managed to stop himself from spitting it out.

'Christ!' he muttered when he could speak again. He wiped tears from his eyes with his sleeve. 'What in God's name did you put in it?'

'Spices,' replied Maude vaguely, taking one herself and chewing without the slightest hint that there was a volcano in her mouth. Too late, Chaloner recalled that she was famous for drinking coffee so powerful that it was rumoured to have killed one of her husbands, and that she liked her pipe tobacco as strong and tarry as it was possible to buy. She was immune to toxic flavours.

'Perhaps you should use them in moderation next time,'

273

said Wiseman, watching. 'Spices in that sort of quantity might give a man a seizure.'

Without further ado, he sailed into the main parlour, crimson robes flowing behind him like some character from the Bible. Temperance's face lit up when she saw him. He bent to whisper something in her ear, and she immediately looked in Chaloner's direction. She nodded, then indicated the cards she was holding. The message was clear: Chaloner could wait until her game was over. Wiseman sauntered off to sit with one of the other women, a jaded whore named Snowflake, who also beamed a friendly greeting at him.

'He seems at home here,' remarked Chaloner to Maude.

Maude nodded. 'We all like Richard. Have you heard the latest news, by the way? The old king's ghost was seen on Cheapside last night. It means something terrible is going to happen.'

'What kind of something?' asked Chaloner, hopeful for some solid intelligence. 'A rebellion?'

'Perhaps. Or maybe a war or a plague. Or even a fire. It is enough to drive a decent woman to church. I have been three times this year alone.'

'Have you heard rumours of any pending unrest? Or plots against the government?'

'No more than usual, although your Earl is unpopular in many quarters, because of his nasty laws against non-Anglicans. And I have heard tell that Lord Bristol is in the country.'

'Do you know where?'

'No. But here is Temperance, so I shall leave you to talk. Be nice to her, Tom. You two are always fighting these days, and she does not have so many friends that she can afford to lose them.'

274

Chaloner gestured around him. 'She has lots of friends.'

'These are clients,' corrected Maude. 'Her friends are me, you and Richard. She may not appreciate that yet, but she is young. Do not despair of her – she is worth your patience.'

Chaloner regarded Temperance unhappily as she approached, and thought that if Maude were truly her friend, she would have advised her to wear a different dress. And she had donned the wig he so hated, too, giving her the appearance of a portly Medusa.

'Richard said you have something to say to me,' she said without preamble. 'What is it?'

It was a sly tactic on Wiseman's part, but Chaloner was not going to be pressured. 'I think he is sorry we are no longer as close as we once were,' he said instead.

Temperance looked disappointed. 'Oh. I thought it was going to be something interesting.'

'He thinks I do not pay you proper attention,' Chaloner went on. 'Do not visit enough.'

'I do not care whether you come or not,' said Temperance carelessly. He could not tell if she meant it. 'I have plenty of other people to keep me amused. Especially Richard. Do you happen to know if he is married?'

'That is something you should ask him yourself,' said Chaloner uncomfortably.

'I would like to, but he might think I am prying.' She took Chaloner's arm and hauled him roughly to one side. Her expression was fiercely intense, and her grip was hard enough to be painful. 'Has he said anything about me? This is important, Tom. *Really* important.'

'He is fond of you,' he said, glancing at the door and

275

wondering whether he could bolt through it before she stopped him. He was acutely uneasy with the discussion.

Her face lit up. 'You are not saying that to please me?'

Chaloner took a deep breath and forged on, supposing she had a right to know what Wiseman had in mind. 'He mentioned looking for a . . . a *companion*. Someone to share his bed, I mean.'

He braced himself for indignation, but Temperance clasped her hands together and gazed adoringly at the great red bulk that was Wiseman. 'You have made me the happiest woman alive!'

Chaloner gaped at her. 'You are interested in such an arrangement? You will not hold out for something more . . .' He hesitated, not sure how to phrase it.

'I do not want to marry him, if that is what you are asking. But I would not mind taking him as a lover. He is handsome, kind and has a magnificent body. What more could a woman ask?'

'I really have no idea,' said Chaloner weakly. He was aware of Wiseman looking in their direction, and could tell by the surgeon's ecstatic expression that he knew the question had been asked and a favourable reply received. He held out his arms, and Temperance flew towards them. Chaloner winced at the sound made by the collision. They were two very large people.

When Temperance had gone, Chaloner left quickly. One card game was turning rancorous, and the situation was not improved when a number of Court debauchees arrived. They exploded into the club like monkeys, grabbing women and food, and making loud demands for attention. Among them were the three Penderel brothers and Progers. Chaloner ducked behind a pillar, certain they would fight him if they knew he

276

was there. He made his escape through the kitchens, ignoring the curious looks of labouring scullions as he weaved his way through them.

Once outside, he breathed in deeply of the cool night air. Wiseman and Maude were wrong to try to repair his friendship with Temperance, he thought sourly, because it was unsalvageable.

Chaloner slept badly for what remained of the night, because of the wind. It rattled the loose tiles on the roof, howled down the chimney, and whistled through the gap between window-frame and wall. It rained, too, and he gave up trying to place bowls under all the drips in the ceiling.

He rose before dawn, dressed, and, recalling his invitation to Winter's soiree the following day, took his second-best viol and practised several pieces he thought the man might like. He felt his spirits lift as the music soared around him. He might be struggling to make sense of his investigations, but on the bright side, he would soon be married, and that morning he would tell the Earl about the prospect of gold in Chapel House. The tale would delight his master, who was fond of treasure.

He forced himself to stop playing after an hour. The sky was just turning light, and it was the time when Thurloe took his daily stroll in Lincoln's Inn's gardens. Chaloner walked there briskly.

He found the ex-Spymaster standing under a tree, staring up at the winter-bare branches. Thurloe seemed oblivious to the drops that pattered down as they swayed in the wind, which was unlike him – he disliked being wet, because he claimed it was bad for a man with a fragile constitution.

'Did your mother never tell you not to stand around in the damp?' asked Chaloner.

He had not meant to make his friend jump, but he had approached with his usual stealth, and Thurloe's thoughts had been a long way off. The ex-Spymaster almost leapt out of his skin.

'Lord, Thomas!' he exclaimed, hand to his heart. 'Did *your* mother never tell *you* that it is rude to creep up on a man and startle him out of his wits?'

Chaloner grinned. 'She did, but then you came along and taught me how to do it even better.'

Thurloe smiled back, but the expression was distant. 'You were my best student. But you look tired. Have you come for one of my tonics, to restore you to your customary vigour?'

'Perhaps you should take one yourself,' suggested Chaloner, studying his friend's grey, exhausted face. 'Or you may find yourself unable to sparkle when Lady Castlemaine comes a-visiting, and I am told she quickly becomes bored with lacklustre men.'

Thurloe shot him a pained glance. 'I am sure I shall manage, thank you.'

They were silent for a while, watching the wind play through the upper branches of the trees. Then it occurred to Chaloner that he should mention his forthcoming marriage.

'Hannah and I will be wed in the spring,' he said, aware of how odd the words felt on his tongue.

Thurloe smiled again, genuinely this time. 'Then I hope you will both be very happy. However, most prospective grooms are rather more cheerful when imparting such news. What is wrong?'

'Nothing,' said Chaloner, unsettled that Thurloe should

read him so easily. Then he shrugged. 'It is a second marriage for us both, and we are neither of us moon-struck youths.'

'You mean you are marrying for convenience, not love? Is she pregnant, then?'

'No! And I do . . . I *am* fond of her.' Chaloner itched to change the subject to one that was less discomfiting, but it occurred to him that sharing his thoughts with Thurloe might help him understand them better, so he blurted them out. 'But we are so different! Will we continue to make each other happy after the initial . . . enthusiasm has died away?'

Thurloe smiled kindly at him. 'In other words, you have fallen in love with someone you consider unsuit-able. Love is like that, Tom – it strikes at random, and there is nothing we can do about it. Yet it does not happen often, so do not be too ready to ignore your feelings. I had nothing in common with my Ann, and we are still happily married.'

Chaloner forbore to point out that Ann and Thurloe spent most of their lives apart, and Thurloe had recently taken to entertaining Court strumpets in his chambers. It was hardly an ideal example.

'So you think we *should* wed?'

'Why not?' asked Thurloe. 'Sometimes, one just has to take a chance, and Hannah has many virtues. You could do a lot worse.'

It was hardly a resounding endorsement, but Chaloner supposed it was the best he could expect. Thurloe's occu-pation, like Chaloner's own, had taught him to be cautious when assessing people.

'Is that why you came this morning?' asked Thurloe, when Chaloner could think of nothing more to say on the matter, and lapsed into silence again. 'Or are you here to tell me you have solved Blue Dick's murder?'

'You ask that every time we meet,' said Chaloner, relieved to be discussing something else. 'Why are you so keen to know?'

'No reason. I am merely expressing an interest in your affairs, just as I always do,' replied Thurloe evenly. 'There is no need to be suspicious.'

Chaloner had not been suspicious, but the remark made him wonder whether he should be. 'I might make better progress when you decode those ciphers I gave you. Have you done it yet?'

'I have studied them *ad nauseam*, but to no avail.' Thurloe sounded frustrated. 'I am not ready to give up yet, though. May I keep them a while longer?'

Chaloner nodded, then studied his friend with concern. 'Each time we see each other, I grow more worried about you. You consort with the likes of Herring, and solicit the company of the King's whore. And neither is doing you any good, because you look terrible.'

Thurloe closed his eyes. 'I feel terrible, but it cannot be helped. And it will not be for much longer, anyway. By Shrove Tuesday, none of it will matter.'

'None of what?' asked Chaloner, confused and alarmed.

'I cannot say,' whispered Thurloe, although Chaloner was under the distinct impression that there was nothing he would have liked more than to unburden himself. 'Will you promise me something? As a friend?'

'I will not leave London and turn a blind eye to your rebellion,' warned Chaloner, predicting what was about to come. 'You always say you will do as your conscience dictates. Well, so must I.'

'Pity,' said Thurloe softly. 'But I cannot say I am surprised.'

His mind churning with anxiety, Chaloner made his way to White Hall. Thurloe was an ethical man, so why was he willing to plunge his country into yet more civil unrest? Chaloner sighed, and reminded himself that the ex-Spymaster had played a vital role in maintaining a military dictatorship. He was hardly a stranger to dark politics and radical opinions.

It was still early, but the Earl was already in his office, issuing a stream of orders that had servants scurrying up and down the stairs at a furious rate. Bulteel was at his desk, writing feverishly, while Leigh, clad in a vivid green jacket, hovered nearby, small feet tapping impatiently.

'He cannot talk to you, Chaloner,' the little soldier said, indicating Bulteel with a jerk of his thumb. 'He has letters to write – letters *I* must see delivered without the loss of a single moment.'

'I can spare a minute,' said Bulteel resentfully, stopping to flex cramped fingers. He moved them with difficulty, indicating he had been at his task for some time.

'No, you cannot,' countered the Earl, making a rare foray into the icy chill of Bulteel's office. He shivered, and tugged up the collar of his coat. 'Keep writing, or I shall hire someone else.'

Chaloner knew Bulteel was indispensable, and so did the Earl, but the secretary looked suitably alarmed and bent his head to his work again.

'What do you want?' demanded the Earl, pulling Chaloner away, so he could distract Bulteel no further. Leigh followed. 'Is Edward Penderel behind bars yet?

281

Have you found the masked men from St Mary Overie who helped him escape?'

'No, sir,' replied Chaloner. 'But—'

'Then have you discovered what Somerset House is plotting for Shrove Tuesday?'

Chaloner shook his head slowly. 'Not specifically, although—'

The Earl sighed noisily. 'What about Lord Bristol? Have you located him, and you are here to ask Leigh to organise his arrest?'

'No,' said Chaloner tiredly.

'Then why did you come, other than to waste the time of my secretary? But you cannot disturb him, because I have just learned that the Archbishop of Canterbury needs to leave my dinner early, so I have been obliged to bring the occasion forward by two hours. Bulteel needs to write to every prelate and explain – as a matter of urgency.'

'*And* we have just heard that there is no green salad to be had,' added Leigh. 'The Dowager has bribed all the best costermongers to sell it to her instead – for her ball.'

'Then waylay them before they can deliver it,' suggested Chaloner. 'A few shillings should convince them that they misheard Somerset House for Worcester House.'

The Earl pursed his lips disapprovingly. 'That would be sly.'

'How badly do you want green salad?' asked Chaloner.

'See to it,' said the Earl to Leigh. 'We cannot have a dinner without green salad. Of course, no one ever eats it, but it adds the necessary splash of colour. Why are you still here, Chaloner?'

Chaloner stifled a sigh, wishing the man would stop issuing orders and listen. 'I believe there is something valuable hidden in Chapel House. Gold, perhaps. I tried to locate it, but crowbars will—'

'Gold?' pounced the Earl. There was an acquisitive gleam in his eye. 'Explain yourself.'

'There are some barrels in the cellar, and it may be inside one of them.'

The Earl grabbed Leigh's arm. 'Forget the bishops' letters – I will find someone else to deliver them. Go to Chapel House and lay hold of this gold before someone else does. You will need an excuse . . . Tell the Wardens that we have a villain in custody, who confesses to hiding stolen property there.'

Leigh frowned. 'Why would a villain hide property in Chapel House, sir? I do not mean to be obtuse, but we need a story that is plausible, or people will think we are just after the money.'

Chaloner suspected they would think that anyway, unless they were totally stupid.

'It is an empty house, and this thief was being pursued by the forces of law and order,' said the Earl, improvising wildly. 'He hid it there and made his escape, but was later captured by you. We want to recover what he stole and return it to its rightful owners. Well, do not stand there! Go!'

'Come with me, Chaloner,' said Leigh unhappily. 'This excuse has flaws, and you are a better—'

'He has other matters to attend,' said the Earl sharply. 'Now get about your business.'

And with that, he stalked away and slammed the door behind him.

Chaloner met Wiseman as he was crossing the Great Court. The surgeon was wearing a grin that made people give him a wide berth. Chaloner understood why: there was blood on his hands, and he looked as if he had been doing something grisly and probably illegal. He tried to grip Chaloner's shoulder when their paths met, but the intelligencer managed to slither away.

'I owe you a great deal, Chaloner,' said Wiseman happily. 'Temperance and I sealed our arrangement last night.' The grin grew wider. 'I feel as though I am walking on air.'

'You once told me that walking on air was a symptom of the French pox.'

Wiseman's mood was far too jubilant to be punctured by acid remarks. 'I believe I said walking on *wool*. And now I shall do something for you in return. Name it, and it shall be yours.'

Chaloner was tempted to ask him to decline Hannah's invitation to dine the following week, but could not bring himself to do it.

'How about telling me any rumours you might have heard about iconoclasts, rebellion, the Dowager's ball or the whereabouts of Edward Penderel?' he asked instead.

Wiseman was silent for a moment, then lowered his voice. 'One of my patients is John Rider – of Rider's Coffee House in Chancery Lane. He summoned me to bleed him this morning, and who should I see there, sipping tea and reading the newsbooks? Herring the iconoclast!'

'Was he alone?' asked Chaloner uneasily, thinking of Thurloe.

'Yes, but he looked as though he was waiting for someone, and I overheard him telling Rider that he was meeting a friend later. But there was a furtive cant to his eyes – and I do not refer to the fact that they are crossed.

If he is not intending to cause mischief, I will dance naked in St Paul's.'

It was intelligence Chaloner half wished he had not been given.

White Hall's Stone Gallery was a long, sumptuously decorated chamber where people went to be seen. It was alive with gossip, rumour and speculation, and it was said that more policy was decided there than in meetings of the Privy Council. The King was present that day, which meant it was more than usually crowded. Chaloner lurked at the fringes of the company, waiting for the Dowager's people to make their appearance, so he could eavesdrop on them. It was not the best way to garner information, but the direct approach had failed with Luckin, and he did not want to put the others on their guard by alerting them to his interest in their dealings.

While he lurked, he heard that the old king's ghost had not been seen the previous night, and people were trying to determine whether its absence was significant. He also discovered that the Thames continued to perplex with its erratic behaviour, and that another of the cathedral's gargoyles had been found smashed on the ground that morning.

Eventually, Luckin appeared, purple nose flaring from the cold. Rudely snubbing the people who tried to greet him, he strode the length of the room, looking for someone. Moments later, Progers arrived, pale and bleary eyed. The vicar of Wimbledon descended on him like a hawk on a sparrow.

'You are late,' he hissed. 'And I cannot afford to waste time, not when there is so much to do.'

Progers took his arm and dragged him into a corner.

Luckin was angry, and the King's pimp was fragile, so neither man noticed Chaloner sidle behind the large statue that stood nearby. It made eavesdropping absurdly easy, and Chaloner thanked God that the pair were not professionals, who would never have made such a basic mistake.

'She asks me every other minute,' Luckin was saying. 'She will not accept that I do not know.'

'Well, there is nothing I can do about it,' snapped Progers. 'You will just have to weather it out.'

'You could tell her that I am as much in the dark as the rest of you. She does not pester anyone else with questions about Lord Bristol's whereabouts, so why does she insist on picking on me?'

'Because *you* are the one who heard him renounce his faith and agree to become an Anglican again,' replied Progers impatiently. 'That tells her he trusts you.'

'He *does* trust me,' averred Luckin. 'But not with details of his whereabouts.'

Progers hesitated, then lowered his voice. 'Is it true? Did Lord Bristol *really* take communion with you, and swear to follow the Book of Common Prayer?'

'Of course he did,' replied Luckin irritably. 'Do you think I would lie about that sort of thing? I am a vicar – I do not fabricate tales about religion.'

Progers sighed. 'Yet I understand the Dowager's eagerness to be certain that Bristol is to hand. We have worked hard these last few days, and it would be a pity if all our efforts were wasted because he is in France.'

Luckin allowed himself a smug smile. 'He is not in France. When I say I do not know where he is, I speak the literal truth – I have no idea where he is hiding. However, I do know he is *very* close, and that he will be ready to appear the moment we pass the word.'

286

'Thank God!' Progers breathed. 'Then why not tell the Dowager so?'

'Because it is safer for Bristol if she is kept in the dark. There is a spy in her household – someone is leaking information to our enemies. Personally, I suspect the Capuchins. Brother Pascal, for example. Catholics cannot be trusted.'

'I am Catholic,' said Progers coolly.

'Yes, but you are an *English* Catholic. They are foreign. But here comes another man I distrust. Quick! Discuss the weather, lest he thinks we have been plotting.'

'You distrust Father Stephen?' breathed Progers, looking to where Luckin pointed. 'But he is the Dowager's chaplain! He would never betray us – he does not have the courage for a start.'

'Yes, the weather has been *dreadful* these last few days, Progers. Horribly cold.'

'There you are, Luckin,' said Stephen with a sickly smile. 'Apparently, the Earl's Sergeant at Arms is searching Chapel House, and the Dowager wants you to monitor the situation.'

'Me?' asked Luckin indignantly. 'I am no errand boy, to be sent hither and thither. *I* am a priest!'

'So am I, but here I am, delivering messages.' Stephen turned to Progers. 'Meanwhile, the costermongers have announced a sudden shortage of green salad. She wants you to find out why.'

'And what will *you* be doing while we perform these menial tasks?' demanded Luckin angrily.

'Praying to St Thomas Becket on her behalf,' replied Stephen unhappily. 'All day.'

Luckin continued to grumble, but Progers pulled him away, muttering about it being wise to do as they were

287

told where the Dowager was concerned. Chaloner slipped out of his hiding place and waylaid Stephen in a deserted corridor. The priest looked around in alarm.

'Please!' he hissed. 'Someone may see us, and I am already under suspicion.'

'I would not have approached you unless it was safe,' said Chaloner. 'Where is Bristol hiding?'

'I do not know,' gulped Stephen. He looked as though he might be sick; the strain of spying was clearly taking a heavy toll on his health. 'I have tried to find out, but no one will tell me.'

'Hannah is worried that ordinary Catholics will be blamed for whatever the Somerset House Catholics are planning to do,' said Chaloner urgently. 'It is a valid concern. What can you tell me about their schemes?'

'Nothing! I am not an intimate of these people, just someone who is tolerated because I am the Dowager's chaplain. I will try to find out, but please do not approach me again. I will send word when I have something to report.'

When he had gone, Chaloner thought about Lord Bristol. Luckin had made it sound as though he was much nearer than Wimbledon, and that meant only one place: Great Queen Street. The Earl had declared the London mansion off limits, but it was a foolish order, and it was time it was disobeyed. Chaloner decided to visit it at once, but had taken no more than a few steps before he met Leigh. The little soldier looked tired and out of sorts.

'What a waste of time!' he grumbled. 'There was no gold in Chapel House. Only salted fish.'

'Are you sure?' Chaloner's heart sank. The Earl was going to be disappointed when he learned he was not going to be presented with any treasure.

'Of course I am sure,' snapped Leigh. 'We opened every barrel and crate, and even prised up a few floorboards. The place is empty.'

Chaloner rubbed his eyes. Had the dial-makers returned after he had left the previous night, and spirited the treasure away? Or, more likely, was there nothing to find in the first place, and the rumour of buried gold was false – everyone was scrabbling after something that did not exist?

'Incidentally, you might want to go to the charnel house,' Leigh was saying. 'Some beggar from Southwark is there, and he was fished out of the river wearing a hat that Kersey says is yours.'

Chaloner stared at Nat's pinched, water-logged features and felt anger boil inside him. Wiseman was there, too – Nat had no one to pay for his funeral, and the surgeon usually took such cases off the charnel-house keeper's hands. Chaloner slammed down a handful of coins, and ordered Kersey to make the necessary arrangements. Wiseman was not going to have Nat.

'I did not know he was your friend,' began the surgeon apologetically. 'Or I would never—'

'He was not my friend,' snapped Chaloner.

Wiseman and Kersey exchanged a glance. 'Then why are you—' began Kersey tentatively.

'What happened to him?' demanded Chaloner. 'He did not kill himself. I am certain of that.'

'No, he did not,' agreed Wiseman. He loomed over the body, dwarfing the frail remains with his powerful bulk. 'Do you see this line around his neck? It is consistent with strangulation.'

Chaloner stared at the mark. Had Nat been killed

because someone had seen them talking together? He was suddenly sick of the whole business. It was Friday – two more days and Nat would have been safely on his way to Manchester.

'When did he die?' he asked tiredly.

'I would estimate yesterday,' replied Wiseman. 'Probably last night.'

'Is there anything to identify his killer?'

Wiseman shook his head. 'I found these coins secreted in his hat – *your* hat – though. It looks as though he was hoarding them for some reason.'

Chaloner turned on his heel and left the charnel house without another word, ignoring the questions Wiseman hollered after him. There was no reason not to go to Southwark now, to look for the cottage Nat said was rented by the St Mary Overie men, so he flagged down a hackney carriage, wondering what sort of villain would strangle a beggar. Poor Nat had already been frightened into leaving his home, so why could it not have been left at that?

He looked at Chapel House as his carriage rumbled past. Labourers milled outside, and it seemed Leigh's invasion had caused considerable consternation. Hussey was ordering them back to work, but they were downing tools and beginning to walk away. Their faces bore uneasy expressions, and it occurred to Chaloner that they sensed something untoward afoot, and wanted nothing to do with it.

Nat had said the masked men's cottage was located near Winchester Palace, so Chaloner directed the driver there, and alighted outside it. The elegant Tudor mansion bore a stark contrast to the row of rude hovels opposite, but Southwark had always been a disparate place.

Chaloner was just assessing the shacks with a professional eye, trying to determine which looked as though it might be leased for dubious purposes, when a coach pulled up. It was a royal one, and he thought he could see the Dowager inside. He ducked into an alleyway to watch.

Within seconds, a young man darted out of one of the cottages and ran towards the carriage. The boy exchanged a few words with the vehicle's occupants, after which it turned around and travelled back the way it had come. Chaloner frowned. What was going on?

The lad watched the coach disappear around the corner, then returned to his hovel. He was well dressed, and clearly wealthy enough to afford better accommodation. Chaloner waited until the door closed, then stalked toward it. Because his temper was up, he did not exercise his usual restraint, which would have been to watch the place and ascertain how many people were inside it. Instead, he felt like fighting, to exact revenge on the men who had murdered poor Nat and tossed his body away like so much rubbish.

He kicked the door as hard as he could, gratified when the wood flew apart under the impact. Then he whipped out his sword and strode inside, ignoring the warning voice in his head that said if all seven masked men were there, he was going to be in serious trouble, especially if they had guns.

But there were not seven, there were two, and both raised their hands the moment they saw him.

'Please!' cried one, terrified. 'Do not hurt us! We are only Edwin and John Barker from Dover. We have done nothing wrong, I swear!'

They were little more than boys, with fair, floppy hair

and the lacy elegance of the would-be Cavalier. Both wore swords, and there were loaded dags on the table, but it had not occurred to either to use them. They were children, thought Chaloner in disgust, knowing they had not been among the men he had fought in St Mary Overie.

'Who employs you?' he demanded.

'Our uncle,' bleated Edwin, the elder of the two. 'He tells us what to do.'

'And what is that, exactly?'

'He told us never to say,' whispered John, close to tears. 'On pain of death.'

'Is that what you want?' demanded Chaloner, taking a threatening step towards them. 'To die?'

He would do no such thing, of course, because he was not in the habit of murdering youngsters. But they did not know that, and exchanged petrified glances. Chaloner made for an unnerving figure when he was angry and armed.

'We watch for the bishop, sir,' gulped John. 'And when the Dowager comes, we have to run to her coach and tell her whether he is in. If he is out, she visits his palace. If he is home, she goes away again.'

Chaloner was not sure whether to believe him, although he recalled Nat saying much the same thing the first time they had chatted. 'Why would she do that?'

'We have no idea,' said Edwin miserably. 'All we know is that she does not like to go in when he is there.'

'Does she take anything with her when she leaves?' asked Chaloner, wondering whether she was in the process of plundering the bishop's palace for art or fine furnishings.

Edwin shook his head fervently. 'Nothing! And she is never there for long.'

Chaloner could see he was telling the truth. 'What is your uncle's name?'

'Thomas Luckin, sir,' John squeaked. 'He is the vicar of Wimbledon. He summoned us here after he was released from the Tower – he was arrested for giving Lord Bristol holy communion.'

Chaloner was not surprised to learn the purple-nosed cleric was embroiled in the affair. 'Tell me about Luckin's friends – the ones who swathe their faces in scarves,' he ordered.

'We have no idea of *their* names,' said John. 'They met in St Mary Overie until a few days ago, but there was some kind of trouble. Then Uncle found somewhere better. We do not know where.'

'This is a peculiar state of affairs,' said Chaloner warningly. 'And one that smacks of treason and insurgency. If you want to save your necks, you must tell me what they are planning.'

'But we do not know, sir!' cried John, frightened. 'They never tell us anything. The only thing I can tell you is that something big is going to happen on Shrove Tuesday. I heard Uncle say so.'

Edwin was also eager to please. 'We think it concerns Somerset House. Uncle spends a lot of time there, despite him being Anglican and most of them being Catholic.'

It was clear they knew nothing more, and Chaloner despised Luckin for entangling them in his dark business. He sheathed his sword and nodded towards the shattered door.

'Go home to Dover, and do not come back. And do not attempt to contact your uncle, either.'

John bolted for freedom before the offer was retracted, but Edwin hesitated. 'Uncle said we should be ready to die for the cause,' he said. 'But he will not tell us what the cause is. He said we are too young.'

'Too young to know, but not too young to die?' Chaloner was disgusted. 'Go home, Edwin. You do not belong here.'

It was not many moments before Edwin and John emerged from the hovel's yard on horseback. They galloped off down the south-bound road, and Chaloner saw they were relieved to be away, not just from sword-toting maniacs who burst in asking questions, but from dangerous politics they did not understand. He spent a few minutes exploring the hovel, but found nothing of interest.

He crossed the road, and peered through Winchester Palace's iron gates, wondering why the Dowager only visited when its owner was out. Feeling the answer might hold a key to at least some of his mysteries, he walked to the side of the mansion, climbed over a wall and dropped lightly into the garden. As he landed, he saw a fountain, which he assumed to be the one in which Edward had rinsed Blue Dick's blood from his hands, watched by the Earl.

The palace grounds were pleasant, full of herb beds and carefully sculpted trees. Chaloner started to move through them, towards the house, but spun around in alarm when he heard the distinct click of a gun being wound. The weapon was being held by a slight, dark-haired man wearing the robes of a high-ranking cleric, and it was pointed right at him.

He recognised George Morley, the Bishop of Winchester, immediately, because Morley was a friend of the Earl's. He raised his hands quickly, not liking the way the dag trembled in the churchman's inexperienced grasp. Morley frowned, then let the firearm drop to his side.

'Chaloner? What are you doing here?'

'The Dowager has been visiting your house while you are away, sir,' explained Chaloner. There was no reason not to tell the truth. 'I came to find out why.'

'Then why not go to the front door and ask to speak to me? Why enter my domain like a thief?'

Chaloner had no good answer. 'I was intent on Clarendon's business, and did not think . . .'

Morley pulled a disapproving face. 'You mean you are so used to breaking into buildings on his behalf that you just did what comes naturally to you?'

Chaloner supposed it was exactly what he meant, although it sounded sordid when put like that. 'Not exactly,' he hedged. 'It was—'

'Clarendon is a good man, and I am proud to count him among my friends. You must never hesitate to ask for my help on his account. But please do not sneak in through the garden next time, because I might have blasted you into oblivion.'

'Do you often shoot intruders, then?' asked Chaloner, a little coolly.

'Not often.' Morley smothered a smile, and Chaloner recalled that the Earl often extolled his friend's sense of humour. Combined with his mild manners and moderate opinions, it made the bishop popular among clergy and laymen alike. 'But Southwark is not very safe, and my walls are easily scaled, as you have so ably demonstrated. I rarely walk around these grounds unarmed.'

'Does your caution have anything to do with the Dowager's visits?'

Morley laughed. 'No! And I doubt the King would be

amused if I shot his mother! Of course, he may turn a blind eye if I dispatched some of her companions – Progers, Luckin or the Penderels.'

'Do you know why she comes here when you are out?' persisted Chaloner.

'Of course. Follow me, and I shall show you.'

When they reached the house, Morley tossed the gun carelessly on to a table, and started to chat about the Earl's upcoming dinner as he led the way along a corridor. He was looking forward to it, not only for the company of his fellow prelates, but for the fine fare that was going to be provided. Shyly, he asked whether Chaloner would be so kind as to ensure that the feast included a pickled ling pie, for which he had a particular fondness.

'I will do my best,' promised Chaloner. Pickled ling pie? Was the man mad?

Morley beamed. 'The Bishops' Dinner is the highlight of the year for us. No one else is invited, so we do not need to worry about appearing gluttonous or drunk, because there is no one to witness it. And we can say what we like, too – we do not have to weigh every remark for its political implications. It is a wonderful opportunity for learning what my colleagues *really* think.'

'About matters like the Clarendon Code?' asked Chaloner, sincerely hoping the prelates would not be encouraged by each other's bigotry and emerge more radical than ever.

Morley nodded. 'Naturally.'

'What about iconoclasm?'

Morley stopped walking and regarded him in surprise. 'Why should we discuss that? Statue-smashing has not been an issue since the wars.'

'You have not heard of anyone gathering statues recently, perhaps to keep them safe?'

Morley frowned. 'No. Why? If you know of some plot to harm churches, then I beg you to tell me. It would be a wicked shame to lose any more of our medieval heritage.'

'It would,' agreed Chaloner evasively. 'Is this what you wanted to show me?'

Morley had opened the door to a tiny room that was bare, except for a prie-dieu in one corner. It had ancient wooden panels on the walls, and the floor was stone and very worn.

'This is said to be the chamber in which Archbishop Becket stayed before he made his fateful journey to Canterbury,' Morley explained. 'He was murdered not long after, in his own cathedral, for challenging a tyrant king.'

'St Thomas Becket was here?' asked Chaloner, his mind spinning.

The chapel on the Bridge had been dedicated to Becket, while the Queen claimed she had heard the Dowager discussing his bones. Could a long-dead saint be the reason for the Dowager's interest in Chapel House and Winchester Palace?

'So the story goes,' nodded Morley. 'I have no idea if it is true.'

'Becket's body,' began Chaloner, trying to make sense of it all. 'Could some of it have been taken to the old chapel on the Bridge?'

'No.' Morley shook his head. 'Canterbury was proud of its shrine, and would not have parted with a single hair from the tomb. But it was all destroyed by Henry the Eighth, anyway. Becket's relics no longer exist.'

Chaloner looked around the room. 'What does the Dowager do here?'

'She says her prayers, but only when I am out. Apparently, the presence of an Anglican minister disturbs her Catholic sensibilities.'

'Is that why Luckin leaves his nephews on guard? So she can pray without risk of disturbance?'

Morley nodded. 'Especially this week, when I am in London for the Bishops' Dinner. She is itching for me to return to my See, so she can have the place to herself again.'

'Is she really so devout?'

'I have rarely met a woman more concerned for her soul, although she will be in for a shock when it is weighed. She will learn too late that God is unlikely to approve of her malicious efforts to harm poor Clarendon.'

'Perhaps she would not dislike poor Clarendon so much if he moderated his opinions about her religion.'

Morley raised his eyebrows at the remark. 'He is wary of Catholics in England because they have a nasty tendency to favour each other and form powerful cliques. He does not want that sort of thing to damage the Anglican Church. *That* is why he supports the Clarendon Code.'

'There is a big difference between controlling nepotism, and religious suppression.'

'He does not think so.'

'No,' acknowledged Chaloner unhappily. 'And therein lies the problem.'

Chapter 9

Chaloner left Bishop Morley with his mind full of questions. He now understood the basis of the Dowager's interest in Winchester Palace, and perhaps Chapel House, too, but why had Phillippes and Kaltoff been digging up the vault? And, despite the assurances of Brother Pascal and Father Stephen that nothing foul was planned for Shrove Tuesday, Chaloner knew in his bones that they were wrong, and that Luckin and the masked men at St Mary Overie were at the heart of it.

Feeling it was time for another crack at the feisty vicar of Wimbledon, using more inventive means to make him talk, Chaloner began the long walk to Somerset House. But when he arrived, the place was in darkness, and he was told by a lone and rather resentful guard that the Dowager and her entourage had been invited to spend the evening with the King in White Hall. Chaloner met Leigh when he arrived there, and confided his suspicions about Luckin.

'Perhaps that is why his nephews were abducted,' said the little soldier thoughtfully. 'Although obviously, it has nothing to do with us, and he is wrong to be so free with his accusations.'

Chaloner gazed at him. 'What?'

'They are missing, but he says they cannot have left London of their own free will, because their belongings are still in his house. He has been rampaging around White Hall, telling all and sundry that *we* are responsible for their disappearance. His is fond of them, apparently.'

'Is that so?' muttered Chaloner, thinking that hauling boys from their home and embroiling them in dark politics was not the way *he* would show affection for young kin.

'But his blaming of the Earl is revealing,' Leigh went on. 'Because it means he *is* involved in something vile – something *he* believes warrants kidnap. He has a guilty conscience, in other words.'

'I am sure of it. Is he still here?'

Leigh shook his head. 'He jumped into a carriage and rode off. I asked around, but no one knows where he went. Incidentally, the Earl was livid when I reported there was no gold in Chapel House, so I recommend you stay out of his way for a day or two, until his temper cools.'

Chaloner thanked him for the advice, and they parted company outside White Hall's main gate. He was exasperated that Luckin was unavailable, but there was no point rushing after the man when he might have gone anywhere. Irritably, it occurred to him that he had never worked on a case that was quite so maddeningly frustrating. Moreover, time was ticking past – it was already Friday, which meant he had less than four days to thwart whatever Luckin was plotting.

It was too early to go to Great Queen Street – it would be best to search Bristol's house when its occupants were asleep – so he decided to call on Hannah first. But when he arrived in Tothill Street, it was to discover her entertaining again; he could hear Buckingham's distinctive laugh within. Chaloner's heart sank, and he realised how much he had been looking forward to seeing Hannah, to telling her what he had learned, and perhaps even to confide his distress over what had happened to Nat. Assuming he could find the words to describe such intimate feelings, of course.

He was about to leave when the door opened and Buckingham emerged. A servant with horses hurried forward, and the Duke swung himself into the saddle, waving at Hannah before wheeling around and galloping off. Chaloner watched him go, then knocked on the door.

'Tom!' exclaimed Hannah, reaching out to grab his hand and haul him inside. 'Thank God you are here! I was beginning to think I would have to go out to find you, because I have news.'

'It would not be from Buckingham, would it?' asked Chaloner rather coolly. He was not sure he liked her entertaining the Duke without a chaperone. The man was not noted for his restraint, and it was clear he considered Hannah an attractive woman.

'Actually, it is,' said Hannah, seemingly oblivious to his ill humour as she closed the door and led him into her cosy parlour. A fire had been lit, sending a warm amber light around the room. 'I know you speak French, Dutch and Portuguese, but what about Latin?'

'Of course.' It was the language of learning, and

everyone who had attended a university or an inn of court had to have a working knowledge of it. 'Why?'

With a flourish, Hannah presented him with a book. The title was embossed in gold on the spine.

'*Acta pontificum Cantuariensis ecclesie*,' read Chaloner, mystified. 'It is Gervase of Canterbury's account of his cathedral's early archbishops. If I recall correctly, it includes a section about St Thomas Becket's martyrdom, which he claims to have witnessed.'

'Does it?' asked Hannah. She seemed neither interested nor impressed that he should be familiar with such a scholarly tract. 'Look at the inscription in the inside cover. What does *that* say?'

Chaloner opened the book, and scanned what had been written there. 'It says this is a gift from the Dowager to Luckin, and is essentially a plea for him to forsake his sinful Anglican ways and become a Catholic. I suspect Father Stephen wrote it for her, because the grammar is perfect.'

'Oh!' cried Hannah, disappointed. 'Is that all? I thought it was something important. You see, I saw her slip it to him – secretly – earlier today, and then I watched him read the message and grin. I thought it might be a clue about whatever is going to happen on Shrove Tuesday.'

'How did you get it?' asked Chaloner uneasily.

Hannah had the grace to blush. 'He left it unattended on a chair. But I need not have bothered! The Dowager is always trying to convert people, so no wonder he smirked when he read her note. Damn! I was *so* pleased with myself, too! I do not suppose you have learned anything, have you?'

'Just that Luckin is one of the St Mary Overie men,

and I suspect he will use the others in his Shrove Tuesday plans. I will hunt him down tomorrow, and force him to answer questions.'

Hannah looked unhappy. 'You can try, but I doubt you will succeed. He was arrested and taken to the Tower, if you recall, which tends to loosen most men's tongues. But all he did was complain about the food and the view from the window. He is not easily intimidated.' She brightened suddenly. 'But I have *some* news for you. There is going to be a demonstration.'

Chaloner regarded her blankly. 'A demonstration of what?'

'A rally, in which right-minded people will stage a peaceful protest against the Clarendon Code. It is to take place on Shrove Tuesday.'

'Shrove Tuesday? Then *this* is what Somerset House has been planning!'

'No,' interrupted Hannah. 'The Dowager's people *are* plotting something evil, but the rally is just a gathering of decent people who want their voices heard. The Duke is organising it – I *told* you he has nothing to do with the other business – and he just paid me a visit, to ask me to join him.'

Chaloner raised his eyebrows. 'I hope you declined.'

To his horror, she shook her head. 'Someone must take a stand against these nasty laws, and—'

'But surely you can see what will happen? Your "peaceful rally" will transpire to be anything but, especially if Buckingham is involved. Then everything you feared will come to pass – innocent Catholics will be blamed for what Somerset House has done.'

'No!' stated Hannah vehemently. 'The Duke would never entice me into danger. Besides, he explained his motives. He said his conscience is urging him to act, because the Clarendon Code is such a wicked piece of legislation, and it is a matter of honour to see it repealed.'

Chaloner gaped at her, wondering how she could believe such nonsense. Then he reminded himself that she had known Buckingham for years, and the two were friends. Incomprehensibly naïve though it seemed to him, it had not occurred to her that friends might lie.

'The Code *is* unjust,' he acknowledged, forcing himself to be patient. 'But a rally will not see it repealed. On the contrary, it is likely to be tightened, so similar events cannot take place in future.'

'You are right.' Hannah smiled when she saw his confusion. 'I would have made the point myself, but you started maligning the Duke before I had a chance. You sidetracked me.'

Chaloner rubbed his head. 'So what are we arguing about?'

'I am wholly convinced that the Duke's demonstration is innocent.' Hannah raised her hand when Chaloner began to disagree. 'Let me finish! However, he frequents Somerset House, and others there are less scrupulous. I think they will use his rally as a vehicle for their own means – that they will attempt to turn it into something wicked.'

'So why did you agree to go?'

'Because it is a way to earn their confidence. To learn something that will let you thwart them.'

'No,' said Chaloner. 'These are dangerous men, and if they realise you are spying—'

'Yes,' said Hannah, equally firm. 'You are not the only one who will do anything to avert a catastrophe, and I am ready to do my part. You cannot stop me, so do not try.' He could see from the determined jut of her chin that she meant it. 'And there is the meeting at Somerset House tomorrow night. I intend to spy for you there, too.'

Chaloner swallowed hard, feeling the stakes had just been raised rather higher than he was willing to pay. He *was* eager to avert a crisis and protect his Earl, but not at the expense of exposing Hannah to such terrible danger. Unhappily, he listened as she began to outline her plans.

By the time Chaloner left Hannah, it was so late that most decent citizens were in bed, and only those with devious business were about. Two men materialised in the darkness ahead of him when he crossed Covent Garden, one holding a knife, but they melted away when he drew his sword.

He had been inside Lord Bristol's Great Queen Street house before – he had broken in then, too, he recalled – so he knew its layout. A wall separated its rear garden from the road, which he scaled quickly. There was an onion patch on the other side, and he remembered Bristol had a liking for that particular vegetable. He noticed the ground around them had been recently disturbed. Did it mean Bristol *was* in London, and had been sampling the home-grown produce?

The building itself was in darkness, and its shuttered windows lent it an abandoned air. However, the laundry on a line near the pantry was damp and smelled fresh. He picked the lock on the back door, and heard voices coming from the front of the house, so he crept towards them, careful not to give himself away with creaking floorboards. Eventually, he reached a parlour. Its door

305

was badly warped, so he was able to see directly into the room through a crack in one of the panels.

Five people sat around a table, but Bristol was not among them. One was Luckin, who slumped disconsolately with his head on his arms. Another was Rupert Penderel. The rest were men Chaloner had never seen before. A pile of face-scarves lay on a chair – the same kind that the St Mary Overie men had worn. They had stopped speaking, and were sitting in silence. After a while, Chaloner backed away, loath to waste time eavesdropping on men who were not saying anything.

He recalled that Bristol had an office overlooking the garden, so he went there first. It was clean, neat and a pile of dustsheets were folded on a chest – if the master was not back already, then it was clear he was expected soon. There were no documents to read or steal, so Chaloner prowled on. A handsome bedchamber was next door, and warming pans had been placed on the mattress to air it.

As he explored, he became aware that there was something odd about the place: one wall was too thick and the adjoining room too short. He regarded them thoughtfully. Bristol was Catholic. Was there a priest-hole in his home? He began to search, and it was not long before he discovered the secret chamber. Here, a bed had been slept in, and clothes were draped across a chair. Someone had been hiding there, and he could only suppose it was the missing nobleman.

He retraced his steps to the parlour, where the five men still sat in gloomy silence.

'I will kill the villain who took them,' said Luckin, raising his head from his arms. 'I will!'

'I wonder if they were stolen by the same scoundrel

who has Edward,' mused Rupert. 'Or do you think your lads are just off sampling the brothels. I know *I* did, when I first arrived in London.'

'My nephews are good boys,' snapped Luckin with an angry scowl. 'And I taught them Christian virtues. *They* do not go about whoring like common louts.'

Rupert bristled. 'I am sure they are veritable cherubs. However, red-blooded lads—'

'Clarendon has them,' snarled Luckin, overriding him. 'We all know his spy has been asking questions. *He* ordered them snatched, because he thinks it will deter me. But it will not.'

'Deter you from what?' asked Rupert innocently. 'We still do not know what—'

'I will tell you when the time is right,' snapped Luckin. 'And not before.'

Chaloner pulled back into the shadows. What should he do? Storm the place, and hope he had better luck than the last time they had fought? He *might* win – there had been more of them at St Mary Overie, and he had been hampered by Leigh's bungling presence. But then the back door opened, and voices began to echo along the corridor. More people were coming. Chaloner ducked into an under-stairs cupboard and held his breath as at least ten men filed past.

'We cannot find them,' announced one testily, pulling off his face-scarf and flopping into a chair. It was Oliver. Neville was with him, and so were several more minor courtiers from Somerset House. 'We have looked everywhere.'

'Perhaps the others will have better luck,' said Rupert encouragingly.

Chaloner listened in alarm. Others? How many were

there? As if to answer his question, more men began to dribble back in twos and threes, until the number exceeded forty. Clearly, Chaloner was not going to be doing any single-handed storming that night.

It was drizzling when Chaloner awoke the following morning. He stared into the wet street outside, and experienced a surge of anxiety for Hannah. And for Thurloe, too, assuming the ex-Spymaster had also thrown in his lot with Buckingham's 'peaceful demonstration'.

He frowned. But *were* they on the same side? Resentment against the Clarendon Code was so widespread that who knew how many revolts were fermenting? Perhaps there were several, and they would all fall over each other in their eagerness to do the right thing.

He yawned as he dressed. The two hours sleep he had managed to snatch were scarcely enough, and had left him far from refreshed. On leaving Great Queen Street, he had run all the way to White Hall, to tell the Palace Guard that rebels were massing and should be apprehended before they could do any harm. But there was only a skeleton squad on duty, and they would neither go with him to assess for themselves what was happening, nor wake their fellows. Curtly, he had been ordered to return in the morning, when his request could be put through the proper channels.

Proper channels! Chaloner thought in disgust. Did they *want* the rebellion to succeed? Still fuming, he walked across the road to the Golden Lion tavern, where he drank a jug of breakfast ale as he considered the day to come. First, he needed to arrange the raid on Great Queen Street, and at one o'clock, he had to attend Winter's soiree, to see if he could learn more about whatever was fermenting on the Bridge. And in the evening, the Earl wanted him to invade Somerset House. His stomach lurched when he recalled that Hannah intended use the occasion to do some spying, too.

When he reached White Hall, it was so early that the Earl had not yet arrived for work. Chaloner paced the corridor outside, fretting at the lost time. When his master did appear, he was hobbling with gout and was in a foul mood. Moreover, Chaloner had forgotten Leigh's injunction to keep a low profile, and the Earl greeted him with considerable hostility.

'You misled me,' he said accusingly, before Chaloner could speak. Leigh was with him, and rolled his eyes when he saw his advice had been ignored. 'And you caused Leigh to waste a good part of his day. There was no gold in Chapel House.'

'I heard,' said Chaloner sheepishly. 'I am sorry, sir.'

'Sorry is not good enough. I expect more from my people. What are you doing here, anyway? Have you found Edward Penderel? Learned the plans of my foes? No? Then you had better get to work. It is Saturday today, so you have only three days left – and if my Bishops' Dinner is disrupted by villains, I am holding *you* personally responsible.'

'Will you be having pickled ling pie?' asked Chaloner, recalling the promise he had made to the Bishop of Winchester. It was something of a non-sequitur, but he was tired and not thinking clearly.

The Earl was taken off guard by the question. 'I sincerely hope not. Why?'

'Bishop Morley wants one.'

'Does he?' breathed the Earl in distaste. 'There is no accounting for taste. Still, I suppose we had better accommodate him. You can buy me one this morning. And I want it delivered by sunset.'

'Lord Bristol is hiding in Great Queen Street,' said Chaloner. There were more important issues at stake than food, and he realised he should not have initiated the subject. 'There were—'

'Wait a minute,' interrupted the Earl, eyes flashing dangerously. 'Are you telling me you *went* there? I thought I told you to stay away from the place.'

'You did, but—'

'No buts!' exploded the Earl, beside himself with rage. 'I issued a direct order, and you disobeyed it. And how do you know he is there, anyway? Did you *see* him? In person?'

'No, but there are signs that someone has been sleeping in a—'

'Then did you spot any item that is definitely his? Something that indicates, beyond the shadow of a doubt, that *he* is there?'

Chaloner considered the question carefully. All the signs pointed to the fact that someone was hiding. But direct evidence that it was Bristol? He was obliged to shake his head.

'Then I refuse to squander valuable resources on another of your wild theories,' snarled the Earl. 'I *know* Bristol. He will *not* be in Great Queen Street. He is not a fool. Unlike you, it seems.'

'But men who played a role in Blue Dick's murder were there. They must be arrested and—'

'Then *you* do it,' shouted the Earl. 'It is what I pay you for.'

'I cannot tackle forty men on my own,' objected Chaloner, beginning to lose patience himself. 'I need Leigh to—'

'Leigh's men are needed elsewhere today,' yelled the Earl. 'I am *not* sending them on another frivolous mission. You were wrong about the gold, and you will be wrong about whatever is going on in Bristol's house. Besides, I cannot invade his property on a whim. What would the King say?'

'You invaded it when you sent me to Wimbledon,' Chaloner pointed out, finally driven to insolence. Leigh screwed his eyes shut in a wince, preparing for fireworks.

But the Earl was too angry to notice. 'That was different! Wimbledon is a long way from London, but Great Queen Street is a stone's throw from White Hall. If you are wrong, I shall appear petty and vengeful, and I refuse to take that risk, not when you cannot be certain that he is there.'

'Even if he is not, the St Mary Overie men still need to be interrogated,' persisted Chaloner stubbornly. 'You said you wanted Blue Dick's murder solved, and they are—'

'Then interrogate them,' bellowed the Earl. 'But you will not do it in Bristol's house, and you cannot have Leigh's troops. However, first you will buy me a pickled ling pie. That is far more important than following dubious avenues of enquiry.'

'It is not dubious, sir. Forty men represents a sizeable fighting force, and—'

'Enough!' roared the Earl, his plump face turning from white to scarlet. 'Why must you always argue? Now do as I say, or you can look for another post. *Leave Bristol's house alone!*'

He turned on his heel and stalked away, slamming his office door so hard that a painting dropped off the wall and all the glass rattled in the windows.

'I told you to stay out of his way,' said Leigh accusingly. 'He had decided how to spend that gold, and I thought he was going to have a seizure when I told him there was none.'

Chaloner sighed. 'Will you lend me a few soldiers? I *know* something dire is being planned – something that might damage the Earl. And for all his stupidity, I do not want him harmed.'

'I cannot help you until tonight. But woe betide you if you are wrong and you waste my time again. In the meantime, buy him a pickled ling pie. It may put you back in his good graces.'

Chaloner hated the notion that the St Mary Overie men were be left to their own devices for the day, so decided he had no choice but to challenge Luckin on his own. He stopped at Bulteel's chilly little office on his way out.

'I do not suppose Spymaster Williamson has confided anything about Shrove Tuesday, has he?' he asked hopefully. 'About plots or rebellions in the making?'

Bulteel regarded him uneasily. 'No, why? Is there something he should know? Or something that might interfere with the smooth running of the Bishops' Dinner?'

'Just a small army of rebels in Great Queen Street, whom no one is willing to confront.'

'Do you mean in Lord Bristol's mansion?' asked Bulteel, wide-eyed. 'Williamson will not go there! Bristol may be disgraced, but he still has powerful friends, and only a fool would risk antagonising them. And Williamson is not a fool.'

'No,' agreed Chaloner bitterly, thinking he was the only one of those, for persisting in his efforts to avert a crisis when no one else seemed to care. He changed the subject. 'White Hall is very quiet this morning. Where is everyone?'

'Watching the King show off at tennis. All the Court sycophants are there.'

Luckin was a Court sycophant, so Chaloner went directly to His Majesty's tennis court. The Dowager was among the elegant throng, but there was no sign of Luckin. Within moments, she declared the building too stuffy, and rose to leave. Chaloner thought one or two of those who traipsed dutifully after her had been at Great Queen Street the night before, but was not sufficiently sure to risk waylaying them.

Next he hurried to Tothill Street, intending to prise Luckin's possible whereabouts from the Penderel brothers, but learned from a helpfully garrulous neighbour that they had left an hour before. They had horses and saddle-bags, and the fellow was under the impression that they planned to be gone for some time. A purple-nosed vicar had been with them, he added, and all four had galloped away in the direction of Hampstead.

Chaloner slumped against the wall. An hour! If he had not wasted time trying to make the Earl see sense, he would have caught them. But why had they left so abruptly? Had they sensed the net tightening around them, and fled before they were caught? Had the disappearance of Luckin's nephews and Edward served to drive home the fact that they were playing a very dangerous game? Or had they gone on an errand to further their plot, perhaps by fetching Bristol or additional troops?

Angry and frustrated, Chaloner returned to Great Queen Street, thinking to ambush one of the masked man and force him to reveal Luckin's whereabouts.

He was sufficiently preoccupied that he almost missed the look-outs that had been posted there – they loitered in doorways and behind garden walls, and he knew he could not reach Bristol's house undetected, at least in daylight. He hid behind a tree, looking for a weakness in their defences, but there was none that he could see: they were well-placed and vigilant.

There was no point embarking on a mission in which the odds were quite so heavily stacked against him, and he was forced to concede that he had no choice but to wait for Leigh's help later.

Resentfully – there were so many more important things he should be doing – he went to the market in Covent Garden, supposing he had better locate a pickled ling pie. Unfortunately, this was easier said than done. The traders informed him that pickled ling pie was not a commodity that was in very great demand, and they had none to hand. In despair, he sought out Hannah, who was walking with the Queen in St James's Park.

'You want me to make you one *now*?' Hannah asked incredulously. 'But I have my duties to attend. Besides, the last time I baked one, you made excuses not to eat it.'

'It is not for me. The Earl needs one for his Bishops' Dinner.'

Hannah regarded him askance. 'You want me to cook a pie for the man who keeps sending my husband-to-be on missions that put his life in danger, and who has given his name to the laws that are suppressing my faith?'

Chaloner grinned ruefully at her. 'If you would not mind.'

She put her hands on her hips. 'Make one yourself. The recipe is nailed on the scullery wall, and it is not difficult to follow. At least that way you can be sure I do not poison it.'

Gritting his teeth with suppressed agitation, Chaloner bought the necessary ingredients, and set off back towards Tothill Street. Then, sleeves rolled up and an apron around his waist, he followed the instructions pinned in the scullery. Was this any sort of task for a spy of his experience, he thought bitterly, to bake treats for prelates whose laws were causing good people like Thurloe and Hannah to dabble in dangerous waters?

But there was something unexpectedly calming about preparing the fish and rolling the pastry, and he was surprised to find himself relaxing. Inspired to improvise, he added pepper and spices to the simmering ling, and even sculpted some decorative pastry leaves for the pie lid. The bells were striking noon by the time stood back to admire his handiwork. He pulled off the apron, rolled down his sleeves, and left the mess for Hannah to clean up.

After donning some suitably foppish clothes, he took his creation to the nearest cookshop – hoping the baker would be as good as his word and have it ready by sunset – then flagged down a hackney to take him to Winter's home on the Bridge.

When Chaloner reached Nonesuch House, he was careful to ensure that his arrival coincided with that of several other guests. While the servants were busy taking coats and pouring cups of welcoming wine, Chaloner slipped away from the general hubbub. He liked Winter, but the man kept ciphered messages in his desk and he frequented Somerset House. It was time his home was thoroughly searched, and when better to do it than at the time the household was preoccupied with his soiree?

Despite its fancy exterior, Nonesuch House was comparatively simple on the inside. It comprised four floors, all of which had two rooms and a hallway, and a single basement. Chaloner explored the latter first, and found it low-ceilinged, full of coal, and much smaller than he would have expected given the size of the building above. Then he recalled that Nonesuch House was perched atop a starling, and there would be no space for anything bigger or deeper.

The next three storeys comprised a kitchen, parlours and bedchambers, but there was nothing in any of them to help his investigation, with the possible exception of a card propped boldly on a mantelpiece. It was a formal invitation to the gathering at Somerset House that evening. The one Hannah had also been asked to attend, Chaloner thought with a pang.

'Hah!' exclaimed Winter, when Chaloner eventually abandoned his explorations, and joined the party on the top floor. His moustache had been subjected to some sort of beauty treatment, because it gleamed greasily and not a hair was out of place. Chaloner hoped he would not go near any naked flames, sure it was a fire hazard. 'You are here at last. Now we shall have some decent music!'

'Dowland?' asked Chaloner, examining the other guests quickly, and disappointed when he saw no one he wanted to question. Fortunately, more visitors were arriving by the minute, and he was hopeful that Winter had extended his hospitality to friends at Somerset House.

Winter's brown eyes gleamed at the suggestion, and he set about arranging chairs and instruments. While he was occupied, Phillippes and Kaltoff walked in. Phillippes, suave, confident and dressed like an aristocrat, immediately homed in on a group of pretty young ladies, who were delighted by his attentions. Kaltoff hovered self-consciously by the door, wearing a coat that was unsuitable for a man with a stoop and a wig that was too small for his head. Hoping he would not be recognised from the chase in Chapel House, Chaloner edged towards him.

'I know you!' exclaimed the dial-maker immediately. Chaloner braced himself for trouble, but Kaltoff smiled. 'We met at Clarendon House – you and Phillippes discussed the Earl's tide-ring.'

'Yes,' replied Chaloner cautiously. 'It is supposed to be ready in less than a week.'

A pained expression crossed Kaltoff's face. 'These instruments are delicate – it is not just a case of shoving a few bits of metal together, you know. If Clarendon wants a quality piece, then he must be patient. I may be a mere mechanic' – here he sent a glare in Winter's direction – 'but I am proud of my art. The Royal Society has praised the precision of *my* instruments.'

'Oh,' said Chaloner. He saw Kaltoff girding himself up for a good grumble now he had someone to listen to him, and hastened to change the subject. 'I was passing Chapel House the other day, and—'

'I never go near that place,' interrupted Kaltoff, his expression suddenly furtive. He began to move away, the opportunity to rant forgotten. 'It is dangerous, what with all that scaffolding.'

Chaloner flailed around for a way to keep him talking. 'Really? I would have thought—'

'Excuse me,' said Kaltoff, turning away. He found

317

himself next to the Bridge's haberdasher, and immediately began holding forth about buttons, to the man's evident bemusement.

Chaloner considered pursuing Kaltoff, but it was clear he would not discuss Chapel House willingly, and Winter's parlour was hardly the place for forceful interrogations. He turned to Phillippes instead, but the man was surrounded by women, and was effectively unreachable.

'Come and choose an instrument, Chaloner,' called Winter, opening a cupboard. 'It is time we had a little—'

He was interrupted by the arrival of Senior Warden Hussey, who was red-faced, beaming and full of the news that his good wife had delivered him a healthy son. He was to be baptised Robert.

'I thought he already had a son called Robert,' said Chaloner to Winter, selecting a bow.

'All his sons are called Robert,' explained Winter, handing him a viol. 'It is his own name, you see, and he wants it perpetuated. They all play the violin, too, although he will insist on teaching them himself, and he is not very good at it. Their massed practices are a foretaste of Hell.'

Hussey was a dismal player in his own right, and his fellow performers were obliged to change tempo constantly, as the Senior Warden sped up for the bits he knew, and slowed down for anything he considered difficult. Winter grimaced and winced, but was far too polite to complain.

Eventually, more guests arrived in the form of three Capuchins and Father Stephen. Stephen looked agitated, as usual, and although his eyes flashed a greeting at Chaloner, he made no other effort to communicate. Bossily, Winter inserted the friars into the little orchestra,

318

and Chaloner was pleasantly surprised when all three transpired to be excellent violists.

Chaloner quickly lost himself in the music, and when he happened to glance at the windows some time later, he was amazed to see it was almost dark. He became acutely aware that he had neglected his duties, and it was high time he had another crack at Phillippes and Kaltoff. But the dial-makers were nowhere to be seen, and he was dismayed when Winter told him they had left the party more than an hour before.

'No!' cried Winter, when Chaloner set down his bow. 'You cannot stop yet! We have not had any Gibbons!'

'Gibbons is my favourite composer,' said Father Stephen shyly. The music had soothed him, too, because there was colour in his cheeks and he seemed much more relaxed. 'And it is a pleasure to see Catholics and Anglicans enjoying themselves together.'

Winter frowned his bemusement, then smiled. 'You are right! It had not occurred to me that I had invited a combination of both. I am not a fellow who cares about another man's religion.'

'No, you are not,' agreed Brother Pascal. He looked wistful. 'If only everyone were as liberal.'

'The fact that music transcends prejudice should not surprise you,' said Winter. 'I once sang with a regicide and an iconoclast, and we never had a sour word. Music can do wonders for concord. So sit down, all of you, and take up your bows again. This city needs as much peace as it can get.'

'But I must leave, too,' said Pascal apologetically. 'My brethren and I are expected at Somerset House, and we must say vespers and compline first.'

'Is there an event in Somerset House tonight?' asked

Chaloner innocently, when Winter and Father Stephen had gone to round up the other two Capuchins and he was alone with Pascal.

The friar nodded unhappily. 'Yes, more is the pity. The Dowager's guests behave while she is there, but she tends to retire early, and then the occasions turn debauched.'

'Folk are saying that the old king's ghost, oddities in the tides and the crumbling cathedral are all signs that God does not approve of such wild antics,' said Chaloner, adding provocatively, 'And some see it as good cause for rebellion.'

Pascal shrugged. 'Well, *I* have heard that a lot of Puritans have started to gather – iconoclasts, no less. Perhaps these omens relate to what *they* are planning, and the Court has nothing to do with it.'

'Do you have any idea what that might be?'

'If I did, I would tell Spymaster Williamson, because no good can come of insurgency,' replied the friar piously. 'However, there is an especially odious iconoclast called Herring, and I have seen him in dubious company on several occasions. Perhaps I should report that.'

'You mean with other iconoclasts?'

'I mean with a high-ranking Puritan who lost all at the Restoration – namely John Thurloe. He and Herring met with a third fellow, who kept his face covered with a scarf.'

'You have seen Herring and Thurloe together *several* times?' asked Chaloner, stomach churning.

Pascal nodded. 'The most recent being in Rider's Coffee House yesterday morning.'

'I do not suppose you heard what they said to each other, did you?' asked Chaloner, struggling to keep his voice even.

Pascal's expression was pained. 'I heard them mention Shrove Tuesday. I shall pray for calm, but I sense something dark and deadly has been unleashed, and we shall be powerless to stop it.'

'I thought you told me that there was nothing sinister about the Dowager's plans,' said Chaloner, rather accusingly.

Pascal sighed. 'I did, and I stand by that claim: her ball is just a ball. However, that does not mean others are not hatching deadly plots. There *will* be trouble on Shrove Tuesday, and I only wish there was something I could do to prevent it.'

He was not the only one, thought Chaloner unhappily.

Chaloner left Nonesuch House with his mind in turmoil. He already knew that Thurloe had met Herring in Rider's Coffee House, but he had assumed it was an isolated incident. Now Pascal was saying he did it on a frequent basis. What was his friend thinking?

He went immediately to Lincoln's Inn, but Thurloe was out, so he borrowed pen and paper, and scribbled a message. He used a cipher known only to them, and warned Thurloe that his activities had been observed and that he should take care. As an afterthought, he added a sentence saying that Blue Dick's killer was likely to be Edward Penderel.

Then he jogged all the way to the King's Street cookshop and collected his pie. It was golden brown, and the baker declared himself delighted with the result. Chaloner grabbed it and ran, arriving breathless to plant the thing in front of the Earl's critical gaze a few minutes later.

'I suppose it will do,' conceded the Earl, after studying it for so long that Chaloner thought he might have to go and make another. 'But I stipulated sunset, and you are late. Where have you been?'

'Trying to locate Luckin and the Penderel brothers. Asking questions about the iconoclasts. Learning more about whatever is going to happen on Shrove Tuesday.'

The Earl regarded him balefully. 'I hope you are not suggesting that I have given you too much to do. But are you ready to go to Somerset House later tonight? It is imperative that you are there.'

Not for the first time, Chaloner was suspicious. Why was the Earl so intent on him going? But asking would be a waste of time, so he did not demean himself by trying.

Leigh was waiting near the palace gate, and had ten men with him. They were more a rabble than a detachment, and Chaloner wondered whether they would be equal to confronting determined and deadly opponents like the St Mary Overie men. He was tempted to call it off before anyone was killed, but there was too much at stake. Besides, even if they only managed to grab one or two of Luckin's secret army, it might be enough. Men were often willing to talk when the alternative was a traitor's death.

But when they arrived at Great Queen Street, there was no sign of the look-outs he had seen earlier, and Bristol's house was in darkness. A maidservant answered the door to Leigh's insistent hammering, then blinked in surprise when the little soldier pushed past her and made his way to the parlour. Chaloner followed, then looked around in dismay. The room had been cleaned so thoroughly that there was no trace of the masked warriors – the floor had been swept, the table washed, and there was not so much as a goblet in sight.

He ran up the stairs and looked into the priest-hole, but that had also been purged. The bed and a few sticks of furniture had been left, but there were no blankets and no clothes – and certainly no sign that anyone had slept there. Leigh regarded it all in stony silence.

'They *were* here last night,' said Chaloner tightly. He was angry – not with Luckin, but with himself, for allowing something to be postponed that should have been done straight away. He should have made more of a fuss, although the rational part of his mind told him he had done all he could. 'The delay gave someone time to warn them.'

'Who?' asked Leigh coolly. 'You and I are the only ones who knew what we planned.'

Chaloner gestured around him. 'This level of cleansing must have taken hours – it was probably going on when I saw those look-outs this morning. So someone not only told them *that* we were coming, but *when* we were coming, too. They knew they had time to eliminate the evidence.'

'If you say so,' said Leigh. His voice was distinctly unfriendly. 'But I am leaving now.'

Outside in the street, he dismissed his men, reminding them that the evening's adventure was not to be mentioned to anyone else. They nodded acquiescence, but Chaloner knew it was only a matter of time before the escapade reached the Earl's ears. He sighed. It had not been a good day.

'Be careful at Somerset House tonight,' said Leigh, clearly struggling to remain pleasant. 'Additional guards have been hired, and the Dowager has promised two shillings to anyone who catches a spy. Two shillings is a lot of money, so you can be sure they will be vigilant.'

* * *

323

'I do not like this,' said Chaloner worriedly, watching Hannah put the finishing touches to her face paints later that evening. They were in her parlour, and she was preparing for the soiree in Somerset House. 'Why do you have to go?'

'To spy,' explained Hannah, a little impatiently. It was not the first time they had been over his concerns. 'To learn what atrocity is planned, so you can prevent it.'

'I will be there anyway, because the Earl has ordered me to go. There is no need for you to—'

'You will not get close enough to the people who matter,' argued Hannah. 'Whereas I am a friend of the Duke. But I am not discussing it any longer. I am going, and that is that. But what about you? How will you get inside? Will you adopt a disguise and pretend you have an invitation?'

'I imagine they will have people watching the doors for that sort of thing. I have a plan, but it would be safer for us both if you did not know it.'

Hannah pulled a disagreeable face. 'Very well. But you must promise to be careful. It is quite possible that Luckin and his cronies will be there, and I do not want you falling into their hands.'

Chaloner was counting on the fact that they *would* be present, because it would be an opportunity to monitor them. 'And you must promise likewise.'

The hug she gave him was brief and dispassionate, and he supposed her mind was already on what she was about to do. They took a hackney carriage to Somerset House, and pulled up near the front door, where, as they had arranged beforehand, Hannah pretended to catch her skirts in the steps. Chaloner used the distraction to slip out of the coach and take refuge in the shadows.

He ran into trouble almost immediately. Leigh was right about the increased security, and there were guards with dogs. One started barking when it scented him, and he was obliged to dash for cover. It tore after him, ripping away from its handler, but when it caught him, it did not know what to do, so stood wagging its tail. Chaloner lobbed a stick into the undergrowth, which it gambolled after with a series of delighted yips.

While it and its owner were distracted, Chaloner raced towards the back of the house, panting heavily as he reached the denser shadows cast by the walls. He began to hunt for chinks in the curtains, aiming to look inside before turning his attention to the dangerous business of actually gaining access. He found one eventually, and saw the gathering in the Great Chamber was far larger than he had expected, with nigh on three-hundred people present.

The Capuchins were there, standing with Father Stephen, who was sweating heavily and looked as though he might faint. Brother Pascal was urging him to drink wine in a caring, kindly manner. There were others Chaloner recognised, too, although he was sorry to note there was no sign of the Penderel brothers or Luckin. Progers was already drunk, his ugly face flushed red, while Winter was paying solicitous attention to the Dowager.

Nearby, Phillippes had cornered Lady Castlemaine, while Kaltoff was with several men whose eccentricity of dress and manner suggested they were scientists from the Royal Society. Kaltoff drew a sheaf of papers from his pocket, and his companions clustered around eagerly. Chaloner assumed he was showing them technical diagrams until they started to laugh. Then he suspected they were being treated to a viewing of his latest caricatures.

Gradually, as he recognised other people he knew, it occurred to Chaloner that everyone was Catholic. Were these Hannah's 'decent folk', who would take a stand on Shrove Tuesday by joining Buckingham's rally? Or were they people willing to do rather more to get their message across?

A stab of anxiety went through him when the door opened, and Hannah entered on Buckingham's arm. She was chatting gaily, and the Duke was obviously relishing her company. Would he be so amiable when he learned she was conspiring to prevent whatever he and his cronies were planning? Somehow, Chaloner did not think so, and longed with all his heart to storm in, grab her and whisk her away before she was hurt.

But what *of* the demonstration? Chaloner peered through the curtain and saw merchants, soldiers, lawyers, members of the medical profession and men of learning. Many had brought their wives, astute, intelligent women with opinions of their own. He had no doubt that every person present would oppose the Clarendon Code, and that they believed in their right to worship God as they saw fit. Was that so wrong? Certainly, Thurloe did not think so. Chaloner backed away and closed his eyes in growing despair. These were no rebels, yet they were certainly going to be treated as such unless he did something to stop whatever was unfolding.

He took a deep breath and fought his anxieties down. He had a job to do that night, and dwelling on the uncomfortable ethics of the situation was going to help no one. He began to prowl, hunting for a point of entry. It was some time before he found what he was looking

326

for – a tiny opening near the ground that was probably a vent to a basement.

Getting through it was a tight squeeze, and he heard something rip on his coat as he went. It was also a bigger drop to the floor than he had anticipated, and he knew he would not be leaving the same way – he could not reach it, even on tiptoe. Brushing himself down, he began to explore.

He was in the Dowager's wine cellar. It was full of casks, some ancient and dusty, but most new, and there were so many of them that he began to understand exactly why the Court debauchees enjoyed her parties.

He made his way up the steps to a dimly lit corridor. Then he waited until a liveried servant came past, hitting the fellow hard enough to knock him out of his senses. He dragged him down to the cellar, where he quickly removed his own clothes and donned his victim's, completing the disguise with some of Hannah's face paints. Then he bound and gagged the servant with some rope he had brought. The man would not remain undiscovered for long, because someone was sure to come for more wine, but the ruse might give Chaloner the time he needed to complete his mission. And if the alarm were raised, then he would just have to rely on his wits to escape.

He knew from experience that adopting a confident swagger meant he was less likely to be stopped, so he strode up the corridor and marched into the kitchens. A scullery-maid smiled, but no one else gave him a second glance. He grabbed a tray of glasses, and headed for the Great Chamber.

'Hey!'

Chaloner kept walking. There were running footsteps,

and someone grabbed his shoulder. He turned slowly, ready to use the tray as a weapon. A fat man stood there, face flushed with anger.

'What is wrong with you? Did you hear nothing I said? Cloths over arms, to be ready in the event of spillages.' He shoved a clean white towel in Chaloner's spare hand. 'Now go.'

Chaloner took a deep breath as he entered the Great Chamber, hoping his disguise would be good enough to fool the people who knew him. He began to circulate, careful not to stop near anyone who might take one of his goblets – if he ran out of them, he would have to return to the kitchen for more, and that was a risk he did not need to take.

The chatter was light, about such matters as the acting in *The Indian Queen*, the sorry state of St Paul's Cathedral and the rising cost of fish. A few discussed politics, and one even mentioned the Clarendon Code, but the conversation was no more seditious than anything that might be heard in a market place. Phillippes was talking about himself, Winter about the music at his soiree, and Kaltoff was answering questions about his drawings. Buckingham had attracted an appreciative audience with a fair imitation of the Earl's distinctive waddle, while Progers was discussing women.

Chaloner became bolder, and edged towards Buckingham's circle. Hannah was there. It took a moment for her to recognise him and when she did, her eyes widened fractionally, but she made no other sign that she knew him. Instead, she turned to the Duke.

'You are a clever fellow with your mimicry,' she said, tapping her fan playfully on his chest. 'But will you take me to meet the people who feel as I do about the Clarendon Code? People who are prepared to take a stand against them?'

Chaloner winced and held his breath at the blunt question, but Buckingham only laughed and gestured around him. 'But these *are* those people, Mrs Cotton!'

Hannah frowned her confusion. 'But they are all ordinary folk, and I know most of them from church. None of them will . . . do anything interesting.'

Chaloner was appalled. As an interrogation, it was hardly subtle, and she might just as well have asked him to lead her to the dangerous ringleaders who intended to perpetrate an atrocity. Fortunately, Buckingham only laughed again.

'Exactly! I am not interested in recruiting rebels and fanatics. My demonstration will comprise normal folk with consciences. That is the purpose of this evening – to show you and your fellow Catholics that we are not violent dissidents, and that they have nothing to fear by joining our Shrove Tuesday protest.'

Hannah shot Chaloner a triumphant look, pleased he should hear this categorical denial for himself. When the Duke went to rescue Lady Castlemaine from Phillippes, Hannah ambled casually towards Chaloner and pretended to choose one of the glasses from his tray.

'Christ, Hannah!' Chaloner breathed, horrified by her performance. 'A little discretion, please! You will not learn anything by charging at the situation like a wild bull.'

She grimaced. 'I know the Duke – if you dance around with him, you will never have an honest answer. But do not worry: he will not take my questions amiss. Look! Here come some friends of Surgeon Wiseman's. I shall ask *them* if they are in the market for an uprising.'

'No!' Chaloner was aghast, but then saw mischief twinkling in her eyes and knew she was teasing him. He did not smile back: the situation was far too nerve-racking for humour. He moved away abruptly when Wiseman's colleagues expressed a desire for wine, then stood in a corner, pretending to clean the tray under his goblets while he listened to five merchants discuss interest rates and index linking.

'You?' came a low voice behind him.

Chaloner turned cautiously. It was Father Stephen, hiding behind a curtain in a way that would have been amusing under other circumstances.

'God save me, but you are brave!' breathed the priest. 'When the Earl said he was sending someone to meet me, I did not think he meant you would come *right inside*. I thought I would have to go out, and perhaps scour the gardens for you. It is very good of you to accommodate me.'

Chaloner had no idea what he was talking about. 'We try to oblige,' he said vaguely.

'Here it is.' Stephen looked around furtively before sliding a piece of paper into Chaloner's pocket. 'Now go. If you are caught with that, it will mean both our deaths.'

Chaloner supposed all would become clear when he read it.

'One more thing.' The priest caught his arm as he started to move away. 'I was wrong and you were right about Shrove Tuesday: something dire *is* in the offing. From what I understand, it will involve the Drury Lane theatre – I keep hearing mention of *The Indian Queen*.'

Chaloner regarded him sharply. Was that why so many members of Somerset House had been in attendance the other day? They had been assessing the venue for a massacre?

'Perhaps I should stay and try to find out more,' said Chaloner. It was risky, because the servant he had punched was going to be found soon.

'If you do, you will be wasting your time. The plotters will not discuss it tonight, not with all these strangers present. They will wait until they are alone again. Now go, before you are caught.'

Leaving Somerset House was much easier than entering it. Still in his stolen uniform, Chaloner walked boldly through the main gate, nodding greetings to the guards as he went. All smiled back, and he heaved a sigh of relief when he was out in the street. He only wished Hannah was with him, and sincerely hoped she would not get herself in trouble with more reckless questions.

Supposing he had better deliver what Father Stephen had given him to the Earl, he walked to Worcester House and broke in through a side door. In the darkness of the hall beyond, he saw the barrel of a gun waving in his general direction. He dived away, whipped out his dagger, and only his last-minute recognition of Leigh's neat little silhouette prevented the Sergeant at Arms from losing hand and weapon at the same time.

'Lord!' breathed Leigh, lowering the gun when Chaloner identified himself. 'I thought you were one of the Dowager's horde – that her copious amounts of wine had encouraged one to venture over for mischief. Perhaps I should scout around the grounds, to make sure all is secure. Will you stay here, and guard the door until I come back?'

When he had gone, Chaloner lit a lamp and took the

paper from his pocket. He was bemused to see it was a list of fireworks, all with names like Scarlet Rockets, Purple Fountains, and White Candles. Calculations were written in both margins, but they meant nothing to him.

Leigh's inspection did not last long, so it was not many moments before Chaloner was knocking at the door to the Earl's parlour. Clarendon was sitting at his desk, looking pale and out of sorts.

'I thought I told you to visit Somerset House,' he snapped. Then his eyes widened as Chaloner stepped into the halo of light cast by the lamp. 'Is that the Dowager's livery you are wearing?'

'Father Stephen asked me to give you this.' Chaloner handed over the folded paper.

The Earl's eyebrows shot up. 'You have completed the mission already? But I expected to be up for hours before you returned – *if* you returned. I was not sure Stephen had the courage to go through with it.'

'Go through with what?' asked Chaloner icily. 'The plan whereby he passed me an incriminating document in a room full of people, some of whom might have killed us, had we been seen?'

The Earl nodded, unrepentant. 'I was not worried about you – you know how to handle yourself in such situations. So I invented a strategy that represented minimum risk to him.'

A strategy that was criminally reckless, Chaloner thought. 'But you did not *tell* me I was supposed to collect something from him,' he said, not bothering to hide his exasperation. 'I was in disguise: he might have gone all night without recognising me.'

The Earl glared at him. 'Do not criticise me, Chaloner, especially as I was following a rule *you* taught me – namely that one spy should never know the identity of another. I promised Stephen he would not have to carry this document out of Somerset House himself – that I would send a courier. All he knew was that he had to look for one of my most trusted officers.'

Chaloner rubbed his head, wishing his master would leave such matters to him. He was sure he could have devised something much less hazardous – for Stephen and himself.

The Earl tapped the paper when he did not reply. 'This is a list of all the fireworks that will make appearances at the Dowager's ball.'

'Is that all?' Chaloner was appalled. Father Stephen had risked his life for an inventory that could have been acquired much more easily.

The Earl smiled and beckoned him forward. 'Not quite. Look at these formulae. The ones in the left-hand margin are recipes for common fireworks. Here you see one for a Purple Fountain – a cone-shaped creation that stands on the ground and releases a spray of mauve sparks.'

'And the figures in the right-hand margin?'

'They are what concern me. They are *adapted* recipes. Look at the Purple Fountain again. Now it contains half an ounce of copper sulphate and—'

'Ten pounds of powder!' exclaimed Chaloner, unable to help himself. 'Christ! That will not be a fountain, it will be a volcano!'

'Precisely,' said the Earl, leaning back. 'And here you see that twenty pounds of powder are to be used in a Red Rocket. I suspect that would render it somewhat heavy for flying. Do you agree?'

Chaloner nodded, staring at the numbers. 'But I still

do not understand. Are you saying the fireworks at the Dowager's ball will be these adapted ones? That she intends to awe her guests with creations that will do rather more than produce coloured smoke and pretty sparks?'

The Earl was silent for a moment. 'There is nothing to suggest that she, personally, is aware of any of this. Or that these modified fireworks have even been made. It may all be theory.'

'Winter?' asked Chaloner, hoping it was untrue – he liked the man. 'He has been charged to generate the display. Are these his "theories"?'

'Winter wants to be elected Green Man, so I cannot see him doing anything to jeopardise his prospects. The King will attend this ball, and His Majesty is unlikely to be impressed by Purple Fountains that blow great holes in his mother's garden.'

Chaloner was growing confused. 'But if you are sceptical about whether these inventions exist, why did you put Father Stephen through the agony of passing you the formulae?'

'Because of a conversation I had with Phillippes, my dial-maker. I told him I was amused by the learned men of Gresham College weighing air, and to ingratiate himself, he responded by telling me some silly things *he* had done. One was increasing the amount of gunpowder in fireworks to—'

'The incident in the Beggar's Bush!' exclaimed Chaloner in understanding. 'It blew the landlord off his feet.'

Clarendon nodded. 'Quite. Phillippes said all he wanted to know was whether more powder would make for a more spectacular firework, but his experiment demonstrated that the manufacture of these things is rather more complex than that. However, he then went on to say that the folk at Somerset House had howled with laughter at the tale, and that several – he did not know their names – had expressed an eager interest in his formulae.'

'How about Father Stephen? Did *he* know who these men might be?'

'No, but he admitted to knowing where the formulae might be kept, so I charged him to get them.' The Earl tapped the paper with a chubby forefinger. 'You will appreciate that I would rather this sort of information was *not* in the hands of men who would like to see me blown to pieces.'

Once again, Chaloner thought there were better and more reliable ways to have acquired the information, but he kept his opinion to himself.

'Was it Phillippes who told you that Winter had been acquiring gunpowder?' he asked, thinking about another piece of intelligence, the origin of which the Earl had declined to share.

The Earl nodded reluctantly. 'But I did not want to tell anyone, lest he builds me a tide-ring that does not work in revenge. The information was irrelevant, anyway – we know now that Winter only wanted the powder for making the Dowager's fireworks.'

'Stephen confirmed that something terrible will happen on Shrove Tuesday,' said Chaloner, changing the subject. 'He thinks the Duke's Theatre may be attacked.'

The Earl looked dubious. 'I doubt there is anything in *The Indian Queen* to warrant violence. If *I* were a fanatic, I would choose a more noteworthy target. White Hall, perhaps. Or the Tower.'

'Or the Bridge,' said Chaloner, recalling what the Queen believed she had heard. Hundreds of people lived on the Bridge, so the carnage would be unimaginable, not to mention the disruption to commerce and the expense of repairs. 'Are you sure these adapted fireworks do not exist, sir?'

The Earl regarded him uneasily. 'Well, no, I am not *sure*. I just made the assumption that no one would do it, because Phillippes said it would be dangerous. And I thought we had just decided that Winter would not take the risk.'

'Winter is not the only man who knows about explosives.' Chaloner thought about the number of questionable people who had converged on the city – Lord Bristol, Herring and his iconoclasts, Will Goff the regicide, Luckin and the masked men from St Mary Overie. The list was endless.

The Earl regarded him in horror. 'You think someone might actually have *made* these terrible things?'

Chaloner frowned as he studied the formulae again. 'If these figures are correct, then we are talking about a huge amount of gunpowder. Such bulk will not be easy to conceal. You had better issue an order for the Bridge and the theatre to be evacuated while a search—'

'I cannot!' The Earl was appalled. 'Do you have any idea of the panic it would cause? And if word got out that religious fanatics are stockpiling items that explode, there will be a bloodbath.'

He had a point. 'Then what do you suggest, sir?'

'*You* must locate this powder. You said yourself that there will be a lot of it, and if we can narrow the search to the Bridge or the theatre, it should not be too difficult to locate. Moreover, we have two full days to do it, assuming that its owners are saving it for Shrove Tuesday.'

Chaloner rubbed his chin. Could gunpowder be the reason for the sudden interest in Chapel House? But where could it be? He had searched the building thoroughly, and so had Leigh. Or was there a false wall or some such device that they had missed? Grimly, Chaloner saw he was going to have a busy night.

Chapter 10

When Chaloner left Worcester House, it was to find Hannah outside, waiting for him in a hackney carriage. She beckoned him in, and began to speak before he was properly seated.

'Well, that was a waste of time!' she declared in disgust. 'I interrogated all manner of people I thought might want to do more than demonstrate peacefully, but no one would tell me a thing.'

'Did you expect them to confide in the first woman who approached them, then?' asked Chaloner. 'That they would reveal all, just because you happen to enquire?'

Hannah glared. 'Of course not. But if someone *is* plotting something big and violent, then he will need plenty of help to ensure all goes according to plan. Allies do not grow on trees, and he will be only too glad of loyal assistants, such as I was pretending to be.'

'Yes,' agreed Chaloner, 'but not ones who storm up and offer their services at soirees. He will be terrified of betrayal, and it will take more than a few words at a party to make him trust you.'

Hannah sighed heavily. 'Oh, well. I did my best. Are we going home now?'

'I wish we could, but Father Stephen gave the Earl intelligence that suggests large quantities of gunpowder might be at large. I need to visit the theatre in Drury Lane, and then the Bridge, to see if I can locate it. It may be hidden inside a stockpile of fireworks.'

'Gunpowder?' Hannah was appalled. 'Their plan involves blowing something up? But explosions are indiscriminate and violent! There will be untold killing if—'

'Yes,' interrupted Chaloner, not wanting to think about it. In his mind, he could still hear the thumps and crashes of the cannons at the Battle of Naseby. 'Which is why I had better start hunting. I will take you to Tothill Street, and then I must go.'

'We will go home,' acknowledged Hannah, glancing at him. 'So you can change your clothes – it is not a good idea to wander about in the Dowager's livery. But then I am coming with you.' She raised her hand to quell the objection he started to make. '*You* need help, and *I* am determined to prevent Catholics from being blamed for the work of fanatics. So we shall work together.'

Chaloner had no intention of letting her join him, and saw he would have to find a way to make her think she was helping while keeping her out of danger. When they arrived at Tothill Street, and he exchanged the uniform for some of his own clothes, she questioned him about his investigations, and he found he was glad to answer, because it consolidated the answers – and the remaining questions – in his mind.

'I still do not know for certain what Phillippes and Kaltoff hope to find in Chapel House,' he said. 'But now I think it must be gunpowder. The formulae for making the enhanced fireworks are Phillippes's, and perhaps he does not want to be blamed for whatever is going to be done with them.'

'That assumes he is not part of the plot,' Hannah pointed out. 'But he might be – he bears a grudge for not being elected to the Royal Society, and bitter men often turn vicious. However, do not forget that Father Stephen said there is gold buried there. Perhaps he was after that.'

Chaloner tugged on a coat and aimed for the door. 'Everything is beginning to merge,' he said, beginning to walk towards Drury Lane. Hannah fell in at his side, trotting every few steps to keep up with him. 'The Earl told me to look into plots fermenting at Somerset House and learn the whereabouts of Lord Bristol. But they are connected.'

'Yes,' agreed Hannah. 'It would seem that *some* of the Dowager's cronies have summoned Bristol home for the purposes of rebellion. Of course, the Duke will know nothing about it.'

Chaloner would reserve judgement on that. 'And a few of the same cronies are implicated in Blue Dick Culmer's death,' he continued. 'Namely Luckin and his masked friends, who include the Penderel brothers.'

'Moreover,' Hannah continued, 'Junior Warden Scarlet is linked to Blue Dick by ciphered messages, and the more I think about it, the more I become certain that the attack on Jane was anything but random. You are right: all your enquiries do seem to be part of the same whole.'

The streets were deserted as they walked, but they were just passing the New Exchange on The Strand, when Chaloner heard scuffling in a nearby alley. He grabbed

Hannah's hand and slipped into a recessed doorway, all his senses on high alert. But the rustling gave way to muted sniggers, and he forced himself to relax. Some drunken jape was in progress.

For a few moments, nothing happened. Then three portly merchants emerged from a nearby tavern called the Sun. Immediately, a pale figure materialised from the alley and undulated towards them. Hannah gulped in terror, and Chaloner could feel her trembling against him.

'It is the old king's ghost!' she said in a strangled whisper.

There was an instant when Chaloner thought she was right, because the wan features, elaborate dress and pointed beard did indeed look like those of the executed monarch. But then he saw the face had been made up with pastes, and the beard was false.

The merchants took to their heels with howls of fright. Two accomplices lurched from the alley to join the prankster, and all three collapsed with helpless laughter. Indicating that Hannah was to stay where she was, Chaloner abandoned his hiding place and stood in front of the 'apparition'.

'Oh, Christ!' muttered the prankster when he saw Chaloner. His crown slipped, obliging him to make a grab for it before it fell. It put him in the light shining from the tavern, and with a shock Chaloner recognised the youthful features beneath the face paints. It was the printer from the Rainbow Coffee House, and the two apprentices with whom he had 'shot' the Bridge a few days before.

'*You* are responsible for all these ghostly sightings, Stedman?' asked Chaloner, stunned.

Stedman was unable to suppress a grin. 'We have been

doing it for more than a week now, and no one has even mentioned the possibility that the "ghost" might be a hoax. It is incredible!'

'And brilliant fun,' added one of his cronies. 'We have a few beers in a tavern, then Stedman emerges from the shadows when some likely victims come past.'

Chaloner was amazed they had not been caught – most of their pranks had been in front of witnesses, which was why the tales had gained so much credence. He doubted they had been careful, so he could only suppose they had been incredibly lucky.

'It has been fun,' agreed the other lad. He regarded Chaloner uncomfortably. 'But now we have been seen, and if this fellow tells anyone, we will be in trouble for certain.'

Stedman regarded Chaloner through bloodshot eyes. 'Chaloner will not give us away. He likes a joke as much as the next man, or he would not spend so much time listening to the ridiculous opinions spouted in the Rainbow Coffee House.'

'You are likely to get yourself killed if you persist with this charade,' warned Chaloner. 'Some of your victims may decide to respond to your spectre with their swords.'

Stedman's grin faded and he looked uneasy. 'You are not one of them, are you?'

'Go home,' said Chaloner, struggling not to smile. 'You have successfully hoodwinked an entire city, so abandon the game while you are still winning.'

'It is probably good advice,' said the friend, when Stedman looked ready to argue. 'If we quit now, no one will ever know the truth, and shall be able to gloat about it for years to come.'

They flung their arms around each others' shoulders

and lurched off, laughing and full of lively good spirits. Hannah stepped out of the shadows, and came to stand next to Chaloner.

'What a wonderful jape!' she exclaimed in admiration. 'They certainly had me convinced. But we are wasting time here, and there is a great hoard of gunpowder to locate. We had better hurry.'

Most of London was sleeping, so it did not take Chaloner and Hannah long to reach the theatre in Drury Lane. When they arrived, a party was in full swing, complete with a lot of raucous laughter and womanly shrieks. Chaloner deposited Hannah in a secluded alley, ostensibly to keep watch, then picked the lock on the theatre's door, and slipped inside.

A few moments of eavesdropping told him that Buckingham had provided the troupe with wine, to express his admiration for *The Indian Queen*. There was still a lot left, and Chaloner was under the impression that no one was going anywhere until the last cask was dry.

He sighed. The sensible thing would have been to solicit the actors' help to look for hidden fireworks – theatres were a jumble of cupboards, crates and awkward spaces, and it would take more time than he had to explore them all. But drunks were hardly ideal companions to go hunting explosives with, so he decided it would be safer if he did it alone.

It did not take him long to realise the task was impossible, though: the area beneath the stage alone was an enormous storage facility. He started to crawl through it, but someone had stowed spare curtains there, and it was impossible to conduct a proper search without first hauling them out. He tried, but they were too heavy, and the noise he made brought several people lurching to see what was happening. They did not find him, but he decided to leave when they went for reinforcements.

While they were summoning their comrades, he took a bucket of paint, and daubed a message on the wall – a threat saying the building would be blown up unless its players abandoned their sinful lives and became followers of the Prophet Elijah. There was no such sect, as far as he knew, so no one was likely to be blamed for the damage, but hopefully the words would serve to frighten everyone off the premises until they could be secured.

He left the theatre when the performers discovered the warning, and there was a concerted dash for the exits. Then he flagged down a lone hackney carriage that happened to be passing, and directed the driver to take him and Hannah to the Bridge.

'What happened?' asked Hannah as they went. 'Did you tell them the place might be full of explosives? Is that why they all came racing outside? Did you find anything amiss?'

Chaloner shook his head. 'So if the gunpowder is not in Chapel House, we shall have to return there tomorrow and search it properly. In daylight.'

'But I thought you said you had already searched Chapel House, and it was empty. *And* you said such large quantities of powder will not be easy to conceal, so it is not as if it is going to be slipped between the floorboards.'

'Actually, it might. False floors and artificial walls are not unknown, and the place has been full of builders for the last couple of weeks. And if we have no luck in Chapel House, there is only one other place I can think of: St Mary Overie, the masked men's erstwhile meeting place.'

Reluctant to leave Hannah alone on the Bridge, Chaloner took her with him when he forced the lock on Chapel House's front door. Once inside, she wrinkled her nose at the foul smell that pervaded the place. They soon discovered the source – the barrels of salted fish Leigh's men had opened in their hunt for gold. Trying not to breathe too deeply, they searched the place from top to bottom, measuring and tapping walls, and even prising up the floorboards. But there was no concealed cavity, and they were forced to admit defeat.

The trapdoor that led to the vault was open, though, and someone had been digging down there again. The statues in the crates had been decanted, too, and left scattered across the floor. Chaloner inspected one. It was a carving of a bishop, holding a Bible in one hand and a model church in the other. It was old, weathered and, to his mind, unremarkable.

'Why would anyone go to the trouble of storing this?' he demanded, frustration with their lack of progress making him irritable. 'It is damaged, ugly and poorly made.'

'I like it,' said Hannah, reaching down to touch the ancient features. 'It was carved in a time when England was Catholic, and artisans knew how to build *proper* churches. Not like these modern things, which are all white walls, silly domes and plain glass windows.'

'Becket,' said Chaloner suddenly. 'Could this be a statue of St Thomas Becket?'

Hannah studied it carefully. 'Yes, I suppose it might. He was an archbishop, and they were often depicted with Bibles and models of their cathedrals in their hands. But

345

if it is him, then so what? How does that knowledge help you?'

'I am not sure, only that it is another connection. The Dowager visits Winchester Palace to pray in the room where Becket was supposed to have stayed, and she has taken an obsessive interest in this house, which stands on the site of his chapel. Perhaps it is significant that these statues might depict him. But perhaps it is not.'

Aware that time was passing, he led Hannah at a brisk trot to St Mary Overie. They roused the vicar, and Hannah concocted a very convincing tale about a much-loved ring that had fallen through a grate into the crypt below. A little bemused that this should warrant a pre-dawn search, but sympathetic to her tears, Feake conducted them down the stairs to a damp, cobweb-draped vault. It was full of broken benches, mouldering altar clothes and ancient tables that no one seemed inclined to throw away. But there was no gunpowder.

There was, however, a large pile of muskets and swords, all carefully wrapped in blankets. Feake stared at them in horror. 'Those are not mine!'

'When were you last down here?' asked Chaloner coolly.

Feake shook his head helplessly, white-faced with shock. 'Months ago. These must belong to . . .' He trailed off and shot Chaloner an uneasy glance.

'To the men who used your church for meetings? The ones who said they would not be back?'

'They have not been back,' whispered Feake. There was an agonised expression on his face.

'No? Then you must take responsibility for these weapons yourself. I would not have taken you for a rebel, but in these uncertain times—'

'I am not a rebel!' cried Feake, appalled. 'And neither are they. At least, they do not seem like rebels. But if they are, then it is nothing to do with me. I did it for the poor . . . the money . . .'

'So they bought your silence, as well as your church,' said Chaloner coldly. Hannah was signalling for him to ease off, sorry for the agitated cleric, but the situation was far too urgent for a gentler approach, and they needed information. 'And you turned a blind eye as they amassed an armoury. That is treason.'

Feake was terrified. 'No! I admit they paid me to say nothing about their meetings, but I had no idea they were stockpiling weapons. Please! You *must* believe me!'

Chaloner did believe him, although he thought the man was guilty of just as grave a crime – namely looking the other way while something flagrantly untoward was going on. It was obvious the men were no angels, and Feake should have had the sense to refuse their bribes.

'Lock the crypt,' he ordered curtly. 'And go about your business as if nothing has happened. Do as I say, and you may yet redeem yourself.'

Feake began to cry, but Chaloner was not thinking about the vicar as he strode from the church, Hannah in tow. He was considering the implications of the cache.

'There is going to be some kind of armed uprising,' he said sharply, when Hannah began to berate him for his harsh treatment of a man who was, when all was said and done, a priest. 'And we must do whatever is necessary to stop it. If that involves upsetting Feake, then so be it.'

He expected her to argue, but she was silent. 'Do you think this uprising is going to coincide with the ignition of these deadly fireworks?' she asked eventually. 'You said the masked men include members of the Dowager's retinue.'

'I imagine so, yes.'

'Blue Dick,' said Hannah. 'Do you think Edward Penderel murdered him because he stumbled across their plot? He was killed to ensure he did not tell anyone?'

'It would make sense.'

Aware that time was running out fast – there were now only two days left before Shrove Tuesday, and dawn was already beginning to lighten the eastern sky – Chaloner flagged down a hackney carriage, and went to tell the Earl what he had found.

As it was Sunday, Hannah was obliged to escort the Queen to chapel, so she parted from Chaloner in the Great Court. He was relieved that she would be occupied for the rest of the day – it meant she could not sidle away on some investigation of her own, because although his mind was still full of questions, he was absolutely certain about one thing: they were dealing with some very ruthless and determined individuals, and he wanted her as far away from them as possible.

The Lord Chancellor was at church when Chaloner arrived, so he told Leigh about the discovery in St Mary Overie instead. The little soldier was not very interested, although he promised to send two men to claim the weapons before they could be used.

'No,' said Chaloner, wishing Leigh had a more tactical mind. 'We need to put St Mary Overie under surveillance, and see who comes to collect them.'

'You mean just look on, while villains grab this arsenal?' asked Leigh, regarding him warily.

'Of course not,' snapped Chaloner. Weariness and

tension were beginning to fray his nerves. 'Your men arrest whoever comes. Then they can be questioned about their plans.'

'But I do not have the troops for that sort of operation,' Leigh barked back. 'The Earl is ordering me here, there and everywhere for his Bishops' Dinner, and I can barely keep up with him. I will send two fellows to collect this cache, but I cannot keep them standing around indefinitely.'

'Surely, thwarting an uprising is more important than—'

'I do not trust your theories,' interrupted Leigh angrily. 'You were wrong about Great Queen Street, and you were wrong about the gold. I am wasting no more time on your fancies.'

And that was the end of the discussion. Chaloner watched him stamp away with a rising sense of despair. Was no one, other than Hannah, willing to help? Bulteel came to stand next to him.

'The Earl told me about these adapted fireworks,' he said. 'And I understand his reluctance to authorise a major search. If he does order one, Somerset House will say he is making spiteful allegations because he wants the Dowager to cancel her ball.'

'That is better than the alternative,' Chaloner pointed out acidly. 'Namely that Luckin and his cronies succeed in their objective, and the resulting outrage gives rise to innocent Catholics being attacked in the streets. Not to mention the carnage that might ensue, should these fireworks ignite.'

'You have no evidence that they exist *or* that it is Luckin who intends to use them,' Bulteel pointed out quietly. 'It is only a theory.'

'The Earl seemed ready to accept the possibility last night,' retorted Chaloner bitterly. 'But I have no idea where they might be. I have looked in Chapel House and St Mary Overie, and will return to the Drury Lane theatre later today. But there is no sign of the wretched things.'

Bulteel was thoughtful. 'The Earl has been saying for weeks that something odd is happening on the Bridge, and I understand that the wife of one of its wardens was attacked. Have you considered looking in Bridge House? I was shown around the place once, and it has huge, deep cellars. Moreover, it is not far from Chapel House, which you say has seen some suspicious activity.'

Chaloner stared at him. He was right! Angry that he had not seen it for himself, he ran out of White Hall, leapt into a hackney carriage, and ordered the driver to take him to Southwark as quickly as possible.

When he arrived, it was to find Bridge House deserted. The clerks did not work on Sundays, and the maid who answered the door said Hussey had taken his children to church, to give thanks for the birth of the latest Robert. She invited Chaloner to wait in the parlour, then pottered off on business of her own, leaving him unattended. It was too good an opportunity to miss, so he began to explore.

He had finished searching the upper chambers and was heading for the cellar, when Hussey and his brood arrived home. Loath to be caught somewhere he was not meant to be, Chaloner hid in a cupboard and waited while they stampeded past to the kitchen, intending to return to the parlour and wait for the maid to inform Hussey that he was there. But he could hear knives rattling on plates and the maid's agitated shrieks as the brats mobbed her for food, and had a feeling he might be waiting some time before she remembered him. It would not take a moment to investigate the basement, and there was no point in wasting time.

He padded to the cellar door and opened it. But it was to find himself confronted by a long, dark, stone stairway that reminded him painfully and unexpectedly of a French prison in which he had once been incarcerated. As the time he had spent there still gave him occasional nightmares, he froze in shock.

'Keep going,' came a soft whisper from behind. 'If you turn around, I will blow your head off.'

Chaloner recognised Hussey's voice, and also recognised the feel of a gun-barrel against his neck. He cursed the weakness that had turned him momentarily deaf, although he was not unduly alarmed by his predicament. Hussey would know him the moment he saw his face, and would let him go.

'I can explain,' he said, looking at the steps and thinking wild horses would not induce him to go down them. 'The Earl of Clar—'

But Hussey was not in the mood for chatter. He shoved Chaloner hard, sending him head over heels into the darkness. Chaloner's senses reeled as he hit the bottom, and he was only dimly aware of being grabbed by the collar and hauled forward. Then he was deposited on a floor, and heard a door slam and a bolt shot into place. Prison sounds. Chaloner's wits snapped clear.

'Hey!' he shouted to the retreating footsteps. 'Wait!'

'You can stay there until I summon the constables tomorrow,' Hussey called back. 'Burglars are the scourge of this fine city, and I mean to see justice done with the one I have caught.'

'I am not a burglar,' objected Chaloner. 'I am on the Lord Chancellor's staff, and—'

'A likely story,' sneered Hussey. His voice was already a long way away – he was climbing the stairs. 'The Earl of Clarendon is the last man to employ thieves.'

'We have met before,' called Chaloner, appalled by the turn of events. 'I visited you in your parlour, and your children—'

'I do not fraternise with criminals,' came Hussey's distant reply. 'And neither do they.'

'Please!' yelled Chaloner desperately, not liking the notion of being locked up, especially when there was so much to do outside. 'Contact Clarendon, tell him I am here. He will confirm my story.'

But Hussey had gone, and there was only silence.

Chaloner resisted the urge to hammer on the door and howl for release, and forced himself to explore his surroundings instead. Hussey had closed the door at the top of the stairs, leaving him in pitch blackness, but Chaloner estimated he was in a room that was perhaps twelve feet long by ten wide. Its walls were stone, and there were no loose or crumbling sections. The ceiling was low and dripped moisture, and the floor was beaten earth. There was no way out except through the door.

The chamber was empty, except for a long crate. Its lid was nailed down, and Chaloner fumbled to prise it open, fully expecting it to contain fireworks. But when his questing fingers slipped inside, they encountered something long and hard. At first, he thought it was a weapon, and his hopes rose. But it was short and uneven, and felt more like wood than metal. He groped his way along it, until he reached something akin to a basket. And further along again was something domed.

He yanked his hand away in horror. It was a skeleton! Was this what had happened to the last 'burglar' Hussey had caught? Panic overcame him then, and he spent several minutes kicking the door in an effort to break through it. But it was made of thick wood reinforced with iron; he could no more batter it down than he could dig his way through the stone walls. Moreover, the silence was absolute, and he knew he could shout himself hoarse, but no one would hear. He was trapped until Hussey came back. *If* Hussey came back.

Then he smiled. Hussey would talk to the maid, who would tell him a visitor was waiting in the parlour. When they found it empty, they would put two and two together and he would be released. The smile faded. Or would they? Hussey might simply conclude that the 'visitor' had requested an interview to get inside the house, and would be even more inclined to forget about him.

The hopelessness of his situation overwhelmed him at that point. He could not imagine a worse fate than being locked for ever in an underground chamber with no light. He slumped to the ground, pulled his knees up in front of him, and rested his head on his arms. What would Hannah say when he failed to return? And Thurloe? How long would the Earl take to find a replacement?

He supposed he must have dozed, because he came to his senses with a start some time later. Had he heard a sound? He listened intently, and became aware of a faint light shining under the door. It was not a large light – a candle, rather than a lamp. Then there was a scrape, and his room was suddenly brighter. With

353

horror, he saw there was a grille in the door. He *was* in a prison cell!

'There he is.' It was the exaggerated whisper of a child. 'He does not *look* like a burglar.'

'They never look like burglars,' came a scornful reply of another boy. 'If they went round looking like burglars, everyone would know what they were, and they would all be arrested.'

'Robert?' asked Chaloner, recognising the lad who had been berated for doing something ungenteel on the Bridge. How long ago was that? He could not say, because he had no idea how long he had been incarcerated. He was hungry, so he suspected several hours had passed.

'How do you know our names?' demanded the second speaker, the older of the pair.

'Will you take a message to the Lord Chancellor?' asked Chaloner, climbing to his feet. 'I will pay you. Bring me pen and paper, and I will write—'

'We had better not, because father will not like it,' said the younger of the pair. 'What did you steal?'

'Nothing,' replied Chaloner, squinting when the candle was thrust through the grille to allow the brats a better look at him. 'What is the time?'

'Eight o'clock,' replied the older Robert. 'In the evening. We brought you some food, because father will not remember, and we do not like to think of anyone going hungry.'

Something sailed through the grille, and then the lads were gone, taking their candle with them. Chaloner crawled across the floor, and groped around for what they had thrown him. It was a lump of cake, although it had suffered from bouncing across the floor, and was wet and gritty. He ate it anyway.

He slept again, but woke shivering. It was icy cold in the cellar, and the damp had penetrated his clothes. He warmed himself by pacing for a while, and tried to take his mind off the fix he was in by thinking about his investigations. Then he slipped into another series of restless dozes, waking every so often to wonder how many precious hours were slipping past. Or was it days by now?

Eventually, for something to do, he groped his way towards the box, intending to replace the lid as a mark of respect. His fingers brushed the skull as he did so. It felt fragile and dusty. Did that mean it was someone who had been dead for a long time? Or had the victim died recently, but corpses simply decayed faster in dank cellars?

He was startled out of his grim reverie by the re-appearance of the light. He stood quickly, and braced himself. If he grabbed a Robert, he could threaten to break the lad's neck unless their father released him. It was hardly a noble means of escape, but he was desperate enough to try it. The grille opened, revealing a plump face beyond. There was only one child this time, the smaller one.

'Do not make a sound,' the boy whispered. 'I have come to let you out.'

Chaloner was taken aback, and his hands dropped to his sides. 'Have you? Why?'

'Because father says you will hang, and I went to a hanging once and I did not like it. But you must promise never to burgle anyone again.'

'I was not burgling this time,' said Chaloner, as Robert began to struggle with the bolt. 'The Lord Chancellor ordered me to look for fireworks. I do not suppose you have seen any, have you? You seem an observant lad.'

Robert was flattered. 'Sir John Winter has plenty.

He keeps them in a warehouse by the river, but someone came in a cart yesterday and took them all away. The driver probably carried them to Somerset House, because Sir John is organising a display there.'

With a snap, the bolt finally opened and the door swung open. Chaloner shot through it before Robert could change his mind, and aimed for the stairs. He paused at the top, listening hard.

'It is all right,' said Robert from behind him. 'Father and the others have all gone for breakfast in the cookshop.'

'Breakfast?' asked Chaloner uneasily. 'What time is it?'

'Just past ten o'clock,' replied Robert, adding helpfully, 'On Monday morning. I would have let you out sooner, but this was the first opportunity.'

Christ!' muttered Chaloner, appalled by the lost time.

He thought fast. He had to be at the Bear tavern by noon, because that was the time stipulated in the note he had found in Winter's house, when someone was instructed to meet 'Goff'. There was just enough time to ask Leigh to search the Drury Lane theatre, and to send a message telling Hannah he was safe.

Leigh said he was too busy to talk, but was able to report that his men had collected the arms from St Mary Overie. They had admitted to a curious feeling of being watched, but had done nothing about it. Chaloner closed his eyes in despair.

'People are going to die if we do not stop this,' he whispered.

'Stop what?' demanded Leigh irritably. 'You have no evidence that anything is going to happen, just a lot of rumour, conjecture and disconnected facts. Have you considered the possibility that it is all a ruse? That

Somerset House *wants* us to think some diabolical plot is in the offing, to make sure the Earl does not enjoy his dinner tomorrow?'

'I wish that were true,' said Chaloner. 'But I *know* Luckin is behind something deadly. Will you search the theatre in Drury Lane, while I—'

'No,' interrupted Leigh firmly. 'I have neither the time nor the men. Where are you going?'

'The Bear tavern,' called Chaloner over his shoulder. 'If you will not explore the theatre, then will you tell Hannah you have seen me?'

'I certainly will,' muttered Leigh. 'Because perhaps *she* can talk some sense into you.'

The Bear at the Bridge Foot was full of smoke from a blocked chimney, and the resulting fug was unpleasant enough that its patrons were leaving in droves. Chaloner sat at the back, settling on a bench and pulling his hat over his eyes. He sat so still, and the room was so hazy, that he was soon invisible in the murk. Not that it mattered, because the smoke had ensured the place was empty, except for two men who sat together in a booth with high-backed benches.

On the stroke of noon, Winter burst in, flapping his hand in front of his face.

'God's saints!' he declared, coughing and gagging. 'The air in here is more poisonous than the glue-works around the Fleet River. I can barely breathe.'

'We know,' said one of the men in the booth. Chaloner recognised his voice as that of the man who had ambushed him when he had been following Herring. 'It is our way of ensuring we have the place to ourselves. Check it for lingerers, will you, Crow, and oust them?

357

And then tell the landlord to wait outside. He has already been paid.'

It was not difficult to elude Crow, because the fellow was so certain the ploy with the smoking chimney had worked that his search was cursory to say the least. When he had finished, he returned to the booth, joining Winter and the man who had issued the order. Undetected, Chaloner edged closer.

'My fireworks have been stolen!' Winter was saying angrily. 'Can you credit it? They were in my Southwark warehouse, but I arrived yesterday to discover thieves have been. They left me nothing but five Red Dragons, and I cannot imagine the Dowager being impressed with *those* when I promised her a spectacle. Damn the villains! If I ever catch them, I shall see them hanged.'

Crow murmured something too low for Chaloner to hear.

'Never mind that,' Winter went on furiously. 'What am I going to tell the Dowager? She—'

'We are sorry for you,' said Crow, speaking more loudly in an effort to stem the tirade. 'But we are not here to discuss your misfortunes.'

'Then why *are* we here?' demanded Winter. 'Why summon me with ciphered messages? What was wrong with coming to my house like civilised men? I wish you had, because then we could have had some music, and I—'

'That would have been rash,' interrupted Crow shortly. 'But let us get down to business. You are Catholic, and you have been heard expressing your dissatisfaction with the Clarendon Code. Are you willing to act on your principles and see these laws overturned?'

'I am not sure,' said Winter. His voice was much lower

now, and he sounded confused and uncertain. 'I *am* unhappy with the Code in its current form, but—'

'No buts,' snapped Crow. 'You either stand up for religious freedom, or you skulk like a dog and let others do it for you. Which will it be?'

'I am no rebel—'

'It is not rebellion. It is asking for what the King promised before we let him have his throne back. So, can we count on you?'

'All right,' said Winter, although he did not sound very convincing. 'But I want your assurance that there will be no violence—'

'We will contact you when you are needed,' said Crow. 'Goodbye, for now.'

Moustache quivering with indignation at the curt dismissal, Winter stood, bowed stiffly, and left. Chaloner was equally bemused. Such a question could have been asked anywhere, and it seemed unnecessarily circumspect to send coded notes. He was about to ease into a position where he might see the men's faces, when the back door opened and a heavily cloaked man shouldered his way towards the booth. He was someone Chaloner *did* know.

'Well?' Herring demanded. 'What did he say? Is he with us?'

'It was a mistake approaching him,' said Crow. 'He may know about gunpowder, but his heart is not with us. Thank God we held back today, and did not tell him our real intentions.'

'Thank God, indeed,' said the last of the trio.

'Nothing is going according to plan,' said Crow bitterly. 'And to top it all, the Lord Chancellor has wind of it. His spy would have caught us at Great Queen Street, had we not been warned.'

'It is Father Stephen's fault,' said Herring, exasperated. 'He is so nervous all the time that people are beginning to regard him with suspicion. His jittery behaviour will see us all hanged, and I vote we deal with him before he damages—'

'You mean kill him?' demanded the third man uneasily. 'No. I shall never agree to that.'

'But his escalating anxiety represents a danger to us all,' argued Herring. 'Moreover, he may be your brother, but I do not trust him.'

So the third member of the trio was Will Goff, thought Chaloner, although he had already surmised as much – the 'Goff' Winter had been summoned to meet was not the priest, so it stood to reason that it was his regicide brother. He eased to one side, to gain a glimpse of the man.

Goff had changed little since he had been in Buckinghamshire all those years before – greyer and leaner perhaps, but still tall, strong, arrogant and harsh. Chaloner's stomach churned at the notion that the plot was serious enough to warrant a convicted king-killer sneaking back into London. He ducked out of sight again.

'I agree with Herring,' Crow was saying. 'And anyway, I am not sure of Father Stephen's loyalty to his fellow Catholics – I think he may be blabbing information to the Anglicans.'

'Do not be ridiculous!' declared Goff contemptuously. 'There *is* a traitor in our midst, who passes secrets to the enemy, but it is not Stephen. He does not have the mettle.'

He spoke with considerable force, and Crow hastily changed the subject. 'Do we know yet who killed Blue Dick?' he asked. 'He was useful to us, and it vexes me that he is gone.'

360

'It was Edward Penderel,' replied Goff. 'Thurloe told me – and he had it from the Earl's spy, so it is likely to be true. But we should not stay here. I have the uncomfortable feeling that we are being watched. I know I say that every time we meet, but you cannot blame me for being cautious – if I am caught, I will be hanged, drawn and quartered, like so many of our old friends.'

The three men fastened coats and adjusted hats in readiness for leaving. Crow went first, heading for the Bridge and Southwark. Chaloner did not bother with him, feeling he was a comparatively lowly cog in the wheel. Meanwhile, Herring and Goff went towards Thames Street, where they climbed into a carriage. Goff was limping, perhaps from when Chaloner had stabbed him in the leg during the ambush in the dark lanes by Charing Cross.

Chaloner hired another hackney to follow the rebels' coach. The driver was delighted, claiming he had always wanted to be involved in a chase, and Chaloner was hard-pressed to keep him from making the pursuit obvious. They rattled across the Fleet Bridge, then turned right into Chancery Lane. Chaloner indicated his driver was to pull into an alley, and watched, stomach churning, as a heavily disguised – but to his mind still recognisable – figure stepped out of the shadows to join them. It was Thurloe.

Chaloner felt physically sick. He had known Thurloe was embroiled in something dangerous, but it was still a shock to see him in company with iconoclasts and regicides. He leaned against the side of the coach, and closed his eyes.

'Well?' demanded his driver. 'Do we follow them again?'

Numbly, Chaloner nodded, knowing he needed to see the thing through, no matter where it took him. The driver had learned fast, and kept a respectable distance between him and his quarry, so Chaloner was sure Thurloe and his confederates would have no idea they were being tailed as they turned left along Holborn, past the Church of St Giles-in-the-Fields, and towards Tyburn Gibbet.

There was apparently going to be a hanging that day, because the heath on which the scaffold stood was full of people. Both carriages were obliged to slow, and Chaloner heard snippets of conversation through his window. Apparently, two robbers and a witch were going to be executed. People did not care about the robbers – these were dispatched on a regular basis – but the witch was unusual. Eventually, Chaloner's carriage rolled to a standstill.

'There,' said the driver, pointing to where Thurloe, Herring and Goff were alighting.

Chaloner paid him, although his inclination was to stay in the vehicle and ask to be taken home. He had no desire to witness hangings, and was astonished that Thurloe should attend one – the ex-Spymaster had always claimed to find them distasteful.

He could see Thurloe some distance ahead, walking between the regicide and the iconoclast, smaller than both. Goff moved like a panther, all coiled energy and power, while Herring was like a bull. The trio were heading towards a series of cartwheels, semi-permanent fixtures placed to give anyone who could afford them a good view of the entertainment. Thurloe paid a fee, and a cartwheel was his. He and Herring stepped behind it, positioning themselves so they would not be seen by passers-by, while Goff pulled his hat lower over his face and slipped away into the crowd.

So now what? Chaloner could not eavesdrop, because Thurloe had chosen a wheel that would be impossible to approach without being spotted. But Chaloner had had enough of subterfuge, anyway. He desperately needed to know what was going on, and the only way to find out was by asking direct questions of men with answers. He walked boldly towards them.

Thurloe spun around at the sound of his footsteps, and Herring drew his sword. A flicker of horror crossed Thurloe's face, but was quickly suppressed and replaced by impassivity.

'I know him,' came a voice from behind. Chaloner knew it was Will Goff, and also knew exhaustion and confusion had led him to lower his guard, because he had not heard him approach. He felt the cold muzzle of a gun press against his neck for the second time in as many days.

'I doubt it,' said Thurloe. His voice was casual, but there was alarm in his eyes. 'He is just someone of no consequence from Lincoln's Inn. Do not cause a scene, Will. Let him go.'

'But he looks familiar,' insisted Goff. 'I never forget a face.'

Chaloner could only suppose he remembered the boy with the viol, because they had never met otherwise, except during the fracas near Charing Cross, when it had been too dark to see.

'*He* may never forget a face, either,' said Herring, stepping forward grimly. 'And I do not want him remembering ours. I shall run him through – no one will see me, hidden behind this wheel. No, do not shoot him,

363

Goff! A gunshot here would see us all in the Tower for certain.'

Suddenly, there was a dagger in Thurloe's hand. Chaloner was so startled, he could not move fast enough to avoid the blow that came slicing towards him. He felt the knife cut through his jerkin and stumbled forward. Thurloe held him for a moment, then let him drop to the ground.

'He is not related to Tom Chaloner, is he?' came Goff's voice. 'My dear old fellow regicide?'

'No,' replied Thurloe shortly, sheathing his blade. 'But we cannot stay here now. Mingle with the crowd, Herring, to see whether it really is Edward Penderel who is being hanged today. Will and I shall leave, and you can catch up with us later.'

The wheel creaked as Herring stepped on to it. 'There is no need for mingling. It *is* Edward. He is trying to make a speech, protesting the verdict, but no one is listening.'

There was a sudden cheer from the mob. 'I take it he has been tipped from the ladder,' said Thurloe bleakly. 'I cannot look. I detest these spectacles.'

'We should go,' said Herring, climbing down. 'We do not want to be caught with a body.'

When Chaloner was sure Thurloe, Herring and Goff had gone, he opened his eyes, and eased up on one elbow. Thurloe had taught him 'fake killings' years before, when he had been in training – a blow that looked deadly, but that actually passed harmlessly under the arm. The manoeuvre had not gone entirely to plan, because Thurloe had not been strong enough to pull him into the proper position, and had scored a scratch across his ribs. He winced as he scrambled to his feet.

Thurloe had certainly saved his life, probably at considerable risk to himself. However, the company he was keeping did not bode well for a happy ending – Goff and Herring had barely raised an eyebrow when a man had been 'murdered' in front of them, suggesting they regarded violence as an acceptable means to whatever end they were working towards.

And what end was that? To see the Clarendon Code abolished and religious freedom in its place? Or to overthrow the government that had devised it, and replace it with a Puritan regime? Were they working with Luckin? Chaloner sincerely hoped they were – the notion of two uprisings, headed by such dangerous and determined men, was too dreadful to contemplate.

Now the hangings were over, people were beginning to disperse, and he joined the stream of folk aiming for the gates. He glanced up at the gibbet as he passed, and saw one of the dead men was indeed Edward Penderel.

'What did he do?' he asked the executioner.

'Burglary,' the hangman replied. 'He was caught red-handed by Spymaster Williamson, just as he was coming out of Chapel House, all loaded down with gold.'

Chaloner looked sharply at him. 'When was this?'

'Last Saturday morning. Were you not listening to the charges that were read out before he swung? It was at half-past eight exactly, and he was unlucky that the Spymaster happened to be passing with a few of his soldiers.'

Unlucky indeed, thought Chaloner, because he knew for a fact that Edward had been in White Hall at that particular time. It was indelibly fixed in his mind, because it was when he had escorted the Earl to the King's Presence Chamber, and all four Penderels had refused to let him pass.

His mind a whirl of confusion, he watched the hangman cut the bodies down. Friends and relatives were waiting to collect them – three women for the witch, a buxom lady for her husband, and two men for Edward, although neither were his brothers. Chaloner frowned. Both wore large hats that concealed their faces, but their postures were familiar . . .

His mind focused sharply for the first time since he had seen Thurloe climb into the carriage with Goff and Herring. Angrily, he decided he had had enough of being buffeted this way and that by an investigation that made no sense, and it was high time he had some answers. He crawled beneath the gibbet and emerged on the other side, standing quickly to press his dagger into Swaddell's side before either he or Spymaster Williamson realised what was happening.

'There is no need for that,' cried Williamson, when he saw his henchman's predicament. 'Swaddell is unwell – he should not even be out of bed. He is no threat to you, so put down your knife.'

The Spymaster was a tall, aloof man, who had a reputation for being ruthless and greedy. Swaddell was his favourite assassin, a small, dark fellow who always wore black, and whose eyes were never still. Swaddell was an extremely dangerous man, and Chaloner had no intention of following the order to disarm. Then he frowned.

'Is Swaddell unwell because the Penderel brothers trounced him?' he asked.

Swaddell grimaced, obviously disgusted with himself. 'They caught me unawares.'

'Is that why you arranged to have Edward hanged?' asked Chaloner. 'To repay them for besting you?'

'No, we did that because I am not in a position to

dispatch him more discreetly,' said Swaddell sullenly. 'Williamson is right about the fragile state of my health.'

Slowly, he raised his hand and removed his hat. His face was so swollen that it was all but unrecognisable. He nodded his gratitude when Chaloner, seeing he was in no state to cause trouble, stepped back and sheathed his blade.

'And why should you want Edward dead?' Chaloner asked.

'Because he was a killer,' replied Williamson coldly. 'And how do I know? Well, first, Phillippes the dial-maker saw a Penderel stab Blue Dick. Second, Swaddell searched their house and found Edward's bloodstained clothes. And third, I heard him brag about the crime with my own ears – to a whore, when he was in his cups. It was as black and white a case as I have ever encountered.'

'Then why not charge him with it?' asked Chaloner. 'Why invent accusations of burglary?'

'It is better this way.'

Chaloner was about to demand a more enlightening answer, when all became clear. 'Blue Dick was working for you!' he exclaimed in understanding. 'You recruited him to spy on his fellow iconoclasts. My God! You must have some remarkable powers of persuasion, because such men tend to be deeply committed to their causes.'

Williamson smirked. 'He proved very valuable to me for several weeks. Unfortunately, my other spies are unsettled by his murder, so I decided to make Edward an example. Now my people see what happens to those who harm them, they know I take their welfare seriously.'

There was a certain shabby plausibility about his explanation – Williamson did *not* care about his intelligencers, with the possible exception of Swaddell, but he would

367

not want them too frightened to work for him. Edward might well have been used to make them feel better about their master.

'And the tale about Edward's theft of gold from Chapel House?' Chaloner asked. 'Is there any truth in it at all?'

'Not really,' replied Swaddell. 'Blue Dick told us that Edward visited the place on occasion, but we were unable to ascertain why. We settled on saying Edward stole gold, because what else can one remove from an empty house?'

'So, this vile killer is dead,' said Williamson, regarding Edward's body contemptuously. 'But unfortunately, he murdered Blue Dick before I could learn what these damned fanatics are planning to do. I am in the dark and very worried.'

Chaloner rubbed his chin. It went against the grain to share intelligence with Williamson, but he could not avert a catastrophe on his own. Besides, it was the Spymaster's job to prevent trouble. So, he told him about the arms cache in St Mary Overie, his suspicion that Lord Bristol was in the city, the populace's growing objection to the Clarendon Code, and the possibility that deadly fireworks were waiting to be ignited. He named Luckin as his chief suspect, but said nothing about Herring and Will Goff, lest they led to Thurloe.

'I shall arrange for the Bridge and the Drury Lane theatre to be searched today,' promised Williamson when he had finished. 'Of course, I shall have to fabricate an excuse that will not have half of London baying for Catholic blood.'

'Blame it on a sect devoted to the Prophet Elijah,' suggested Chaloner.

The Spymaster looked puzzled. 'I have never heard of such a faction.'

'It does not exist,' explained Chaloner, a little impatiently. 'That is the point – no one will be held accountable and attacked because of it.'

Williamson nodded assent. 'Meanwhile, I suggest you look in Somerset House for these fireworks. My spies saw a lot of green salad being delivered there yesterday. Now, I know the Dowager is having a ball tomorrow, but there is a limit to the amount of green salad that can be consumed, and this went well past it. *Ergo*, I surmise something was hidden beneath the stuff.'

'*You* look,' objected Chaloner. 'Preventing explosions is your responsibility, not mine.'

Williamson's expression hardened. 'I cannot do everything myself. How many spies do you think I have? *You* tackle Somerset House; *I* will take the Bridge and Drury Lane.'

'But Somerset House is full of my master's enemies,' Chaloner pointed out. 'I cannot just march in and ask to poke through her green salad. It will be much better if you do it.'

'Better for whom?' demanded Williamson archly. 'The intelligence may be faulty, and I do not want to incur the wrath of that rabble, thank you very much. It is different for you – they hate you already.'

'You should talk to the Penderel brothers first though,' said Swaddell, before Chaloner could argue further. 'Our sources say they arrived back in London late last night. Perhaps Luckin has finally confided in them, and they will be able to tell you precisely what is being planned.'

'Me?' asked Chaloner, not liking the way the assignments were being allocated. '*You* do it.'

Swaddell shot him a reproachful glance. 'In my condition?'

'And I cannot manage it, either,' added Williamson. 'You may think Luckin's uprising is important, but it is not the only devilry currently in progress, and my hands are extremely full at the moment. You speak to the Penderels – and send me word if you learn anything pertinent.'

'There is one other thing you may find useful,' said Swaddell, cutting through Chaloner's objections a second time. 'The Dowager's devotion to St Thomas Becket is significant. Unfortunately, we do not know why.'

Williamson shot Chaloner a nasty little smile as he began to walk away. 'This is a very dangerous business. I do hope you will be careful.'

Chaloner watched them go, feeling that he was just as much alone as he had been before he had told the Spymaster General and his most dedicated henchman everything he had learned.

Chapter 11

Chaloner decided to follow Swaddell's recommendation and visit the surviving Penderels straight away, lest they disappeared again. He flagged down a hackney to take him to Tothill Street, and when he arrived, his knock was answered by Oliver, who grinned evilly and gestured with one of his scarred fists that he was to enter their house. Chaloner declined.

'I came to bring you news,' he said quietly, when Rupert and Neville came to stand with their brother on the doorstep. 'Edward is dead.'

'You lie!' cried Oliver. He started to reach for Chaloner, but Rupert stopped him with a look.

'How do you know?' Rupert asked.

'I have just seen his body.'

'No!' snarled Oliver. This time Rupert's glare was to no avail, and Neville was obliged to leap forward and restrain him. The knife from Chaloner's sleeve slipped into his hand.

'Enough,' barked Rupert. He lowered his voice when Oliver stopped struggling and fixed him with a stricken expression. 'Edward has been gone too long, Oliver, and we guessed something dreadful had happened. He would have come home, had he been able.'

'You are all in very deep trouble,' said Chaloner. 'But you may yet save yourselves from a traitors' death, if you answer some questions.'

'We are not telling you anything,' shouted Oliver, trying to break free of Neville's hold.

'Yes, we are,' said Rupert softly. Oliver gaped at him, and he continued. 'Neville was right all along – we are out of our depth in this place, and we should not have come. It is time to cut our losses and do what we can to extricate ourselves.'

'Thank God!' breathed Neville, sagging in relief. 'Sense at last!'

Rupert turned to Chaloner. 'Do you *promise* that talking to you will save us from the scaffold?' Chaloner nodded, although it was hardly in his power to make such an arrangement. 'Very well, then. Ask your questions, and let us be done with it.'

'The evidence for Edward's guilt is overwhelming,' Chaloner began. 'He *did* kill Blue Dick—'

'Yes!' bellowed Oliver, tears of anguish and rage beginning to flow down his cheeks. 'Yes, he did stab that vile iconoclast and I am glad he did his duty. I am proud of him!'

'Take him inside,' Rupert ordered Neville. 'We will work with the Earl's man, but we do not have to dig ourselves into a deeper hole with foolish defiance. *I* will do the talking.'

Neville did as he was told, although Oliver fought him every step of the way. When they had gone, Rupert turned to Chaloner, his expression haunted.

'As you have probably surmised – there are enough

rumours circulating about it – there is a plan afoot to rally anyone who disagrees with the Clarendon Code. It is an unpopular set of laws, so the number of people expected to take part in the demonstration will be enormous. The problem is . . .'

'Yes?'

'The problem is . . . Luckin told us last night that the protest will not stop with the Clarendon Code. Some people dislike other things about the government, too.'

'So insurgents plan to hijack a peaceful protest, and transform it into something it was never intended to be? A rebellion?'

'In essence,' agreed Rupert unhappily. 'Anyone who has lived through the wars knows how easy it is to turn a passive crowd into a horde of vengeful zealots. All it needs are a few explosions and some rumours, and the thing will take on a life of its own.'

'Explosions?' pounced Chaloner. 'Where will these be?'

'We have not been told. I thought at first that Luckin planned to sabotage Winter's firework display, but now I am not so sure. There is a rumour that Drury Lane will be attacked, and Luckin has never liked theatres. Or perhaps he will pick on Clarendon House – everyone is appalled that your Earl should be building himself such a fancy new mansion at tax-payers' expense.'

'I thought you were a Royalist,' said Chaloner in disgust. 'Yet you see a plot like this in the making, and you do nothing to stop it?'

'I *am* a Royalist,' objected Rupert. 'We would never do anything to harm the King. But Luckin says this is not about the King, it is about his government—'

'You think the King will emerge unscathed if his government is deposed? That is not how these things work.'

'But we did not know who we could trust!' cried Rupert desperately. 'It would not do to go to the wrong person, and I cannot read anyone at White Hall – cannot tell traitors from loyalists. Besides, I am Catholic. Why *should* I help to prevent an event that may see my religion benefit?'

'Because you do not condone bloodshed? Or the vengeful slaughter of your co-religionists when this misguided plot fails? Jesus wept, man! How could you go along with such dark mischief?'

Rupert looked away. 'It started out as a simple plot to give your Earl a bit of a fright. But suddenly, other people were involved – killers, zealots and rabble-rousers, with whom we would never normally associate.' He turned back to Chaloner, holding out his hands in entreaty. 'We are guilty of following stupid orders in return for money, but we are not traitors.'

There was no point wasting time by continuing to point out the folly of what they had done.

'I am sure killing Blue Dick was not Edward's idea,' said Chaloner instead. 'So who ordered the murder?'

'I do not know. The instruction came in a letter – the culprit took care to keep his identity secret. Edward was well rewarded, though, so it was someone wealthy. The message said Blue Dick was a traitor to the cause. Well, that was true – we have since learned that he was telling our secrets to the Spymaster.'

'Tell me what happened on the day Blue Dick was stabbed. He visited Chapel House briefly . . .'

'He was monitoring it for Williamson, and he often slipped in to poke around, although I do not know why. When he came out, Edward killed him. Unfortunately, you saw the whole thing.'

'He fled to St Mary Overie. Were you among the masked men I fought there?'

Rupert hesitated, but then nodded. 'Yes. With Neville, Oliver and three courtiers from Somerset House. I wanted to shoot you, but I found I could not do it. I am not a natural killer.'

No, he was not, thought Chaloner, and was grateful that Oliver or Edward had not been holding the gun, because he suspected neither of them would have hesitated to pull the trigger.

'Edward never told us he was going to kill Blue Dick,' Rupert went on. 'We were horrified when he confessed to what he had done. But killing came easier to him than the rest of us – even Oliver baulks at inflicting a fatal blow, which is why the Spymaster's creature still lives.'

'Nat,' said Chaloner, changing the subject abruptly. He was not interested in Rupert's attempts to distance himself from his brother's excesses. 'The beggar who was strangled and tossed in the river for asking questions. Who murdered him?'

Rupert looked away again. 'Luckin. For a vicar, he is a turbulent soul. I think he enjoyed it.'

'Tell me about Luckin. And about your clandestine meetings in Lord Bristol's house.'

Rupert paled at the notion that Chaloner knew so much about his activities, and his voice was unsteady when he replied. 'Luckin has gathered quite an army, and when St Mary Overie became unsafe, he told us to use the Great Queen Street mansion instead.'

'Was he one of the swordsmen in St Mary Overie on the day Blue Dick was killed?'

'No. If he had been, you and Leigh would be dead.'

'The last I heard of him was when he galloped away intent on mischief – in company with you.'

'That was not mischief! We were warned that there would be a raid on Great Queen Street – do not ask me by whom, because I do not know – so Luckin said it was a good time to bring some fireworks to London. That was innocent, at least. They are a surprise for the Dowager, in addition to the ones Winter is making.'

'Did you take them to Somerset House?'

'Well, no. Luckin took them elsewhere. Why? What is so important about a few Red Rockets?'

'Are you sure it was Red Rockets on Luckin's cart? Did you see them?'

'They were covered with tarpaulin, to protect them from the rain.' Rupert blanched as the realisation dawned that Luckin could have been transporting anything. 'You must think us fools.'

Chaloner nodded.

Rupert gave a strained smile. 'So what happens now? Will you arrest us?'

Chaloner did not have time. He pointed to the kitchen, which, like Hannah's, possessed a door with a substantial bolt. Without a word, Rupert walked towards it and took a seat at the table next to Neville. Oliver leapt to his feet, scowling as he tried to work out what was happening.

'You are facing some very dangerous and committed people,' said Rupert, as Chaloner started to close the door. 'And Luckin has vowed to kill you.'

'I imagine he will have more important things to occupy his time for the next few hours,' said Chaloner grimly.

'Perhaps, but a man matching your description was seen in Southwark just before his nephews disappeared.

376

Watch him, Chaloner. I have never met a man with a greater love for vengeance.'

With the warning ringing in his ears, Chaloner bolted the kitchen door, then ran to the back of the house, where he secured the rear entrance by bracing it with planks of wood. Oliver bawled obscenities all the while, but Neville and Rupert were silent. The moment Chaloner was sure they could not escape, he went to Hannah's home, relieved to find her safe.

'Tom!' she exclaimed. 'Thank God! Where have you been? I have been worried!'

'Williamson is searching the Bridge and Drury Lane for the adapted fireworks,' said Chaloner, sinking down on to a chair. He tried to remember the last time he had eaten a proper meal, and was hungry enough that he even took a piece of Hannah's homemade gingerbread. He gagged on its fiery flavour. 'And I must do the same at Somerset House.'

'I have news for you, too,' she said, sitting next to him. 'The Duke came earlier, to tell me the plan for tomorrow. We are all to make black bands. Then, when he gives the signal, we are to leave the Somerset House ball, and assemble outside White Hall with these ribbons covering our eyes. It is to symbolise the government's blind refusal to see justice.'

'Explosions and rumours will be used to turn it into a riot,' Chaloner explained tiredly. 'And while troops struggle to quell the trouble, Luckin will be causing mischief elsewhere, using his army of masked men. The weapons stored in St Mary Overie will not be his only cache. *And* there are the fireworks, which we have so far failed to locate.'

Hannah swallowed hard, but then her face flooded

with resolve. 'We must stop him, Tom. He cannot get away with this! Do you see what he is doing? His vile deeds will be blamed on the poor, innocent Catholics who met at Somerset House on Saturday night. If they are not massacred immediately, there will be lynchings and persecutions for weeks to come.'

'Yes,' agreed Chaloner. 'You say the rally will be at White Hall. Perhaps *that* is Luckin's target – the firework-bombs will be ignited there.'

'No.' Hannah's voice was unsteady. 'For two reasons. First, because the demonstrators will be there, and Luckin will not kill the people he wants blamed for whatever happens. And second, it is the King's home. Luckin's fight is not with His Majesty.'

'No? How do you know? I imagine fanatics like Luckin, Will Goff and Herring are more than willing to sacrifice lives to achieve whatever it is they want, including that of the King.'

Hannah's expression was bitter. 'These men *are* extreme, but the Earl of Clarendon is just as bad – he is the one who passed all these repressive laws to start with. And the Dowager is a fanatic, too, with her peculiar fascination for St Thomas Becket. She does not seem to care about anything else.'

'Becket,' said Chaloner softly, recalling Swaddell's conviction that the Dowager's devotion to the saint was significant.

Hannah was chattering on. 'The Duke told me that her fixation with him started when someone sent her a message, saying that his bones had been spirited out of Canterbury Cathedral during the Reformation, and secretly buried in the chapel on the Bridge. Of course, the tale is untrue, because it is a matter of record that

378

they were destroyed, but . . . Tom? What is wrong? What have I said?'

Chaloner was staring at her. '*Who* sent her the message saying Becket's relics were on the Bridge?'

'The letter was anonymous. The Duke was delighted, though, because as long as the Dowager has Becket's mortal remains to occupy her, she is blind to all else, which means he can organise his rally without her interference. He said he could not have planned it better, had he sent this missive himself.'

Finally, Chaloner saw the beginnings of a solution. He stood abruptly. 'I must speak to the Earl immediately. I will try to come back later, but if I am busy, please swear to me that you will not attend Buckingham's demonstration tomorrow.'

Hannah regarded him askance. 'I cannot promise that! Supposing there comes an opportunity to ask questions, or even to expose the plot before it can ignite? I would have to break my word!'

'No!' Chaloner took her in his arms. 'You have done more than enough already, and if you try to interfere now, all you will do is put yourself in danger. I could not bear it if . . .'

'I will be careful.' Hannah patted his cheek, then kissed him in a businesslike way. 'And so will you. Oh, do not look so horrified! Did you really expect me to sit at home while such devilry is at work? As I have said before, I shall do as my conscience dictates.'

Her and Thurloe both, thought Chaloner unhappily as he took his leave.

Dusk came early that night, because of the rain. It was not the hard, drenching stuff, but a persistent drizzle that

379

encouraged shopkeepers to close early and people to hurry along with their hats pulled low. The dampness trapped the smoke from the thousands of homes with coal fires, and it turned the streets dull and foggy. Chaloner coughed, feeling particles of grit catch at the back of his throat.

'Edward Penderel is dead,' he said without preamble, as he entered the Earl's office. Leigh was there, too, and looked up in surprise at the abrupt intrusion. 'And you were right: he did kill Blue Dick, although he was acting on the orders of another.'

'Who?' demanded the Earl.

Chaloner shrugged. 'It could be anyone. Blue Dick associated with a lot of unsavoury people, and he betrayed them. Or perhaps someone objected to what he had done in his past.'

'It will be a fanatic,' predicted Leigh sagely. 'From one end of the spectrum or the other.'

'What?' demanded the Earl irritably. 'What are you talking about? What spectrum?'

'The religious spectrum,' elaborated Leigh. 'On the one hand, you have fervent Catholics, like Progers, the Penderels, Phillippes and Kaltoff, Junior Warden Scarlet and those Capuchins. And on the other, there are Anglican maniacs like Herring and that horrible vicar from Wimbledon. Any one of them might be responsible for ordering Blue Dick killed.'

'Do you really think there will be an armed uprising tomorrow?' asked the Earl uneasily, ignoring the little soldier and turning back to Chaloner. 'I confess, I have been rather absorbed with my Bishops' Dinner. Perhaps I should have given the matter more thought.'

'If so, then all these religious lunatics must have banded

380

together,' said Leigh, before Chaloner could agree. 'There cannot be more than one rebellion planned for the same day, so the two extremes must have united.'

Chaloner supposed it was possible, although it would take a lot of tolerance and understanding from men not normally noted for either.

'Lord Bristol,' said the Earl bitterly. 'At least we know why *he* is rumoured to be home. He has wind of this plot, and is standing in the wings, ready to turn it to his advantage. Or perhaps the whole thing was his idea. God knows, he is wicked enough.'

Chaloner turned to another matter, the one that had driven him so quickly from Hannah's house a few moments before. 'What do you know about St Thomas Becket, sir?'

The Earl blinked at him, then looked decidedly furtive. 'Why?'

'Because someone sent the Dowager a letter, telling her his bones were buried on the Bridge – in the chapel dedicated to him before it was demolished. She ordered Scarlet and his wife out of their house, ostensibly so it could be renovated, but really so she could search it properly.'

The Earl smirked. 'I cannot see the Dowager on her hands and knees with a trowel.'

'She sent someone else to do it – the dial-makers, Phillippes and Kaltoff.'

'You may be right,' conceded the Earl. 'They are Catholic, they live on the Bridge and they are sometimes invited to soirees in Somerset House. She will know them well enough to beg favours.'

'The Dowager is determined to find these relics,' Chaloner went on. 'She prays in Winchester Palace, and has even started collecting old statues of him.'

The Earl nodded smugly. 'Catholics do that sort of thing.'

Chaloner took a deep breath. 'It was you who sent that letter, sir,' he said quietly. 'You did it to distract her from her campaign to damage you. Unfortunately, she has taken it rather more seriously than you anticipated.'

'How dare you!' cried the Earl, incensed. 'I did nothing of the kind!'

'Steady, Chaloner,' breathed Leigh, also shocked. 'You go too far.'

But Chaloner forged on. 'Unfortunately, the deception has done more harm than good. Her obsession has rendered her oblivious to what else is going on in her household. In other words, Luckin's plot has gained momentum because she has been too distracted to stop it. She hates the Clarendon Code, but she would never use a rebellion to see it overturned.'

The Earl's indignation turned to disquiet. 'What are you saying?'

'Buckingham crowed that he could not have arranged it any better himself. In other words, you diverted the one person who might have knocked some sense into these schemers.'

The Earl's face was ashen. 'No! I *did* want her to stop criticising our new laws and think about something else. But I did not intend . . .'

'I wish I had known all this last week,' said Chaloner. 'Because then I would not have wasted time looking into the curious happenings at Chapel House. I thought it was all part of the same plot, but it is not – the searches of that building have nothing to do with Luckin's uprising.'

'And if you *had* known, you could have planted a bone for her minions to find,' said Leigh brightly. 'Then she would have worshipped it, and turned her attention back to more important matters.'

The Earl regarded Chaloner with hopeful eyes. 'Can you lay your hands on a few bones today?'

'No,' replied Chaloner. 'And even I could, it would be too late to prevent this crisis.'

'But what about in the longer term?' pressed the Earl. 'You are right in that she took my letter more seriously than I anticipated, and now you have me worried. If you worked out that I am the culprit, then others might, too. She will come after me like a Fury.'

'We cannot let that happen,' said Leigh anxiously. 'Send her another anonymous note, saying you were mistaken – that all Becket's relics are accounted for, and she is wasting her time.'

'I have already considered that,' said the Earl miserably. 'But it will not work. You see, she *wants* the tale to be true, and hope is a very powerful thing. I cannot dissuade her now.'

'The King will be furious when he hears his mother was hoodwinked,' mused Leigh tactlessly. 'Especially on a matter concerning religion.'

'Lord!' groaned the Earl, covering his face. 'What have I done?'

The Earl only had himself to blame for his predicament, thought Chaloner, and he was far more worried about Luckin than what the Dowager might say when she learned she had been the victim of a hoax. He left White Hall, aiming for Somerset House and his resumption of the search for deadly fireworks, but had not gone far before he met Wiseman. The surgeon rushed towards him and grabbed his arm urgently.

'Thank God I have found you! Someone sent me this, and I need your help.'

He shoved a letter in Chaloner's hand. Chaloner walked towards the nearest house, to read it in the faint light that filtered through the window. It warned the surgeon that Warden Scarlet and his wife were in imminent danger, and should be removed from Wych Street immediately.

'Do you know who sent this?' asked Chaloner warily. 'The writer has left it unsigned.'

'Of course,' snapped Wiseman. 'I would recognise Brother Pascal's writing anywhere. He is a good man, despite his unfortunate choice of religion.'

'Tell Leigh,' suggested Chaloner, handing the letter back. 'He can send soldiers to protect Jane.'

'Leigh is no good,' snapped Wiseman. 'He is too preoccupied with the Bishops' Dinner. But poor Jane has suffered enough, and while I am more than a match for most men, I am not skilled in the kind of dirty, sly warfare employed by ruffians. You are, though.'

It was hardly a remark destined to win friends. 'I have work to do.'

'Then it will have to wait,' snapped Wiseman, waving frantically at an approaching carriage. 'Jane is far more important than week-dead iconoclasts.'

'You refused to let me talk to her earlier,' mused Chaloner. 'But if you had, she might have provided clues to show that week-dead iconoclasts and the attack on her are connected. And she would be safe already.'

Wiseman gaped at him, and the hackney thundered past without stopping. 'What?'

'Scarlet and Jane live in Chapel House,' explained Chaloner. 'Where the Dowager hopes to locate the relics of St Thomas Becket. The Dowager is a determined lady, and when she did not find what she wanted, she dispatched henchmen to question the Scarlets.'

'Are you saying the *Dowager* is responsible for what happened to Jane?' Wiseman was appalled and disbelieving. 'She would never stoop so low, not even for saintly bones.'

'No,' agreed Chaloner. 'And I suspect she was as shocked by the assault as anyone. But she employs ruthless men, and they are not always easy to control once they have been given free rein.'

Wiseman turned his attention to the road again. 'We shall discuss this later, when Jane is safe. I think the best place to take her is Chyrurgeons' Hall. She can have my rooms.'

'Where will you stay?'

Wiseman blushed a little. 'Temperance will find me a corner.'

Chaloner cringed when the surgeon leapt in front of a carriage, forcing the driver to rein in sharply. It already had a passenger, but Wiseman hauled the fellow out by the scruff of the neck, simultaneously promising the astonished hackneyman a fabulously generous reward for driving to Wych Street with all possible speed. The driver accepted with alacrity, leaving his previous customer waving his fist in impotent fury as the coach rattled away.

The journey was a wild one, with Wiseman yelling for more speed, and the driver determined to oblige. They tore along The Strand like the wind. Chaloner hung on grimly, expecting at every moment for the vehicle to overturn. When they arrived at Wych Street, the horse's flanks were slippery with sweat, and it was gasping for breath. Wiseman shoved a heavy purse at the driver.

'We must hurry,' he said, grabbing Chaloner's arm and hauling him towards the Scarlets' lodgings. 'Pascal's note did not specify a time for the attack, but the sooner we have Jane safely ensconced in Chyrurgeons' Hall, the happier I will be.'

He rapped on a downstairs window. Next door, the Shakespeare's Head rang with acrimonious voices. They were discussing the late king's ghost, and someone was braying that His Majesty was attempting to warn his loyal subjects about the sinister increase of Catholics in the city. After all, a Capuchin had been seen lurking in Wych Street that very night!

'Brother Pascal,' explained Wiseman to Chaloner. 'He agreed to sit with the Scarlets until I had fetched you. I thought the villains might hold off if they saw a religious habit.'

'I imagine that depends on who is doing the attacking,' said Chaloner, suspecting the garb of a Catholic priest might have the opposite effect on some people.

The door opened, and Pascal ushered them inside.

'I cannot stay here any longer,' he said urgently. 'A situation is brewing at Somerset House, and I am needed to cool hot heads.' He called the next words over his shoulder as he hurried away. 'I sense foul mischief, and it must be stopped.'

Chaloner had a bad feeling it was too late, and that the 'foul mischief' was already underway. While Wiseman disappeared up the stairs to prepare Jane for the journey, Chaloner drew his sword and took up position by the door, peering out into the street and willing the surgeon to hurry. Scarlet came to stand next to him, lost and frightened.

'Pack what you need,' Chaloner ordered, to give him something to do. 'Hurry.'

Numbly, Scarlet began dropping articles into a sack, but there was no rationale to his selection, and Chaloner saw he would be useless in the event of trouble. The Junior Warden abandoned the bag and ran towards the stairs when footsteps heralded the arrival of Jane.

She was a small, dark-haired woman who might have been pretty, but her ghastly experiences had turned her gaunt and hollow-eyed. She could barely stand, and Wiseman was carrying her. She looked past terror, and Chaloner wondered whether she would ever recover.

'Sit down while I wrap you in these blankets,' ordered Wiseman. 'And then we shall be ready.'

'Do not take long,' warned Chaloner. He did not like the fact that the racket from the Shakespeare's Head meant it was difficult to hear anything else outside, nor the fact that Wych Street was poorly lit. Combined, they conferred a significant advantage on an attacker.

'There is no point whisking her to safety if she catches a chill on the journey,' said Wiseman, turning to scowl at him. 'I will not be a moment.'

'I hate them,' said Scarlet, watching dully. 'Them and their silence.'

Chaloner frowned. 'Their silence?' he asked, wondering what the man was talking about.

'They said nothing the whole time they were here,' whispered Jane. 'Not one word.'

'Do not dwell on it,' advised Wiseman, taking another blanket. 'I shall give you both a sleeping draft when we arrive at Chyrurgeons' Hall, and my apprentices will be outside all night, guarding you. Do not worry, you will soon be safe.'

'We will never be safe,' gulped Scarlet. 'They said they would be back and they will, even though we have kept our end of the bargain and said nothing to anyone. They are evil!'

'You just said they did not speak,' said Chaloner suspiciously. 'So how did you make a bargain with them?'

Scarlet and Jane exchanged a brief glance. 'They made gestures,' she said weakly.

But Chaloner understood why they felt the need to lie. 'I imagine they said that if you breathed a word about them, they would come back for you,' he surmised. 'And when you say you hate their silence, you mean you have been *sworn* to silence, not that *they* were silent. In other words, you know – or suspect you know – who they are.'

'No!' cried Scarlet, alarmed. 'We do not! They did not ask us any questions. Please believe us!'

And there was another slip, thought Chaloner: their attackers *did not ask questions*. But that was exactly what they had done, of course.

'They came because they wanted information,' Chaloner went on. 'You were ordered out of Chapel House, so it could be torn apart in the hunt for Becket's bones. Phillippes and Kaltoff could not find them, so someone came to question you, to see if *you* knew where they were hidden.'

'The dial-makers?' asked Wiseman, jaw dropping in shock. Chaloner gestured that he was to hurry; the wrapping process was taking far too long. 'They are responsible for this outrage?'

Chaloner shook his head. 'It was two of the Dowager's other minions.'

'But we do not know where these bones lie!' cried Scarlet, no longer bothering to contest Chaloner's conclusions. 'We did not even know they still existed, until those men accused us of choosing to live in Chapel House *because* Becket was there. We are Catholic, you see, and they thought . . ."

'We told them all Junior Wardens live in Chapel House,' added Jane. 'But they did not listen.'

'In the end, I made something up, just to make them go away,' said Scarlet miserably. ' I said they were buried in the vault beneath the cellar.'

'And we have been expecting them to come back ever since,' finished Jane. 'Because we lied.'

Chaloner felt sorry for them, but he also knew that expressing sympathy would probably see the vestiges of their resolve crumble, and he could not afford Scarlet to go to pieces yet.

'Your assailants had French accents,' he said, keeping his voice businesslike and professional. 'That is why you said they never spoke – lest investigators asked for details of their speech.'

'Doucett and Martin!' exclaimed Wiseman. 'I should have known, because I have seen the results of their handiwork before – hushed up, of course, with reparation to the victims; the Dowager is loyal to her people. But they have never done anything this bad before.'

'We should go,' said Chaloner. 'They may not come alone, and we cannot fend off an army.'

'One more minute.' Wiseman took the last of his blankets and tied it around Jane's legs. He had her wrapped like a cocoon, although he had left her arms free.

'They will kill us when they find out you know,' said Scarlet tearfully. He slumped on to a bench, as if his legs would no longer hold him up. 'What have we done to deserve this?'

'Well, you have engaged in treasonous plots,' said Chaloner bluntly, aiming to shock him from his paralysing helplessness. 'In your Turnstile house, there was a message written in a complex form of cipher. It was similar to one found in the clothing of a dead iconoclast.'

But the ploy did not work, and Scarlet put his hands over his face, more dejected than ever. 'It was from someone at Somerset House,' he whispered. 'Not the Dowager, but one of her cronies. Luckin, probably. It told us to be ready to take a stand against religious oppression.'

'Then why did Blue Dick have one?' asked Wiseman, indicating he had finished, and Jane was ready to go. 'He was not Catholic – he was a Puritan who liked smashing popish images.'

'Because he, like us, disliked being forced to pray in Anglican churches,' explained Jane. 'He was Mr Williamson's spy, but that did not mean he was unwilling to take a stand against tyranny.'

Chaloner felt the rest of the discussion could wait until they reached Chyrurgeons' Hall, and indicated that Scarlet should help him lift Jane. Wiseman hauled open the door, but then raised his hands above his head, and backed inside again. He was followed by Doucett and Martin, both of whom held swords to his throat. And behind them was Kaltoff, gripping a gun.

Chaloner lowered Jane down again, and stood between her and the invaders. Next to him, Scarlet was shaking so violently that he was obliged to grip the back of a chair to prevent his knees from buckling. He made it rattle, and for a moment, it was the only sound in the room. Kaltoff closed the door, and indicated with an awkward jerk of his dag that Chaloner was to drop his sword.

While Kaltoff took up position in the middle of the room, Chaloner took a moment to assess the situation. The knife he kept in his sleeve was in the palm of his hand, although he could not use it as long as Kaltoff had a gun trained on him. Meanwhile, the Scarlets were too cowed to be of use, and Wiseman was pinned against the wall by the two Frenchmen.

'I should have risked the fever,' the surgeon murmured. There was a stricken expression on his face at the notion that his patients should suffer yet more terror. 'We should not have lingered.'

'Do not berate yourself,' said Kaltoff. He did not look comfortable with the situation, unlike Doucett and Martin, who were clearly itching to explode into violence. 'We have been outside for some time, listening to what you have deduced. More haste would have made no difference.'

Wiseman glowered at him. 'What do you want? We cannot tell you the whereabouts of these damned bones, because they do not exist!'

'Oh, they exist,' said Kaltoff softly, crossing himself. 'Of course they do.'

'Where is Phillippes?' demanded Wiseman coldly. 'Or does he consider bullying sick women beneath him, and has given you the task, because *he* is a gentleman and you are not?'

Kaltoff blanched and the hand with the gun trembled. 'We do not do everything together, you know,' he said stiffly. 'I am quite capable of acting for myself.'

'Let Jane and Scarlet go,' said Chaloner quietly, trying not to flinch as the firearm wobbled about. 'They kept your secret, and there is no need to terrorise them any longer.'

'Not *my* secret,' objected Kaltoff hastily. 'Doucett and Martin attacked Jane, not me. And I wish I could let you all go, but that is impossible. I overheard what you deduced, and it is too much – the Dowager will not want her good name sullied with this unfortunate business, so I am afraid you must die tonight.'

Scarlet released a muffled sob, although Jane made no sound.

'It is too late for silencing,' argued Chaloner. 'Others have noticed the Dowager's curious interest in Becket, and it is only a matter of time before the holes you dug in Chapel House are associated with her hunt for his relics. And then everyone will draw the obvious conclusion: that it was *she* who ordered questions to be asked of Scarlet and Jane.'

Kaltoff swallowed hard, and his eyes flicked towards the Frenchmen. 'It is a pity she was impatient, and involved others in the hunt. Phillippes and I *told* her we would find the bones. And we did. Or *I* did, at least. I discovered them on Friday. They have been in Chapel House all along.'

Scarlet gaped at him. 'No! I do not believe you. There is nowhere they *can* be!'

Kaltoff smiled, but sadly. 'They have been in the vault all these years, just where you told Doucett and Martin they would be, although I suspect that was a lucky guess on your part. I shall present them to the Dowager tomorrow. She has already promised the finder a fabulous reward.'

'Is that what all this is about?' asked Chaloner in disgust. 'Money?'

Kaltoff shook his head. 'No, it is about what money can buy. Namely membership to the Royal Society. Phillippes has made it perfectly clear that he intends to take all the credit for the tide-ring himself, and I will never be elected on its account. And that is a great injustice.'

'So is murdering innocent people,' argued Chaloner. 'It is not—'

But Kaltoff was intelligent enough to know his resolve would fail if the discussion was prolonged. He turned to Doucett and Martin. 'You know what to do. Please make it quick.'

Moving fast, he strode across the room and pressed the barrel of his gun against Wiseman's temple, leaving Doucett and Martin free to deal with Chaloner. The Frenchmen immediately began to circle the spy, stabbing at him with their swords. They ignored the Scarlets, dismissing them as of no consequence.

The situation might have seemed hopeless, but Chaloner had a knife in his hand. In one swift movement, he sent it flying towards Doucett, where it embedded itself in his thigh. The man howled in pain, and fell to the floor. Chaloner took advantage of Martin's momentary surprise to retrieve his sword, so they were more evenly matched. Kaltoff was horrified.

'Finish him,' he shouted in alarm. 'We have already lingered here too long.'

'You are the one who has been doing all the dallying,' muttered Martin resentfully. 'We wanted to kill them straight away, and it was *you* who wanted to listen to their deductions.'

'Because we needed to know whether they had told anyone else,' explained Kaltoff impatiently. 'For the

Dowager's sake. And for St Thomas's, bless his sainted soul. Neither can be tainted by this bloody business.'

As long as Martin was arguing with Kaltoff, he was not concentrating on the fight, and Chaloner used his inattention to launch an attack that sent him staggering backwards. Wiseman stepped forward to help, but Kaltoff struck him with the gun, and he dropped to his knees, dazed. Too late to be useful, Chaloner saw Kaltoff was reluctant to discharge the dag, presumably because there was a tavern full of nosy intellectuals next door. He wished he had realised it sooner.

But there were more immediate problems to concern him. Martin was advancing with murder in his eyes, and Kaltoff, now that the surgeon was incapacitated, drew his own blade and joined him.

Kaltoff was a surprisingly competent swordsman, and it was difficult to repel him with Martin jabbing away from the opposite side. Chaloner could hear Scarlet sobbing, while Jane's face was corpse-white.

'Run!' he shouted, hoping he could keep their attackers busy long enough to let the Scarlets escape. But the couple were beyond helping themselves, and could only watch the skirmish with horrified eyes.

Kaltoff came at Chaloner again, and as they fought, Chaloner was vaguely aware that Wiseman had recovered, and was involved in a violent tussle with Doucett – the surgeon had grabbed the dagger in the Frenchman's leg, and was trying to pull it out; Doucett was trying equally hard to prevent it. Martin was distracted by the howls of agony, so Chaloner stabbed him, just above the collar bone. Martin screamed and reeled away.

Sensing defeat, Kaltoff began to fight harder. Chaloner avoided the hacking blow that would have disembowelled him, but Kaltoff followed it with a left-handed punch that caught him on the side of the head. It was a heavy clout, and Chaloner dropped to his knees. He tried to keep hold of his sword, but the room tipped and swayed, and he could not stop Kaltoff from kicking it out of his hand. And then the dial-maker moved in to finish him off.

Chaloner's vision was still blurred when Kaltoff came to loom over him. He tried to twist away, but the dial-maker pressed the tip of his sword into his chest and began to push down. There was no escape, and Chaloner saw he was going to die.

Suddenly, the door crashed open and something flew through the air. Kaltoff released a short bark of agony, then pitched forward. Chaloner fought his way free of the heavy body, struggling to understand what had just happened. There was a dagger protruding from Kaltoff's back, and he knew from its angle and depth that the wound was a fatal one.

He tore his gaze away from it and looked towards the door. Phillippes was standing there, surveying the scene with distaste. Meanwhile, Wiseman had gained control of the knife he had pulled from Doucett's leg, and for a moment, the only sounds were Kaltoff's laboured breathing and Doucett's whimpers. Chaloner grabbed his sword and staggered to his feet.

'Why?' Kaltoff gasped. His eyes were fixed on Phillippes. 'We are . . . friends.'

'Are we?' asked Phillippes coldly. 'Then why did you betray me?'

'I was going to tell you . . .' gurgled Kaltoff, 'that I found . . .'

'When?' demanded Phillippes. 'You did not mention

it when we met yesterday. And the note you wrote to the Dowager – the one I happened to intercept – informed her that *you*, not *we*, had found the Blessed Becket's body. On Friday. You were going to keep the Dowager's reward for yourself, you wretched little worm.'

Kaltoff tried to say more, but no words came. Phillippes shook his head, then deliberately turned his back on the dying man. He bowed formally to Jane and Scarlet.

'I am sorry for your suffering,' he said stiffly. 'Had I known it was Doucett and Martin who assaulted you in so monstrous a manner, I would have run them through myself.'

'Doucett will not be bothering anyone else,' said Wiseman grimly. 'He seems to have exsanguinated. And I see my services are not required for Martin, either.'

Chaloner glanced at the other Frenchman, and saw Martin had been rash enough to lurch towards the Scarlets. The Junior Warden had not moved, but Jane was standing, blankets cascading around her. She held a poker, and the back of her tormentor's head had been caved in. She was pale, but the blank helplessness had gone from her eyes, to be replaced by another emotion entirely. It was rage. Chaloner suspected she would now recover a lot more quickly than her husband.

'You are safe now, madam,' said Phillippes. 'Go upstairs and rest. We will clean up this mess.'

Obediently, Scarlet escorted Jane away, although he was the one who needed support. Meanwhile, Chaloner watched Phillippes warily, not sure what to make of his timely appearance.

Wiseman was less shy about satisfying his curiosity. 'We are delighted to see you, Phillippes, believe me. But why are you here?'

Phillippes held up a piece of paper, and his expression was bitter. 'Because I intercepted my so-called friend's letter to the Dowager. I have been hunting him all day, to give him a piece of my mind. Then Brother Pascal told me he had seen him lingering near this house, but I did not for a moment imagine he might be involved in . . .' He waved his hand, to encompass all around him.

'I did not have him marked down as that sort of fellow, either,' admitted Wiseman. He went to crouch next to Kaltoff, resting a hand on his neck and shaking his head when he could detect no life-beat there. 'Although in his defence, he did not seem entirely comfortable with the course of action he had embarked upon.'

'I did not associate the attack on Jane with our hunt for relics in Chapel House,' said Phillippes. 'And I am appalled that I have been dragged into such murky waters by association.'

'Very murky,' agreed Chaloner, not sure what to believe. 'Will you answer some questions?'

Phillippes inclined his head. 'I shall try.'

Chaloner scarcely knew where to begin. 'Why did the Dowager choose you to look for the bones? Why not her faithful Frenchmen? Or some of her other cronies?'

'That is easy! Because Kaltoff and I are men of science – painstaking, methodical and thorough. Moreover, we have access to certain tools – large ones for hacking, and more delicate ones for excavating. In short, there is no one in London better qualified for the task. She promised us money if we were successful. I was going to use my share to design a more accurate tide-ring.'

'Winter,' said Chaloner moving to a more urgent subject. 'You were seen conferring with him. Why? Was it anything to do with fireworks?'

Phillippes nodded, then looked sheepish. 'I thought I had devised a way to make bigger, more spectacular displays by using larger amounts of gunpowder, but all I did was design what is effectively a bomb. Winter told me my formulae would not work, and I should have listened to him. He is an expert on the matter, after all.'

'You mentioned these fireworks to Clarendon,' said Chaloner, recalling how his master had then ordered Father Stephen to go a-spying.

Phillippes nodded again. 'Just in passing. I thought it might make him smile. I cannot say I admire his perse-cution of non-Anglicans, but even bigots deserve to laugh occasionally.'

'What happens now?' asked Wiseman, looking from one to the other when Chaloner struggled to think of what else needed to be asked. 'Will you tell the Dowager all we have learned?'

Phillippes winced. 'She will be horrified. But first, we had better locate these bones before they disappear for another hundred years. Will you come to the Bridge, and help me look for them?'

'Me?' asked Wiseman, startled.

'Actually, I meant Chaloner. But you should come, too. The Scarlets do not need you, and you are said to be good with corpses. If we find them, you can tell us whether they really do belong to Becket, or whether Kaltoff was on the verge of perpetrating some monstrous hoax.'

He would not be the only one, thought Chaloner, thinking of his Earl's anonymous letter. 'Becket is not on the Bridge,' he said tiredly. 'He is in Warden Hussey's cellar.'

Phillippes stared at him. 'Kaltoff hid his find with the Senior Warden? How do you know?'

Chaloner did *not* know for certain, so he only smiled enigmatically and declined to elaborate.

Phillippes had hired a few Southwark louts when he had gone hunting Kaltoff. He ordered them to clear up the carnage in the Wych Street house, and when they went to work without demur, Chaloner could only suppose they were being very well paid.

'I do not understand any of this, Chaloner,' said Wiseman in a low voice. 'But are you *sure* it is wise for us to jaunt off with this man? There is something about him that I do not trust at all.'

'No, I am not sure,' replied Chaloner. 'But what else can we do? I need answers about what is going to happen tomorrow, and this may provide some.'

Wiseman did not look convinced, but said no more. He nodded his satisfaction when the Southwark men had righted the furniture, concealed spilled blood with rugs, and carried the bodies to the nearest church. Then he, Phillippes and Chaloner walked to the end of Wych Street, where a line of hackney carriages was waiting.

Chaloner was as taut as a bow as they rode through the darkness, bracing himself for mischief, but the dial-maker sat with his hands folded in his lap, and seemed perfectly at ease. Given that he had just killed his friend, Chaloner thought the calm rather unnerving.

The Bridge was all but deserted when their carriage rattled across it. Even so, Chaloner saw Williamson's men knocking on doors. The Spymaster had been as good as his word regarding the searches. Of course, they were not being discreet, and any self-respecting saboteur would have had his deadly cache whisked away hours before. Was it deliberate, Chaloner wondered, because the

Spymaster felt empathy towards the plotters, or was it simple incompetence?

'The last time I was here, Hussey accused me of burglary,' he said, when the hackney drew up outside Bridge House. For the first time, it occurred to him that returning there was not a good idea.

Both Phillippes and Wiseman shot him curious looks, but neither asked for an explanation. Phillippes knocked on the door, which was eventually answered by the Senior Warden himself, resplendent in nightcap and bed-gown. His portly brats were ranged behind him, similarly attired. Chaloner retreated behind Phillippes when he saw Hussey's gun.

'Put that away,' Phillippes ordered haughtily. 'We are here on official business.'

'Are you indeed?' asked Hussey coolly. 'What manner of business?' He glanced up at the black sky, and added pointedly, 'In the middle of the night.'

'You have a box of bones in your cellar,' Phillippes replied. 'We want to inspect them.'

Hussey frowned his surprise. 'Well, yes, I do. I found them when I was preparing Chapel House for its renovation, and brought them here for safekeeping – I did not want workmen to tip them into the river, because that would have been disrespectful. But it is odd you should be asking after them, because you are the second. I happened to mention them to Mr Kaltoff on Friday, and—'

'So *you* found them?' interrupted Phillippes, rather dangerously. 'Kaltoff did not? And this was on Friday?'

'Yes,' said Hussey warily. 'He told me not to tell anyone else, but I cannot imagine he will mind *you* knowing, as you are friends. Can this not wait until morning? It is an odd hour to be looking—'

'It cannot wait,' said Phillippes firmly. 'I carry the Dowager's authority, as you know from our previous encounters.'

'Yes, yes,' said Hussey hurriedly. 'You do not need to remind me of the perils of crossing the Dowager. You had better come in.'

They trooped inside the house, where Hussey showed no sign of recognising his 'burglar'. When the door was closed behind them, he turned to his children.

'I am disinclined to wander about dark basements at this hour of the night, so which one of you will show them the way to the box?'

There was an eager clamour of voices and a forest of raised hands. Chaloner pointed to the Robert who had helped him escape. The boy grinned his delight as he grabbed his father's lamp and danced towards the cellar door. Phillippes was next, with the rest of the children. Chaloner started to follow, but when he saw the dark stairs, he faltered. Wiseman prodded him impatiently, so he forced himself to take a step. And then another, and eventually he reached the cell in which he had spent so many hours.

Phillippes was already on his knees, levering off the crate's lid with his dagger. Fat Roberts knelt all around him, and Wiseman had to jostle a couple aside to make room for himself.

'These are old bones,' the surgeon said, rubbing his hands together before beginning his inspection. Chaloner thought he looked like a fly alighting on ripe meat. 'Very old.'

'You mean they really do belong to Becket?' asked Phillippes. His voice was flat, and Chaloner could not tell if he was pleased, surprised, disappointed or merely indifferent.

Wiseman began to rummage around rather roughly, like a child in a toy-box. 'I am afraid my skills do not extend to determining a man's name from his bones, so I cannot answer that question. Of course, that is no reflection on my brilliance as a *medicus*, and . . . But what is this?'

He inspected something he had dragged out, but then shrugged and shoved it into Chaloner's hands, before digging back into the treasure trove in search of something more interesting.

'It is a metal plaque,' said Chaloner, rubbing off the dirt with his sleeve. 'Engraved in Latin.'

'That was on top of him, along with some rotten wood,' supplied Robert helpfully. 'Father said it might be a coffin plate.'

'Tell us what it says,' pleaded another Robert. 'We are not very good at Latin.'

'*Hic sepultus est Petrus de Cole* . . . the rest of the name is missing. *Requiescat in pace . . . Anno Domini MCC* . . . no, it is too corroded.' Seeing the Roberts' blank expressions, he translated it for them. 'Here is buried Peter de Cole–something. May he rest in peace. And then there is part of a date.'

'Peter de Colechurch!' chanted the children as one. They looked at each other and giggled.

'Who is Peter de Colechurch?' asked Chaloner.

'The first builder of the stone bridge, in the year twelve hundred and . . .' Robert waved an airy hand to indicate details were unimportant. 'It is something all wardens know. And all wardens' sons, too. Legend says he was buried in the chapel, but that was demolished a long time ago, and no one knows what happened to his coffin. It makes sense that he should still be in the vault.'

'Peter de Colechurch was the only person ever to be buried on the Bridge,' added another Robert helpfully. 'It says so in Father's records.'

'So these are not Becket's relics?' asked Phillippes. Once again, it was impossible to gauge what he was thinking.

'It would seem not,' said Wiseman, lifting the skull and inspecting it. 'This is the head of a very old man. Becket was much younger when he died.'

'When work on Chapel House is finished, we are going to put him back,' piped Robert. 'Father said that to do otherwise might bring the Bridge bad luck.'

'Fair enough,' said Phillippes, standing and brushing dust from his clothes. 'Then see to it.'

'And the Dowager?' asked Wiseman doubtfully. 'What will you tell her?'

Phillippes sighed. 'The truth. I have no idea who wrote the letter telling her that Becket's relics were on the Bridge, but it was a cruel thing to have done. Her disappointment will be monumental.'

'She may decide not to believe you,' warned Wiseman. 'Why would she, when it means the end of all her hopes and dreams?'

'I will tell her that the skeleton has been found, but that it cannot be Becket's,' said Phillippes. 'And I shall bring her here, if she does not accept my testimony. Hussey and his boys make for convincing witnesses, and so do you. Do not worry: her relic hunt ends tonight.'

'How do we know we can trust you?' asked Wiseman baldly. 'That you will not slip back later, and lay claim to these remains for your own purposes?'

Phillippes was silent for a moment, staring at his feet.

When he looked up, his expression was haunted. 'Because they have cost me a friend – Kaltoff was not a bad man, and it was the prospect of the Dowager's reward that turned him against me. They have also brought about the deaths of her two Frenchmen and done untold harm to the Scarlets. The Dowager will not want more blood on her conscience. We Catholics try to keep that sort of thing to a minimum.'

Chaloner was relieved to be out of Bridge House and into the open air. He watched Phillippes climb into a carriage, and stood with Wiseman as it rattled towards Somerset House. Its wheels were very loud in the silence of the night.

'Are you *sure* we can believe what he says?' asked Wiseman worriedly. 'Because I would not like him to renege and cause trouble for the Earl.'

Chaloner did not reply, because he had no idea whether Phillippes could be trusted. The dial-maker had seemed sincere, but who knew what he was really thinking?

Chaloner glanced up at the sky, sensing dawn was not far off. He was exhausted, and envied Wiseman when the surgeon said he was going home to bed. But it was no time to be thinking of sleep, because it was Shrove Tuesday. How many people would wake for the last time that morning? What was going to happen to Hannah and Thurloe?

He shivered as he ran towards Lincoln's Inn. It was bitterly cold, but the chill that had settled inside him had nothing to do with the weather. He forced himself to listen outside Chamber XIII for several minutes, to ensure Thurloe was alone, then he picked the lock and let himself in. Thurloe was sitting at his table, writing, and whipped around quickly when he became aware that someone was standing behind him.

'Tom! Thank God!' he exclaimed. 'I have not performed that knife manoeuvre in a very long time, and you are heavier than I remember, less easy to manipulate. I fear I hurt you.'

'You did,' agreed Chaloner. 'But never mind that. All my efforts to prevent trouble today have failed, and I need your help. Lives are at stake, and the only way we can save them is by working together. There is no one else I trust.'

Thurloe set his pen on the table. 'Do you have a plan?'

'No. But I might be able to devise one if you tell me what is going on. For a start, you can explain what has induced you to keep company with a regicide, an iconoclast and the King's mistress.'

Thurloe regarded him soberly. 'I have done nothing that is not for the good of my country.'

Chaloner slumped in the chair next to him. 'I imagine hundreds of people all over the city will wake up today, and think exactly the same thing. But among them are those who do not care whether innocent blood is spilled in the process.'

'I am not one of them,' said Thurloe quietly.

'I know. I also know you are loath to confide because you do not want to put me in danger. But it is too late for that. There will be a rebellion today, and I cannot stop it alone. I need your help.'

Thurloe closed his eyes, and suddenly his face was haggard. 'The Clarendon Code is not a sensible piece of legislation, and it is causing dismay in many quarters. But because it is foolish, it will be repealed in time. It is just a question of waiting it out.'

Chaloner was bewildered by the enigmatic statement. 'But if you know it is going to be overturned, then why have you been so vocal about it? Why make noisy declarations in coffee houses that . . .' Understanding came in a blinding flash. 'It was a ploy! Your outspokenness was designed to encourage dissidents to approach you – you, a high-ranking member of a former regime!'

Thurloe winced. 'I was obliged to be embarrassingly brazen to attract them. It was painful.'

'So, you were never a rebel, you are a spy! Do not tell me you work for Williamson?'

Thurloe made a moue of disgust. 'Credit me with some standards, Thomas.'

'The King,' surmised Chaloner. Thurloe would not have dabbled in politics for anyone less.

'I was not very happy about it, but I could not refuse a direct request from His Majesty. Not without looking like an insurgent myself.'

Chaloner was uneasy. 'I hope you do not intend to tell him that Lady Castlemaine is among the plotters. I assume that is why she was here? To recruit you to her cause?'

'She came to ask whether I would be interested in toppling your Earl, on the grounds that he lends his name to the Clarendon Code – the laws I have been railing against. However, she and her friends at Somerset House are not interested in the rights and wrongs of religious repression. They just want to destroy your master.'

'That may be *her* intention,' said Chaloner. 'And perhaps Buckingham's, too. But there are others whose plans are rather more wide-ranging. Luckin has armed men awaiting his instructions; most of Winter's fireworks have been stolen; and firework-bombs have probably been manufactured. Father Stephen thinks their target is the theatre, but I still believe it is the Bridge.'

Thurloe stared at him, aghast. 'The Bridge? But the loss of life will be appalling!'

Chaloner raised his eyebrows. 'You do not know all this? But Will Goff and Herring are deeply involved, and you have been consorting with them.'

Thurloe grimaced. 'People tend not to trust ex-Spymasters – the King was wrong to have placed so much faith in me. Several dangerous men *have* been eager to secure my support, but I am told very little in return. You have learned far more than I, despite my best efforts.'

'But still not nearly enough. What can you tell me about your fellow conspirators? Start with Will Goff. Did he come from New England with the express intention of leading a rebellion?'

Thurloe shook his head slowly, and Chaloner saw the wretched position he was in – caught between loyalty to old friends and his vow to support the new government. 'He says he had wind of the trouble in letters sent to him, and is here to prevent it. I have no idea if he is telling the truth, despite my attempts to inveigle my way into his confidence.'

'And Herring?'

'I recruited him to work for me – to infiltrate the rebels' ranks. He maintains the illusion that he is a radical, but his opinions have moderated since the heady days of his iconoclasm. I believe he is on our side.'

'You *believe*? You are not sure?'

Thurloe looked tired. 'There is so much treachery in this business that I am not sure of anything.'

'Then who do you trust?'

'You,' replied Thurloe simply.

'Good,' said Chaloner. 'Then talk to your contacts and prise as much information from them as you can, no matter what you have to do to get it. Then I suppose I had better search Somerset House. I doubt the plotters are foolish enough to hide gunpowder under green salad, but you never know with fanatics.'

'Go to Nonesuch House first,' suggested Thurloe. 'Winter knows more about explosives than any man alive. He may be able to tell you how to prevent these powerful fireworks from igniting. If I discover anything, I shall send you a message.'

Chapter 12

It was just growing light when Chaloner ran into the street. One or two churches were open, inviting parish- ioners to pray on the last morning before Lent, but other than that, Shrove Tuesday was much like any other day of the year.

When he arrived at the Bridge, there was no sign of Williamson's soldiers, and he assumed they had either given up their search or had finished it empty handed. He heard the residents discussing it, though. They were furious to have been disturbed in the middle of the night, just because a dangerous sect called the Followers of the Prophet Elijah were at large.

'I have never heard of them,' Tyus remarked to his wife as Chaloner passed. 'But Williamson's men said they recite incantations to interrupt the tides, and make bits of the cathedral drop off.'

'And they called up the ghost of the old king,' added Sarah.

Chaloner hurried on, marvelling at the power of rumour. He slowed when he reached Nonesuch House, because something was happening there. A guard had been posted on the door – he was dressed as a servant, but he carried himself like a soldier – and although lights flickered in several rooms and every chimney was smoking furiously, the curtains were drawn. Chaloner regarded the place in alarm. There had not been guards, smoke and closed draperies before. He crossed the street and approached the guard.

'Sir John Winter asked me to tune his viols today,' he said.

The fellow barely glanced at him. 'Come back tomorrow.'

Was Winter being held captive inside, wondered Chaloner, seized by people who wanted to make use of his expertise?

'Very well,' he said, feigning nonchalance. 'But the Dowager will be vexed when Winter arrives at her ball with discordant instruments. I would not want to be in *your* shoes later.'

The guard gulped, and promptly stood aside. 'Top floor,' he said gruffly. 'Go up, do your work and come straight back down again.'

Chaloner began his search the moment the door closed behind him, knowing he would not have long before the guard came looking for him. The ground-floor was hot to the point of suffocating, and fires blazed in both hearths, although neither of the rooms were occupied. Deciding to leave the cellar for last, he headed for the upper chambers.

The door to the parlour on the first floor was closed, but voices emanated from within. He crept towards it, and pressed his ear to the wood. But it was thick, and he could not hear what was being said. Moving with the utmost care, he released the latch and eased it open. Then, not only could he hear, but he could see, too.

A dozen men sat around a table, but the one who caught his attention was Lord Bristol. The peer was thinner and paler than the last time Chaloner had seen him, but the handsome face was unmistakeable. On either side of him were Luckin and Father Stephen. Stephen looked terrified, while Luckin's eyes flashed vengefully, as if he was glad his day had come at last. Herring was there, too, sitting at the far end of the table with his arms folded. The others Chaloner recognised as men he had seen in Great Queen Street, although Winter was not among them.

'I do not feel comfortable here,' Bristol was saying. He was eating a dish of onions. 'I should have stayed longer with my brother. Or better still, remained at my own home in Great Queen Street. No one would have thought to look for me there.'

'On the contrary,' argued Luckin. 'It was the subject of a raid on Sunday. Fortunately, Clarendon has a tendency to shriek when agitated, and Progers overheard him – and then his staff – debating the matter. We were able to eradicate all evidence of your presence there, but it was a close thing. We spirited you away just in time.'

Chaloner was disgusted with himself. How could he have let an amateur like Progers eavesdrop on the plans he had made with Leigh? He had been tired and dispirited with the lack of cooperation from the Earl, but that was no excuse.

'Tell me about the cached weapons,' ordered Bristol, changing the subject. 'What do we have?'

'Enough to arm anyone who rallies to our call,' replied Herring. 'We lost the stash in St Mary Overie – I watched Clarendon's men collect it myself – but one out of twenty is an acceptable loss.'

411

Twenty? Chaloner was appalled. Just how widespread was the uprising going to be?

'Lord, it is hot in here!' exclaimed Bristol, running his sleeve across his forehead. 'Do we have to keep the fire so high? I know there is a lot of coal in the cellars to get rid of, but—'

'It is almost time,' interrupted Luckin. He grinned. 'We have worked hard for this.'

'It is an impressive achievement, given that you only had the idea a few weeks ago,' agreed Bristol. 'However, I wish the King had been more forgiving. If he had let me back into his fold after I renounced my religion, there would have been no need for . . . this.' He waved his hand, encompassing the men at the table.

'And Luckin would not have been sent to the Tower for failing to arrest you,' agreed Father Stephen, apparently thinking it was time he voiced an opinion. But he spoke with such misgiving that Chaloner thought he would have been better to keep his mouth shut.

'There *would* have been a need,' countered Luckin, ignoring the priest and fixing his attention on Bristol. 'It is time the government knows we are in earnest about these vile laws. And who better to lead our fight than you, My Lord? By this evening, we shall be toasting our success.'

'I hope so,' said Bristol uneasily. 'Yet I cannot help but feel the whole business is rushed.'

'Since when have you allowed that to stop you?' asked one of the others. 'You have always been a man for seizing the day.'

Bristol did have a reputation for impetuosity, but Chaloner thought the scheme sounded recklessly eleventh-hour, even for him. So what did they intend to do *exactly*? He willed them to say something that would tell him.

'Is everything ready, then?' asked Bristol, looking around at his companions. 'All the weapons have been taken to Somerset House, waiting to be distributed to those willing to wield them?'

There were nods from around the table. 'And over the last two weeks, I have been sending encrypted messages to anyone I think will side with us,' said Father Stephen, trying yet again to curry favour. 'Some have confirmed their allegiance, although others have remained silent.'

'That is because the code you used was too complex,' said Herring critically. 'It took me hours to translate mine, while Blue Dick never did break his. Moreover, Thurloe managed to acquire a couple, but even he is struggling – and he can decipher virtually anything. I imagine a lot of folk will have given up and thrown them away.'

'But I needed to be sure only the most devoted followers would understand,' objected Stephen, stung. 'We do not want anyone who is uncertain, because they may spread doubt and scepticism among the ranks. And that might prove fatal to us.'

'Thurloe?' demanded Bristol at the same time. 'I do not like the notion that *he* might know our business. I know he opposes the Clarendon Code, but I do not trust him. Perhaps we should call the whole thing off, and give ourselves more time to—'

'We have had more than enough time,' snapped Luckin angrily. 'But run back to France if you must. We can manage without you.'

Bristol sneered at him. 'You cannot!' He turned away from Luckin and addressed the others. 'Where is Blue

Dick? He has been monitoring Spymaster Williamson for me, and I want a report before we start.'

'Dead,' said Luckin coldly. 'I gave the order for his execution when I realised he was betraying us to Williamson, rather than watching Williamson for us. Edward Penderel obliged.'

'The powder and fuses are in place,' said Herring in the silence that followed. He grinned suddenly. 'The Dowager will be in for a surprise when her firework display begins.'

'Perhaps we should reconsider,' said Father Stephen in a small voice. 'The carnage—'

'The carnage is unavoidable,' snapped Luckin impatiently. 'And you are either with us or against us, Father. If you are against us, then tell us now.'

'I am with you,' squeaked the priest, when hands dropped to daggers. He addressed the group in a voice that was far from steady. 'In a few hours, our enemies will be dead and the Clarendon Code will die with them. Let us drink to our success.'

So the powder was ready to be detonated, thought Chaloner in growing despair as he watched the conspirators raise their glasses. But where? Surely, *some* would have been found if it was on the Bridge? He ducked into the room opposite when the door opened and the plotters began to emerge.

'Stay here,' said Luckin to Bristol, when the nobleman started to follow. 'It is safer for you.'

Bristol did not look convinced, but nodded acquiescence. The rest of the insurgents made for the front door, some aiming for Southwark, and others heading for the City.

* * *

Chaloner remained hidden until the house became quiet again. Would the guard assume he had left with the conspirators, or would he come looking? Either way, there was not much time. He was about to resume his search when Luckin reappeared, a number of burly warriors at his heels. Chaloner ducked into a cupboard, heart thudding as more minutes ticked away.

'The weapons are in place,' Luckin was saying. 'You must be ready to act on my command in less than two hours. Do I make myself clear? And do not forget the blindfolds I gave you.'

'Why must we wear them?' asked one of the men. 'I know you cut holes for our eyes, but I still cannot see properly, and it is stupid to be half-blind when you are waving a musket about.'

Luckin glared. 'I have explained this already. Buckingham has arranged a rally of liberal-minded moderates today. Hundreds of them will converge on White Hall, and they will be wearing these blindfolds. It is a symbolic act, to express their disapproval for the Clarendon Code.'

'But why should *we* wear them?' pressed the man. 'We are not liberal-minded moderates.'

'It is what is known as a disguise,' said Luckin, bitingly sarcastic. 'You will look like everyone else, and no one will suspect what you intend to do. You do *know* what you are supposed to do, I take it? You paid attention when I briefed you last night?'

The soldier bristled. 'Of course. We are to cause panic and confusion by shooting into the crowd. Those who are armed will retaliate, and there will be a fight. It is to be a diversion, although you have declined to tell us for what.'

The vicar patted him on the shoulder. 'Go. I want you in position by nine o'clock. But do *not* act until you hear the first explosion. Then you may kill as many moderates as you please.'

Chaloner watched Luckin usher the soldiers out, then make for the basement. Keeping a safe distance, he followed the vicar to the small cellar he had searched once before. Then it had been full of coal, but now the fuel had either been piled to one side or removed completely. It explained why so many fires had been lit, and Chaloner cursed himself for not realising sooner that it was significant.

A table had been placed in the space that had been cleared, and Winter sat at it. The man called Crow, who had been in the smoky Bear tavern with Goff and Herring, stood behind him, holding a gun to his head. The floor around them was knee-deep in paper, which had a curious waxy appearance, and there was a barrel to one side. Chaloner immediately understood what was happening: Winter was dismantling fireworks to retrieve the powder.

'How is he doing?' Luckin asked, as Winter looked up and scowled.

Crow grimaced. 'He is taking too long.'

'I admire your courage in trying to delay us, Winter,' said Luckin pleasantly. 'But it is too late for heroics. The plot is underway, and nothing can stop it now.'

Winter glowered, moustache bristling with furious indignation. 'Do you have any idea how long it took me to make these things? And now you order me to tear them apart! What will the Dowager say, when she sits down to enjoy a pyrotechnic spectacle, and all she gets is a fizzle?'

'She will not be disappointed, believe me,' said Luckin smugly. 'Although I doubt you will be appointed as Green Man afterwards. Still, it cannot be helped.'

'So it was you who broke into my Southwark warehouse and stole my creations?'

'It was.' Luckin looked smug. 'The ones you are kindly demolishing for me are just a few of them. I have something else in mind for the rest. And I have something even better in mind for the ones I made using Phillippes's formulae.'

'Please do not do this,' begged Winter, defiance crumbling abruptly. 'It is wrong.'

'I do not care.' Luckin glanced at Crow. 'How much longer?'

'Two more Purple Fountains to go, and then we shall have enough powder to see St Paul's Cathedral turned into rubble. And what a powerful statement *that* will be!'

'Is that what you intend to do?' asked Winter, appalled. 'Destroy a church? A house of God?'

'It is a monument to authoritarian oppression,' declared Luckin, eyes flashing. 'And—'

He did not finish what he was going to say, because Winter dived at him. Crow aimed his gun, but could not use it, because vicar and prisoner were too close together. Luckin shoved Winter away, and he stumbled into the table. The lamp fell off and smashed. Immediately, sparks danced across the firework papers. They began to splutter as the gunpowder impregnated in them ignited.

Crow screeched in terror, and tried to pat out the flames with his hands. More sensibly, Luckin ripped off his coat and hurled it over them, aiming to smother them before they could reach the barrel. While they were distracted, Chaloner darted into the cellar, grabbed

Winter's arm and hauled him outside. Then he slammed the door closed, and threw the bolt across it.

'Chaloner!' howled Luckin. He leapt up and began pounding on the door with his fists. 'You murdering bastard! What have you done with my nephews?'

Crow was screaming at the vicar, urging him to help put out the flames before the whole place went up. Between them, they were making a lot of noise, and Chaloner heard footsteps hammer on the floor above. The guards were coming.

'This way!' hissed Winter, moving deeper into the cellars. 'There is another exit. Hurry!'

Chaloner followed him along a narrow passage, to a filthy and none-too-stable ladder. There was a trapdoor in the ceiling. Winter bellowed with the effort of raising it, and for a moment, Chaloner thought it was locked from the other side. But then it flew open with a resounding crash, and daylight flooded in. Winter scrambled out, but guards were grabbing Chaloner's feet by the time he started to climb, dragging him down.

He kicked out as hard as he could, knocking the hands away. Then he made a last, desperate scramble upwards, and was out. Winter slammed the trapdoor shut, and Chaloner secured it with a metal bar. The guards began to pound on it, but it held fast. They were safe – temporarily at least.

'If you came for music, you picked a bad day,' gasped Winter, slumping against the wall and rubbing his eyes with a hand that shook. He glanced at Chaloner. 'Or are you on another mission? I should have known that a friend of Will Goff's would be more than a talented violist.'

'The same goes for you,' retorted Chaloner. 'You met him and his cronies in the Bear tavern—'

'They invited me to join their venture,' agreed Winter. 'But did not say *what* I was joining . . .'

There was no time for an analysis of Winter's ill-advised actions. 'Did you retrieve enough powder from your fireworks to bring down the Bridge?' asked Chaloner urgently, wondering whether it could be evacuated in time.

'No. Well, Luckin and Crow will not survive, and it will make a mess of my house, but—'

'Then what about St Paul's? Is there enough to destroy that?'

Winter shook his head. 'It may damage a small section, but that is a massive building, and the volume of powder needed to destroy it would be enormous. They will need barrels of the stuff.'

'They might *have* barrels. Luckin has all the fireworks from your Southwark warehouse—'

'Still nowhere near enough, not for St Paul's. Of course, there will be plenty to demolish something smaller. Damned villains! Gunpowder is difficult to obtain, and it is ingenious to—'

'Adapted fireworks,' interrupted Chaloner urgently. The trapdoor shuddered as the guards struggled to batter it open. 'Purple Fountains with ten pounds of powder. Have you made any?'

'No!' Winter's expression was agonised. 'Those would be bombs, not items of entertainment. But Luckin has manufactured some – he just told me. And I have an awful feeling that St Paul's is not his only target – that another building will be reduced to rubble today, too.'

'I think it is Somerset House,' said Chaloner, recalling Herring's words – that the Dowager was going to be in for a surprise when the display started. 'Her ball is today, and it will be full of people. You have fireworks there, do you not?'

Winter regarded him in horror. 'A few. I took them there when the rest were stolen, because I thought they would be safer. However, I saw Luckin driving a large cart around the back of the building the other day . . .'

Chaloner groaned. 'It almost certainly contained the "bombs", and the Somerset House guards will not have searched it, because Luckin is one of the Dowager's inner circle. They would have assumed he was bringing something for her ball.'

Winter's face was white. 'You must be wrong! Luckin would never harm her, or her property. The folk at Somerset House befriended him, and invited him to their soirees. They *like* him.'

'That does not mean he likes them back,' Chaloner pointed out. 'And he is dangerous, capricious and unpredictable. Who knows what he might do in the name of whatever cause he has embraced?'

He flagged down a carriage, and took a leaf from Wiseman's book by hauling out the astonished passenger and offering the hackneyman a princely reward for driving as fast as he could to White Hall. He pulled Winter in beside him.

'When we arrive, you must find Spymaster Williamson and tell him all that has happened.'

Winter regarded him uneasily. 'I will. But what if he already knows, and has decided to turn a blind eye? He is not a fellow to back the losing side, and who knows how all this will end?'

It was a terrifying thought.

* * *

Despite the driver's best efforts, progress along Thames Street was painfully slow. It was too slow for Chaloner, so he abandoned Winter and dived out, knowing he would be quicker on foot. He ran like he had never run before. His lame leg burned, and his breath came in short, agonised gasps.

He tore along Fleet Street, where he found traffic moving more freely. There were no hackney carriages to hire, so he leapt on the back of a private coach, displacing a startled footman to do so. The man bellowed his fury, but the driver did not hear, and continued to rattle westwards.

Chaloner used the time to consider what he was going to do. First and foremost was to tell Buckingham to call off his protest. That would deprive Luckin of his diversion, and would put Hannah out of danger. Second, someone had to go to St Paul's, to prevent the conspirators from damaging London's most famous church. And lastly, Somerset House needed to be searched for Luckin's 'bombs' and the rest of Winter's fireworks.

He jumped off the carriage outside White Hall's main gate, and tore into the courtyard. The first person he saw was Leigh, wearing a splendid dress uniform in anticipation for his duties at the Bishops' Dinner. Father Stephen was with him. Chaloner skidded to a halt, but the priest began gabbling at him before he could find the breath to speak himself.

'I have just been to see Clarendon.' The priest's eyes were wide and frightened. 'Apparently, your suspicions were right. My regicide brother *is* back, and he has joined the criminals who want to see our streets soaked in blood. He must be stopped. They all must! Lord Bristol is with them, and they have weapons and rebels and . . . Oh, it is all too dreadful!'

'I have alerted the palace guard to be on the lookout for trouble,' added Leigh. 'But the Earl says the best way for *him* to combat these lunatics is by continuing his day as though nothing has happened. So I am on my way to Worcester House, to greet the bishops.'

'Forget the bishops,' ordered Chaloner. 'Go to Buckingham and tell him fanatics plan to shoot his demonstrators. Force him to cancel the protest. Then send word to St Paul's that there is a plot afoot to blow it to kingdom come.'

'Their target is the cathedral?' gulped Stephen, appalled. 'I thought it was the theatre!'

'Winter is warning Williamson,' Chaloner went on. 'And I am going to Somerset House.'

'Why there?' asked Father Stephen, horrified. 'I assure you, the Dowager knows nothing of—'

'Probably not,' agreed Chaloner tersely. 'She prays for plagues to kill Anglicans and condones Lord Bristol's illegal return, but she would never countenance rebellion – not when it might put her son's throne in danger. I am going there to look for fireworks.'

'Fireworks?' asked Leigh. 'Not these adapted ones that Phillippes designed? But I thought they did not exist – that they were just a theory.'

'They exist,' said Chaloner grimly. 'And they will do untold harm unless we can find them.'

He started to move away, but Leigh stopped him. 'I do not understand! Are you saying that the conspirators are turning on the Dowager? That they plan to harm *her* with these fireworks?'

Chaloner struggled for patience. 'Not her specifically – anyone at her ball. I suspect it will happen during Buckingham's rally, so his peaceful demonstrators will be blamed for the atrocity.'

'Security at Somerset House is intense,' said Stephen, grabbing Chaloner's arm when he tried to leave a second time. 'You will never get inside, and there are orders to shoot intruders.' He swallowed hard, and resolve suffused his white, terrified face. 'So *I* will go. I will pour water over these nasty things if need be, and when Winter arrives with Williamson, *he* can make them safe.'

It was a sensible plan, and Chaloner sagged with relief at the priest's new-found courage. He only hoped it would last long enough to avert a massacre.

'So what will you do, Chaloner?' asked Leigh. 'While we dash around preventing trouble?'

Chaloner intended to gain access to the Dowager's ball by whatever means necessary and drag Hannah out. But disappearing on personal errands would not be seen as a suitable course of action under the circumstances, so he waved a vague hand, too tense and fraught to invent a lie.

'I almost forgot,' said Leigh, shoving a piece of paper at him. 'This was delivered a few moments ago, and the courier said it was urgent. But we cannot wait while you read it. Come, Father. There is not a moment to lose.'

Chaloner watched them hurry away, then studied the missive. Rain had seeped into it, causing the ink to run, so it was all but illegible. He struggled to decipher it:

Vital inform..tion has b..n left at yr rooms in Fetter La ... Go ther ... immed ... tely. Jo ... Thurl ...

Thurloe had news!

* * *

423

Chaloner raced out of White Hall, and looked up and down King Street wildly, hunting for a carriage. There were none to be seen, so he started to run. As he went, he reflected on the message. Thurloe had promised to send word when he had learned something, and the note certainly looked like his handwriting, but why had he chosen Fetter Lane? And why had he not used cipher, as he usually did when communicating? Chaloner stopped abruptly. It was a trap.

Common sense told him to ignore the letter and rescue Hannah. But the lure was also an unlooked for opportunity – a chance to outwit the plotters and question them about their plans. He decided it was worth the risk to himself for the benefits that might ensue, and began running again.

When he arrived in Fetter Lane, he forced himself to take refuge in the doorway opposite, and spend several minutes watching his house. There was nothing to see, so he could only suppose they were waiting inside. He crept up the stairs to his garret with a stealth born of long experience, and found the door ajar. He relaxed slightly when his cat walked through it and began to wind around his legs, purring. It would not behave that way if there were intruders within. Carefully, he pushed open the door and looked inside.

The room was strangely dark, because someone had put a curtain over the window. It was also full of acrid smoke, and there was a low hissing sound that he could not immediately identify. In the dimness, he saw a patch of white on the table. It was another note. He grabbed it, and took it to the window to read, ripping down the curtain as he did so.

Thus will all mine enemies perish.

He gazed at it in confusion, then looked around the room. He recognised the pungent scent of burning gunpowder at almost the exact same time that he saw the tell-tale scorch-marks leading across the floor. They ended in two large cylinders, partially hidden under the table, on each of which was written the words 'Purple Fountain'.

He turned, grabbed his cat and ran. The instrument-maker – Spong – who lived on the floor below, heard the crashing footfalls, and poked his head around his door to see what was happening. Chaloner seized his wrist and hauled him down the stairs, too. He was just wondering how long a fuse had been placed, when there was a resounding boom that hurled him from his feet and made him lose his grip on the cat. Fragments of plaster pattered down around him, and then there was silence. But it did not last long. The house started to creak, louder and deeper than it had ever done before.

'Hurry!' he yelled, pulling the dazed Spong upright.

Spong did not need to be told a second time. He fled. Chaloner glanced around for the cat, but it was nowhere to be seen. With a pang of regret, he followed Spong. Meanwhile, their landlord had long been aware of his house's losing battle with gravity, and was already tugging the box containing his valuables to safety. Pieces of rubble dropped all around them, and there was a groan so intense that Chaloner was sure the place was going to fall before they reached the street.

But then they were outside, lurching through a hail of tiles that were sliding from the tilting roof. Chaloner was just congratulating himself on his escape when he saw Luckin. The vicar was breathing heavily, as though he had been running, and he was holding a gun. He was exchanging urgent words with a man Chaloner recognised from Great Queen Street. The fellow held a tinderbox, indicating he was the one who had set the explosion.

Then Luckin spotted Chaloner, and his face went taut with rage. He took aim. There was nowhere to hide in the street, and sword and dagger were no defence against a bullet. So Chaloner did the only thing he could: he turned and raced back inside the house. Something cracked, and the doorframe exploded into pieces. Had Luckin shot at him, or was it just the building's death throes?

'Stop!' Spong bellowed after him. 'A cat is not worth your life!'

Chaloner tore along the corridor, aiming for the back garden. The rear door was blocked, and he lost vital seconds kicking rubble away, so he could drag it open. A chunk of ceiling struck his shoulder, knocking him to his knees, and the air was full of dust.

He struggled upright and thrust through the gap between door and frame, but his coat caught on the shattered wood. There was a tremendous crash as a supporting beam came down, bringing more of the ceiling with it. Using every ounce of his strength, Chaloner ripped free and staggered outside. And then the building was falling in earnest. Dust enveloped him, and he could not see where he was going. He put his hands over his head, and blundered on blindly.

Suddenly, he was clear. He reached the end of the garden and looked backwards just as the house that had been his home collapsed in on itself with a groaning sigh.

*   *   *

It was several minutes before Chaloner's eyes stopped smarting enough to allow him to locate the back gate. He hauled it open and stumbled into the lane. It was deserted, and he was grateful Luckin was an amateur – a professional would have posted a guard at the rear of the house.

He happened to glance up at a wall as he made his way through the maze of alleys that led to Fleet Street. His cat was sitting on top of it, regarding him with bored amber eyes. Then a child's voice called, and it jumped into a garden. Chaloner watched as it was swept into the arms of a little girl, and given a protective cuddle. He sagged, feeling betrayed. It was bad enough that he had lost his home – and worse yet, his second-best viol – but did his cat have to abandon him for better accommodation quite so soon?

He headed for St Dunstan-in-the-West, and found a quiet spot in the churchyard, where he shook the dust from his hair and wiped his face with a handful of wet grass. As he brushed the filth from his jacket, he heard the crackle of paper. He withdrew the two notes.

He supposed Luckin had laid the powder the previous night, and Rupert Penderel had not been exaggerating when he had warned him of the vicar's murderous intentions. But how had Luckin delivered the forged missive to the Earl's offices? Did he have access to them? And if so, what else had he left there? The moment he did not look as if he had been in an explosion, Chaloner set off for White Hall, cursing the unsteadiness in his legs that slowed him down.

After what felt like an age, he reached the main gate, raced across the courtyard and pounded up the staircase to the Earl's domain. It was empty, and the fires that always burned in the hearths had been allowed to go out. The curtains were drawn, too, and the rooms were chillier and darker than Chaloner had ever seen them. He searched them quickly, supposing that any firework intended to do serious damage could not be too small.

But there was nothing to find, and he was about to leave and go to Somerset House when he heard footfalls on the stairs. They were moving in a way that was distinctly furtive, so he darted back into the office and slipped behind the curtains. The door opened and three men entered.

Chaloner's stomach lurched when he saw Father Stephen between Luckin and Herring. How had the priest managed to fall into their clutches? Was he a total incompetent?

' . . . as Chaloner is dead,' Luckin was saying, peering around. 'I saw him run back inside the building myself, and no one could have survived the collapse that followed.'

'Why would he run back inside?' asked Herring dubiously.

'Because he saw me.' Luckin replied. 'I have no love for blood, but he deserved to die for killing my nephews.'

Father Stephen regarded him askance. 'You have no love for blood? But you are about to perpetrate one of the greatest massacres the city has ever known.'

'That is different,' said Luckin haughtily. 'The government will not listen to reasoned demands, so it will have to listen to violence instead.'

'I cannot see what I am doing in here,' said Herring. The taut excitement in his voice told Chaloner that Thurloe had been wrong to think the iconoclast had changed. He was still a radical, and his enjoyment of the chaos Luckin was bringing about was palpable. 'We need light.'

He strode to the window and opened the curtain.

Exposed, Chaloner drew his dagger. 'Perhaps I can help you,' he said pleasantly. 'What are you looking for?'

'You are supposed to be dead,' cried Herring, shocked.

He started to reach for his weapon, but Chaloner did not give him the chance. He spun the iconoclast around, wrapped one arm around his neck to keep him still, and pressed the knife to his side, using him as a shield against the gun Luckin had drawn.

'What are you looking for?' he repeated, more forcefully.

'Tell him,' said Stephen with one of his sickly smiles. 'He knows his way around Clarendon's offices, and it will be quicker to secure his help than to hunt for it on our own.'

'I am not telling him anything,' snarled Luckin. 'And he is hardly in a position to make us.'

'He will kill Herring if we do not comply,' said Stephen. He turned to Chaloner. 'We are looking for information about Clarendon House. Where does your Earl keep his private papers?'

'Why do you want to know about Clarendon House?' asked Chaloner, bewildered.

'We do not have time for this,' declared Luckin. He took a second gun from his belt and tossed it towards Stephen. The priest fumbled as he caught it, and everyone in the room flinched. 'You move to the left, I will go right. He cannot use Herring to protect himself from both of us at once.'

'It is over, Luckin,' said Chaloner, tightening his grip on the struggling iconoclast. 'Spymaster Williamson knows what you intend to do, and so does the Earl. Even as I speak, troops are moving into position at Somerset House and St Paul's Cathedral—'

'Lies!' cried Herring in a strangled voice. 'No one can have guessed our plans. Ignore him, Luckin! He is trying to disconcert you.'

'You do not need to pretend any longer, Father,' said Chaloner, indicating Stephen was to disarm the vicar. 'And there is no time for games, because we must prevent this pair of traitors from—'

'Traitors, are we?' demanded Luckin. 'Why? Because we object to repression?'

'Father!' said Chaloner urgently. 'Take the—'

'How can you think I am on Clarendon's side?' snarled Stephen, rounding on him suddenly. 'That wicked heathen who is crushing the life out of the True Church! He is a massive obstacle in the way of religious toleration, and it would be unethical *not* to stop him.'

Chaloner gaped at him. 'But you have been passing Somerset House's secrets to the Earl for—'

'Wrong!' Stephen smiled, although it was a deeply unpleasant expression. 'I have been passing *his* secrets to *Somerset House*. I am a spy, but *he* has not been the beneficiary of my expertise.'

Chaloner gaped at the priest in disbelief, his thoughts tumbling in confusion. How could Stephen be a rebel? He had revealed too many of the conspirators' plans.

'I lied, too,' said Herring smugly, sensing his captor's bafflement. 'I told you I had moderated my opinions, but I have not. It was Blue Dick who advocated restraint – and who acted on his new-found principles by spying for Williamson.'

But Chaloner was more concerned with Father Stephen. He noticed that the hand holding the gun was suddenly steady, and the timid, anxious expression had been replaced by something calm and purposeful. Chaloner was disgusted with himself. The man was brother to a regicide, and felt strongly enough about his convictions not only to convert to Rome, but to become one of its priests. How could he have thought such a fellow was a timorous nonentity?

'Is this about Becket's bones?' he asked, shifting Herring to cover him better.

'They do not exist,' replied Stephen scornfully. 'And I never believed they did. But the business had its advantages. It kept your attention divided, so you failed to learn about our work.'

'It distracted the Dowager, too,' added Luckin gloatingly. 'Because she would not approve of what we are doing.'

'You told me there was gold in Chapel House,' said Chaloner to Stephen, more strands of the mystery beginning to make sense. 'But it was to divert me from your real—'

'Yes, it was,' said Stephen, edging to his right, the gun held in front of him. 'I lied about the theatre, too. There were never any plans to destroy it.'

Chaloner was impressed: the man had been convincing. 'It was all an act?' he asked. 'This pretence of nervousness?'

'Oh, I was nervous,' said Stephen. 'Of course I was – I was deceiving not only Clarendon, but the likes of Buckingham, Lady Castlemaine and Progers, too. They can be lethal when crossed, so it was not an act, I assure you.'

'Those dissipated rogues at Somerset House are nothing,' spat Luckin contemptuously, climbing over a desk to gain a clear shot. 'We are *using* them – persuading

431

them to stage a rally, which they think will turn people against Clarendon. They are blinded by their hatred for him. Fools!'

'We will rid ourselves of the lot of them today,' crowed Herring, still trying to wriggle free of Chaloner's grasp. 'And those left will think twice about inventing repressive religious laws in the future.'

'You will not succeed,' said Chaloner quietly. 'Thanks to Father Stephen here, and the secrets he passed to the Earl, too many people know what you plan to—'

'It makes no difference what they know,' sneered Luckin. 'Weapons and special fireworks are in place, and no one can stop what we have started. Do you really think the bombs in Somerset House can be made safe with a few pails of water? What we have arranged will reduce the place to rubble.'

'Enough chatter,' barked Stephen. He glared at Chaloner and raised the gun. 'Where are the Clarendon House plans?'

Chaloner quickly shifted position again. 'Why do you want them?' They were hardly something *he* would have considered important.

'So we can make them public after the massacre,' replied Herring. There was a confident timbre to his voice: he fully expected his companions to defeat Chaloner and save him. 'When people see the extent of the Earl's greed – a vast mansion paid for by public taxes – he will be become a figure of hatred. And the Clarendon Code will fall with him.'

Suddenly, Stephen's arm jerked and there was a deafening report. Herring gasped, then went limp. Chaloner tried to hold him, but blood was gushing, and there was no point in clutching a corpse. He let Herring fall, aiming to capitalise on the fact that Stephen would need to reload, but Luckin reacted fast, and had his own dag trained on Chaloner before his colleague's body had hit the floor. Chaloner expected to be dispatched immediately, and braced himself, but Luckin was frowning his puzzlement.

'Did you do that on purpose?' he asked of Stephen, indicating that Chaloner was to drop his dagger. With no choice, Chaloner did as he was told. He felt for the one in his sleeve, but he had thrown that at Doucett in Wych Street, and had neglected to reclaim it.

'Herring was a liability,' replied Stephen dispassionately, turning the key on his gun to wind it. 'Why do you think I told Clarendon about him and the other statue-smashers? You encouraged me to accept their help, but I do not approve of iconoclasm. I never wanted them involved.'

'You gave the Earl information about the adapted fireworks, too,' said Chaloner, hoping to cause division in the ranks. 'Phillippes's formulae, which—'

'So what?' demanded Stephen. 'Has it allowed you to stop us? No, it has made no difference whatsoever.' He regarded Chaloner coolly. 'The Earl was not always an avaricious bigot, and I am sorry for what he has become. When he is dead, he will not be well remembered.'

'Dead?' asked Luckin, regarding him askance. 'Unless he is in Somerset House or the cathedral, he will survive. Of course, he may be ripped limb from limb when London learns the truth about Clarendon House, but that is for the future.'

Yet Chaloner knew from the dark, malignant expression on Stephen's face that Luckin was not party to all that would transpire that day. Then the awful truth hit him like a physical blow, and he wondered why he had not seen it before.

'You do not care about St Paul's and Somerset House,' he said, appalled. 'Your target is the Earl and his Bishops' Dinner – the men responsible for the Clarendon Code.'

'Do not be ridiculous!' exclaimed Luckin. He glanced at Stephen for confirmation, and his jaw dropped when he saw it was not going to be forthcoming. 'No! How did you . . . but that would—'

'Chaloner is not going to tell us where the Earl keeps his plans,' interrupted Stephen shortly. 'And we *must* have them, or people will make him a martyr and the Clarendon Code never be repealed. Shoot Chaloner before he pulls some kind of trick. We will find them without his help.'

Luckin had been gaping in astonishment, staggered by what he had just learned. But he quickly pulled himself together. 'Oh, well,' he said, raising his weapon and taking aim. 'I suppose you know what you are doing.'

He could not miss at such close range, and there was nothing Chaloner could do but grit his teeth and hope the kill was a clean one.

'Stand away, Luckin,' came a stern voice from the door. Chaloner spun around to see Thurloe, who was holding a gun. It was levelled at the vicar.

Behind him were Will Goff and several palace guards. With a howl of fury, Stephen gave the firing mechanism one last, vicious twist and turned towards his brother. But there was a sharp crack, and he dropped to the floor. Smoke issued from the end of Thurloe's gun. Luckin gaped in horror, and while he was distracted, Chaloner rushed him, bowling him off his feet and silencing the stream of foul curses that poured from his mouth with a punch.

'Tom, what did they tell you?' demanded Thurloe urgently, wasting no time on explanations.

'That they mean to kill the bishops. And blow up Somerset House and St Paul's Cathedral.'

'Damned fanatics!' muttered Will Goff. 'Have they not had enough of bloodshed and chaos?'

Chaloner raced towards The Strand, aware that he faced an agonising decision. Who should he try to save? The bishops, without whom the country might be plunged into the kind of anarchy from which it was difficult to recover? Or Hannah? But there was no real choice. He wanted to rescue the woman he was going to marry. Thurloe had other ideas, though.

'Do your duty,' he ordered, catching up with him. 'See to your master. Winter has warned Williamson, who is already at the cathedral, so we do not need to worry about that.'

'But Hannah is at the Dowager's ball, waiting for orders to don a blindfold and—'

'I will go to Somerset House,' said Thurloe. 'You and Will must save the Church.'

Chaloner wanted to argue, but Thurloe shoved him in the direction of Worcester House, and he knew the ex-Spymaster was right. Lady Castlemaine would arrange for Thurloe to be admitted to the ball, but the courtesy was unlikely to be extended to Clarendon's spy.

'Come,' said Goff urgently, tugging on his arm. 'We do not have much time, and I would rather not be blown to pieces with these prelates, if it can be avoided.'

The Bishops' Dinner was in full swing, and the Earl's garden was jam-packed with coaches, all bearing ecclesiastical coats of arms. Chaloner began to weave through them, wondering how long it would be before the place went up.

'I am sorry about your brother,' he said, aware that Goff was matching him step for step. He did not want the man to assume he was responsible for his kinsman's death, and try to kill him while he was grappling with other fanatics.

'I am not,' said Goff grimly. 'As soon as I heard the Dowager had made him a favourite, I knew it boded ill. I hurried from New England as fast as I could, and informed the King of my concerns. He drafted me into his service, but it was too late: Stephen's plot was already in motion.'

'I thought you were part of it,' confessed Chaloner.

'You were meant to – everyone was. I hoped it would encourage traitors to confide their secrets in me, but I found, as did Thurloe, that people are wary of ex-Cromwellians.'

They reached the house's main entrance, where the guards recognised Chaloner and stood aside for him to enter. The Earl's dining room was directly ahead, and through the door, Chaloner could see Bishop Morley tucking into his pickled ling pie. He also saw the Earl, whose jaw tightened in annoyance at his spy's dirty, unkempt appearance. Chaloner ignored him. There was no time to do otherwise.

'Where shall we look?' demanded Goff, looking around breathlessly.

'Cellar first.' Chaloner began to head in that direction.

But the Earl had left the celebrations and was blocking his way. 'What are you—' he began. Then his hands flew to his mouth in horror when he recognised the tall, hawk-featured man who stood in his hallway. 'Good God, Chaloner! What have you—'

Explaining would take too long. Chaloner dodged

around him, and ran towards the basement, taking the steps three at a time. The first room he dashed into was empty, and so was the second, but the third was full of barrels. And someone was standing to one side, holding a lamp above a trail of dark powder that snaked across the floor towards them. Chaloner gazed at him, struggling to understand.

'I thought you . . .'

'I have nothing to do with blowing up the cathedral or Somerset House,' said Winter quietly. 'But this is different. These bishops are trying to eradicate my religion. I cannot let that happen.'

'It is not different,' said Chaloner, acutely aware that he was weaponless, but Winter had a sword. 'Both will result in carnage followed by chaos. And if you light the fuse, you will die, too.'

Winter nodded. 'I know. But the last man who attempted to assassinate Clarendon ran away, and the powder failed to detonate. That was on Bonfire Night. The lesson is learned, though: whoever sets flame to fuse this time must wait with it, to ensure it does not splutter out. Father Stephen has absolved me of my sins, and I am ready to face my God.'

Chaloner dived forward when Winter touched his lamp to the powder, and stamped on the flame. It flickered for a moment, but then burned on, and Chaloner's second stamp went wide as Winter punched him. It was a clumsy blow, delivered more in exasperation than with any real intent to harm, but it knocked Chaloner to one knee. Chaloner promptly dived on top of the burning powder, and tried to smother it with his body. With a groan of despair, Winter came to skewer him.

'I wish you had not come, Chaloner,' he whispered.

437

'I have no wish to kill a violist. But I cannot let you stop me, not when Father Stephen and I have worked so hard to plan this day.'

As the weapon descended, Chaloner reached up and grabbed it. As they struggled, he was aware of the Earl waddling into the cellar, Leigh and Goff at his heels, and heard his exclamation of horror when he saw the amount of gunpowder that had been smuggled into his home.

'Get out, sir!' he managed to gasp. 'Now!'

In a massive display of strength, Winter ripped away the sword, but Chaloner leapt at him before he could regain his balance, and then they were both rolling on the floor. Chaloner heard the Earl shouting, but could not make out the words. Then Winter scored a lucky punch, and Chaloner's senses began to darken. He was going to lose the fight, and Worcester House and all the bishops were going to be destroyed.

Then there was a distant boom, followed immediately by another. Thurloe was too late! Luckin's firework-bombs were igniting, and Hannah . . .

The notion that lunatics were going to kill her filled Chaloner with a white, burning fury, and he found a reserve of strength he did not know he had. He lashed out wildly, and felt his fist connect once, and then twice. He thought he heard Winter howl, but sounds had become a meaningless buzz and his vision was blurred. He struck out a third time, but his arm was as heavy as lead, and he knew there was no power in the blow. Then darkness overtook him.

Slowly, Chaloner's wits cleared. He was lying on his back on a cold stone floor, and someone was kneeling next to him. He blinked trying to focus. It was Thurloe.

438

'It is over, Tom,' the ex-Spymaster said gently. 'Winter is arrested, and the bishops are safe.'

'Hannah?' gasped Chaloner, struggling to sit up. 'Somerset House?'

'The Dowager cancelled her ball when Phillippes told her there were no relics to be had. She did not feel like celebrating, apparently. Everyone was being turned away when I arrived.'

'I heard explosions—'

'That was Buckingham. He decided the best way to render the fireworks safe was to ignite them all by shooting at them. And in the streets outside, a lot of people removed black blindfolds to coo appreciatively at the resulting display.'

'Thurloe says the enhanced ones have made rather a mess of the Dowager's parterres.' It was the Earl speaking, a spiteful grin plastered on his chubby face. 'And her box hedges will never be the same again.'

'They were placed so as to cause the greatest injury to spectators,' said Thurloe in distaste. 'There would have been a bloodbath, had the plan succeeded.'

Chaloner became aware that other people were in the cellar, too – Will Goff, Leigh, Bulteel and several servants. 'They should not be here,' he said urgently, trying to stand. Thurloe helped him. 'The gunpowder . . .'

'Far too damp to explode,' said Goff cheerfully. 'It has been down here too long. Winter should be ashamed of himself for not realising it straight away.'

Chaloner was not sure he believed him. 'The fuse burned well enough.'

'That was from a new barrel,' explained Goff. 'And Clarendon did the right thing anyway: he kicked a gap in its trail, which is far more effective than stamping or lying on it.'

The Earl preened at the praise. 'I had better return to my guests. They will be wondering what is going on, but I do not think I shall tell them. I shall invent a tale about a kitchen fire.'

'That is probably wise,' agreed Goff. 'The news that religious fanatics tried to murder every bishop in the country is not the sort of thing that will help the cause of peace.'

The Earl regarded him balefully. 'The King should have told *me* that he had ordered you and Thurloe to infiltrate these villains. Then I could have told Chaloner, and the affair need never have gone so far.'

'His Majesty told no one,' said Thurloe. 'Not even his own Spymaster. And he swore us to secrecy, so we had no choice but to keep our silence.'

'He swore Herring to secrecy, too, but that did not stop him from betraying us,' said Goff bitterly. 'Damned zealot! But, Lord, I shall be glad to leave this country! No one tells a man how to pray in New England. This has been a dirty business, and I am glad it is over.'

'Is it over?' asked Chaloner unhappily. 'We prevented these massacres, but how long will it be before the next band of lunatics stirs itself up? Especially if the government persists with its policy of intolerance. And some of the plotters are still free – Lord Bristol, for example.'

'But they are not for us to fight,' said Thurloe kindly. 'At least, not today.'

Epilogue

Two men stood on Botolph's Wharf and watched the ship unfurl her sails as she started her journey towards the sea. It was early morning, and fog shifted on the silvery surface of the river like a veil. The Bridge loomed above them, strong and timeless.

'Will Goff will do well in New England,' said Thurloe, as the vessel gathered momentum. 'He is a hero there, a man who stood against the oppression of the state.'

'Yes,' said Chaloner, glancing around uneasily. It was not the sort of statement he wanted anyone else to hear. 'But I am glad he has gone. It was dangerous for you to hide him in Lincoln's Inn.'

'It was not his fault the tides prevented him from leaving sooner,' said Thurloe. 'But your fears were groundless. The King would have protected us, had he been discovered.'

'Would he? I do not think I have ever known an affair to be so completely covered up. There has not been so much as a whisper about it in the coffee houses, which is amazing, given that it involved such a large number of people.'

'All of whom are glad to have escaped unscathed. Folk like Buckingham, Progers and the Lady have learned it is unwise to dabble with fanatics, and Bristol has slithered across to Holland. They will not dabble in such deadly business again.'

Chaloner was not so sure. The Earl's enemies had been openly disappointed when they had learned that their plot to harm him had failed, and had not cared who had seen it.

'The Clarendon Code will cause a lot of trouble before it is repealed,' Thurloe went on. 'But repealed it will be. Popular opinion is against Catholics and nonconformists at the moment, but that will not last for ever. Tolerance will come, although I doubt it will be in our lifetimes.'

'It is amazing how religion can turn sane men into lunatics. And Stedman's pranks did not help – the old king's ghost started all manner of panicky rumours.'

'Not just Stedman,' said Thurloe. 'Phillippes also added to the unease by telling folk that the Thames was disturbed. But the reality is that his tide-ring is not very accurate, and he was reporting greater variation than was actually the case.'

'St Paul's Cathedral really is falling to pieces, though. It will not be long before it collapses completely. Like my house. And there is another story that has been mis-reported. People believe it fell down because it was unstable, despite witnesses reporting a loud bang before it went. There has not been the slightest whisper that gunpowder might have helped it along.'

'It is better that way,' said Thurloe, as they began to walk back towards Thames Street. 'But you have been subdued since all this happened. Is something wrong?'

'The Earl has still not forgiven me for the fact that there was no gold in Chapel House. Past investigations uncovered money that went into his coffers, but this one did not. He feels cheated.'

'That is hardly your fault,' said Thurloe, indignant on his behalf.

'He is angry about Winter, too. I rescued him from Nonesuch House and . . .'

'And he promptly tried to blow up the Bishops' Dinner,' finished Thurloe. 'But again, that was not your fault. You thought he was going to warn Williamson, and that all would be well.'

'He *did* warn Williamson – he did not want Somerset House or St Paul's destroyed. But the assembled bishops represented far too attractive a target, and he agreed readily when Father Stephen invited him to finish what the last Green Man had started.'

'The last Green Man,' mused Thurloe, 'who smuggled enough powder inside Worcester House to flatten half The Strand, and tried to ignite it on Bonfire Night.' He turned, and stared intently at Chaloner. 'But the case is not all that is worrying you. Do you still have questions about *my* actions? You are vexed that I did not confide in you sooner?'

Chaloner shook his head. 'It was exasperating, but I know now that your hands were tied.'

'I wish we could have worked together, but the King made me swear to shun everyone's allegiance. I felt terrible about taking advantage of you.'

'You took advantage of me?' asked Chaloner, surprised. He had not noticed.

'I was eager to learn the identity of Blue Dick's killer, because I thought it might help me understand the rebels' plans. I kept asking you about it, but gave you nothing in return.'

Chaloner smiled ruefully. 'Even when I did find the answer, it came too late to help.'

'Well, we averted disaster, regardless, so all's well that ends well. I am sorry about your home, by the way, although the place was dismal, and you must be far more comfortable with Hannah.'

'My second-best viol was in it,' said Chaloner gloomily. And so was the jug from his mother and the cracked mirror from his dead wife, although he had not felt able to mention these to anyone.

Thurloe frowned, concerned. 'But the loss of a much-loved musical instrument is not the cause of your despondency, either. Tell me what ails you, Tom. I may be able to help.'

'I am beyond help with this,' said Chaloner. 'Hannah has invited Temperance and Wiseman to dine tonight, because our previous arrangement had to be cancelled. I cannot imagine a worse combination of people. And she is going to make one of those appalling pickled ling pies.'

'Wiseman is a decent soul, and he likes you. Do not reject his friendship, because he is a better man than Bulteel. You are aware that Bulteel grows ever closer to Spymaster Williamson, and that everything you say and do is reported to him, are you not?'

They had discussed Thurloe's reservations about Bulteel on several occasions, but the reality was that Chaloner liked the shy secretary a lot more than he did the arrogant surgeon. He changed the subject, not wanting to argue.

'Will you come tonight?' he asked hopefully. 'That would make it bearable.'

Thurloe regarded him askance. 'I do not think a Court Catholic, a brothel-keeper and a man who loves anatomy are the kind of company an honest ex-Spymaster should keep. But do not worry. It will not go on too late, because Temperance will need to open her brothel. Besides, you will have to acquire a taste for pickled ling pies if you are to marry Hannah. It is all she can cook.'

'Christ!' muttered Chaloner. It was not an appealing prospect for his stomach, although his heart was content with the arrangement.

'Incidentally, Bishop Morley claims the Earl's pickled ling pie was the best he has ever eaten,' said Thurloe, amused. 'He wants the name of the supplier, so he can order a regular supply.'

'I know,' said Chaloner unhappily. 'And I am running out of excuses not to tell him.'

'Perhaps you should confess. Life as a bishop's baker cannot be any worse than life as an earl's spy. At least there will not be any explosives involved.'

Hannah had decorated her parlour beautifully, and it looked cosy and welcoming. Temperance was ill-at-ease at first, and clung to Wiseman's arm for moral support, but soon began to relax. The surgeon was in his element, though, with two ladies hanging on his every word. Listening to the grisly stories with growing revulsion, Chaloner thought the evening would never end.

'I owe you a great deal,' Wiseman said, when Temperance had gone to help Hannah prepare the syllabub. 'I was lonely and miserable before you introduced me to Temperance, but now my life is a round of unending happiness. How is yours?'

'The Earl is sending me to Holland tomorrow, to hunt

for Lord Bristol. I have not told Hannah yet. Still, I imagine Buckingham will be ready to step in and comfort her while I am away.'

'Buckingham will not bother Hannah. The King has suggested an extended stay in the country for him, until all danger of repercussions from the recent Somerset House debacle has faded.'

'The debacle no one knows about,' said Chaloner flatly.

Wiseman nodded. 'I find myself a little confused about the details, and while common sense tells me that I should keep it that way, my scientific curiosity is piqued. Will you go through it with me?'

Chaloner obliged. 'There were a large number of plotters, but because they were such a disparate group – fervent Catholics, dedicated Puritans and hedonistic mischief-makers – they were all pulling in different directions. They owed each other no loyalty, and they had different objectives.'

'Which is why Father Stephen had no compunction in shooting his fellow-conspirator Herring – an iconoclast who liked smashing the popish images that Stephen revered,' surmised Wiseman.

Chaloner nodded. 'Father Stephen was the most complex. He enlisted Winter to blow up the Bishops' Dinner, he joined Luckin and Herring in their plan to destroy St Paul's and Somerset House, and he was quite happy to assist the Lady and Buckingham in their petty tricks to harm the Earl. He spied on them all, and played each against the other.'

'An evil villain,' mused Wiseman. 'Or perhaps just insane. Like my wife, he belongs in Bedlam. So did Luckin, by all accounts. I heard he assembled a small army, and ordered them to shoot innocent demonstrators. And he tried to kill you because he thought you had kidnapped his nephews.'

'There was spying and treachery galore,' said Chaloner softly. 'Will Goff and Thurloe looked to be rebels, but were actually agents of the King; Blue Dick was a reformed iconoclast who agreed to watch his former associates for Williamson; and Kaltoff betrayed Phillippes, by planning to take the credit for finding Becket's bones.'

Wiseman frowned. 'Did you hear the Dowager is going to France as soon as there is a favourable wind? And good riddance! I shall never forgive her for what happened to Jane Scarlet.'

'No,' agreed Chaloner. 'Her obsession with Becket meant she did not notice the plot unfurling in her home, but she still bears some responsibility for what happened. She probably did *not* know Bristol planned to overthrow the government – she thought he was just here to cause trouble for the Earl, which she applauded – but she still should have reported his return to Williamson.'

'Explain how Becket's bones tie into all this.'

'They do not – they were a totally separate matter, although it took me a long time to realise it. It was Blue Dick's fault – *he* knew something odd was happening on the Bridge, and was monitoring Chapel House to find out what. I saw him enter the place just before he was murdered, and it led me to afford it too great a significance – Becket's relics were nothing compared to the rebellion.'

'They were nothing anyway,' said Wiseman. 'They do not exist.'

Chaloner nodded, but did not tell the surgeon that the whole affair owed its origins to a spiteful letter penned by the Earl of Clarendon.

'Did I tell you Jane was offered three hundred pounds to keep quiet about the fact that it was the Dowager's men who attacked her?' asked Wiseman after a moment. 'I told her to accept. Well, why not? She will never be able to tell anyone what really happened, so she may as well get something for her suffering.'

'And the culprits are dead anyway,' said Chaloner. 'Martin at her hands, and Doucett at yours.'

Wiseman nodded cheerfully. 'But they were better deaths than the alternative they faced – prison-fever in one of London's dungeons.'

'There is a lot of that about. Luckin and Winter have succumbed to that particular ailment.'

'Well, what do you expect? The government is right to keep the affair quiet, and all the perpetrators have been brought to one kind of justice or another. But perhaps some good will come of it. The authors of the Clarendon Code may see their laws are unpopular, and agree to relax them.'

'On the contrary. It has given them a glimpse of how dangerous religious dissenters can be, and they will slam a lid on ferment harder than ever in future. This nasty little plot has done the cause of religious tolerance no favours whatsoever.'

Wiseman sighed. 'You are probably right. But this is maudlin talk, and we are supposed to be enjoying ourselves. Let us drink to each other's health, and thank God we survived all this fuss.'

Chaloner smiled and raised his glass.

Not many miles away, on a ship that rocked gently on the restless sea, two men stood at the rail and smoked their pipes in companionable silence. The night was very

448

dark, and there was no moon, but several lanterns had been lit and swung lazily with the movement of the vessel. The only sounds were the soft lap of water, the creak of timber and rope, and the occasional muttered order issued by the officer of the watch.

'What a damned waste of time,' said one eventually. 'All that effort and planning.'

'Not much effort and planning on my part,' said Bristol ruefully. 'I only received word a month ago that there was a rebellion in the making, and that the time might be ripe for me to return.'

Will Goff sniffed. 'Well, it took *me* nigh on two years. I had to gather the iconoclasts, assemble my troop of masked men, indoctrinate the likes of Luckin to my way of thinking, arrange safe places for caches of arms. And then there was my brother.'

'Your brother,' said Bristol flatly. 'I heard he tried to kill you, and that wretched ex-Spymaster saved your life.'

'Stephen would never have harmed me – he was aiming for Thurloe.'

Bristol turned to look at him. 'There is one thing I still do not understand, though: why you failed to help Winter destroy Clarendon and the bishops. The powder was in place, and all you had to do was make sure one barrel blew. The others would have followed, regardless of their dampness.'

'And I would have been dead,' said Goff flatly. 'Besides, Leigh was behind me with a gun – I would have been shot. Like poor Stephen. Still, perhaps it is just as well my brother is gone. He was too fervent a supporter of our cause, and played too complex a game. We are better off without him.'

449

Bristol gaped at him. 'You mean to try again? You will not return to New England?'

Will Goff smiled. 'We may not have succeeded this time, but London is deeply discontented with the current regime, and there will be other opportunities. Besides, I plan to spend a few weeks with you in Holland. We shall have plenty of time to discuss it.'

Bristol frowned. 'That is not a good idea. I have been warned that the Earl's spy will be coming to hunt me down. And being discovered plotting more rebellion is unlikely to endear me to the King. I will never win back his favour!'

'Do not worry about Chaloner,' said Goff contentedly. 'I shall ensure he does not carry tales of our plans back to his Earl.'

'You will?' asked Bristol dubiously. 'How? I understand he is rather good at his job.'

'But so am I,' said Goff softly. 'So am I.'

Historical Note

In February 1664, a woman was assaulted in her Turnstile home. Two Frenchmen broke into her house, bound her husband in his shirt, raped her, and then abused her with a link (a torch) that was said to have been lit. The villains were caught, and the first rumour was that the affair was hushed up for £300, because the culprits were servants of the King's mother.

The Dowager, Queen Henrietta Maria, was a woman of strong religious faith and decided opinions. Her haughty manner, along with her Catholicism, made her an unpopular figure in Restoration London, and her home, Somerset House on The Strand, became a focal point not only for prominent Catholics – including her group of Capuchin friars – but also for people who disliked the Earl of Clarendon. The portly, fussy, disapproving Earl had made an enemy of her, and she was only too happy to entertain his opponents. The Duke of Buckingham, Lady Castlemaine and the King's pimp, Edward Progers, were among them. She left London for her native France in 1665, and never returned.

Another eminent Catholic of the time was Sir John

Winter. He was a wealthy purveyor of lead and timber, who also possessed an extensive knowledge of gunpowder. Doubtless, this would have been seen as a worrying combination in an age of religious intolerance.

Lord Bristol, also Catholic, had been in disgrace since July 1663, partly for a reckless attempt to impeach the Earl of Clarendon in Parliament. A warrant for his arrest was issued on 23 August for 'crimes of a high nature against the King's person and government', but he promptly went into hiding. Then, on 17 January 1664, he arrived at Wimbledon parish church and renounced his Catholicism in front of the vicar and witnesses. The hapless cleric, Thomas Luckin, was later arrested and taken to the Tower for failing to take the fugitive into custody. Also present at the incident were Abraham Doucett and William Martin.

Meanwhile, the Clarendon Code comprised four acts of Parliament that were passed between 1661 and 1665, during Clarendon's Lord Chancellorship. All were designed to curb nonconformists. They comprised the Corporation Act (1661), which forbade municipal office to anyone not taking the sacraments at a parish church; the Act of Conformity (1662), which excluded them from Church offices; the Conventicle Act (also 1662) which made nonconformist worship illegal, even in private houses; and the Five-Mile Act (1665), which forbade nonconformist ministers to live or visit any place within five miles of somewhere they had preached. Some of these restrictions were loosened in 1689, but others were not repealed until the nineteenth century. They were bitterly opposed in 1660s London, because the King had promised religious tolerance and 'liberty to tender consciences' in a statement given in

Breda in 1660, shortly before he was invited to reclaim his throne.

Many other people in *A Murder on London Bridge* were real. John Thurloe, Cromwell's Spymaster General and Secretary of State, was living in quiet retirement between Lincoln's Inn and his Oxfordshire estates in the mid 1660s, the rabid pamphleteer William Prynne was his London neighbour, and Richard Wiseman was appointed as Surgeon to the Person in June 1660. John Bulteel was the Earl of Clarendon's private secretary, and the clever, ruthless Joseph Williamson was Spymaster General. Humphrey Leigh was Sergeant at Arms to the Lord Chancellor from 1660 to 1673.

William Goff was a regicide, and his brother Stephen converted to Catholicism while in exile with the Royalists during the Commonwealth; he was later chaplain to the Dowager at Somerset House. William Goff left England at the Restoration, but was followed by Royalists determined to make him face justice. He was said to have lived in a cave in New England to avoid them. Thomas Chaloner, uncle of the fictional Thomas Chaloner of *A Murder on London Bridge*, was another regicide; he died in exile in 1662.

The Wardens of the London Bridge in 1664 were Robert Hussey and Anthony Scarlet, and the bookseller Charles Tyus and his wife Sarah were Bridge tenants. Henry Phillippes also lived on the Bridge, and was a mathematician–surveyor. His home allowed him to study the tides of the Thames, and he was a prolific writer of textbooks on them. He invented something known as the Phillippes Tide Ring, an instrument for measuring tidal variation. He gave a paper to the Royal Society in 1665, and died in 1677. Casper Kaltoff was a mechanic, who probably died in 1664.

Richard Culmer, vicar and iconoclast, was proud of the fact that he had despoiled Canterbury Cathedral, smashing its medieval stained glass with a pike as he stood on a long ladder. In his own words, he 'rattled down proud Becket's glassy bones'. The probability is that Becket's relics, like so many others, had been destroyed during the Reformation – King Henry VIII certainly ordered them burned. Culmer was known by his contemporaries as Blue Dick, presumably for his penchant for blue clothes. He died in 1662. Another famous iconoclast of the time was Michael Herring, the zealous churchwarden of St Mary Woolchurch in London.

Five brave Penderel brothers did help the King escape after the Battle of Worcester. They belonged to an ancient and much-respected Catholic family, and did not, unlike many others, flock to London to take advantage of the King's gratitude. The King rewarded them for their courage, anyway.

The London Bridge of 1664 was a very different place to the neatly functional late-nineteenth-century structure that bears its name today. It was the city's only crossing of the river, and was topped by medieval houses, although a fire in 1663 had denuded its northern end. Above the Stone Gate were displayed the severed heads of men associated with the execution of Charles I, and the glorious Nonesuch House was an exotic mansion with onion domes.

Originally, the Bridge boasted its own chapel, too, dedicated to St Thomas Becket (who was said to have spent a night in Winchester Palace before travelling to his martyrdom in Canterbury). The chapel was demolished in 1533 and a secular house raised on its foundations.

Peter de Colechurch, credited with raising the first stone bridge in the late twelfth century, is thought to have been the only person ever buried in the chapel. Bones were discovered in the remnants of the old crypt when the Bridge was finally demolished in the early 1830s, which may well have been de Colechurch's. It seems they were tipped unceremoniously into the river.

Other bestselling titles available by mail:

☐ A Plague on Both Your Houses	Susanna Gregory	£7.99
☐ An Unholy Alliance	Susanna Gregory	£7.99
☐ A Bone of Contention	Susanna Gregory	£7.99
☐ A Deadly Brew	Susanna Gregory	£7.99
☐ A Wicked Deed	Susanna Gregory	£7.99
☐ A Masterly Murder	Susanna Gregory	£7.99
☐ An Order for Death	Susanna Gregory	£7.99
☐ A Summer of Discontent	Susanna Gregory	£7.99
☐ A Killer in Winter	Susanna Gregory	£7.99
☐ The Hand of Justice	Susanna Gregory	£7.99
☐ The Mark of a Murderer	Susanna Gregory	£7.99
☐ The Tarnished Chalice	Susanna Gregory	£7.99
☐ To Kill or Cure	Susanna Gregory	£7.99
☐ A Vein of Deceit	Susanna Gregory	£7.99
☐ A Conspiracy of Violence	Susanna Gregory	£7.99
☐ Blood on the Strand	Susanna Gregory	£7.99
☐ The Butcher of Smithfield	Susanna Gregory	£7.99
☐ The Westminster Poisoner	Susanna Gregory	£7.99

The prices shown above are correct at time of going to press. However, the publishers reserve the right to increase prices on covers from those previously advertised, without further notice.

— sphere —

Please allow for postage and packing: **Free UK delivery.**
Europe; add 25% of retail price; Rest of World; 45% of retail price.

To order any of the above or any other Sphere titles, please call our credit card orderline or fill in this coupon and send/fax it to:

Sphere, P.O. Box 121, Kettering, Northants NN14 4ZQ
Fax: 01832 733076   Tel: 01832 737526
Email: aspenhouse@FSBDial.co.uk

☐ I enclose a UK bank cheque made payable to Sphere for £ . . . .
☐ Please charge £ . . . . . . to my Visa, Delta, Maestro.

Expiry Date ☐☐☐☐   Maestro Issue No. ☐☐

NAME (BLOCK LETTERS please) . . . .

ADDRESS . . . .

. . . .

. . . .

Postcode . . . . Telephone . . . .

Signature . . . .

Please allow 28 days for delivery within the UK. Offer subject to price and availability.